For I Could Lift My Finger and Black Out the Sun

A John Black novel
Omnibus edition

KEITH SOARES

Erin -
To my #1 fan!
Keith

Bufflegoat Books

First edition April 2015
ISBN 978-0-9906542-7-8
Original publication date April 17, 2015

Edited by Christopher Durso

Many thanks to my wife, Layla, who gave me a huge hug when she finished reading this. Best review ever. Additional thanks to Dee Gazda, Bill Setzer, John Childs, Susan Clutter, Dan Halter, and Jeff Yeatman.

Dedicated in memoriam to my mom, Betty Soares,
who could always save the day.

PART ONE

DAWN

KEITH SOARES

Prologue

Walter Ivory was a son of a bitch. Walter, the neighborhood nuisance. I knew my parents couldn't stand the guy, and my sister and I were terrified of him. But I guess it came down to this: He never actually *did* much of anything, so it wasn't like you could have him arrested or something like that. He was just a creep. He'd come around, like the time Mom and my six-year-old sister, Holly, were playing with the sprinkler. He stopped, hanging over our little iron fence, leering at my Mom, her shirt wet. Or when Dad was changing the oil of the car while I looked on, my head poking under the hood. "Oh you got a *real man* to help you, finally, eh, Phil?" Walter said with a chuckle. He was the kind of guy who would look good with a black eye. Preferably one you gave him yourself.

One time we were having a cookout at our picnic table in the backyard, late summer. Dad was grilling burgers and dogs, and Mom had made corn on the cob and all the other stuff. Holly and I were setting the table. Holly was still tiny then, wearing some pink frilly dress. She had jet-black hair and pale skin, like Mom and me. People said our last name was appropriate for the hair alone: Holly Black and John Black, the kids with the inky hair, so dark it sometimes looked blue in the light. As I set plates and utensils at each seat, Holly walked behind me laying checked napkins.

Dad was at the grill when we saw him look up. Aimless as always, Walter Ivory was strolling along the sidewalk past our house again. Dad tried to look away, just let him pass, but Walter wasn't like that. "Looks lovely!" he exclaimed from down the street, picking up his pace as soon as he saw the blue smoke of Dad's grill. Walter was a tall, ropy guy with skin darkened by sun and grime from his job with the county road crew. He had apparently tried to clean up on this particular occasion. His dirty-blond hair was slicked back, and he was wearing a faded button-up denim shirt, but it was sort of like putting a shine on a turd.

Dad hesitated. "Uh... thanks," he said. He gave Mom a look, away from Walter's direction: *Dammit. This guy again?* She missed it.

Walter strode right up to our fence, directly opposite Dad, and stood shaded by a dogwood tree from our yard. Walter's house was surrounded by a wooden fence so rotten that we expected it to turn to dust at any moment. On several occasions, he'd brought up our iron fence as evidence that we thought we were better than him. But not today. "Whew, it's a hot one, eh, Phil? And you, slaving over that grill." Walter dramatically waved his hand to fan his face, showing dirty, chewed fingernails. "What're you grilling? Probably that ground sirloin shit, right? Not that ground beef I buy. You buy the good stuff."

"Walter..." Dad began with a sigh.

"Nothing's too good, too expensive for your family, Phil. You deserve it! You work *hard*. You must be sitting at your desk for, what? Eight hours a day? Not me. I get 15 minutes to sit at work. Through a 12-hour shift. But I've got a *shitty* job, right, Phil?" He laughed an empty, vicious little laugh.

"Can you watch the language?" Dad said, pointing his spatula at Holly and me.

"I'm sorry. I am truly sorry. I certainly didn't come down the street on this fine day to interrupt your family picnic. You've had a tough day today, Phil, and slaving over that grill in this heat makes it even harder. I understand." He smirked. "But you can take it! You're a tough guy, aren't you, Phil?" He turned to my mom, standing there in a pretty polka-dotted sundress, her black hair pulled back by a red band. "He's a tough guy, right, Andy? You like tough guys?" Phil and Andrea Black. Those were my parents. Although no one called my mom "Andy." Not even Dad.

Walter winked, suggestively. Mom turned away. She gave Dad a sidelong glance with a tilt toward us kids that told him to get rid of this guy.

"That's enough, Walter," Dad said, wiping a wisp of his fading light hair out of his eyes. He didn't quite have a comb-over, but it was close. It didn't help that he was decked out in a light-blue dress shirt covered by a white apron on which a cartoon chef declared, "I'm *En Fuego!*"

"Oh, sorry, tough guy." Walter stared at Dad, clearly willing him to start a fight. Dad looked at him for a minute, looked at us, took a deep breath, and went back to grilling.

Walter grinned. Under his breath, he muttered, "That's what I thought." He muttered another word, too, even lower. But it was loud enough that we all heard it. A slur that made Holly, Mom, and me gasp with shock, and Dad instantly furious.

Holly slid over behind me. She seemed to be holding her breath. Her grip on my arm was tight, nearly painful. "Johnny…," she said to me in a low voice, like a question, unanswered.

"You *watch it!*" Dad shouted at Walter. Whoa. He was pissed. "My kids are out here!"

Walter said… nothing. He just stood there next to the fence, looking at us. Smug, staring at Dad. He made a small huffing sound and nodded. A tense moment passed. Very low, very deep, Walter grumbled, "Any time, Phil." And he stared.

Dad was boiling over. But Mom was there. We were there. He wasn't a hotheaded teenager, or a witless adult like Walter, looking for trouble. What was Dad supposed to do? He just stood there. So Walter upped the ante. He turned back toward Mom, rolling his eyes. Walter was in a particularly good mood this day, it seemed.

"You're looking *good* tonight, Andy." He let his eyes linger.

"My name is Andrea, Walter," she turned away, and that made it worse. Walter's eyes slid down her body.

Dad blew up, stalked to the fence. For a moment, Walter stood his ground, gleeful in his ability to push other people's buttons. He even seemed to lean in toward the fence, awaiting Dad. But when my father reached the iron bars, Walter collapsed backward.

"Whoa, whoa, whoa, friend! I mean no harm." He mockingly cowered on the other side of the fence, grabbing at a tree branch and pulling it back, as if holding on to it for security. He stood there, waiting. That was the true Walter. A total coward when confronted. His toughness was directly related to whether he outgunned you, or how much he thought he could get away with, without the bravery of really doing anything. The fence helped him feel very brave, and the tree branch was an almost infantile gesture, like cuddling a teddy bear with teary eyes.

Dad stopped. I could see he was ashamed — in front of his kids, he'd been about to hit another person. He turned around and started back toward the grill.

And like a true coward, Walter released the branch.

It hit Dad in the back. His feet slipped in the mulch by the fence and he fell. He wasn't hurt, but dirt and mulch clung to his otherwise pristine shirt and khaki pants. His apron, which Holly and I had given him, was streaked with thick dark stains.

"Oh, sorry about that, buddy! Have a nice night!" Walter shouted as he scurried down the street. Dad pushed himself up and gave one exasperated punch to the ground, but that only succeeded in splattering more dirt on his formerly clean clothes.

Mom stooped to help Dad as he tried to get up and brush off, while I just stood with my mouth wide open. In the commotion, it took us nearly a minute to notice the sound.

Holly was convulsing on the patio in a seizure.

KEITH SOARES

1

It was snowing. I was eleven, and although the word was forbidden to me by my parents, I thought, *Shit!* It was snowing. There were easily six inches already on the ground. It was a Friday, Dad was at work, and Mom had just gotten Holly and me out the door. School was canceled; the day was mine.

I turned to wave bye to Mom and Holly, and a moment of guilt passed over me. Holly, now nearly eight, wouldn't be running through the snow. She sat in the special chair that half supported her and half constrained her, snowflakes landing on her hair, her clothes, at the side of her slack mouth. She hadn't been the same since that day. Mom saw my eyes, read my thoughts. She gave me a melancholy little smile, but then shook it off. She waved me away. "Go," she said. "Have fun." I hesitated. But I was young, and heavy thoughts don't weigh down eleven-year-olds for long. I pressed my forehead lightly against Holly's for a moment. I think it was the first time I'd ever done it, but over time it came to be our little thing. Then I turned and ran into the snow.

I gasped for joy, running down the street with my thick winter coat blazing like a red streak, mittens — mittens, for God's sake! — clamped to my sleeves, and I even had a knit blue hat jammed down over my mop of black hair, although I'd told my mom, *my head does NOT get cold!*

I tilted my head up and opened my mouth, and the cool flakes of snow landed gently on my tongue and immediately melted. A gift. A gift from the heavens. A gift that, beyond all comprehension, would change the very course of my life.

I enjoyed the sensation for maybe seven seconds before my next great idea surfaced. I decided to run to my friend Steve's house so we could pelt each other with snowballs. Racing past the similar rows of suburban homes, I turned the corner and slid to a stop. The road was empty; there weren't even any tire tracks in the new snow yet. But something — someone — blocked my path: Bobby Graden. He hadn't noticed me yet; he was tipping his head back, collecting snowflakes on his tongue, just as I'd been doing a moment before. He must've felt someone nearby, my presence. Slowly, he closed his mouth and swung his head downward, looking directly at me.

Bobby had the kind of big, animal look that screamed "elementary school bully." So, thankfully, he didn't disappoint, living up to his appearance in all aspects of life. You could be assured that any contact with Bobby would involve him trying to put you down, mentally, physically, or both. With me, it was usually physical. I'd probably been hit, slapped, kicked, grabbed, or shoved by Bobby more times than anyone else at school. Standing in the road in front of me, his messy brown twirl of hair becoming frosted with snowflakes, he started to grin. His teeth went in various directions, the perfect complement to his rat-like eyes and ruddy cheeks. In general, Bobby looked like a very large mole. I never mentioned this to him; I'd had enough bruises without inviting more trouble.

"Well, well," he began. "What's up, dopey?"

I looked to the side, gauging where to run to get away. I stepped backward with my left foot, scuffing the new snow.

"Whoa, whoa, whoa — where ya goin', buddy? You just got here." His grin got even bigger. I stepped back again. I didn't bother to say a word; there wasn't anything I could say that would change Bobby's mind about anything. He came closer. I wondered for a second why my family seemed to invite bullies to bother us so much. In my head, I imagined those Sunday-morning panel shows that my dad watched, but instead of talking politics or the economy, they discussed the pressing issue of assholes in our society. I smirked.

"Something funny, John Boy?" Like all bullies, Bobby thought everything was about him, so he naturally assumed I was laughing at him. This didn't improve his disposition.

I figured escape was my best and only option, so I dodged to the right and ducked. If I could just get past him, I'd run to Steve's house.

Bobby didn't bother being artful; he outweighed me by probably 30 pounds. It wasn't David versus Goliath, it was David versus Godzilla. He simply reached out and put his hand on my hunched back as I ducked, and pushed. I fell face first into the snow in the middle of the street.

"Have a nice trip?" He laughed and grabbed the back of my coat to lift me out of the snow. "See you next fall!" He pushed me down again, puffing up a cloud of snow.

"Come on, Bobby, leave me alone!" My voice was muffled by a mouthful of snow.

He put on a mocking look of concern. "Where's the fun in that?" If I could have, I would happily have slapped the look off his face. He grabbed my arm, raising me up as he twisted it backward. "Now where are you headed? To that other dork Steve's house, I bet. You two are sweet on each other, aren't you?" He pushed my arm farther until something went *ping* inside my shoulder.

The pain made me snap. I wheeled and hit him directly in the Adam's apple. He let go of my arm as he began spasming and coughing, clutching his throat in pain. I ran.

After only a moment, Bobby gave a harsh cough and shouted, "You're *dead,*

John! *Dead!*" He came after me, fast but silent, like he was gliding over the padding of snow. My heart raced and I ran toward Steve's house, hoping to God he would let me in immediately, or maybe even his mom would be home. Turning the corner, I saw their white two-story house just down the block.

Bobby must have cut through someone's yard, because suddenly he appeared on my right, cutting me off. I shot down another street to the left, now having no idea what to do other than run. Bobby was hot behind me. I zigged and zagged down side streets, headed out toward the main road, panting heavily.

"You can run all you want, little John! You're not getting away this time. *I owe you one today!*" Bobby chuckled as he ran. He could probably run all day. I felt like my heart was about to burst. As we approached the main road, I could almost feel his breath on the back of my neck. I charged out across the road, through the carved tracks of the cars that had passed before.

His hand grabbed the back of my coat as we heard a loud *beeeeeeeeep*. Looking left, I saw a two-door red hatchback driven by a woman about my mom's age. She looked like she was standing on her brakes as she snapped the wheel hard to her left, trying to cross the median without hitting us. Her car ignored her. The wheels, now turned sideways, became skis on the snowy surface and kept the car moving directly at us, eerily silent in the fallen snow. Bobby let go of my coat and started to dive back toward the curb. I stood frozen. The car hit both of us, sliding like a cherry-colored battering ram into our bodies. There was a double *whump-whump* as we collided with the front and passenger sides of the car. I don't remember anything else about that morning.

Years later, I know what really brought us together. But at that time, you can see how it made no sense that Bobby and I became best friends.

2

I later found out that it was Walter Ivory himself who called 911. He saw the whole thing from across the street as he was walking out of a convenience store with his morning coffee. Three fire trucks and two ambulances arrived. There wasn't anything for the firefighters to do except watch. The EMTs made sure we weren't quite dead, then put us each in an ambulance and sped us to the local hospital. Davidson Regional was a huge tan brick building, just off the highway, where the land was cheaper. It loomed over six lanes of traffic with its glowing sign in large, white letters. Bobby and I were admitted with haste, ER doctors and nurses in a frenzy to help the two little kids who'd been hit by a car. It was an unusual event in our area — we didn't have drive-bys, hit-and-runs, those sorts of big-ticket emergencies, very often — so it made the staff perk up. Or maybe the doctors were bored from another typical day of ear infections and croup. In any event, we got a lot of attention.

The snow probably saved both of our asses. If we'd hit raw pavement, the impact might've killed us.

Bobby was banged up pretty bad, bleeding like crazy from a slash to the side of his neck, sporting a nice dark shiner under his left eye, but he was mostly fine. I had to have emergency surgery on my right knee; it had shattered on the front bumper of the hatchback. Caught me at just the right angle to lock my knee straight, so the impact was especially hard, snapping the joint like a twig. I also had an ugly gash on my chin from where my face slammed onto the hood of the car. That needed about a million stitches. But the knee was the real mess. I'm sure the doctors at our regional hospital did their best, but car-shattered kneecap wasn't a common issue for them to resolve, so my results were less than ideal.

After surgery, they put me and Bobby in the same room. I guess they figured we were joined at the hip. Looking back now, it makes me laugh to think how accurate that was.

My parents were waiting when I got out of surgery, and Holly was there in her wheelchair. I was groggy, but at least I knew who they were. My knee was in a big wrap of bandages that Mom maneuvered around to give me a huge hug. Dad followed suit, but where Mom had an almost heart-wrenching look of concern on her face, Dad looked... suspicious.

"John," he said to me in a low voice, "this isn't one of your typical friends." He gestured over his shoulder toward Bobby. "What happened here?"

I hesitated. Bobby was no friend of mine, but he was *right there*, in the same room. If I said it was all his fault, he'd just wait until some other day when we were alone again, and pummel me in retaliation. I gave a sideways glance toward Bobby, who seemed to be pretending not to eavesdrop on our conversation. That's when I noticed he was alone; no one from his family had bothered to show up yet.

"We were just playing around," Bobby said suddenly, speaking up. He looked me in the eye. We both knew it was a lie, and I opened my mouth to protest.

Dad turned toward Bobby in surprise and blurted out, "You guys were just *playing around* and got hit by a car?" Looking back at me, he asked, "Is this true, John?"

Bobby interjected again. "Yeah. It's stupid, but we were just playing in the snow and BOOM, you know? There was the car." What was Bobby doing? I stared with my mouth open. And he looked at me in a decidedly... *human* way. Was that *fear* in his eyes?

Dad was flummoxed. "Jesus! Do you have any idea how lucky you are? You boys could have been killed!" He paused, looking back and forth at us both.

"Dad...," I started, but got no further.

At that moment, Bobby's parents burst through the door.

3

"What the hell have you been up to this time?" raged Bobby's mother. His father just stood back and somewhat smugly awaited the answer. Bobby's demeanor changed in an instant. The over-the-top bully I had always known became a mere sheep in front of his parents. It actually made me feel bad for him. That was a first. The tinge of fear I'd seen in Bobby a moment before became panic, almost terror.

"I didn't do *anything*, Mom. I got hit by a car!" He was pleading. It wasn't a tone I'd ever heard from him before that day. But I'd hear it again.

"What were you doing fooling around in the road, *boy?*" Bobby's father asked. He was mostly bald, with fringes of red on the sides of his pasty head, a large man who I imagined had an equally large appetite. Perhaps he'd been lean and strong in the past, but now it seemed that appetite had won. He was nearly as wide as he was tall. Nonetheless, given his old muscle and the serious amount of weight behind it, I wouldn't risk even one punch from him. I envisioned his fists snapping my bones, an unyielding force like the fender of an oncoming car. Meanwhile, Bobby's mom looked like she'd just come from a small-town beauty pageant. She had swirls of curly platinum hair all done up in some kind of clip, eyes as big as a doll's, dark makeup accentuating them, and an hourglass figure shown off by a tightly fitted pink top. The only problem was that when she opened her mouth, everyone in the room cowered. She was a woman who was used to getting her way. She was what my grandmother would call *a witch, with a capital B.*

"Bobby, tell your Daddy what happened," she said, batting those huge dark eyelashes with an almost sympathetic cadence. Somehow, she made it clear that this was a threat.

Bobby hesitated. He looked toward me. In that instant, I knew what his fear was: If he told his parents what really happened, they'd kill him. I noticed Bobby's father balling his fists, and imagined them being used against his son. Suddenly the school bully looked small against the meaty orbs of his father's clenched hands. But if Bobby kept up the lie he began with my dad, what would stop me from protesting? The punishment would come. Either way, Bobby was screwed.

For a glorious moment, I basked in this power. I, John Black, could finally seek my revenge against the bully Bobby Graden. I could either sit back gleefully and watch him hang himself with the truth, or wait for him to lie. Then I'd dive in with the fatal blow, revealing his deceit and making him pay nonetheless. It was fantastic! What kid gets to do this? I thought about the generations of downtrodden before me; the meek and cowardly who never got the chance to revel in their tormentor's defeat. I considered every humiliation, every taunt, every blow. I thought it would be sweet to send Bobby to the flames to roast, and then jab him in the ribs while he was on the spit. I might've even cracked a smile. I imagined legions of the small and weak lifting me onto their collective shoulders, their hero.

Bobby must have noticed my smug look, and he was worried. He licked his lips, nervously. "Ma, I…" he trailed off, hanging his head, stealing a look toward me.

No longer tough, he just looked… beaten. And terrified. My smile cracked. Was I feeling sympathy for Bobby? What the hell was going on? In my daydream, my legions of fans suddenly dropped me rudely to the street, no longer a hero, now the goat. I considered what would happen if I let Bobby off the hook. He'd feign humility as he got away with it all, and later we'd see each other again at school. I dreamed of Bobby mocking my sympathy as he came up with clever new ways to harm me. My brow furrowed as my focus returned to the moment. I was newly determined to watch him fall. A sinister sneer came over my face. And Bobby's mom saw it.

She cocked her head like a dog hearing a high-pitched noise. Her eyes squinted as she focused her attention on me. Did she suspect what I was thinking? Or worse, did she think that I'd been the one responsible for what had happened? She started to walk over to me, wearing a toothy grin that I didn't trust one bit. As my parents looked curiously at her, she reached the side of my bed. "Are you okay, honey?" she asked, dripping false sympathy.

"I… I guess," was my only reply. She leaned in close.

So close, in fact, that only I could hear her. "Are you trying to get my boy in trouble?" she whispered, barely moving her lips, smile still cemented on her face. Her eyes held mine, gleaming, predatory. I felt a lump lodged in my throat.

"No! No, ma'am! We were… just playing around. Throwing snowballs. We accidentally went into the street, and didn't hear the car until it was too late." I said it too loud and too abruptly, feeling like the lie was written all over my face.

Bobby's mom still had her head cocked to one side as she questioned me. "You were *playing?* Together?" Both of my parents looked at me with suspicion.

"Yeah, John. *You guys?*" my dad said. "The two of you, were … playing?"

I froze. I needed to make them believe it. "Yes." I looked at Bobby. *Please,* I thought. *Back me up here!* My eyes would have burned holes into him if they could. He stared for a second, not understanding why I wouldn't tell them the truth, why I wouldn't give him up. Then, with an almost nonexistent shrug that only I could see, he chimed in.

"Yeah. Me and Johnny, we were just … playing around." *Oh good, Bobby, call me Johnny. No one calls me that except Holly, and sometimes Mom.* "You know, throwing snowballs. Running around. We should have realized we were getting too close to the road, but with the snow, we couldn't hear any cars." *Okay, I had to admit Bobby was a better liar than me by far.* "Johnny was about to smash me with a big snowball when we suddenly realized a car was gonna hit us." *Nice touch, Bobby. Make them think I was going after you, even if it was in a game.*

My mom turned to me with that Mom stare that says, *this is when I want you to really, truly tell me the truth.* "Are you sure, John?" she said. She waited, looking deep into my eyes for the answer. Bobby's mother had backed away, but continued to stare directly at me with her cold, unsettling gaze.

If there's one thing that parents deserve more credit for, it's their bullshit-detection skills. I didn't know what to do. I just about blurted out the truth. That would have gotten Bobby in a ton of trouble, but I would have had my share of it in return when he showed up to school to find me later. My feeling of being caught in a trap intensified. I looked into my mom's probing eyes, then over to the terrifying gaze of Bobby's mother. I was certain my mom could smell the lie. I was terrified of Bobby's mother. I shut my eyes, twisting my face in a grimace.

I wished for all of it to. Just. *Stop.*

And it did.

4

Mom blinked. Then she blinked again. Then her face... *shifted.*

Her Mom stare vanished, replaced by a look of pure motherly concern. "My poor Johnny. I'm so glad you're okay." She leaned close, eyes welling. "I heard what happened, and I just started to shake. We raced right over here. My *baby!*" She wrapped me up in a big hug.

"Ow, Mom! The knee!" Even through whatever painkillers the doctors had given me, it hurt as she brushed up against my bandages. My yelp made her smother me even more with her affection.

What just happened? My mother did *not* just give up on something like that once she'd sunk her teeth into it. Even my dad was giving me this dopey sympathetic look.

Still, the most startling thing I saw was Bobby's parents hovering over him with concern. Bobby's mother had softened, like someone had changed a channel in her mind. Where before she had been set to News Reporter Bulldog Interviewer, now she was more Sitcom Mom. It was really weird, and seemed unnatural on her.

Bobby caught my eye. He raised his eyebrows slightly, saying, *What was that?* With the tiniest motion, I shrugged. *I have no idea.*

Then I looked over at Holly, sitting to one side in her wheelchair. Her normal detachment was gone. She was staring directly at me, unwavering.

Her lip twitched at the corner. And she looked into my eyes like the entirety of my soul was a story for her to read. Which I suppose it was.

5

Bobby, strangely, felt a connection to me after that day. He'd say things offhandedly, like, "You know, we've been through a lot together, Johnny," or "Maybe someone was looking out for us both that day." I think he was covering up the fact that he knew he owed me one, and that he couldn't quite figure out how I did it. In truth, I couldn't figure it out either. I had willed people to change their minds, and somehow they did. Bobby knew it. I knew it. And I think Holly knew it, too, even if she couldn't say anything.

So Bobby and I became friends. He was released from the hospital well before I was, but came back to visit several times. It was really bizarre, especially since most boys that age can be total inconsiderate dicks. Case in point: None of my other friends came to visit me even once.

After about a week, I was allowed to go home. So finally, my lazy "real" friends came over to my house to see me. Guess the trip to the hospital was too far. My friends had already heard rumors about me and Bobby, from where I had no idea. They were incredulous.

"Bobby. Bobby Graden? You're hanging out with him? For real?" Tom Shafer didn't mince words. Okay, that's a sugarcoated way of describing Tom. The truth is that he could be a pain in the ass.

But Steve Martucci felt the same. "What the hell, John?"

I shrugged. "He's been really nice to me ever since the accident. I mean, I guess we both could've been killed together." I shrugged again. I didn't have any better explanation.

"Yeah, well, screw that if you think I'm gonna hang out with him. He's just waiting for the right moment to beat the crap out of you, you know?" Tom had a truly insightful mind.

"Look, I know he used to be like that, but he's different now," I said. "Ever since the car crash —"

"*Ever since the car crash! Ever since the car crash!*" Tom was pitiless. "One little car crash and you make such a big deal about it." Yeah, that was a pretty crappy thing to say. "Ever since the car crash, you've been a little nuts," Tom said, rolling his eyes.

"Look, if you wanna be friends with Bobby, go ahead." Steve brimmed with disgust. "But we'll see you around. Come on, Tom." He turned to leave.

"You guys! Come on, this is ridiculous!" I shouted as Tom turned to go, too. "I'm not asking you to marry Bobby Graden — just give him a chance!"

"Why don't you marry him?" Tom said with his back to me. "That's a great idea. Freakin' superb."

"Okay, fine," I said. "Just walk away. But when I become an international superstar, don't come knocking on my door. The role of 'posse' will already be filled." Even I winced at the lameness of my joke. Tom and Steve left without another word.

Of course, like with most kids our age, this was a momentary disruption. We fought, stormed off, then hung out again within a day or two. Tom and Steve would simply make fun of me for hanging out with my "girlfriend" Bobby, knowing full well that if word of that got back to Bobby it might restart the full-on beat-down process he used to administer to them. (Bobby had been an equal-opportunity bully.) So they kept the brave words between the three of us, and we all stayed friends. To the degree that snarky, self-centered punks can be friends.

As for Bobby, it was interesting. At first, I don't think there was much of anything in common between us. He'd just show up at my house. He was terrified of his parents, although we never talked about them. It was clear that hanging around at his own house wasn't an option, so he'd appear at my door. After the second or third time we hung out playing videogames next to each other, never saying a word, I thought, *I'm not gonna do this again.* But he kept coming back, for reasons I couldn't figure out back then. And I kept letting him in.

* * *

My knee was a pretty serious problem. I'm sure there's no good age to have a reconstructed knee, but eleven was a particularly challenging one. I was in physical therapy until a few months after my twelfth birthday. In the meantime, I had to learn to gimp along on my busted-up leg as best as I could. The therapist would bend and twist my knee all sorts of ways, making me want to either give up and die on the spot or find an axe so I could murder him. At school, people wanted to make fun of my limp, and I'm sure they did behind my back, but no one dared to do it to my face. The benefits of being friends with the school bully.

More than anything, my knee just hurt. Morning, noon, night. Sitting, standing, running, sleeping, watching TV. If I got distracted, which I tried to do as often as I could, it would fade from my mind, but God help me if I thought about it. There was an intense throb underneath my kneecap that no rubbing or ointment could ease. My worst nights were the ones when, for whatever reason, I started to think about my knee before falling asleep. I often stayed awake almost until dawn, writhing in pain, and many times got out of bed covered in a sheen of sweat.

And then one day, something changed.

It was warm out, but not too much so, with the kind of puffy white clouds that look more like a painting than reality. It was fall already, the new school year still as fresh as an open wound. We were seventh graders now, moved on to the middle school at last. You know what that mostly meant? More homework. But Bobby kept coming around. I had to admit, he was good at pulling me out of my head, distracting me with some low-stakes adventure or another. Around that time, he'd been bugging me about sneaking into the local self-storage building. A place he called Mount Trashmore because, according to Bobby, it was where "people pay a lot of money to store junk they don't want or need." He mostly thought they paid their money so they didn't have to look at all their crappy stuff anymore. I think he may have been right. The tall brick building was just a short way from his house, and had become something of a fixation for him. Because it loomed so high above the strip malls and walk-up apartments clustered around it, it promised a vantage point from which to look out at the world beyond. You could see maybe five or 10 miles on a clear day, but more importantly, you could see there was a world outside of your parents' house. It let you dream, to look so far. And it was high enough that you couldn't quite smell the dumpsters that sat behind the building, festering on hot days.

Did I mention it was completely forbidden for us kids to be anywhere near the building? No, we weren't supposed to be in the self-storage compound at all. Off limits. That just made Bobby want to do it more. He cajoled me until I gave in. We snuck over the tall metal fence in an inconspicuous corner, then ran across the lot into a door on the back side of the building that Bobby said was always left unlocked. By this time, he was completely healed — you'd never look at him and think he'd been hit by a car. Outwardly, I looked fine, but my knee was still killing me.

I tried to ignore it, and managed to drag myself about halfway up the climb inside Mount Trashmore. We took the stark cement stairs, floor by floor. Bobby knew I was in pain, but goaded me on, using words clinically proven to be able to coax a 12-year-old into doing anything: wuss, pansy, wimp. I plodded on. Under my breath, I muttered, "Now batting for Team Jerk, Bobby Graden."

Two floors from the top, I missed a step. And fell.

Of course it was my bad leg that took the brunt of it. I slid down toward the right before catching myself. I heard a small pop. I had visions of a return visit to the hospital, lying in that bed with nothing to do, day after day. I tried to take a step, but it seemed impossible. Hell, *standing* was a challenge.

Bobby trotted back. "You okay?" he asked, peering down at me.

"Yeah, yeah, sure," I said through clenched teeth. "I just thought I saw the rare mottled bufflegoat through the window, and I simply had to get a closer look. I'm fine." Sarcasm is a tool. Use it whenever you can.

"Hmmph," he snorted. "Fine, my ass. You hurt your knee again, didn't you?"

"I'm *fine*," I replied, with a little too much conviction.

"Listen, dumbass. I may not be trying to beat you up every day anymore, but that doesn't make me stupid." He grinned and hopped back up a few steps. "If you're okay, walk up this flight of stairs."

"Okay, sure," I huffed. I took a step. If a sewing needle had been dropped directly in front of my foot, I might have cleared it with this colossal step forward. But I doubt it.

"Johnny?" Bobby said. "Seriously?"

"What?" I looked at him in that exaggerated way kids do, when it's clear they're full of crap.

He came back down to look at my knee. "You need help," he decided.

"For what?" I mocked. "Walking up the stairs? What am I, your grandma?"

Bobby looked at me in an eerily serious way, head tilted downward, eyes still locked on me. "I want you to stop feeling the pain in your knee and finish climbing these stairs with me," he said in an almost chant-like voice.

"With me. *Now.*"

I felt a *shift*. I wanted to move. I wanted to climb the stairs. I wanted to be at the top of the building, looking down. I forgot about my knee. Was there pain anymore? I didn't care. I took one step, then a second. A calm expression came over my face as I continued upward, step by step, gaining strength.

We moved, first slowly, then faster and faster. Finally we rocketed up the last flight and burst through a door onto the roof. I stood looking out as far as I could see.

"*On top of Mount Traaaash-more!*" Bobby sang, way off-key. "Look at this view, Johnny." He glowed. "How far do you think you can see?"

Looking around, I took in the whole town. Hell, I could see *other* towns. Past the tall pines out west, I could see the interstate, people traveling fast to somewhere else, nowhere near our little world. An RV buzzed past, a white blotch against the black ribbon of road, heading south.

I held up a second, realizing that something strange had happened. Where moments before I'd thought I would need someone to take me back to the hospital, I'd come to realize that I felt fine. How? I experienced a tinge of joy, almost elation. I'd done it, despite my bad knee. But something about how it happened bothered me. Nonetheless, I felt completely happy. I was giddy, in fact.

I gave Bobby a look, stern, serious. Sensing something changing about my mood, he wrinkled his brow. "What is it now, Johnny?" he asked. "Something wrong?"

After a pause long enough to fool him, I spoke. "Out there." I pointed, dramatically. "I think I can see… Uranus."

Bobby erupted in laughter.

Interlude

Voices. Small, very quiet, but many all at once, coalescing into a buzz. Only in the dead of night, drifting in and out of sleep. Coming from somewhere close, all around me. Not saying words, but yet… communicating. Not with me, with each other. Like the static on a distant radio transmission being intercepted, vaguely electronic, squeals and hisses.

I hear you.

6

My knee improved quite a lot after that, to the surprise of my doctors. When my mom heard about my fall down the stairs — by *accident*, I assured her, completely vague about *where* those stairs were — she immediately rushed to get me checked out. The orthopedic specialist I was seeing then was named Dr. Mathers. He looked at me with great skepticism, assuming that he'd find a new tear. Instead, he reported that my knee seemed to have *regained* some mobility, and that the muscles around it seemed to be compensating. As a doctor, he felt he had to explain it. "Kids run around all day," he said, his overly confident tone suggesting he was trying to convince himself as much as us. "They get exercise and improve their muscles and don't even think about it." Mom seemed happy and satisfied. That kept her from hovering over me, at least for a couple days.

I knew it was something else, but I simply didn't want to tell anyone that my knee felt *healed*. Not *healed*, actually, but *reconfigured*. That was the best word for it. How was that possible? Much like the moment in the hospital where my mom suddenly changed, had Bobby done something to me? In my gut, I felt like whatever happened had originated inside me, and that maybe he just prodded it a little more. Or maybe my body was already healing, but my timid nature and conservative brain held me back. Maybe Bobby's push got me past that point.

It was all very confusing. My knee felt great. No pain, no stiffness. And yet mentally, I felt *guilty*. Like I shouldn't be doing so well. But why? My improvement was no harm to anyone. If anything, it meant less time and money spent on doctors. I should be glad to rid my parents of the burden. But somehow it was unnatural.

Bobby, meanwhile, had gotten to like the privacy of the self-storage building. He'd drop by my house and we'd go there for hours. It was our playground, hideout, and private world, all in one. Bobby knew something radical had happened with my knee. In fact, he told me, he felt changes himself, like the injuries he suffered in the car accident had been erased. Something had changed in our bodies, something important. And we could do things with our minds, too, make people change their minds. So far, it seemed like it was happening accidentally, but Bobby starting working on that, to channel it. Both his mind and his body.

I had to slow things down. To figure out what was going on.

"Bobby, what's happening with us?" I asked, jangling a knee that should have been restrained to a 45-degree arc. Bobby was trying to mentally influence a cockroach climbing up the cinder-block wall of the self-storage building, but he stopped and looked my way.

He had a smile on his face. "Does it matter? We're badasses!"

There certainly was no arguing with that logic. And this underscored one of the more fundamental differences between me and Bobby. I worried. He didn't give a damn. There was no one for me to talk to about the reasons behind the change, so I found myself just going with the flow.

By this time, we were well versed in the art of avoiding Mr. Gerald, the guy who ran the self-storage facility. We came to find that Mr. Gerald was a die-hard fan of what he called his "stories." As in, he'd be diligently at work, then look at his watch and say "Ah, fer crap's sake, almost time for m' stories!" Mr. Gerald said bizarre things like that. Then he'd run off, back to his office. His "stories" were the afternoon soap operas. So for several hours every weekday, we were relatively sure we'd see no sign of him. And most weekends he watched golf, so those were wide open, too. But we couldn't avoid Ike and Izzy, the two Rottweilers he kept around to guard the place. That was okay. Living close to the self-storage building his whole life, Bobby had become friends with the dogs, through a slow process of giving them little treats every once in a while. Out of training and habit, the two dogs would run at us, hackles up, whenever we snuck in. But Bobby would just pet them on the head. They must have accepted me simply because I was with Bobby. As for the occasional people who came around to poke through their storage units piled high with crap, well, worrying about a couple of kids playing in the building wasn't high on their list of concerns. Still we avoided being seen as much as possible.

So we pretty much had the run of the place. One Sunday afternoon in late October, Bobby noticed one of the storage pods had been left open. In it, a plastic cigarette lighter lay amid a pile of someone's important trash. Picking up the lighter, its yellow body glinting in the setting sun from the window, Bobby spun the mechanism to spark a fire. Then he put his finger into the flame.

"Ow, son of a *bitch!*" he yelled, shaking his hand.

"Very clever, Bobby. Next you'll be hitting yourself in the head with a hammer." I smirked. "I'm totally up for the entertainment value of you hurting yourself, so please, go ahead." I don't think Bobby always appreciated my wit. His loss. He flicked the lighter again, and put his finger into the flame a second time. He winced. It was clearly causing him pain. I can't be certain, but I think I smelled burning flesh. Not pretty. But he kept his finger where it was. After a minute, he stopped. His finger was a little singed, but in a couple of minutes, the dark patches went away.

"All right," I said. "That was a treat, but I was thinking about doing something that isn't so... what's the word? *Boring.* What do you say, Bobby?"

In response, he looked at me with gleaming eyes and raised the lighter again. One more flick, and the flame appeared.

"Really?" I sighed. "Come on."

He put the same finger in a third time. This time, he just stared at me while his finger hovered in the middle of the flame. There was no burning smell, no yelling, not even any wincing. He left his finger there for a minute, two, maybe more. I looked closely. The flame appeared to be splitting into a U shape, diverting itself around his finger, so close it was hard to tell, but maybe not even touching his skin.

Bobby pulled his finger out, not the fast pull of someone glad it's done, but the slow draw of someone making a point. "I didn't feel a thing," he said.

"No way, liar," I responded.

"Try it. You'll see."

"Um, no." Despite the previous business with my knee, I assumed this was just some stupid juvenile trick, so I could think of many more interesting things to do. Like watching paint dry or grass grow.

"Johnny," Bobby said. "I just had my finger in a fire for, what? Two minutes? I didn't feel it at all. I'm not kidding."

I squinted at him like a true skeptic. "Look, Bobby, I know something is going on with me and you. But that's just crazy. You *felt that*. You did."

"I didn't."

"You did."

"I did *not*. Try it." He held out the lighter.

"No way. Besides, it's not even summer. Not the right time of year for a good ol' John-B-Cue, I'm afraid," I said with a tired chuckle. Bobby continued to hold the lighter. I looked at it, then at him. Then I grabbed it. "Fine."

I spun the thumb wheel thingy and nothing happened.

"Hold the gas button down, stupid," Bobby said, rolling his eyes.

I cocked one eyebrow back at him. "Yeah, you've been using a lighter for several minutes now, so I'll definitely be considering you for the job of local expert." I bowed slightly in mock deference. He ignored me and made a little wiggling gesture with his thumb — *push the button, stupid.*

So I pushed the button. I spun the wheel. The gas came out. The spark ignited the flame. I decided to try it, putting my finger into the flame the way I'd seen Bobby do.

"*Jesus!*" I shouted.

"Shut up, you idiot!" Bobby chided. "You want someone to find us in here?"

"Well, pardon me, but that really *freaking hurt.*" I grimaced at my charred finger and shook it.

"Just do it again," Bobby said.

I laughed. "Yeah, right. That will *not* be happening." I shook my head.

Bobby got serious, tilting his head down at me. It reminded me of the day on the stairs, with my hurt knee. "Just do it, Johnny," he said in a low monotone. For a moment, I felt compelled. Then...

"Cut it out, Bobby," I said, breaking eye contact.

"What?" he smiled. I think things changed a little then. He wasn't trying overly hard, but I had repelled his mental push. Silently, we both considered what had happened for a second. Then he laughed. "Just do it anyway, jerk." He stood in front of me, a huge goofy grin on his face. Though we both played it off, it seemed like he was a little surprised I hadn't just gone along with his mental demand. We both realized that I could resist when he tried to make me do something, if I really wanted to.

"I'll do it one more time," I said. "That's it."

I flicked the lighter again, and as soon as the flame popped out, I put it right under my finger. To my surprise, the flame bent around my finger. I didn't feel a thing...

For about a minute.

Then it went right back to hurting like hell. I threw the lighter back onto the jumbled pile of someone else's stored crap.

7

Winter passed, a cold mass of air that occasionally turned moisture into snow, but never with enough staying power to interrupt the routine for more than a few days. Other kids got excited about snow days, but for me they came to mean a little bit of humiliation. When school was out, Bobby and I practiced our new skills, and while he got good at all of them quickly, I pretty much sucked. The only thing I seemed to do better than Bobby was the mind thing. I could repel him. If I tried hard, he couldn't repel me. But the idea of mentally forcing my will on a friend seemed unfriendly, so I rarely did it. Unless he was really pissing me off.

Like I said, snow days were the worst. On normal days, we had school, homework, other stuff to take up the time. My parents were music lovers, so they gave me a choice: Pick any instrument to learn. I picked the French horn, mostly because I thought they'd laugh and say no. You know the expression *cut off your nose to spite your face*? Yeah, that. With apologies to anyone who finds the French horn to be a major turn-on, my experience was that it just made me a bigger dork. But when I tried to backpedal and choose something cooler, like say the electric guitar, Mom and Dad were having none of it. French horn it was. Well played, dork.

Anyway, at least French horn lessons had one thing going for them: Bobby wasn't there to make me feel bad about what I couldn't do. My music teacher was paid to handle that role on his own, but at least with him the stakes were scales and sight reading, not warping minds and lighting fingers on fire.

But snow days. Geez. On snow days, Bobby would be over early in the morning, begging me to go "out" — that was our word for the storage building. And every time it was the same. "Try to do something else to hurt me," he'd say.

It was getting annoying. The trick with the lighter got old once Bobby mastered it. For me, it was harder. I spent a lot of time *concentrating*. Maybe that was the problem. Maybe Bobby's seemingly effortless way of just *doing it* was the way it was supposed to work.

Bobby would dare me to do crazy things. Light his hair on fire, smash his finger with a hammer, cut him with a utility blade. I tried to talk to him about *why* this was happening. Why were we able to do these things? Things no one should be able to do? Bobby didn't care. And alone at night, turning it over in my mind, I had no answers.

We did our best to control the process, but in the end it came to seem natural and self-directed. It was something we didn't have to do much about. Once our bodies got used to the various forms of damage we wanted to inflict on ourselves, they learned to adapt and overcome. I was just much more timid about experimenting, so Bobby flourished while I floundered. I could tell that frustrated him. He felt held back. I felt humiliated. He wanted me to move faster, try harder. In a way, he was bullying me all over again.

Thinking back, I don't really know why I was such a stick in the mud. I could push people's minds, at least within reason. I felt no pain from fire. When I relaxed, I could even manage the hammer trick without pain or blood. And yet, because I was a kid, I spent most of my time upset and moping about how Bobby could do it better.

Oh yeah, the hammer trick. That was particularly neat, and certainly not anything I planned to show my mom. She'd have me under round-the-clock psychiatric supervision if she had any idea what we did. What we could do.

When we did the hammer trick, we'd put one hand on a hard, flat surface. There were plenty of those around the storage building, especially when someone left a unit open — old tables, appliances, whatever. We didn't even have a hammer, we just called it the hammer trick. We'd find something else hard and metal, compact enough that we could easily swing it with one hand, similar to a hammer. Then we'd bring it slamming down, crushing our other hand.

And that hand would *shift*.

On its own, with no input from our brain or muscles, it would move out of the way of the falling hammer-like object. Sometimes it was subtle, like a few of our fingers separating themselves to allow the blow to miss. Sometimes more drastic — watching closely, it was like our hand would sluice out of the way, losing distinct form where it sat waiting to be crushed and regaining form in a new place.

It was mind-boggling.

The first time Bobby tried it, I called him out. "You totally moved!" I cried.

Bobby looked back, eyes wide. "Didn't. Honest."

"Shut up, liar."

"You do it," he said, daring me.

"No way."

"Then how about this," Bobby said that first time. "You smash my hand while I'm not looking. No way I can move in time if I'm not watching, right?" I hesitated, then agreed.

Because, like I said, boys could be real dicks as friends. So, in order to call him out, I had to prove he was cheating by smashing his hand into a bloody pulp.

He handed me the hammer, which was actually just a discarded metal pipe. It was pretty heavy. Then he turned away, leaving one hand on the surface of someone's credenza. "Go ahead," he said, looking toward the back wall of the storage unit.

I couldn't resist a joke. "You know," I said, "this is gonna hurt you a lot more than it hurts me."

Bobby turned back for just a second, with a serious but calm expression. "No, it won't." He turned away again.

And I brought the pipe down.

As I stood there, pipe wedged in the crack it had just made in the credenza's mahogany surface, I thought to myself, *How'd he do it? How'd he know when to flinch?*

But eventually Bobby convinced me. It wasn't him, it was his body. It did the work for him. It just knew what to do, on its own, like it was *preserving* itself. Finally, he had me so convinced that I did the trick, too. First, with lighter implements that were unlikely to leave permanent damage. It worked. It wasn't long before I moved up to pipes and other heavy hammers myself.

Still, Bobby was the brave one. More willing to try the next crazy thing. Every time I did the hammer trick, I always assumed, *this time it won't work*, and I'd be in the hospital again like a dunce. But it always worked. Always.

As winter started to fade, Bobby's appetite for stunts increased. One day, he was at my house and we were playing videogames. My mom was sewing at a table across the room. I could tell Bobby was anxious about something.

Finally, Mom got up to get a soda, and Bobby turned to me. "Let's get out of here," he said. "This is boring."

"I don't feel like going to... going out... right now," I said, not taking my eyes off the TV.

"Come on, man. We've played this game like 50 times." He got up and started pacing around the room.

I ignored him.

Then I heard the sewing machine start up. At first, I assumed my mom had returned.

"Johnny," Bobby said. "*John.*" The second time it was more forceful, trying to get my attention. I paused the game and looked over, annoyed.

"*What?*" I asked, exasperated. Then I saw what he was doing. Bobby had one foot on the pedal powering the sewing machine and he was holding his hand out toward the moving needle. "No — cut that out!" I said in a harsh whisper.

He grinned. "I'm gonna do it." I rushed over to stop him, and he thrust his hand under the rapidly bobbing needle.

At just that moment, my mom came back in the room, carrying a glass of fizzing soda and looking at us with alarm. "Boys. What are you doing with my machine?" Bobby quickly took his foot off the pedal and the machine went quiet.

"Um. Ow," he said, not very convincingly. "Ow! Sorry, Mrs. B. Hey, I gotta go." He ran out, holding the hand he had thrust into the moving machine.

Looking down, I saw the needle.

It was bent into a U shape, destroyed.

KEITH SOARES

8

Mom was pissed about the sewing needle, but we were kids. Kids were messy and destructive, particularly boys, so while she was mad and I got in trouble for it, it wasn't a big deal. In a few days, the whole thing was forgotten.

Bobby was fine. No puncture, no blood, nothing. He told me he'd felt the needle — jabbing at him over and over as the sewing machine did its work — but that it was more like a nuisance than actual pain. He also said that when he grabbed his hand and ran out, his skin felt hard, but just for a moment. After a few seconds, he couldn't tell anything had happened at all.

Spring eventually arrived, and so we kept pretty busy. Between soccer, French horn lessons, homework, and school, there wasn't a lot of time to spend at Bobby Graden's Informal Skills Improvement Workshop. Plus, I still hung out with Tom and Steve from time to time. I never told them about any of the strange things I could do. I was a nerd with three friends. I wasn't willing to risk losing two of them by revealing that I was also a circus freak.

I knew Bobby kept working on his physical abilities, but it wasn't something that interested me. There are only so many ways you can creatively try to hurt yourself without making a scene.

But I started to reconsider one hot day toward the end of May. The school year was nearly over. The bus dropped us off at the usual spot, near Steve's house, and we decided to take a side trip to the convenience store. We each had a few bucks in our pocket for just such an occasion, so we wanted to get those slushy frozen sugar drinks that kids love because they're completely lacking in nutritional value or other redeeming qualities. Which, of course, means they're awesome. It was only a few blocks to the store, so Tom, Steve, and I walked.

As kids do, we were talking, razzing each other, kicking rocks, basically doing anything except paying attention to what was happening around us. So we were surprised when, across the street from the convenience store, just a few feet from where I'd been hit by a car all those months ago, we heard an alarm bell. And yelling.

All of a sudden, Walter Ivory, still doing his best to look the part of lanky, greasy dirtball, came running out of the store, cradling something under one arm like a football. It looked like a plastic bag filled with bottles and other things. Right behind him, the door burst open a second time and Mr. Donaldson, the storeowner we'd known for years, ran out.

Mr. Donaldson had a shotgun pointed at Walter's back.

"Dammit it, Walter, stop!" Mr. Donaldson worked the action on the shotgun, but Walter kept running. "I know who you are, you're not getting away with anything. And I'm sure as hell not letting you steal from me, you son of a bitch!" See what I mean? It wasn't just me who thought that about Walter. It was pretty much universal.

Walter and Mr. Donaldson continued along the two-lane road in the world's slowest hot-pursuit chase. The scene was actually comical for a moment. But Mr. Donaldson was a lot older than Walter, and it was clear that he'd be outrun soon.

"I mean it — last chance!" Mr. Donaldson yelled, panting.

Without turning back, Walter shouted, "Go to hell!"

Mr. Donaldson stopped. He was furious but exhausted. In an almost reticent way, he steadied the shotgun, sighted down the barrel, and pulled the trigger.

And Walter Ivory was riddled with pellets from the shotgun blast, knocking him facedown onto the shoulder of the road. The sack flew from his arms, some of the bottles breaking on the ground, spreading beer into the gutter, some rolling away with loud clinking sounds.

"Holy crap!" Steve said. "Mr. Donaldson just freakin' killed Walter Ivory!"

Walter Ivory, town son of a bitch, was dead on the side of the road.

At least for a few moments.

Then, inexplicably, he dragged himself to his feet. Limping, he started running again, gaining speed as he headed away from the exhausted Mr. Donaldson. Jaws hanging open, we all watched as Walter disappeared over the next hill and was gone.

Mr. Donaldson stood gasping for air. But the sack of unpaid items was still on the ground, so he didn't chase Walter any farther. He picked up the bag, mindful of the broken glass poking through the plastic like shrapnel, gathered up the remaining bottles, and slowly walked back to his store.

In the distance, sirens began to wail, so we decided we didn't need slushy drinks after all.

9

Bobby and I were still friends, and to be honest, he was pretty freaking funny. Always cracking jokes about something or other. So it wasn't like I *hated* hanging out with him. I just wished he'd tone down the more abrasive parts of his personality.

But who's perfect? So Bobby always wanted me to try to set him on fire or break his neck. So what? Tom was the kind of guy who'd take your allowance money if you left it sitting out, then plop down next to you for two hours playing videogames, thinking nothing of it. And Steve did these insufferable little dances about everything that he liked, thinking he looked cool. Other than Michael Jackson, can you think of any dancing 12-year-old who looks cool? Yeah, me neither.

I envied my friends for having me as a friend — perfect in every way. Humble. Respectful. Brilliant. Ha ha. I told endless lame jokes, usually on rapid repeat, and complained endlessly about every little thing I *didn't* want to do. So I was a pain in the ass, too.

Where was I? Oh yeah, Walter Ivory got shot, and then stood up and ran off like it was nothing. That was a little odd, right?

A few days went by, and Bobby and I were back at the self-storage building. Bobby was rubbing Izzy's tummy as the dog flopped on the floor of level four, where we'd found an open, abandoned unit. Ike was sniffing around and peeing on a pile of old magazines and other junk. Should he be peeing indoors? I didn't know. Did he have any way to get outdoors? Probably, but I wasn't really sure. In any event, not my dog, not my magazines, not my problem.

I was bored, so I went exploring, a few levels higher.

The building was really big — wide and tall, with eight floors total. I mean, it might be small compared to a New York City skyscraper, or Nova Scotia, or Uranus, or something, but to us kids, it was huge.

From above, the building must have looked like a fat lowercase letter "b." There was a single hall that ran north to south, the longest part of the building. On the north end, there was a small door for people and a much larger door for the mobile storage pods that got moved in and out. Another door stood at the south end — it was the one Bobby had learned to jimmy open. Off the main hall, two long rows of bays shot to the east, connecting at the end with another short north/south hall.

There was plenty of space to explore, plenty of space to get lost. We were never concerned we'd bump into Mr. Gerald. There was just too much space, too many floors. Even on a single level, it was easy to hide, just by disappearing around a corner or ducking behind something large. But usually, the stairs were our primary getaway. When he was actually out doing work, done with his stories for the day, Mr. Gerald almost never took the stairs. He preferred the noisy industrial-strength elevator, meaning we could always hear him coming. Plus, he worked alone and liked to sing to himself, and he was really bad at singing.

The elevator was pretty cool, in a sci-fi-movie kind of way. It was huge — big enough to carry a storage pod plus the big rolling rig Mr. Gerald used to move them — and not the least bit posh. No carpet, tile, or mirrored panels like at my dad's office downtown. This was strictly business: thick corrugated metal floor and sides, with two sections of metal grating serving as the gates, like a chain-link fence on steroids. The gates came down from the ceiling and up from the floor, meeting in the middle. On the rare occasion when Bobby and I used the elevator, it felt like we were boarding a spaceship. But usually we left it alone, because you never knew when Mr. Gerald would be moving a pod.

Pods were the latest craze when it came to the storage of unwanted possessions for the well-to-do materialistic pinhead. Big, heavy metal boxes that could be rolled via a cart, delivered to some glutton's home, filled with crap, and brought back. There were dozens of pods around the building. In fact, there were so many that Mr. Gerald kept a bunch of them on the roof of the building. (In a cleverly economic use of space, the elevator went to every floor, including the roof, allowing all-weather storage up there, too.) Bobby and I got to know a lot of the pods by number and by sight, meaning there were always a couple that we knew how to jimmy. Same thing went for the storage bays, which ranged in size from hall closets to small car garages, but it was harder to get those open. Luckily, people were always moving in or out, or failing to pay the rent and getting tossed. In other words, we always had somebody else's stuff we could rummage through.

Out of habit, I walked as quietly as possible up the stairs. I was looking for Pod A26, which had a particularly bad lock and was usually filled with interesting things. I'd last seen it on the sixth floor, so that's where I ended up. Windows were set in the east and west walls on every floor (another economical decision — it meant less need for electric lights), so as I exited the stairwell on the sixth floor, I turned to look out over the town through the dirty glass.

Out of the corner of my eye, I saw something move behind a pod down the hall.

Instantly, I retreated through the doorway to the stairwell, then peered nervously back down the hallway.

There, in an open bay on the sixth floor, tucked between two pods, was Walter Ivory.

I started to sweat. I mean, my family didn't exactly have a great history with Walter, but now he was wanted by the police for attempted robbery. Oh, and he probably should have been dead.

I watched him for a minute or two. He looked to be setting up a little place for himself, shifting things around, reorganizing the space in some way I didn't understand. But it was clear what I was seeing: a couple of backpacks of gear, a little bedroll, a cooler. All arranged so that a grown man could stretch out on the floor, in the middle of the bay. It wasn't just for storage anymore.

Walter Ivory was living as a fugitive in Bay 6-13.

I had to tell Bobby.

Quietly, I ran down the stairs, to where Bobby was sitting with the dogs in a ray of sun coming from a side window. "Bobby!" I hissed. " Come here, and be quiet!"

Bobby looked up from petting Izzy. "What?" he said, too loudly, and I *shushed* him, gesturing silently for him to follow me. Without another word, we both crept to the sixth floor, crouching like we were in a war movie. Kids are always ready to sneak around.

As soon as Bobby saw Walter, he froze, mouth hanging open. We watched as Walter opened the cooler and pulled something out.

"He's not hurt," Bobby whispered. I just nodded. I'd told Bobby all about the shooting. I mean, it's not like I was going to see that and *not* tell everyone about it, right? I practically gave nightly performances. Bobby continued watching, mouth still slack. "Do you have *any idea what this means?*" he asked.

First I smiled, knowingly. Then my smile faded. I gave a moment's thought, scratching my head. "Um… no?"

Bobby pulled me down to sit beside him, our backs to the wall of the stairwell, so we wouldn't be seen. "He might be *like us*," Bobby said.

I blinked. I hadn't thought of that.

Walter had been shot. But he seemed no worse for wear. And I was pretty sure that if he'd been patched up at Davidson Regional, his next stop would have been the county jail.

But I refused to accept it. First off, I secretly believed that the car accident had something to do with me and Bobby changing, although I didn't know how. I knew there was still a lot to think about, regarding *why* we changed, what it meant. But I was young enough to just go with the flow. More important, I didn't *want* to think of myself as being anything like Walter Ivory. I hated him. "No way," was all I said.

"Then how'd he get shot and then get up and run away?" Bobby asked. For a moment, he looked wistful. "Ah, I wish I'd thought of that, Johnny."

"I don't know," I said. "Maybe he had on a bulletproof vest under his clothes or something." I was grasping at straws. "Wait — what? You wish you'd thought of what?"

"Getting *shot!*" Bobby said, a big smile breaking across his face.

I rolled my eyes. "You're nuts. Besides, we've got more important issues: Walter Ivory. He's wanted by the law. We've got to turn him in." I didn't say it very convincingly. I wish I had. Maybe Bobby would have agreed.

"No way, I wanna see what he's doing." I had to admit, I pretty much wanted to do that, too. Spying? On an adult? In a place we knew like the back of our hand, where we already felt invincible? Hell, yes. Bobby pushed ahead: "Besides, if we turn him in, people will start asking what *we* were doing on the sixth floor of the self-storage building. You want that?"

He had a point. "Okay," I said, nodding. "But, if he does anything illegal, we'll have to think of some way to turn him in." I was still a nerd, in case you forgot.

"Fine," Bobby replied offhandedly.

Just then Ike and Izzy came racing up the stairs toward us.

"Oh crap," Bobby said as the dogs ran past us and into the hall toward Walter Ivory. Bobby tried to grab Ike's collar but missed.

I expected mayhem. Dogs growling and barking, Walter shouting. Maybe he'd get bitten. Maybe he'd hurt one of the dogs. We jumped up and poked our heads around the corner, anticipating the worst.

But Walter didn't budge. He sat on a large cardboard box, pulling something out of his cooler. When Ike and Izzy got close, he tossed something toward them. Some kind of food. They each snatched up a mouthful. Walter absently waved them away, growling, "Now get outta here!" The dogs obeyed.

"Damn," Bobby said, shaking his head in disappointment. "Those dogs really suck at their jobs."

10

"Where can we get a gun?" Bobby asked as we pedaled our bikes down a street of repetitive single-story homes.

"You need to shut up," I replied. "I'm not helping you get a gun, and I'm sure as hell not going to shoot you."

Bobby pushed into an upright sitting position, his grip leaving the handlebars. I turned away with a slight eye roll. Bobby knew I didn't know how to ride no-hands, so he was doing this in front of me to grandstand.

"Come on, wouldn't that just be *amazing*?" he said, opening his arms into the wind. "We could do it safely. Like, you just shoot my foot or something to start. It's really no different than the hammer trick."

"No different?" I said, still refusing to look over at him. "Me stealing a gun and shooting you is *no different* than us playing a little I-dare-you-with-a-hammer-game? Right."

We turned onto another street, down a slight hill, toward a row of small storefronts framed in two-story brick buildings with flat roofs. "But we've *got* to figure out if Walter is like us," Bobby said. "If you shoot me and I'm okay, then, well —"

"Or I could just walk up to Walter and ask, 'Hey, do you mind if I try to smash your hand with this lead pipe?' That would be informative, too." Sarcasm was practically my middle name.

"True. But I doubt he'd do it." Bobby sort of missed my point. Then he got this *expression*. Full of excitement. "Hey, look there!" He put his hands back on the handlebars and started to pedal faster, racing away from me. I pushed to catch up.

"What?" I asked, panting as I came up behind him. He pointed up.

"There," he said with a smile. "I'm totally going to jump that." He was beaming.

We had stopped in an alley between blocks of the two-story brick buildings. Above us, jutting from the top of one of the stores on our right, was the edge of a sheet of plywood. "What're you talking about?" I asked.

"Come on. Around back." It was his only reply. Behind the stores, we saw all the unsavory elements of marginalized small business: dumpsters, grease-stained parking spaces, a part-time employee in a blue uniform smoking a cigarette a few stores over. We waited until blue-uniform went back inside, then Bobby led me to the fire escape that ran up the back of the nearest building. I followed behind like a lost puppy. I was entirely sure Bobby was up to no good, but the combination of youthful exuberance and youthful stupidity got the best of me.

Looking around to make sure no one saw him, Bobby jumped up and grabbed the suspended ladder of the fire escape. He missed. He tried to find something to stand on, but there was nothing. "Johnny," he said, turning back to me, eyes wide. "You grab the ladder. I'll hold you up. Come on, don't be a wuss."

Ah damn. Clever ploy, Bobby. As a 12-year-old boy, "wuss" was one of the magic words I couldn't refuse. I had to help him.

I climbed onto Bobby's shoulders, first in a sort of piggyback, then on my knees, stretching an arm upward. When that wasn't enough, I timidly placed one sneaker on Bobby's back as he hunched over. "It's okay, go ahead," he said with effort. I carefully raised my other leg and stood fully upright on Bobby's curved back, then reached up and easily grabbed the lowest rung of the ladder. It came sliding down, ripping me off Bobby's back.

I held firmly onto the ladder as it descended, until it clanged to a stop and I slammed into the pavement, hard. I was already regretting helping out. As I rolled over, I noticed Bobby was on the ground, too, under the hanging ladder.

Bobby was lying on his back, with his right cheek pressed to the pavement. The foot of the ladder had stopped inches from his head, and his left eye was wide, straining to peek at the rusty metal just inches above him.

But we had done it. The ladder was down. Neither one of us was hurt. Much. Yet. We looked around and confirmed, as far as we knew, that no one had seen or heard us. So Bobby started to climb, carrying his bike.

He did an awkward shuffle, latching one of the handlebars over a rung of the ladder every couple of steps. But he made progress, eventually getting to the first landing of the fire escape. Wrestling the bike onto the platform proved to be more difficult than the climb, but he got it done, then called down to me. "Were you thinking of helping me at all, jerk?"

I snapped out of my daze and climbed up to join him. Bobby was already most of the way to the second landing. I kept expecting him to mess up and drop his bike on my head, but it didn't happen. He moved like he was on a mission.

I reached the second landing as Bobby approached the roofline. "Did I mention help would be nice?" Bobby looked down at me, dripping sweat from humping the bike up so far. I hurried to join him, then held the bike as he hauled himself onto the roof. For a moment, I was certain that I was going to drop the bike two stories to the pavement below, giving me visions of the old Bobby, beating the snot out of me. But I held on. And then he lifted it from above, and I scrambled up the ladder to join him on the roof.

It was exhilarating. And totally illegal, of course. We were only two stories up, but from the flat roof of the anonymous brick building, I felt like we could see everything in town. For a moment I scanned the horizon, looking for our self-storage building, our Mount Trashmore, but Bobby wasn't taken in by the view. He walked over and checked the sheet of plywood that someone had left propped at an angle, one end on the flat asphalt roof, the other on the short brick half-wall that garnished the top of the building. Basically it made a ramp. Bobby shook it with one hand to measure its strength. That seemed like a very scientific test.

Gauging the entire setup, this is what I figured: Each store, though connected, had its own flat roof, with its own surrounding half-wall, perhaps a foot or two high. The angle of the ramp looked relatively low — let's say, 13.57 degrees. As if I had any idea. And the distance to jump across the gaping hole of the alley and onto the next roof was maybe 15 feet. Carry the one, divide by pi. Yep, it was confirmed.

In short, there was no way in hell Bobby could make it.

He started to ride his bike in circles on the roof, getting ready, building up speed.

I was certain he was going to die.

But kids at our age use those words too much, in a disposable way: *You're gonna die! I'm gonna kill you!* They didn't have a lot of weight.

I was 12, after all. If you asked me, for real, whether I'd rather die or go to the principal's office, I'd pick death.

So we were kinda stupid.

Bobby turned toward the ramp, at the best speed he could manage in the small space.

I watched, holding my breath as he hit the ramp. For a split second, I thought, *this is going to be AWESOME!*

As he launched into the air, I was suddenly sure he was going to make it, land on the other roof, skid to a stop, and laugh at my fear. Perhaps fireworks would go off in celebration. They didn't.

He didn't.

Midway through the jump, Bobby and his bike started fading. They'd never make the other side. Bobby let out a wail of fear and anger and surprise. He dropped past the roofline and I rushed to the edge as he fell to the alley below, uttering only a solitary, unsatisfying *oof* as he landed.

His bike, however, made quite a racket. It clattered and rang as it hit the pavement and broke into several unexpected pieces. No doubt the Schwinn corporation would have considered it *totaled*.

Bobby lay splayed in an obscene pose, arms and legs all crooked and wrong. I stared at his head. It seemed *flatter* than it should've been.

Oh Jesus, did he brain himself? I wondered.

But there was no blood. He seemed intact, just crumpled in a weird position.

Then I saw the blood start to pool.

Crap crap crap crap crap, I thought, clanking loudly down the ladders to the alley. "Bobby! Are you all right?" I called out as I descended, not really wanting to hear the answer.

I hit the pavement, turned, and ran over to him. He was still in the same twisted pose I had seen from above, face down on the rough pavement.

One eye looked up at me, but he didn't speak. Maybe he couldn't speak. His head still had that *flattened* look to it.

"Oh my God oh my God OHMYGOD," I chanted. "What the hell am I gonna do?" My mind scanned for options, but for some reason only *You need to kick his stupid butt for being so stupidly stupid!* came through. "I'm getting help," I said, running out of the alley.

Back on the main strip of stores, I looked left and right for someone to help. An old woman, a teenage mother with an infant in a stroller. No, no. Then, down the street. A cop! I ran.

"Hey! Officer!" I yelled, but several cars were passing and he didn't hear me. I kept running.

Listen, adrenaline is great, you know? Nature's little pick-me-up. Works wonders. But even though I was jacked on adrenaline, I wasn't exactly a world-class sprinter. I finally pulled up near the cop, winded, hands on knees.

"What is it, son?" he said, pulling off his reflective sunglasses.

"My frien—," I said, panting. I took two more deep breaths. "My friend hurt himself." The cop stood up taller, realizing this might be serious. Don't you love cops? I mean, that's pretty badass, right? *Someone's in trouble? Point the way!* I'm pretty sure if someone came up to me and said, *Hey, someone's hurt! I need your help!* I'd just start sweating. And maybe cry.

"Where?" he asked.

Still panting, I pointed. From where we were, the alley was only a narrow break in the repetitive facades of stores stretching down the street.

"Take me to him," the officer commanded. I was 12, so being ordered to do something by a police officer was akin to having God himself, clad in the purest shimmering samite, appear in front of me and utter a commandment. I sucked in some air, stood, and started hurrying back to the alley. The officer followed.

Bobby just tried something stupid. We're really sorry. That's what I was planning to say. Then we rounded the corner into the alley.

Bobby was gone.

The cop looked at the bike wreckage, noticing the blood around it. He started checking the area, all the way to the back parking lot. When he found nothing — no one — he looked back to me, part confused, part angry. "What's going on here?"

Oh crap.

Where the hell did Bobby go? I figured he must have pulled himself back together, at least enough that he could walk, but now what was I supposed to do? I hesitated, stammering *ums* and *uhs* at the cop, and basically not doing anything to gain his confidence. He leaned in closer. "I said, *what's going on here?*"

I faked it! Ha ha! I thought. *Yeah, that's an excellent thing to say, if I'd like to rent a room at the Iron Bar Hotel.* My brow furrowed, and still I offered nothing, no explanation.

The cop reached for his radio.

No no no not that, don't call this in! My mind raced. Then I realized what I had to do.

I had to force him to think something else.

Do you have any idea how scary that was? The idea of using some unexplained, mystical *mind power* that I acquired unexpectedly, and on a *cop*? When you're 12? I was sure I'd need new underwear afterward.

His hand lifted the radio. I had about one more second to decide.

Eyes squinted in fear, I *pushed.*

And he shifted.

His hand held steady, then he blinked. Twice. He lowered the radio; it was forgotten. He looked around without really seeing anything, finally resting his gaze back on me. "Oh, uh…." He shook his head, clearing cobwebs. "Um, have a good day, son." He turned and walked out of the alley.

I did a quick check of my underpants to be sure I hadn't crapped myself, then hopped on my bike and pedaled home.

11

When my mom threw open the door just as I reached for the handle, I shrieked like a bleating goat.

"Oh, John! There you are," she said, oblivious to my terrified look and sweaty brow. "Hey, I need you to stay here with Holly for just a bit. I need to run an errand. I'll be back in about an hour, okay?" She was nodding to herself, fumbling with her keys, and walking out before I even had a chance to respond.

Suddenly she turned back. "What's my cellphone number? Just in case?" She paused, awaiting my reply, and I stuttered out the numbers from memory. She gave a small smile and nod and continued out the door, keys in hand.

And just like that, I found myself locked in the house, still wide-eyed with shock. I heard the engine of Mom's car start and then fade as she backed down the driveway and drove away. So I did the only logical thing that a kid my age would do after engaging in a deadly stunt with a friend, watching that friend fall to his obvious death, seeking police help, finding out the friend wasn't dead, using mind powers on the police to send them away, then pedaling fast all the way home, only to get stuck on babysitting duty: I got a glass of water and went to watch TV with Holly.

Holly had been wheelchair-bound since her seizure. I really missed the sound of her voice. I hadn't heard her say an intelligible word since that day. So you can see why I nursed a special sort of hatred for Walter Ivory. Sure, he didn't directly do anything to Holly, but just him *being there* that day, starting things with my Dad. I know I blamed him.

Of course, whatever happened to Holly could have been a ticking bomb. She could very well have had her big seizure the next day at school, or a year later riding her bike, or whatever. Still…

Holly was watching cartoons. She loved cartoons. I could tell because her eyes stayed glued to the TV when they were on, and if I had the gall to stand between her and the set, she'd twitch to look around me, sometimes making little upset noises. Before I sat, I offered her some of my water, and she tilted back her head a bit in acceptance, so I gently poured some into her mouth. She swallowed and bent to look around me at the TV, so I moved out of the way and sat down on the couch.

After a few minutes of cartoons, I realized I wasn't watching the TV at all. I was just thinking about Bobby. Where the hell did he go? Was he actually okay? I figured I needed to check on him, since no one else even knew he'd been hurt.

I looked over at Holly. She hadn't budged since I sat down. Not an inch. Watching the screen like a zombie.

Bobby lived four streets over. If I ran and snuck through backyards, I could be tapping on his bedroom window in maybe five minutes. Five minutes there. A minute or two to make sure he was okay. Five minutes back. Eleven or 12 minutes. I checked the clock hanging over the TV. It was 3:35 p.m. Cartoons would be on for another 25 minutes. I could do it before Holly even knew I was gone.

"I'll be right back," I told Holly. She didn't move or respond. That was what I wanted. *Just keep watching your show*, I thought, knowing my Mom would seriously kill me if she found out I left Holly at home alone. But I was desperate. If Bobby wasn't home, he could really be hurt. I had no idea what I would do if that were the case, but I had to find out.

Getting up, I first went to my room and strapped on my wristwatch. I was going to time this like a military operation. Then I put my glass of water, now about half full, on the counter in the kitchen and made for the back door. I clicked the button to start my stopwatch.

Four minutes, 48 seconds later, I was knocking lightly on Bobby's bedroom window, practically breaking my arm to pat myself on the back at being ahead of schedule.

There was no answer.

12

I rapped my knuckles on the glass again. "Bobby, it's me," I said in a loud whisper.

I heard a groan from inside. *Oh crap.*

Knowing that Bobby kept his window unlocked, I reached up and pushed. I mean, we were boys, after all. We had to be able to sneak out of our houses at a moment's notice. The window slid up, and I leaned in to push away the curtains.

Bobby's bedroom was dim, even though the afternoon was bright — he always kept the curtains closed, to make his room as dark as a tomb. His parents gave him infinite trouble about it, especially his father, who said Bobby just wanted it dark so he could be lazy and sleep in. Which was, of course, correct.

After a moment to let my eyes adjust, I saw him. Flopped on his bed. He looked worse than he had in the hospital after being hit by a car. I crawled in the window.

"Crap, are you okay?" I asked.

Bobby let out a heavy sigh. "Not yet. But… I think I will be soon." His voice sounded ragged.

"Yeah, right. You look awful."

"I know. But…"

"But what?"

He managed to turn his head a bit and give me a smile, through the bruises and dried blood on his face. It was several minutes until he was able to speak. "But I'm *not dead*, Johnny."

"You got freakin' lucky," I said.

"No, Johnny, I didn't. I got hurt. But I can *feel* it getting better. Actually, that's not the right word. I can *hear* it getting better." His eyes were dead serious.

I paused, not understanding. "What the hell does that mean?"

Bobby continued to look at me with a deeply solemn expression. "Tell me you've heard them, too, Johnny. The sounds. The sounds *inside* you."

I was taken aback. Sounds? Sounds inside me?

But, yes. I had heard them, hadn't I? At night, on the edge of sleep, when everything else was quiet. I'd heard something like a buzz. Like a distant radio signal. A sound inside me. Many sounds inside me, an unseen, unknown chorus.

Slowly, I nodded. "Yeah. Yeah, I've heard them. Well, I've heard *something*."

Bobby closed his eyes. "Thank God. I was beginning to think I was going crazy. And it's *loud* now, Johnny. Like me hurting myself woke up the sounds. They sound *busy.*"

They sound busy? Sounds inside me. Sounds inside Bobby. I looked down at my left hand, the one that had dodged our hammer trick so many times. Had I heard a sound back then, doing the trick? I think maybe I had, just for a moment.

Then I noticed my stopwatch.

"Oh no," I said, too loud.

"What?" Bobby asked, as I put a leg up on the windowsill, trying to throw myself outside.

"I've been gone 14 minutes!"

"So?"

I gave Bobby a last look, already half out the window. "So, Holly's at home alone!"

* * *

I didn't time myself on the way home, but as fast as I was going, I assumed it was a new record. I pushed through the back door, half expecting to find Holly in a panic, or Mom waiting for me, or both.

But the house was quiet, except for the sounds of the TV still playing cartoons in the other room. I let out a huge sigh and walked in to join Holly.

She wasn't there.

No wheelchair, no Holly. *I'm dead.*

Holly was able to push herself around, but only rarely, and only for reasons we could never figure out. If we asked her to roll the wheels of the chair, we'd usually get nothing. Then sometimes she'd just cruise here or there, for something she wanted or because an inner voice told her to — hell, I had no idea.

Our house wasn't big. The most obvious possibility was that she went to her room, so I ran there first. Nothing. My room, my parents' room: both empty. *Oh man, she probably had to go to the bathroom, why'd I give her that water!* But the bathroom was also empty. So I went to check the kitchen, now assuming that Holly had somehow gotten out of the house, or had been abducted by aliens, or some other scenario that my parents would definitely kill me for.

And I saw her lying on the floor of the kitchen among shards of broken glass.

She twitched and moaned a bit, and my stomach twisted with the fear that she might be in great pain. Her chair was turned over next to her, right in front of the counter. I quickly realized what had happened: She'd gotten thirsty and somehow maneuvered herself into the kitchen to get my glass of water. Reaching for it, she knocked it over and fell out of her chair.

I was a dead man.

One nick, one scratch on Holly and my mom would know for sure I hadn't been here for her. In fact, Holly wheeling herself somewhere — *anywhere* — was so uncommon that I was certain Mom would know I hadn't even been at home. How else could I have missed it?

Yep. Dead.

I righted her chair and positioned it back up against the counter. Holly was smaller than me, but let's be honest: I wasn't prepared for the dead lift required to get her back into the chair. Still, out of sheer desperation, I tried. And remarkably, it worked.

Once Holly was back in the chair, I checked her over. Any scratch — *any scratch* — and I was doomed.

She seemed... fine.

Then I saw the tear in her shirt, on the left side of her stomach. I straightened and smoothed the shirt, and as I did the hole opened up and I saw that it was stained with blood. I expected to see an equal tear in her skin. But there was nothing. I couldn't believe my luck. The small hole in her shirt — that I could just feign ignorance about, even with the blood. As long as *she* wasn't hurt. She was a little wet, but that could be explained, too.

I brushed some tiny flecks of glass off Holly as she sat in her chair. The floor needed to be cleaned up, so I got to it, using a new trash bag.

When I wheeled Holly back to the living room, I had to admire my work. It looked like nothing had happened.

I took the bag out into the garage and stuffed it deep into our big trashcan.

Coming back in, there was Mom. "Where were you?" she asked.

Oh my God, how could she know! My heart raced. Then... *Wait! She just means* right now. *She just means why was I outside* now.

"Just throwing out some trash," I said, trying to be casual.

"Okay. Hey — thanks for babysitting. Is Holly okay?"

I nodded. "Yeah, she knocked into me and I spilled a little water on her, but that's it," I lied.

Yeah, Holly was just fine.

13

So the one thing I didn't expect the next morning was just the thing that happened. Bobby walked up, like any other day, no sign of injury, and knocked on my door.

"Can Johnny come out and play?" he asked my mom.

* * *

As usual, we hung out at the self-storage building. Ike and Izzy greeted us with wagging tails, then ran off like they had something better to do. Our first order of business: See if Walter was still around.

He was. Still squatting in 6-13.

We figured we needed a plan.

The building was *our* place, dammit, and a place where we did a lot of weird stuff we really weren't all that keen on having someone else know about. We'd have to keep an eye on Walter, if for no other reason than to be sure he wasn't keeping an eye on us.

The first step was to see what Walter would do if Mr. Gerald showed up. Was Walter actually *allowed* to be in the building?

Having snuck around the building for so long, we knew that waiting for Mr. Gerald to show up wasn't an option. His patterns were erratic, and most of the afternoon he'd be glued to the TV. Instead, Bobby stood watch behind a row of pods on the sixth floor, where he could easily keep an eye on 6-13 while staying hidden from both Walter and Mr. Gerald. My job was to use the dogs to get Mr. Gerald's attention, but how was I going to do that without getting caught? Some simple recon had told us that Mr. Gerald was two floors below. He was driving his little forklift, using the elevator to move pods onto the fourth floor, so I'd need to make a lot of noise. I'd need him first to come up two floors, and then head toward Walter's bay in the back corner.

At the open stairwell door on the sixth floor, I waited until I heard quiet from the floors below me, then teased the dogs with some baloney I had stolen from home. They barked like mad. Mr. Gerald, always one to prefer sitting on his ass to doing something, made me keep it up for a solid five minutes before deciding to take the elevator and check on the dogs. As the elevator slowly churned its way upward, I ran down the hall and the dogs followed. I positioned myself at the corner, where Mr. Gerald would see the dogs but not me. The heavy doors of the elevator rasped open, and an angry Mr. Gerald stepped out. "What in the hell are you damn dogs going on about?" he shouted.

I tossed the baloney down the hall in the direction of Walter's bay and the dogs ran off after it. As I hid behind a pod, Mr. Gerald grumbled and lumbered after them. He checked his watch once and I thought *oh damn, are his shows starting already?* But he kept walking toward the sound of the dogs, so I guess there was still a little time before *The Young and the Pouty* or *Days of Our Twisted Discontent* or whatever soap opera he watched first came on.

Bobby told me later that Walter quietly tucked into his bay and rolled down the door before Mr. Gerald got close. So at least we established something: Walter wasn't there with permission.

For a couple of weeks after that, we kept an eye on him. And even though we did all kinds of crazy things in the building, Walter had us beat. The things he did were just nuts.

Our hammer trick was nothing compared to the time Walter purposefully fell head first onto the cement floor from the top of a pod. Or when he started a little fire in his storage unit and just sat there with his lower leg nestled in the flames. He even had his own version of our hammer trick, but he aimed for his forearm. That made it unmistakable. Seeing his entire arm shift to avoid the blow told us for certain that Walter was like us.

But unlike our little games, Walter seemed to have higher stakes in mind. He looked like he was trying to kill himself.

Walter Ivory had gone completely insane.

He talked to himself constantly, muttering in a way we couldn't understand. The only words we ever recognized were "Shut up! Shut up!" He said that a lot, and if he did raise his voice, that was almost always what he'd repeat. Many times, he'd suddenly slam his head against something hard, like he was trying to knock something out of his skull. Like his head was the cookie jar, and he wanted that cookie inside really bad.

Seeing Walter's head sluice and shift for a moment reminded me of Bobby after the failed bike jump, his head oddly flat.

I couldn't shake the sense that Walter was having a darkly mirrored version of my and Bobby's experience. Like watching a movie of my life turned into a horror story. All we needed was the scary music. Even when it came to the self-storage building, which for us was a wonderful place to find just about anything. Whatever people couldn't bear to throw away made it into a bay or a pod, and many of those were easy to break into. In our many visits, Bobby and I had stumbled onto countless treasures. Would you believe I found a crown one time? A *crown*. I mean, I'm not trying to tell you it was real and belonged to the king of England or anything, but it was *metal*, etched, and loaded with things that at least seemed like jewels. I wore it around the building for *days*.

Walter found things, too, but nothing that ever seemed to bring him even the smallest measure of joy. One evening as the sun was setting, shining slantways through the west-facing windows, we saw him pull out something long and dully reflective in the fading light: a very large knife.

There was no warning, just a brutal slash. Walter Ivory quickly and savagely slit his own throat. Blood flew and he fell.

Terrified, we ran.

14

Bobby and I vowed never to return to Mount Trashmore, which was now a vile, terrible place replete with horrors unimaginable. Yeah, sure. You do remember that we were 12-year-old boys, right? We went back as soon as possible the next day.

Walter Ivory was nowhere to be found.

From our normal hiding spot among the pods, we saw his bay was open, but there was no sign of Walter. Our minds turned.

"Oh crap," Bobby said, bug-eyed. "You don't think the *dogs* got to him, do ya?"

"What, like *ate* his dead body or something?"

"Yeah!" Bobby nodded.

"Geez, I hope not," I said. "That's gross." Those dogs *licked* me, for God's sake.

"Then where is he?" Bobby asked, pointing toward Walter's empty bay.

"He's gotta be dead, so I don't know how he could've just walked away," I mused. How does a dead body move? For a moment, I thought of Walter Ivory reanimating, walking himself away as a zombie. I laughed at myself. Everyone knew zombies were hyped-up pop-fiction bullshit. The dogs seemed the most logical option. What else could have gotten to him inside the building?

Bobby hesitated. "What if he's not dead?" he asked, quietly.

"Come on, you saw it — he slashed his own throat!" I couldn't believe he was alive, even if he had the same powers Bobby and I did.

Bobby squared his shoulders. "I'm going over to take a closer look," he announced.

"Are you *nuts?*" But Bobby was already striding down the hall. I hurried to catch up, still protesting, but not too seriously. I wanted to know what the hell was going on, too.

After searching through the open bay, Bobby was convinced. "He's definitely not here. And look." He pointed at the rough floor around us.

A large splash of blood had seeped into the cement. I gagged. "Jesus, that's disgusting."

"If the dogs dragged him away, the blood would show which way he went. But there's nothing." Bobby was right. *Damn.*

At that moment, heavy hands grabbed Bobby and me by the backs of our shirt collars. We both let out a startled shout.

"What're you two doing here?" That voice. *Walter Ivory.* He was alive.

I craned my neck to get a glimpse of his face, and up close I could see the ragged skin of his neck. It was healed, but not just once. There were many scars, knitted and intersecting. Walter must have slashed his throat countless times. We only got to see the first. Or the most recent. Who knew how long he'd been playing this sick game.

Suddenly Walter gave a pained expression as his body shuddered violently. "You…!" he said, staring at us in a strange way, like he recognized us, maybe even was *afraid* of us. He winced, twisting his head like he was hearing some painfully loud noise, then nodded to himself. "I know what to do." Oh goody. A psychopath had taken a keen interest in us. That sounded like it would turn out well.

He began to pull us in the direction of the elevator. *Oh God, he's gonna turn us in*, I thought. We dragged our feet and pleaded, but he kept a firm grip on our shirts and forced us to move along. As we went, Walter found a roll of packing tape and snatched it up.

We were pushed into the elevator as Bobby pleaded with him. "Come on, mister, don't turn us in! We were just looking around! We'll leave and we won't come back, promise!" Walter looked at Bobby with a strangely quizzical expression, and punched a button on the elevator. The doors clanged together and we started to move.

Upward.

He had hit the button marked "R." We were going to the roof.

As the elevator lurched along, we were trapped with him, so he let go of our collars for a minute. Then Walter peeled sections of packing tape and wrapped them around our wrists.

In moments, the elevator doors opened noisily onto the roof. I blinked at the bright, merciless sun as Walter grabbed us each by an arm and dragged us out of the elevator. The roof was surrounded by a low brick wall, and Walter was headed toward the far side. Other than to throw us over the edge, I could think of no reason for him to bring us there. In the middle of the flat roof, I noticed Mr. Gerald's forklift parked to one side. Pods dotted the surface like an obstacle course.

Walter practically slammed us into the half wall, near a section of metal pipe poking up from the roof. Probably some kind of ventilation. I had to slide the last foot to avoid flailing and falling over the wall. Forget the hammer trick, forget Bobby's two-story fall. We were eight stories up. The words *terminal velocity* came to mind. Walter snatched first at my hands, then at Bobby's, using more tape to wrap us tightly to the pipe.

"What do you want with us, mister?" Bobby begged. I just took it all in, wide-eyed with disbelief. Walter ignored the question and walked back to the forklift. Mr. Gerald must've left the key in the ignition, because Walter easily got the thing running, then turned it toward one of the large metal pods. As he drove, Bobby tugged hard on the packing tape holding his hands together, binding him to the pipe. "I can't get out!" he said in a low voice.

Walter slid the tines of the forklift under the pod and lifted it high. Then he wheeled back toward us.

As he drove at us with the pod offered up before him, I could see the look in Walter's eyes. A focused sort of insanity.

Listen, I'd seen a lot of old movies. I knew what he was doing. He was *sacrificing* us.

I nearly wet myself.

I shouted at Bobby. "He's gonna *kill us*! Like a ritual or something!"

"Shit!" Bobby responded, ever the intellectual. "Shitshitshit!"

"We gotta get away, somehow." I pulled hard on the packing tape but couldn't get free. "Maybe we can rock the pipe loose!"

Bobby strained. "Time it with me!" he said. "Left! ... Right! ... Left!" It was no use. The pipe was solid. Walter and the forklift arrived directly in front of us, the giant pod looming above our heads, covering us with its ominous shadow. Walter fiddled with the controls and the pod started to lean downward, toward us. In seconds, I could tell it would slide off the forklift tines and we would be crushed.

84

I had an idea. "Bobby!" I said, gesturing toward my head while turning toward Walter. I used my mind. Told him to *Stop!* For a moment, Walter paused, but only for a moment. He shook his head and continued to move the tines downward. I heard a gritty sound, like the pod was starting to slide. "Bobby, you gotta help me — use your mind to make him stop. Let's do it together." It didn't really hit me at that moment, busy as we were, but later I realized that this was the first time we ever worked our new magic together.

"Okay!" Bobby's brow furrowed as he mentally forced the command onto Walter. I joined him.

Neither of us had ever tried to push so hard. Even the police officer that I'd persuaded to ignore Bobby's broken, bloody bicycle was easy in comparison. But Walter was resisting.

I wondered, as I strained at the effort and sweat began to form on my forehead, if it was because his mind was corrupt already.

Then I got my answer.

Under the blunt force of both my and Bobby's wills, we felt Walter Ivory's mind *snap*. He fell out of the forklift seat and dropped to the roof, rolling in pain, letting loose terrible animal-like sounds. As he fell, he must have jammed the pedal or pulled at the steering wheel, because the forklift gave a jarring lurch, one of its front wheels bumping up onto the half wall of the roof. The pod stayed balanced on the tines, but slid ever farther toward us.

All we could do was watch Walter writhe, scared by the thought of what we had just done. It was like we'd held a fragile egg in our hands, squeezing and pushing on it to test its limits, when suddenly it burst. Always the punster, I thought to myself, *The yolk's on you, John!*

After what seemed like forever, Walter stopped writhing on the ground. He lay still, face to the rooftop. Then slowly, he stood up.

Walter's eyes were no longer human. They were a rabid dog's, a wounded deer's. They were the eyes of a goat bleating as its throat was cut. He began to rage back and forth, flailing his hands.

"We need to get outta here!" Bobby yelled. "Rock the pipe more!" And we rocked, but still it barely moved.

Walter ran at the forklift, slamming his head into one of the metal tines.

We watched as Walter's forehead partially caved in, then shifted around the tine. He pulled back and did it again, and again. We could see that the impacts were doing damage, but each time his head quickly healed. And his failure to hurt himself threw him into an even darker rage.

We rocked back and forth, back and forth. The pipe ignored us.

Walter did anything he could to hurt himself, but nothing helped. "Stop the noise! Stop the noise!" Walter repeated it until the words blurred together.

Still we rocked. And, then, unexpectedly, with no warning, the pipe came free and we fell over. We rolled to get out of the shadow of the dangling pod.

Seeing our movement, Walter scrambled back into the forklift. No, *onto* the forklift, up the front lifter mechanism, to the pod hanging above.

He got his hands on a corner of the pod and pulled himself up to its slanting metal top, then set about trying to dislodge it, to send it down upon us.

In terror, we rolled and rolled, trying to get free. The tape twisted and frayed and fell from our arms, leaving the pipe clanging behind. And we heard that gritty scraping sound again. But the pod was moving away from us, toward the roof's edge. Walter's weight had shifted its balance. In fact, the entire forklift looked to be leaning precariously now.

Glancing up, I saw Walter give a startled look as the surface he stood on angled too sharply for him to remain on his feet. He slipped to the edge of the pod, dropping to his knees and scrambling for some kind of hold.

For a moment, the whole thing — man, pod, forklift — teetered on the edge.

And then Walter Ivory lost what little grip he had and fell, off the pod, over the side of the building, down eight floors to the pavement below.

I had a split second to think of Bobby's own fall, and how Walter might have survived.

And then the pod gave in to gravity and slid off the tines and over the edge, following Walter's descent. To add insult to injury, the forklift, now completely off balance, tipped off the roof as well.

Below, we heard the devastating clangs and crashes as first the pod and then the forklift hit the ground and, presumably, Walter.

Immediately I fell to the rooftop in pain, hardly noticing that Bobby had done the same. Somewhere inside me, there was a screaming. A horrible, pained screaming, like knives stabbing into my ears, only the pain and the sound weren't actually in my ears. I held my hands to my head in vain. It seemed like it lasted forever.

And then the sound disappeared. It didn't fade or die out. It was cut off. One instant it *was* and the next it *was not*.

Like coming out of a dream, I looked around and found Bobby. He, too, seemed to be waking up from something. He stood, slowly, then staggered to the edge of the building. "He's gotta still be alive, right?" Bobby asked in a quiet voice. "I mean, nothing was hurting him before. He's alive under there."

"I don't think so," was all I said, looking over the edge. I didn't know why, precisely, but I was sure.

Somewhere below, Ike and Izzy began to bark, and Mr. Gerald called out, "*What the hell is going on around here?*" We heard the elevator start to move. The sound of the crash had boomed and echoed through the building, enough to pull Mr. Gerald away from his stories for once. He would be headed to the ground floor, to the source of the commotion.

"We need to get outta here, Johnny," Bobby said. "Unless you like being grounded for the rest of your life." But we both hesitated, looking at the wreckage, waiting for some sign of life that didn't come.

"We could go to jail," I said, nodding toward the scene below us.

Bobby's eyes bugged out. He turned and ran toward the stairwell. I followed, and together we raced down eight floors and out the back door, leaving Walter Ivory dead behind us.

PART TWO

MORN

1

Lice.

Pretty much every kid I knew got lice at some point. Around the time I turned 13, Tom did. Steve did.

But not me. Not Bobby.

Why?

Good question. Could it be that the lice bites were like tiny little versions of the hammer trick, and our bodies thwarted them? I mean, if they couldn't eat, they weren't gonna stay, right?

But you know what sucked? I still *felt* like I had lice, for the two weeks while everyone else was getting treatment. I'd constantly scratch my head, sure the little buggers were up there. Yet every time my mom would comb through my scalp... nothing. And I'm pretty sure she did a really good job of looking, because if I had 'em, she'd probably get 'em, too, and she was *very* clear that she didn't want that.

Phantom lice.

The scratching at something that wasn't there. The feeling of being infested with little … *things.*

It was an awful lot like how I came to feel about my entire body after Walter Ivory's death.

When he died, something in him *screamed.* And something in me *screamed back.* Not out loud. But I could feel it.

I had to figure out what was going on inside me, or I'd go insane. I'd be twitching and scratching my head, and as far as anyone else knew it would just be the lice that drove me mad, but actually it felt like my body was trying to turn itself inside out.

I talked to Bobby about it a lot, but he'd just nod and say *uh huh* in a noncommittal kind of way that reminded me of my dad when Mom told him about her latest shopping adventure. In other words, Bobby didn't seem to care.

So that left me on my own to unlock the mystery of my… could I call them *powers*? I had no idea. I only knew I couldn't exactly ask anyone for help. Bobby wasn't interested, like I said. Walter Ivory? Insane. Also, dead. My parents? Yeah, right. Tom or Steve? Did I mention they could be dicks when they wanted to? A teacher or a doctor? They'd put me away, or have me strapped in for experimentation. I imagined myself 20 floors underground, in a sealed room, labeled "Specimen A."

I was on my own.

My first thought was that something was in my brain. How else could I push other people's minds? But then I considered the other physical effects. The sluicing of my hand or fingers as the hammer came down, or the flattening and reshaping of Bobby's head after the fall. No, I realized, my problem wasn't only in my brain. It was *everywhere.*

A week came when Bobby's family took a trip out of town — I think he said he was headed to his Uncle Mike's house a few states away, and he wasn't happy about it. So I had a lot of time to myself. I decided on a simple test. One that even a 13-year-old could do without raising suspicion.

"Dad!" I called to my father as he walked in the door one night after work.

"Hey, John, how's your day?" he asked, hanging up his jacket by the front door, in a move he repeated almost daily.

"Dad! I was wondering if I could get a microscope!" Ah, damn. Way too excited. Way too early. I messed up. Dad frowned.

"A microscope, huh?" He gave a quizzical look and a little chuckle. "What do you want to do with that?" He put his briefcase down by the door and turned to face me.

Oh crap. I hadn't thought I'd need a fake story. I mean, I was asking for a *microscope*, for God's sake, not a crack pipe. Weren't parents supposed to support educational hobbies? I had to think. Other than investigate the possibility of something in my body that gave me strange powers, what would I use a microscope for? What did other kids use microscopes for? Why couldn't I think of anything?

"Um, yeah, I just think it's cool," I said. Internally, I was cursing myself. What a lame reason.

"*Cool?*" Dad repeated. "Well, yeah, it is cool, but how much does it cost? I don't mind getting it for you if you'll really use it, but I don't want to spend the money just to see it sitting on your dresser gathering dust."

"No way, Dad! I'll definitely use it. I promise." I dared to crack a smile. I mean, I *was* going to use it.

"Well, still, what do you want to use it *for?*"

Man, why did parents always have to have *reasons*? Why did things always have to make *sense?*

I blurted out an answer. "I want to study... plant cells!" I said, with the sort of energy one would not normally associate with studying plant cells.

"Really?" Dad said. "That sounds great!" I staggered. He *believed me*? God, parents were a conundrum.

I froze, then stammered, "I... I can have one?"

"Sure, son, why not?" Dad said.

Thanks to the miracles of online shopping, the microscope set arrived three days later.

* * *

So, I thought to myself after tearing open the package in my locked bedroom, *what to test?* Skin cells, blood cells, saliva? Hell, boogers? What should I try first? I decided on skin.

After a little research on the computer, I found that the human body loses between 30 and 40 *thousand* skin cells an hour. I started there, flicking some dead-looking cells off my elbow. I figured they wouldn't be with me long anyway.

I dropped the flakes of skin onto a glass slide from the kit, then slid that into the holding bracket on the microscope. Nervously, I jammed my right eye against the eyepiece to see what there was to see.

I should mention that I spent some of my three waiting days investigating the normal appearance of skin cells. I kept a printed diagram next to the microscope for reference, so I knew the round nucleus, the curved golgi complexes, the tube-like reticulum, the pods of mitochondria, the little starbursts of centrioles. I even memorized their names and basic appearance. I did mention I was a nerd, right? The problem was, under my shitty kid microscope (sorry, Dad), everything just looked like a blob. I could see the shape of the cells, the dark spot of the nucleus, but the rest was a sort of mottled grey.

Scouring the dead cells, I looked for *something*. Anything at all. I almost gave up. Then, on the fourth or fifth batch under my scope, I saw it.

A little triangular thing poking through the plasma membrane of a cell, like a splinter, but pointing out, not in.

Like it was *pushing* out.

What the hell was going on?

I scraped more skin and checked it under the microscope. Again and again, I found nothing unusual.

Then finally, another of the little triangular things. This time it was inside the cell. I strained to study it, twisting the focus knobs to get the best view. I was still new to the whole microscope thing, so I accidentally spun the coarse-focus knob instead of the fine focus, and everything went blurry. Cursing under my breath, I turned the coarse focus back to where it had been.

And saw that the triangular object had *moved*.

It had sort of slid to the edge of the cell. And damned if it wasn't starting to poke out of the membrane. Like it was trying to escape.

I sat bolt upright.

This was *in my body*. This little triangular thing. And now, on the slide under my microscope, it looked like it was trying to get away.

Why?

I considered the possibilities. *Why would this thing want to be in the cells* inside *my body, but not want to be in cells* outside *my body?* And an idea came to me.

Because these cells are dead, I thought. *Or dying.*

A name came to mind, a name for a living thing that survives off another living thing.

Parasite.

I needed to try something other than flecks of dead skin. Blood? Yes, blood. I decided to prick myself and look at my blood. Coming right out of my veins, the cells should be alive. If I had a parasite living in my blood... I didn't want to think about what that would mean.

I looked around the house for some sort of needle. When I couldn't find one — after the incident with Bobby and the sewing machine, my mom seemed to have stashed her needles — I went back to my room disappointed, thinking. And as I looked up from the little desk where I had set up the microscope, I noticed the pushpins holding up pictures on the cork board in front of me. One shot of me with a baseball bat from my single season in Little League, another of me honking away on the French horn.

I yanked out the pin that held the French horn photo and tossed the picture in the trash. Good riddance. Every time I played the thing, I imagined someone was killing a goose with a club. Not pretty. Holding the red plastic end of the pushpin, I prepared to stab my finger with the metal point. For a brief moment, I considered whether it would give me tetanus or something. Then I figured a little tetanus never hurt anyone, and jabbed.

Ow.

A proper needle would've been better. Smaller and sharper. But the pushpin did the trick. A single dot of blood welled up on my fingertip, and I grabbed for a slide.

Smearing the blood on the slide, I wiped my finger and then jammed the slide under the microscope.

Using the highest magnification level, I couldn't believe what I saw.

Every cell had one of those little triangular shapes in it.

* * *

I was in shock. I mean, yeah, I went looking for answers, but I had no idea what to expect. Or that I'd really find anything. The idea that the cells in my body were overrun by some sort of parasite, these little thorns. I didn't know what to say, what to do. Tell Bobby? Would he care? Tell my parents? I'd be strapped to a hospital bed in minutes. Just let it go? My mind couldn't think about anything else, so how could I let that go?

What the hell were those triangles? How did they get in me? What were they doing in my cells? Were they responsible for the strange things I could do? That Bobby could do?

Were they what I heard screaming when Walter Ivory died?

Wait. Bobby.

I had to find out if his cells looked the same, to see if he was infested with this parasite, these odd things like lice inside my cells.

Bobby was still at his Uncle Mike's and wouldn't be back for a couple more days. *Why the hell did I do this when he wasn't around? Oh yeah, because Bobby didn't care about my little theories. But I bet he'd care now.*

Damn. I really needed to talk it over with someone. And while Bobby wasn't exactly Mr. Introspection, he was the only candidate.

Waiting sucked.

* * *

You know what sucks even more than waiting? Someone thinking you've lost your mind, for real.

When Bobby's family got home from their trip, I called him and told him to come over right away.

In my room, with the door shut and locked, I told him what I'd found, what I thought, that our abilities came from these little triangular structures in our cells. I called them *thorns*, because I didn't have a better name.

Bobby was more than a little skeptical, especially hearing the word *parasite*, but that was okay. I'd expected that. All I needed to do was show him my blood cells, then get a sample of his blood to compare.

First, I fired up the light of my microscope.

97

"When'd you get that?" he asked.

"This week," I said breathlessly, "while you were gone." The light came on and I put my eye to the eyepiece.

"Son of a *bitch*!" I shouted, way too loud. Remembering too late that my mom was home.

"Boys?" came the call from somewhere else in the house.

"Yeah, Mom?" I replied sheepishly.

"Watch the language."

"Sorry, Mom!" I rolled my eyes at my own stupidity.

"What's your deal, dude?" Bobby asked.

I paused. This was not going as planned.

"They're gone," I said finally.

Bobby didn't even bother to reply, just smirked in an *of course there are little monsters in your body* kind of way.

"Wait — I'll just do it again." I grabbed the red pushpin.

But no matter what I did, I couldn't get a single drop of blood. My fingertip changed every time I tried. It *sluiced* out of the way. Had I somehow activated the thorns' self-preservation instinct? "Goddamn it!" I shouted breathily, hoping my mom couldn't hear me. "Cut it out!" I yelled at my own body.

I stopped, closing my eyes, not knowing what to do.

"You want me to try my finger?" Bobby asked. My eyes popped open.

"Yes! Let's do that!" I handed him the pin.

But it was useless. Bobby had done so many things trying to hurt himself that his body was even more evasive. Every patch of skin he tried just sluiced around his attempts.

"Wait, let's do skin — the dead skin has fewer thorns — they try to get out — but some should still be there."

"They try to get out..." Bobby repeated, with a strange tone to his voice. He wasn't buying it, not one bit. I noticed his expression out of the corner of my eye. Not ridicule. Not mockery. *Concern.* Maybe even *fear.*

"Johnny..." he started. I paused from scraping my skin onto a slide. "Johnny... are you okay?"

"What? Yeah, sure." I went back to scraping my arm.

"It's just... You're acting kinda weird."

I looked at him. "And so?"

"Well, Walter was acting kinda weird and..."

"Hold on. No. No, no, no. I am *not* losing my mind, Bobby. This is real. Just let me show you." I hurriedly placed the slide under the microscope.

Bobby humored me for over an hour and countless slides, my skin and his.

We found nothing.

2

"Spit!" I yelled, bolting up from a dead sleep that night.

I heard a clamor and a thud. From down the hall, my dad yelled, "Jesus, John, it's the middle of the night! Can you tone it down?" He made a *harumph* and I heard my mom say something muffled. "And watch your language!" Dad added. Their bed creaked as he turned over and I heard swishing noises as he grabbed at the blankets. Then there was silence again.

I didn't say shit, *Dad,* I thought. Spit was the answer, I told myself in the middle of the night. There had to be viable cells in my spit, and it would be easy to extract.

My mind wandered. Spit. It should work. If not, maybe other bodily fluids or excretions? *God,* I thought to myself in the dark, *please don't make me have to test a turd. I'll do pee if I have to, but please not a turd.*

But first, spit. Super easy. Way less disgusting.

As much as I hated to wait, I'd confirm it in the morning.

* * *

Man, I was learning a lot about the human body. Did you know that saliva is 99.5% water? Guess how helpful that was for me? If you guessed *not helpful at all*, you're right!

Still, in the morning, I tried to see what might turn up in that 0.5% remainder. I ended up testing so many samples that I had to keep swirling my tongue around, trying to drum up some new loogie to lather onto a slide. That's when I think I dislodged cells from my cheek or tongue, just a few, floating around in the juicy 99.5% water of my spit. And I found those little triangles, the thorns, again.

They were in my mouth, too. For some reason, this *really* bothered me. *Parasites.* In my skin. In my blood. And now in my mouth. Before I had time to think better of it, I spat on the floor. Of my own room. They were *everywhere.*

I plopped down on my bed. At least I'd have evidence to show Bobby that I wasn't going nuts, but I wanted very badly to know what the hell was going on.

I figured it wouldn't be long until I heard from Bobby again, so rather than look even crazier by calling him and ranting, I'd just wait. By 10 am, he was knocking on my door.

* * *

"Get. Out!" Bobby shouted, not believing his own eyes, not pulling himself away from the microscope. "What are those things?"

I shrugged. "Don't know. But we've both got 'em, and based on what I've seen, they're everywhere. All over our bodies. Inside us."

"What the hell…," Bobby trailed off, squinting into the eyepiece again for another, harder look. "You're sure this is *my* spit?"

"You saw me put it in there. I don't have a secret stash of random spit, so yeah, it's yours." I fell back on the bed, still contemplating, but relieved that Bobby might not be thinking I was nuts anymore.

Bobby straightened his back and turned toward me. "Wait. How do you know this isn't normal? How do you know everyone doesn't have this stuff?"

I gestured toward the computer and printouts on my desk. "Take a look for yourself. There's nothing like it in any of those diagrams."

Bobby picked up the topmost paper, stared at it for a second or two, then dropped it. When artists considered carving the busts of humanity's great scientists, Bobby was unlikely to be top of the list. He waved away all the mumbo jumbo with a backward flick of his hand. "I don't know what the hell I'm looking at here."

"Well, I looked at those a lot, and a bunch of other pictures and descriptions. There's *nothing* like this stuff in normal cells. *Nothing.*"

Bobby furrowed his brow. "And just how is it that you think these little... *thorns*? Is that what you're calling them? How are they responsible for what we can do?"

I shrugged again. "That, I have no idea."

Bobby seemed reassured somehow. "Then you're not sure."

"Of course I'm not sure!" I scoffed. "I'm 13 years old! I'm not a cellular scientist!"

Bobby raised his hands. To himself, he said in a low grumble, "Then why the hell am I listening to you?" Bobby spun around, like he was looking for a place to escape.

"What?" I asked, sitting up on my bed, then turning and flipping my feet onto the floor.

He didn't respond. So I asked again. "What did you say?" I stood and took a step away from the bed.

Bobby whirled on me. "Why the hell am I listening to *you*?" he asked with too much venom.

I flinched, taking a seat again on the bed. "Whoa, what's the problem?"

Without warning, Bobby flew into a rage. "The problem? I don't know, John Boy, what *is* the problem?" Oh man. He hadn't called me *John Boy* since... when? "You know, why can't you just be *happy*? I would think you'd be *really* happy."

"What're you talking about, Bobby?" I have to admit, I was a little scared. This was the old Bobby. The bully.

He leaned down so our noses were almost touching. "You have *powers*, Johnny, and so do I. What does it matter where it comes from, or why, or if there are little doohickeys running around in our bodies? *Powers*. Do you realize what we could do?"

I shook my head slightly, afraid to look away from him.

"*Anything* — we could pretty much do *anything*, Johnny!" He backed up and began pacing around the room. "You wanna get straight A's without trying? Done. Just *push* the teachers' mind! You wanna be a celebrity? Get in front of a camera and show the world how a hammer can't crush your hand! You want to be the coolest kid in school...? Uh," he gestured impatiently. "Just do *anything* we can do." Bobby paused, turned, and grabbed me by the shoulders. "Johnny," he said, his eyes pleading "who *cares* how it happened, or why, because we're the ones in control now." He let go of my arms.

The ones in control.

Is that how I felt? Is that what I wanted?

"Bobby...," I started. He stood waiting for a revelation to happen to me. But it didn't. "I... I don't know." I took a big breath. "I just don't feel in control of anything."

He spun, hands held up on both sides of his head, nearly shouting. "Geez, Johnny, get over it! You know, we're friends, but sometimes I want to give you a good, swift punch like the old days." Bobby balled one fist and I cringed at the memories. "There you go! Why are you so afraid? You can do the physical stuff almost as good as I can. Why do I always have to twist your arm to get you to do it? Why are you afraid of it? And the stuff with your mind, you're good at that, too." He paused to look me in the eye, heaving a sigh. "But even with these abilities, you're too scared to do *anything* most of the time. Why, Johnny?"

"I... I don't know. Maybe because it's not... natural?" It was a question more to myself than Bobby.

"Not natural?" Bobby was incredulous. "Not natural? Why not? It's just you. It's just me. We're still just kids. What's so unnatural? Just *do it*, John. Just *use* your powers."

Once more I flopped backward on the bed, arms wide. "Ugh, I don't know. I mean, I think it's kinda cool to do this stuff, but I can't let my parents know, or teachers, or even other friends. Really, only you can know. And I just don't understand *why* it happened to me." I folded my arms across my eyes, grimacing. Life seemed to have gotten so complicated. Bobby and I could do these things... We had, as he put it, *powers*. But so did Walter Ivory, and it seemed to have driven him crazy. Suicidally crazy. We had to keep the secret not only that we had powers, that there were little thorns in our cells, but also that we had witnessed Walter's death. It was a lot of deep doo-doo for a couple of doofus 13-year-olds to keep bottled up.

But then I began to think it didn't matter. Who cared about all this stuff? All this *thinking*? Bobby was right. I could do amazing things. I should enjoy it.

Wait.

Those seemed like alien thoughts.

I sat up abruptly. "Cut it out, Bobby." I could see him concentrating on me, trying to push my mind.

Again, I thought that I should just let go and welcome the changes I was experiencing.

I shook my head. Bobby again. He wasn't letting up. It was pissing me off.

There was a tingling in my head, as I realized I could *feel* the push happening. It was the last straw.

I stood up. "I said *cut it out!*" I shouted, pushing back with my mind. Hard. Bobby staggered against a bookshelf, sending things thumping to the carpet below. He blinked, twice, then shook his head.

Oh my God, I thought. *Did I break his mind, like we did to Walter Ivory?* Then Bobby looked up at me with a nasty sneer, the perfect incarnation of the old Bobby Graden, school bully. He puffed himself up and stepped toward me, raising one fist.

"That *hurt*, asshole!" He swung, aiming a heavy blow at my right shoulder.

And missed.

Well, not really missed. It was like the hammer trick. My body, keen on self preservation whether I had any input or not.

My shoulder sluiced away as Bobby's fist went by. His eyes popped, not only from the embarrassment of the punch missing, but from the surprise of seeing what my body did. Even knowing about our powers, he didn't expect it.

One important thing to remember about a pissed-off young boy is that embarrassment does *not* make things better. Bobby became even angrier. Without a word, he swung again, trying a cross at my right cheek.

I didn't think. In fact, I would honestly have to say I didn't *do anything*. But my body reacted, bending my neck unnaturally to slide my head out of the path of his punch.

Bobby had now missed twice. He stepped back, seething.

"Come on, Bobby, cut it o—" Before I could finish, he launched himself at me.

I raised one hand, palm flat toward his approach, a lame attempt to stop his hulking body from crashing into me.

And Bobby hit my hand like he was hitting a wall, then fell gasping to the floor. I was several inches shorter and 30 pounds lighter, and I hadn't even budged.

I looked at my hand and realized I couldn't move it. It was like my hand was made of stone. Then I noticed my arm, my shoulder, my midsection, and legs... I couldn't move anything but my head.

After a moment my arm dropped, like ice melting, and I regained control.

But for that moment... just that moment, I had become something hard and impenetrable. I looked at my fingers in amazement.

Bobby coughed and dragged himself up, holding one hand to his chest where it had rammed into my hand. "Nice trick, jerk. How'd you do it?"

I just shrugged.

That was when the first earthquake hit.

3

I didn't see Bobby for a while after that, and he offered no explanation why. Still, I thought I knew.

Up until that moment, while we had used our minds to both push and repel — to attack and defend — our bodies had only been used one way. When we slammed that hammer down to hit our hand, our hand moved out of the way in self-defense. But I'd just done something new.

Even though I was stopping Bobby's charge with my hand, I had turned myself, for the first time, into a *weapon*.

Bobby was jealous.

* * *

Mom and Dad (Andrea and Phil, remember?) were huddled in conversation a few weeks before my fourteenth birthday. As usual, being a kid, I had no idea what they were talking about, or that it might in any way impact me. But it did.

"John, come here," my dad said as I was taking my dishes to the sink after dinner one night. Holly sat next to my parents, all of them still at the dinner table. "We want to tell you something we think you're going to like," Dad announced with a broad smile, taking his glasses off to wipe them clean on his shirt.

"What's up?" I asked, standing beside the table impatiently.

"Son, we're going to take a trip. A vacation. In just a couple weeks."

I took in the information with no response. I was a kid, and didn't know anything about vacations. Hell, as much as I complained about school, pretty much my entire life was a vacation. This just meant doing the same stuff somewhere different. I shrugged. "Okay," I said.

"Well," Dad said, spinning around his laptop so I could see the screen. "I think you're going to be really happy when you hear *where* we're going!" Dad sounded excited. I was no dummy. I was old enough to realize that if my parents were excited about something, there was a 97.8519% chance that I would find it hideously boring and lame. In fact, that figure may have been on the low side.

Still, I humored him. "Where?"

"We're going to go to Playa Beach! Whaddaya say, bud? Excited?" My dad held his arms wide, awaiting some kind of tearful bear hug.

"Is that the beach up north? Isn't it cold there?"

"Yes, it's up north. And no, it's only cold in the wintertime. We're going in the summer, of course. We're going to be there for your big fourteenth birthday!" Still, Dad waited for some big reaction.

I blinked once. Twice. "Uh… Okay, good. Sounds fun," I said calmly, then turned and began walking away.

"John," Dad called behind me. "That's it? *Sounds fun?* Come on, son, I think you're gonna have a blast. Playa Beach has the boardwalk, rides, all kinds of fried foods that are bad for you, but that your mom will still let you eat..." Mom protested slightly at that. "And of course the beach and the ocean."

"I don't get it," I said, blinking.

"Get what? It's vacation, son." Dad was frustrated by my lack of elation.

"No, I get that. It's the name. 'Playa Beach.' Doesn't that mean 'Beach Beach?'"

Dad rolled his eyes at me. "Um. I guess. So?"

"Well, that's weird, isn't it?"

Mom turned her back. I think she was either highly annoyed with me or possibly laughing a bit at my questions. Dad huffed out a response. "No, I don't think so. The area around Playa Beach has been popular with Spanish people for many years."

"*Spanish* people? People from Spain? Or people who speak Spanish but come from many places? Latinos?" Dad just blinked. There was no point in continuing. I shook my head and changed the subject. "Um, sure Dad, like I said, sounds fun." I turned and headed for my room.

But not before I saw Dad and Mom trade an exasperated glance.

* * *

I got ready for bed, teeth brushed, pajamas on (I had taken to wearing a t-shirt and shorts to bed, pretty much same sloppy look as my daytime attire during the summer, but we can just call them pajamas for simplicity). Mom and Dad each came to wish me goodnight. Afterward, I could hear them talking downstairs.

"Geez, I would've thought he'd be thrilled about Playa Beach!" Dad said, voice carrying up the stairs.

"He was, honey. You know he's getting to that age…" Mom sounded tired.

"I mean, none of us get enough time to just have fun. This is important," Dad said. "This could really make a difference in his life." They had sensed something bad had happened to me, even though they didn't know a thing about the self-storage building. They'd heard about Walter Ivory, but of course they had no idea I'd been there. Thankfully. Walter was so universally disliked that no one thought twice about how he had accidentally gotten himself killed. He was hiding from the law after all.

"We'll have fun," Mom offered, sounding a little patronizing.

Dad heard the tone. "We really will," he said, defensively. "This trip could be a game changer."

I thought Dad was giving the trip way too much weight. But in reality, it was a sort of game changer. Just not the way Dad meant.

As I drifted off to sleep, the house shook back and forth slightly, making things clatter and jangle.

"Must be an aftershock," I heard Dad say.

4

The earthquakes were really unexpected. My parents said they could only recall one other quake happening in our area in their lifetimes. Suddenly we'd had two more, one after the other. Or maybe one and one aftershock. Did it matter? Mom said even the experts weren't sure. But for a few days, our town, which they said was the approximate epicenter, made the national TV news.

For the first time, but definitely not the last.

The quakes themselves were hardly noticeable. Very light. Like a 2.4 on the Richter scale (which Bobby always mistakenly called the Litmus test). Maybe more or less. Honestly, I wasn't paying much attention to it all. I had thorns inside me. I'd been threatened with death by a man who'd likely been driven crazy by those same thorns. I'd helped break that man's mind and watched him die. I could make my body into a weapon, albeit accidentally. So you can see I had other things to think about.

A few days after the second quake, I was sitting in front of the television with Mom and Holly. I was zoned out in thought, so it barely registered when Mom suddenly jumped off the couch.

"Phil! I need you! Help!" she shouted, fear in her voice.

From the other room, I heard my dad's muffled reply. "What is it?" Quick footsteps told me Dad was taking her seriously, rushing in. I snapped back to reality.

"Holly!" Mom went to my sister, who sat shaking slightly in her chair. "Phil, she's having another seizure."

Dad knelt beside Holly, taking her by the wrist. I stood and watched, but there was nothing I could do. Nothing Mom or Dad could do either, really, except make sure Holly didn't hurt herself. After a moment, she became still, sitting with her eyes closed. My parents waited a few moments longer, until they felt reassured that it truly was over, then let out small sighs of relief.

The four of us were motionless. The whole world was motionless, it seemed.

Then Holly opened her eyes, staring ahead but not seeing. Why did I feel she was looking right at me?

At that moment, another earthquake shook the house.

5

"Do you think she can sense them coming?" Mom asked.

Dad looked up absently from his newspaper, folded in quarters to read some article, a white mug of coffee proclaiming him to be SUPER DAD! in the other hand. "Huh?" he said.

Mom sat in front of Holly, feeding her spoonfuls of her favorite breakfast, bananas mashed with oatmeal. I always figured it was the brown sugar on top that really made Holly like it. "Do you think that Holly can sense them coming?" When Dad still seemed confused, Mom added in a low whisper, "The earthquakes?" She twisted her hand back and forth to indicate a rocking motion, as if Dad didn't remember what an earthquake was.

Dad set the paper down and looked up thoughtfully. "Never considered that. But... maybe?" It definitely came out as a question.

I paused over my scrambled eggs, fork halfway to my mouth. I guess I sat agape like that for too long. "John," Mom said in that tone that's meant to tell you to watch what you're about to do, but that kids never heed. I shook my head a bit to refocus, and a bite of egg dropped into my lap and onto my clothes. Of course, I wasn't using a napkin. "John! Come on. How many times do I have to tell you to put your napkin in your lap? And eat over your plate?" I behaved as if I'd most certainly never heard these instructions before, huffing as I straightened my posture and dropping the paper napkin haphazardly onto my lap.

It was more than a week later that Holly had another brief seizure. Minutes after, the house shook again.

* * *

Bobby and I hung out a few times before my family went to Playa Beach. Sure, he was still miffed at me for the whole hand-as-a-weapon episode, but we were kids and we were friends, so things blew over quickly. I told him about Holly's seizures seeming to predict the earthquakes. His helpful suggestion was to get her on TV like a weather forecaster. I could just see it: *And now we send it over to Holly Black with your AccuQuake forecast. Any seizures, Holly?*

Bobby didn't bring up my little microscope experiments, or what happened when he tried to hit me. But he was back to pushing the limits of what he could do, only worse, if you can believe it. He kept talking about getting a gun, which I still thought was an insane idea.

But of course, we lived in America. So eventually Bobby was able to get his hands on a gun. Not surprisingly, it was quite easy.

Step one: Find someone in your family, or even just your close surroundings, who owns — and this is important — more than one gun. Go talk to them. You'll never get them to give you their last gun. Never their only gun. But people who have more than one gun like to give them out in a spirit of magnanimous celebration, sort of like shoot-'em-up Halloween.

Step two: Be a kid. Bobby had that covered.

Step three: Express a wholesome and upstanding interest in having your own gun. That's right! Don't hide your desires or try to lie. Get right out there and say you like guns and you want one of your own. This is considered rational teenage behavior, at least in certain parts of the country. Try it!

Step four: As soon as you're done promising your parent/uncle/grand-father/niece/great-aunt/stepbrother/nanny/postman/pastor/cousin-in-law/local gunophile that you'll be careful — run off and don't be careful. After all, you can rest assured, it's what they did, and they lived!

I should mention that we needed a new hangout. After what happened to Walter Ivory, it would've been in poor form to go back to the self-storage place. I kinda missed the dogs, though.

The problem was, where the hell were we going to go to shoot off a gun? Bobby's Uncle Pete, once approached using the four-step method, was thrilled to provide a "loaner pistol," and so Bobby was quite anxious to find a firing range. Since I wasn't very keen on the idea, I didn't try terribly hard to solve the problem. Bobby, on the other hand, was dedicated.

Not far from the self-storage building, there was a lumber yard. That wasn't the place Bobby chose, but it was close. The important thing was that the yard was almost always noisy. Behind it there were three nondescript rows of warehouse bays. Not old, drafty brick warehouses with metal-dinosaur machinery gathering cobwebs inside, like you might see in a movie. These were just rectangular expanses of cinder block and cement, each with a large roll-up door on the front and a single metal walk-in door on the back.

The first row of bays, closest to the lumber yard, was completely abandoned. Well, I shouldn't call it *abandoned*, since in reality it was simply *unwanted*. Signs were plastered on the doors of each bay: For Lease. For Sale. There didn't seem to be many takers.

Two or three of the bays in the other rows were occupied by carpet cleaners or print shops or caterers or something, but it didn't matter. At the end of the first row, Bobby jimmied the lock on Bay 6. He proudly showed me around, like he owned the place.

Inside was a rectangle of grey. I could still hear the whining saws and clatter of other sounds coming from the lumber yard, although they were muted. Looking here and there, I saw drips of something staining the cinder-block walls and making dark little puddles on the cement floor. In the front of the bay, to one side of the large roll-up door, a block of space had been walled off to make a sort of office. There were no windows of any sort in the bay and the power was off, so we had to prop open the back door to get some light. The office was empty, an almost completely dark, square space, shorter than the bay and carpeted with some sort of rough industrial fabric. I imagined some businessman tucked behind a desk in the corner, spending years of his life toiling away. It made me not want to grow up.

"Let's do it, Johnny!" Bobby proclaimed, pulling Uncle Pete's small pistol from his backpack. I rolled my eyes. "Let's start by having you shoot me in the leg. That way, if anything goes wrong, I won't die." He held out the gun. I was pretty sure a person could die from any sort of gunshot wound, but I kept quiet.

Taking it gingerly, like it might go off at any second, I asked, "Is it loaded?"

"Nah, Johnny, I'm not stupid. Didn't want the damn thing going off in my backpack."

I fiddled with the gun until I found out how the clip slid out. It was empty as promised. "Where're the bullets?"

Bobby reached into his front pants pocket and his grin disappeared. "Oh *shit*," he said, franticly patting his shirt and pants. I couldn't help but laugh, and Bobby shot me an angry look. Then he reached into a back pocket and sighed. With a flourish, he pulled out four small, shiny bullets. He took the clip from me and started to slide them into place.

"Uh, just one, please," I said. "To start." Bobby shrugged and passed back the clip holding a single bullet. I jammed it into place. My memory of every shooter video game I'd ever played was pretty clear, so instinctively I worked the slide catch to load the gun.

Suddenly I was nervous. The gun was loaded and ready. I couldn't say the same for myself. I looked at Bobby and could tell he was nervous, too. But

FOR I COULD LIFT MY FINGER AND BLACK OUT THE SUN

he wasn't daunted. He leaned over and patted his left calf. "Okay, shoot me right here," he said with a weak smile.

I raised the gun to aim at his leg. The pistol was small but heavy. Maybe heavier in my mind than its true weight. It felt dangerous and important and powerful and terrifying, all at the same time.

And then too many things happened, too quickly.

Outside, there was a loud clang, an explosion of shouting. I looked back toward the open door, expecting to see someone, but no one was there. My arm was still raised, and involuntarily I tensed in fear. And my finger squeezed the trigger just enough that the gun fired.

Directly into Bobby's belly.

Interlude

A whoosh. An image of the crowd watching a magic show, suddenly amazed by some act of seeming impossibility. Like the sound of a thousand people inhaling quickly, followed by an almost inaudibly calm exhale. Fast and light. In time, coordinated.

It is you.

6

I stared in shock at Bobby, and he looked back at me, equally stunned. I'd seen it happen. With incredible speed, his body momentarily made a *tunnel* from his stomach to his back, allowing the bullet to pass through harmlessly. As I watched, the hole closed and Bobby was back to normal. Even his shirt, at least on the front side, had parted and then returned whole.

I leaned slowly around to look past Bobby, and he twisted to see as well. There was a deeply chipped spot in a cinder block in the wall behind him. In the center of the hole, we saw the metal slug of the bullet that had passed through Bobby's body without leaving a mark.

"That," Bobby started, breathlessly, a slow smile dawning across his face, "was *incredible!*" He laughed and slapped me on the shoulder playfully. "Gotta admit you scared me, though, Johnny. What the hell did you shoot me in the gut for?"

For a minute or two, I couldn't answer. Finally, I realized I'd been holding my breath.

Holy crap, I thought. *Bobby's bulletproof.*

* * *

The following Friday night, my dad had our pale-blue family van packed to the gills, prepped for our trip to Playa Beach. (We'll just agree to ignore the name, okay?) The van was larger than your typical family minivan, because we had to support Holly's wheelchair.

With Holly on board and the van ready to go, I plopped into the rear seat as Dad started the engine.

We rolled through town to start our five-hour drive to the beach. I noticed an old safety pin on the floor of the van, so to pass the time, I idly jabbed it at one hand, watching my skin slide smoothly out of the way. I don't recall noticing whether Holly was watching me or not.

* * *

I have to admit, Playa Beach was a lot of fun. Holly seemed thrilled to sit in a rented big-wheel wheelchair — perfect for traversing the sandy beach — while enjoying the sun, wind, waves, and birds. Mom sat with her, both of them covered by a large umbrella.

Dad and I rode the waves, body surfing, bouncing through the endless swells, tossing our foam football. For three days straight, we woke up, ate breakfast, and then ran into the water. We took the occasional break to eat lunch or lay resting in the sun, but for the most part, we played in the ocean. Together.

Body surfing across the water on the back of a large wave on the afternoon of the third day, I beat Dad to the shore by inches. It was the day before my fourteenth birthday and the last time I ever heard my father laugh.

7

The next day, we hit the boardwalk. I had an enormous amount of fun at the time, but of course now I wish I'd never gone. I'm not sure if things would've gone any differently in my life, but maybe so. Worst of all, the whole day was supposed to be for me — for my birthday. Mom and Dad took turns pushing Holly along, while I was given a somewhat obscene amount of quarters to spend as I wished in the various arcades and amusement parks.

I had just turned 14 — a grown man, in my mind. So of course I pressed my parents to let me take off on my own. They relented and I was about to run. But first, I walked to where Holly sat, pressing my forehead to hers. *I so wish you could come with me, sis*, I thought, as hard as I could. After a moment of our ritual, I stood and without another word raced away down the boardwalk.

There was a blur of videogames, blinking icons and screens, tweeting sounds, salt-water-ruined loudspeakers playing outdated rock music. T-shirts with words on them I knew but my parents thought I didn't. Jocks strutting with their sunglasses shining, bikini-clad girls that caught my eye as they made their own confident strides. People from all stations in life, the snooty and the seedy, the weathered and the pampered. Hours passed.

I stood in line for The Hurlstorm, a twisty mess of a ride that flipped over and over on itself, people locked in little cages of near-death. The area around the ride was, ostensibly, cleared for safety. I assumed it was really cleared to allow for a spew zone. I'd heard the rumors. I suspected at least once a day they got a true hurler, and I didn't want to be their latest statistic. The Hurlstorm was one of the boardwalk's most popular rides, and as such, drew a lot of spectators — and cost a whopping 10 tickets. I had just enough to cover the cost, or so I thought, idly looking around while I waited in line for my turn. At last, the ride slowed and people staggered out, laughing and wide-eyed, some looking like they might need a break for the day or a quick trip to the porcelain god. The Hurlstorm was not a jealous master. It would take your sacrifice any time, now or later. Finally everyone was off the ride and the gate attendant looked for his next batch of victims. I was fourth in line.

I shuffled forward and pulled my remaining tickets out of my pocket. When I reached the attendant, I passed them over without thinking, ready to rush in and find the best seat.

And she stopped me, her mousy hair pulled back, a rash of red sunburn across her nose and cheeks, her mouth screwed up in a grimace. "It's 10 tickets," she said.

I looked at her dully, not comprehending. "Uh-huh?"

"This is nine," she said, holding up my tickets in three ragged batches, annoyed at having to delay the line, or possibly her lunch break. People behind me started to grumble and push forward.

The day was still and hot. I heard a garbled sound, like static on the radio, until it faded into a tinkling of notes like a very distant wind chime coming to rest.

I reached into my pockets and found... nothing. I didn't have any more tickets. Or money. I'd be forced to wander off and find my parents in shame, one measly ticket shy of having a terrifyingly good time on The Hurlstorm. Or worse, I could ride one of the cheaper baby rides.

"Ah, crap," I muttered. Then a figure pushed forward.

The first thing I remember is that he was dark. Dark clothes, dark hair, dark skin. His hand reached out and it, too, was dark, deeply tanned. His fingernails were immaculately manicured. Gleaming arcs of pure white atop bronze fingers. In between two of those fingers was one simple thing: a red, paper ticket.

"Here, my friend, take one of mine," he said with a smile of the same immaculate white as his fingernails, offering the item not to me but to the flushed gate attendant. She took the single ticket and waved me through, so I smiled and gave the man in black a little salute, but that was all.

I rushed to an open seat, not giving much thought to the stranger and his gift of a single red ticket. Not thinking about why. Certainly not thinking about the future. What happened in that split second. Just wanting the visceral thrill.

For a short while, I experienced the one thing amusement park rides do well. I was lost in the moment.

* * *

Jose.

His name was Jose do Branco. He was waiting when the ride was done.

Amid the other lurching, somewhat vomitous riders, I made for the exit. I ducked past two older teenagers, probably on a date. Clearly, the boy had coerced the girl into going on the ride, because she looked like she would live up to The Hurlstorm's name at any step, so I rushed by them and out the gate.

And I bumped directly into *him*.

"Did you enjoy the ride?" he asked with what seemed like true interest, even happiness. I looked up, for a moment not realizing who was speaking to me.

The dark, nearly black jeans. A black, button-up shirt, sleeves rolled up a turn or two, chest exposed at the open neck. Jet-black hair, almost as dark as mine, but slightly wavy, like a mesh. But his skin…

His skin was the even, bronzed color produced only by people with no northern blood in their bodies whatsoever. I looked at the texture and tone of his skin and thought it was beautiful. Yes, that's the actual word I thought. This was high praise. It was a word I normally reserved exclusively to describe the latest videogame graphics.

Then he smiled. Good God, the whiteness of his perfect teeth next to his perfect dark skin. If I had known the name Adonis at that age, I would've thought Adonis was talking to me. I had to try to be eloquent.

"Huh?" I said, unsuccessfully blinking the dumbness out of my eyes.

"Did you enjoy the ride? The…" He looked toward the sign. "*Hurlstorm?*" Again, the bright white smile.

I shook my head. This was an adult and a complete stranger talking to me. I had no idea why. "Uh, yeah." I fidgeted, kicking the ground idly with one sneakered toe.

"Wonderful," he said, with a turn and a slight laugh. He seemed like a movie star to me. "I am so happy to have provided you with the ticket you required, then."

"Oh, yeah, right," I looked down, embarrassed to have forgotten. "Thanks. Um, thank you for that, sir." I shifted my weight awkwardly.

"'*Sir?*' Please." He leaned down in front of me and I realized he was actually pretty young. An adult, sure, and way older than me, no doubt. But maybe just out of college, like my cousin Mick. Not old like my-parents-old. "Don't call me 'sir.' Call me *Branco*. That's what everyone calls me." He paused, and I stood blinking at him, like a cow looks at an oncoming train.

"Well, my full name is Jose do Branco." Not *de* Branco, *do* Branco. Don't ask me why. He pronounced it in a sort of excessively foreign way, using his deep voice to emphasize the sounds, doh *Brrahn* koh. I found myself wishing I knew how to roll my Rs without sounding foolish. "But most people," he continued, pausing to look me in the eye, "people who know me, just call me Branco."

I nodded absently. *Branco. Franko. Monkey-spanko. I'll call you whatever you want, mister. Just either (a) give me more ride tickets, (b) stop creeping me out by acting like a pedophile, or, preferably, (c) both.*

He stood again. "May I ask your name?"

Wow. This guy was either really formal, or really European. Maybe those meant the same thing. "John. John Black," I replied, awkwardly. A second later, I thought that a fake name would've been a really good idea. Apparently, all the work my parents had done trying to drill some sense into my head about strangers was futile.

Branco raised one eyebrow with a small smile, then bowed a bit. "It is my pleasure to meet you, John Black. Are you here on vacation?" It seemed an innocent question.

"Yeah."

He nodded, briskly, then made a circular gesture, indicating the boardwalk around us. "*Playa Beach*. Did you help your family select this place?" he asked, expectantly.

I scoffed. "No." He looked at me with one eyebrow raised. "Stupidest name ever."

Branco and I shared a laugh.

* * *

Branco was one seriously charming guy. I mean, my stupid friends, Bobby included, would probably say I was sweet on him, but really? The guy was too good-looking, too suave, made you want to be friends with him. It wasn't just me. People on the boardwalk turned to look at him. Girls turned twice. Some guys, too.

He asked me about my family, and, like a fool, I told him everything. About my mom, my dad, even Holly. He seemed particularly interested in Holly, how she came to be in her wheelchair. I didn't mention Walter Ivory at all, just said she had a seizure as a little kid. He nodded, but I think he knew I was leaving something out.

"There is a place that serves good Italian food, three blocks or so away," he said, pointing down the boardwalk. "I would like to invite you and your family to be my guests there for dinner."

"Are you Italian?" I asked.

Branco gave a single short, deep laugh. More like a polite gesture than real amusement. "No. I am Portuguese, my friend!" he said with a little flourish of one hand. "But, still, I like Italian food. Do you?"

"Do they have pizza?" I asked suspiciously, tilting my head to the side.

"Only the best in town," he replied with a nod.

I burst into a smile, the way only kids can at the word *pizza*. "I gotta ask my parents!" I said, running off down the boardwalk and through the crowd. Behind me, I think Branco called out, but I was gone.

* * *

"John, come on, we've got to get a move on if we want to make our reservation," my dad said, when I found them. He was packing Holly's chair into the van. Mom and Holly were already waiting inside.

"But Dad!" I complained.

He stopped, turning to look me in the eye. "'But Dad,' nothing. We have reservations at The Rusty Anchor." The name came out like it was important. "Your mother made those reservations weeks ago. You know, for your *birthday*? So we're not breaking all of our plans because some *stranger* told you he'd buy you pizza! I mean, really. Come on, John!" Dad looked flabbergasted. "And like I said, what are you doing talking to strangers, anyway? Be *careful*, John."

My shoulders fell as I exhaled loudly. What else could I do? Parents always won, even when you were fourteen years old. I huffed and jumped in the car, and we slowly drove away from the boardwalk. I figured I'd seen the last of Jose do Branco.

I was very, very wrong.

KEITH SOARES

8

"John, nice to see you again."

Really? I thought. *You've gotta be kidding me.* My morning was already pretty terrible. Dad woke up in some kind of bad mood, maybe still fuming over the service at The Rusty Anchor. As you can imagine, it was terrible. I mean, Mom said her crab cakes were good, and I went for fish sticks. But they were just... fish sticks. Can you really screw that up too bad? Sure, I guess you could, but then the government would need to come and take away all your spatulas and make you close up shop. Because that would be pretty low.

But Dad got the prime rib and wouldn't stop complaining about it. *Looks like it's going to walk off my plate, it's so undercooked,* and *Would you look at all this fat!* Plus, the service was truly horrible. Some poor Eastern European kid just trying to make a few bucks in America, but he was slow. And forgetful. And the kitchen was really backed up. Dad was pissed the whole night. He didn't wake up much better.

So I ate my breakfast and asked if I could hit the boardwalk arcades. A grumble was my only response. Mom was busy with Holly. I left without another word.

And of course, just as I neared the lot where The Hurlstorm loomed above me, I heard his voice.

"Sorry you could not make it last night for pizza," he said.

I shrugged. "Me, too. My folks made *reservations*... and they didn't want to change. Anyway, see ya." I started to run off.

"Hold on just a second, John. I was wondering if you wanted all these extra tickets I have." Branco pulled out a wad that made my head spin.

"Extra? Those are *extra*? That's, like, a hundred tickets!"

"Well, I must admit I purchased them without considering how many I would really need. But they are yours if you want them. Or we could use them together." He eyed me, waiting for a response.

"Listen, mister..."

"Please. *Branco*." He smiled.

"Listen, mister Branco, this is nice of you and all, but it's a little creepy. I'm just a kid and you're... you're not. Makes me wonder if you're up to no good. If you know what I mean." I took a step back.

Branco sighed, with a little laugh. "I am sorry, John, I realize this must look strange. Please believe I have no ulterior motives. You seemed like a nice fellow, and I know so few people around here. If you'd like the tickets, please take them. I will not bother you again, if that's what you wish." He held out the long sections of connected red tickets with one hand.

I reached out and he gave them to me freely. I blinked once or twice, trying to think of all the things I could do. The day was mine, and it was going to be *awesome*. "Thank you, Mr. Bran— , I mean, Branco." I turned and started to run off to find something to ride.

Then, my mind changed. Suddenly, unexpectedly, I found myself stopping. I turned around.

"You know," I said, slowly at first, then gaining steam. "Maybe one ride would be okay. Have you been on The Zipper?"

Branco slowly, theatrically wrinkled his brow and frowned. "I do not think I have." He shrugged. "Do you recommend it?"

I tilted my head back in amazement. "Do I? You've *got* to try it! Come on!"

* * *

Even as early as it was, there was already a line at The Zipper. The ride was a hot mess. A rollercoaster with a tight climbing spiral tower, two loops, and a super-steep drop, all packed into what looked to be 15 parking spaces on the asphalt lot. I'm sure that falling out of any rollercoaster was a certain death sentence, but somehow the idea that you could be flung out and land in the parking lot gave The Zipper an extra air of danger. When it was our turn, I passed the appropriate amount of tickets over with glee and raced for the front car. Branco jogged behind me, seeming amused by it all.

The car was a small, metal shell. Inside there was a borderline-useless seatbelt, a loose strap that we draped over ourselves in a mild attempt at safety. The only thing really keeping us in the car was the pull-down padded harness. But the ride was old and the harness was definitely not the latest design. And it kinda stuck when you latched it. This was a lot of what made The Zipper so much fun. The ride itself was probably fairly tame, if not for the fact that you assumed it would break down, fall apart, and you'd die at any moment. Branco wasn't used to it, and couldn't get the harness to latch. I slammed mine down and it made a loud click, locked in place as securely as it was going to get.

"Hold on, I'll get yours," I said, reaching up to grab his harness.

"All right, thank you, John." Branco sat still, waiting for me. I pulled hard, yanking the harness down over his shoulders.

"Watch your fing—," I started.

And then, as the harness clicked loudly into place, I froze. My mouth hung open, forgetting what I was saying in the middle of the word.

I couldn't help but stare. The harness had slammed hard into its latch… right where the fingers of Branco's left hand were accidentally waiting.

Or, I should say, where they were before they sluiced out of the way.

* * *

Before I could think or react, the ride attendant was there, checking our harnesses and the seatbelt. She gave a half-hearted tug and then stood, giving a thumbs-up to her colleague in the control booth. I was dumbstruck, staring at Branco's hand, and he knew it.

"This is *exciting*, John, isn't it?" He looked straight ahead as the ride lurched and began. After a moment, he turned to look at me. We were almost to the spiral climb. "Is something wrong?"

I stammered. "Your— your *fingers*," I said.

He held up his left hand, wiggling all five fingers. "Oh yes, you almost got me!" He gave a little laugh, and I realized I'd heard that sound a number of times already. A chuckle more than a laugh, actually.

"But how—," I started.

Then the car whipped into the spiral climb and all I could do was scream.

* * *

Back and forth, back and forth, to the top. Then spilling out of the tower, plummeting down. Hitting the first loop, flipping. The world going upside-down.

For me, it was a mirror of what was happening in my mind. *How the hell did that happen? He did the hammer trick. That's... that's impossible.*

Coming out of the loop, I struggled to look over at Branco. But he was gazing straight ahead and smiling, his perfect white teeth gleaming in the sun, his perfect dark hair blowing back in the onrushing wind.

"How the hell did you do that?" I shouted over the wind.

Branco turned, confused. "What?"

"Your fingers!" I yelled. "How did you do that?"

"What, John? What about my fingers?"

Then we hit the crest of the big drop and my stomach flew out of the top of my head. Or so it felt. I turned back to watch where were going as we dropped too fast toward the pavement. I gasped. At the last second, the track curved and we were parallel to the ground. But only for an instant. We hit the second loop and I screamed some more. Beside me, Branco laughed. Not his little polite little laugh, but a big and hearty one.

Finally the loop was done. I took a breath, tried again.

"What happened with your fingers, when I pulled down the harness?" I asked.

"I don't know, John. What do you mean?" He was still half-smiling from the thrill of the ride.

The coaster lurched to a halt as the breaks stopped our movement. One, then two quick jerks, until our speed was near zero.

"When I pulled down your harness, your fingers were in the way. They should've been smashed. But they... *moved.*" I looked at Branco, demanding an answer with my hard stare.

He gave that little laugh again. "They did?" A question. I thought it was a question. But I've replayed this moment countless times in my mind since then. And now I wonder if it wasn't a question at all. *They did.*

All of a sudden, I needed to be off the ride, away from Branco. He could do what I could do. What Bobby could do. What Walter Ivory could do. How was that possible? I didn't care, I just wanted to be away from him.

The Zipper stopped hard, back in its little station, and I jerked and jerked on the harness, trying to pull it up. Finally, there was a hydraulic hiss, and the harness swung free.

I pushed it out of my way and ran.

9

Like everything, whether good or bad, the beach trip had to come to an end.

It was the day after my rollercoaster ride with Branco. I'd simply avoided the boardwalk for the rest of the trip, and thereby avoided Branco. And so finally, unlike most days leaving the beach, I was glad to be going. I didn't want to ever lay eyes on Branco again. He scared me, with his polished appearance and charm, and most of all with his *abilities*. His *powers*. Suddenly, things with Branco didn't seem like they had happened quite so randomly.

I was going to have to talk about this with Bobby.

During the car ride, a long and tedious affair that promised nothing but boredom, I fell asleep. The day was a scorcher, but my dad wanted to keep the windows open rather than use the air conditioning. Hot air whipped my hair around my head as I closed my eyes and dozed off.

And dreamed of a cooler place.

Of winter.

And snow.

I was running through the snow, happy, laughing. I saw the streets and houses of my neighborhood and felt safe and at home.

I turned a corner and stopped, giddily holding out my arms as I opened my mouth to the sky, tongue out, catching snowflakes. I turned in circles for what felt like hours; the icy flakes landed on my tongue and melted.

Then I heard a little laugh. A chuckle.

I dropped my arms and turned toward the sound, mouth snapping shut.

Just down the snow-covered street stood a boy my age. He wore Bobby's winter coat, Bobby's jeans, Bobby's boots. But he wasn't Bobby.

His skin was darker, bronzed. His hair was dark, too. He held his head up, catching snowflakes on his tongue in a mirror of what I'd been doing, his gleaming white teeth seeming brighter than the snow itself.

Where there should've been Bobby's face, in this memory dream I was having, there was someone else's: Branco.

He stopped, and tipped his head back down to look at me.

"Isn't this wonderful, John? This *snow*."

Dream-Branco started to laugh the same hearty laugh I'd heard on the rollercoaster.

I awoke with a loud gasp, still in the hot car, miles from home.

"Geez, John," Dad said, looking at me in the rearview mirror as he drove. "Keep it down, okay? You're going to wake up Holly."

Absently, I turned to look at my sister, and found her eyes, wide awake, locked on mine.

* * *

The dream wouldn't leave me alone. I didn't want to sleep again, for fear of seeing Branco's face, but I couldn't get the images out of my mind.

I realized it was a replay of the day Bobby and I had been hit by that car. My idle mind had simply inserted Branco where Bobby should've been. Why this was even scary, I couldn't quite say, but it was.

That day.

That was the day my life changed.

Everything changed.

Not just getting hit by a car, not just the whole business of becoming friends with Bobby. But the *powers*. I couldn't help but forever link them to that day. So I guess it made sense that my mind took another leap, made another connection between these two things: the day Bobby and I gained our powers, and the new revelation that Branco had them, too. Or at least some of them.

I started to think it might've been my eyes playing tricks on me. That there was no way Branco had our powers. Maybe I was just making it up. Maybe Branco had done nothing at all. But there was me, and Bobby, and even Walter Ivory. Could there be another? I had no idea.

God, I thought. *I'm really losing it, aren't I?*

The powers.

Why me? Why do I have powers? It makes no sense. I thought hard about the day of the accident. The snow falling, and my forehead pressed against Holly's, and then Bobby chasing me, and the terrible hissing slide of the red car that hit us. About those thorns that were deep inside me, inside every cell, and in Bobby's, too. Looking for a way out only when their host cell died. Where did they come from? *How the hell would something infect my entire body?*

141

I paused.

Infect.

Like a disease.

How did a person get a disease? Handed down from their parents, maybe, or even just bad luck. What else? I thought about the warning labels on cigarettes, announcing that if I smoked I could get cancer. I thought about people always telling me what to eat, not to have too much junk food.

That stuff'll kill ya.

How would something get in me and just... *spread.* All over?

I certainly hadn't injected anything into my body, unless they'd done it when I was in the hospital after the accident. Bobby was there, too, so that would definitely explain both of us. But what about Walter? And if Branco was like us, what about him?

What had I eaten that day? I had no idea. Probably a normal kid breakfast of toaster pastries, my go-to wake-up meal for as long as I could remember.

Did toaster pastries make me superhuman?

Think of the marketing they could do! *Kids! Ask Mom and Dad to get you new Acme Toaster Pastries! Now with uber-powerful thorns!*

That was nonsense. But I couldn't think of anything else.

Wait.

The dream.

Tilting my head up. The way Bobby had the day of the accident. The way Branco had in my dream.

The snow.

Come on, now you're really being ridiculous, I thought to myself. *Snow?*

Could there've been something in the snow that infected me?

Hours later, I was no closed to an answer. We finally pulled into our driveway, and I jumped out of the van and went quickly to my room. My parents hollered for me to come help unpack, so grudgingly I went back and moved the bare minimum number of things before they turned me loose.

In my room, I went straight to the computer and started searching for everything about snow. What snow was made of. (Surprise: It's water!)

I found a whole debate about whether Inuit's truly had 50 words for snow. A *debate* about this. The ability for adults to argue about literally anything once again boggled my mind.

As for real answers, I found nothing.

Of course there was nothing; it snowed all the time in the winter. Why would that particular day's snow be special? Wait. What day was that? I thought hard and came up with the date, or at least a close approximation. It was relatively easy to narrow down, what with it being the same day I was hit by a car and admitted to the hospital and all.

I searched for unusual or noteworthy events on that date.

And found nothing. I mean, sure, a lot of stuff happened. Congress failed to accomplish something, the president made a speech, a string of robberies was going on across town and police were stumped… but nothing stood out. I scanned other results. The typically dominant football teams were still dominant that winter; the typically crappy ones were still crappy, even though their fans always expected miracles. In other news, people were, as always, unprepared for the snow when it started to fall that day. What might have been *special* about the snowfall, though? I looked at the weather records.

And that's where I learned about the comet.

P0921/Magellan passed between the Earth and the sun, with Earth drifting through its tail for a couple of days — including the day of my run-in with the hood of a car. There were interviews with astronomers about when the comet might be visible to the naked eye, even a few reports about a bunch of nutjobs holding ceremonies to greet it, to worship it in some way. Making something mystical out of it.

But it was just a comet. Just passing through. So what?

Dejected, I turned off the computer and tried to forget about it. So what if some stupid comet went by. I needed to figure out how the thorns got in my body. I didn't know for sure it happened that day, the day of the accident, but that was my hunch. Everything seemed to trace back to that day. These little things, these thorns. Like parasites, like *alien invaders* in my body.

Hold on.

Aliens.

No way. I quickly flipped the computer on again.

Then, of course, I waited, annoyed, for more than five minutes as it rebooted. Ah, computers. They're making our lives easier, aren't they, folks?

What was a comet's tail made out of? The answer — well *answers* — came quickly. First, there are really two tails: a dust tail and an ion tail. The dust tail is made of, you guessed it, *dust.* The ion tail contains water and other ions like carbon monoxide. Water. Like snow is made of. But still. How would water from a comet reach Earth? And would it even matter if it did?

After a bit more research, I found that some scientists think water on Earth might actually originate *from* comets in the first place. And of course, other scientists think those guys are completely off their rocker, so who knows what to believe, right?

My head was spinning.

So… on or about the day my life changed, the planet passed through a comet's tail, which was made of water ions, and those water ions may or may not have filtered down through the atmosphere to me. A dumb kid, sticking his tongue out in the snow.

I laughed out loud. What a bunch of bullshit.

Flicking off the computer once again, I got ready for bed, all twisted up with confused thoughts.

* * *

A little while later, on the last day of the summer before school started, I decided to go looking for Bobby. I vowed to myself not to mention the whole comet thing. Bobby'd freak for sure.

I'd almost never gone to Bobby's house to find him, for fear of running into his parents. I wasn't going to start this time. Instead, I looked for him at the empty warehouse bay. As I approached the building, the noise from the lumber yard droned behind me. Yet ahead... I thought I heard a sound like a loud slap. Then two more.

I stepped to the back door and found it open.

"Bobby, you in there?" I called into the shadowed interior. There was no answer. The late-afternoon sun was thick and heavy outside, but the bay itself might as well have been a thousand feet under ground, daylight nothing but a bitter memory. I could see almost nothing inside. I went in anyway. If the door was open, I figured Bobby was in there somewhere. He probably couldn't hear me over all the noise from the lumber yard.

Three steps inside the door, I froze.

Something, no, *someone* was lying on the floor, still. I blinked and blinked, squeezing my eyes, willing them to adjust more quickly to the darkness.

"Bobby...?" I stepped forward.

The body moved. Beside it, next to one slowly twitching hand, I saw a glint of metal. It was the gun — Bobby's gun. The person on the ground was definitely Bobby, but why did he look so... strange? The body moved again. Not really moved, but flowed. *Formed.*

145

The irregular shape where Bobby's head should have been shifted and coalesced. As my eyes finally got used to the darkness, I saw Bobby's face staring upward, features swelling and sharpening, like a clay sculpture being smoothed into shape.

"What the…," I began.

His head shook, slightly, and started to rotate toward me. His mouth moved, but only inhuman wet noises came out. He shook his head again, then his eyes focused on me.

"Hey, Johnny," he said, his voice sounding strange, alien, like it was bubbling up from underwater.

My jaw dropped. "Bobby. What the hell are you doing?"

He twisted his head back and forth, like he was working out a kink in his neck, then sat up on the cement floor. "Just… practicing." He reached one hand up and felt his head, then broke out in a smile. Pulling his hand back, he looked at it, amazed.

"What'd you do, Bobby?" I asked, in a near whisper. I felt like I should run, leave the place. I don't know if I wanted to get help or just get away, but I knew I didn't really want to know what Bobby was about to say.

"I shot *myself* this time, Johnny," he said with a smirk. "Here." He pointed to his right thigh. "Here." His abdomen. Then his hand raised higher. "And here."

He put one finger to his forehead, a crazy grin on his face.

10

I don't know exactly how to put this. I'm sorry, it's hard.

Damn it. Of everything that happened, all the crazy stuff, *this* is the thing.

The thing I don't want to talk about.

But it's important.

I staggered out of the dark warehouse and into the bright sunlight, reeling from what I'd seen. What Bobby had done. What he could do, and what I apparently could do, too. I was stunned.

In a daze of emotion and dull, formless thought, I walked out to the side road and headed for home. As I passed behind the lumber yard, I was staring blindly ahead. Barely conscious of my own footfalls, I plodded forward; I was hardly aware of where I was going. I certainly wasn't looking for trouble.

As I followed the deserted road, somehow my eye caught movement off to the left, at the rear of the last building in the lumber yard. Without considering what it might mean, I turned my head and suddenly made eye contact with an older kid, a guy from high school. That's all I did. I wish I'd kept my head down.

The kid jumped up, followed by two more; they stood glaring at me next to a beat-up old green four-door sedan. I recognized them as part of the rough crowd in town, kids a few years older than me, kids I should avoid. I tried to walk by. Whatever they were doing was nothing compared to what I'd just seen.

Is Bobby going crazy? I asked myself. *Is he going to end up like Walter?*

Am I *going to end up like Walter?*

Walter Ivory was the man I blamed for my sister's condition. And he'd tried to kill me and Bobby. I was *glad* that son of a bitch was dead. But if Walter, Bobby, and I shared a connection — the thorns in our bodies — did that mean Walter's descent into madness was just a preview for Bobby? Or me?

I had a very bad feeling that Bobby was already too far gone.

He *shot himself.* Three times. It reminded me of Walter's attempts to hurt himself — or, being honest, to *kill* himself. It wasn't normal. It didn't make sense. I mean, even though I could do things, special things, I was *not* about to shoot myself in the head to prove a point.

"Hey there, John Boy?" a voice called out, sneering and rude. *Really? John Boy? God, was it a rule that bullies had to use* that *name?*

I kept walking, muttering a *hi* under my breath, but keeping my head down. *Don't make eye contact again,* I told myself.

"Talking to *you*, asshole," the voice called again, too angry, too fast. What had I done? Foolishly, I looked over. And saw the bottles. And the lit, hand-rolled joints. *Smoking and drinking behind the lumber yard. As if I care.* I kept going, but already the three were loping over to the small road, cutting off my way home.

The tallest of the boys stepped in front of me, forcing me to stop. I looked up, past his red t-shirt with its black skull printed large in the center, up to his sneering face. Roger Steele. He looked back and forth to the other boys, one on either side of him, his coifed blond hair bouncing across his forehead as he gesticulated. What a freaking name. *Roger Steele.* Between the hair and the name, he should've been a porn star or maybe a super spy. Instead he was just a dope head who bullied other kids whenever he had the chance. He was what Bobby might have grown into if our car accident hadn't seemingly jolted him into a change of heart.

I'd had the misfortune of knowing Roger most of my life. He lived only a few streets over from my house, and his younger sister, Hanna, was in my grade. (For reference, Hanna Steele is also a good porn name.) Still, I was surprised he knew who *I* was. His two henchmen, a couple of other Neanderthals named Lawrence and Zach, were shorter, darker, hairier, like shadows trailing behind their taller, blonder master. Lawrence dropped something into his near-empty bottle as he approached; it was the end of a cigarette, making a faint *hiss* as it went out in the shallow pool of warm beer. I guess Larry didn't smoke the stronger stuff. Thinking this, I almost laughed out loud. Thankfully, I caught myself.

I put my hands up, palms out, in front of me. "Look, guys, I'm just trying to get home. Whatever you all are doing back here is your own business." My eyes flittered to Roger's and Zach's joints, slow curls of smoke tracing upward from the lit ends. The sweet smell was undeniably marijuana.

"You're *damn right* it's our business. You better watch yourself, John Boy," Roger said. He had all the intellect of a ball-peen hammer. He raised a fist to emphasize his point. "You say one word about us back here and *you are dead.*" As he leaned close, I could smell stale smoke on his breath.

My body tensed. I thought of when Bobby tried to hit me, and all at once I was both excited and terrified. I realized that I probably didn't have anything to fear from these guys. That thought was intensely... *liberating.* On the other hand, I was scared. If one of these guys decided to punch me and my body did some crazy bending or shifting, it was going to raise some eyebrows. My little secret wouldn't be so secret. *Everyone* would find out. My friends. Everyone at school. My parents. All this just made me tense up even more. Roger bent his elbow and cocked his fist at my chin.

This is it, I thought. I squinted and winced. But the blow never fell.

Opening my eyes, I saw Roger's goofy grin spread into a full-on laugh, a guffaw. He stayed that way, laughing in my face, for maybe half a minute, braying like a donkey, his wingmen echoing the sound, almost doubling over.

Then Roger turned, taking the last puff of his joint, burning it down to nothing before closing his eyes and letting its effects settle in. He reopened his eyes and gestured for Lawrence's bottle, and Lawrence passed it over, at which point Roger twisted up his face and spat a gooey and discolored blob of phlegm into the bottle. He paused to examine his handiwork. "That's disgusting," he said, gesturing at the slosh of horrors in the clear glass bottle. "You should dump that out," he said nodding toward me then handing the bottle back to Lawrence. Roger walked away, back toward his dated green car.

Lawrence's eyes were glued to the bottle, the dark-stained liquid inside, the stew of spent cigarette, ash, and disgusting slime. Slowly, his eyes came up and met mine. The other one, Zach, toked the small nub of his joint, giggling uncontrollably. When it was finally burned to nothing, he followed Roger toward the car. As Zach walked away, Lawrence took a step toward me. For good measure, he coughed up a generous loogie of his own and hawked it into the bottle, swirling everything together.

Behind him, Roger started the car with a loud, reluctant grumble. Zach hopped in the front passenger's seat, slamming the door with a thud.

Why didn't I just run? I mean, they probably would have chased me, most likely would have caught me, definitely would have tried to give me a beating. But I knew I could take it, or least my body could overcome. Still, I realized that I didn't know what it *felt like* when Bobby wrecked his bike. Or, worse, when he shot himself. If they tried to beat me up, even if my body could avoid the blows or heal itself if it didn't, was it going to *hurt?* Like a chicken, I stood frozen.

And Lawrence dumped the entire disgusting mess of stale beer, tobacco bits, and bubbling saliva on my head. It dripped down, leaving trails of wet stench in my hair, on my face, touching my mouth, running onto my clothes.

I seethed.

Still I was frozen in place. My body didn't move, but my eyes bored holes in Lawrence as he laughed, shook the bottle empty, and then tossed it aside, pumping his fist as it shattered on the cracked pavement. As he turned and walked to the car, my eyes burned like lasers through his back. He opened the rear door and dropped his ugly, ignorant, hateful dumb ass inside, and my eyes blazed fury at him, at them all.

I knew I could kill them with my mind.

I *wanted* to kill them with my mind.

The car dropped into gear and lurched forward, spitting gravel out behind it as Roger revved the engine. Passing close beside me, Roger shouted something inane and vulgar that I don't even remember. The car turned away from me, shooting little rocks into my shins and coughing up dust as it picked up speed. Roger headed out toward the main road, to the stop sign where he could either turn left onto the long straightaway of Route 22, which became Tucker Street downtown, or head right, up and over the hill that led out of town.

Just before Roger reached the stop sign, I saw the police car, far off to the left, coming down Route 22. I was sure Roger could see the cop, too, and I knew his brakes lights would come on in the next second or two. He was going to stop calmly at the intersection, let the police car pass, and be on his way. Off scot-free. That bastard and his bastard friends.

Like an omen, a wet blob of reeking ash and saliva fell from my hair, past my eyes.

Furious, I clenched my teeth and took a half step forward, arms arched back, body leaning ahead, as if I were aiming my mind.

But I didn't kill them. I did something much, much worse.

For just a second, just a split second too long, I made Roger's foot freeze, holding down the gas pedal.

His car flew past the stop sign and out onto Route 22, right in front of the cop. Happy with my little plan, I relented. Suddenly back in control, Roger slammed on the brakes, coming to an awkward, lurching stop in a kind of diagonal roadblock across both lanes of traffic. The cop, too, hit the brakes hard, turning slightly to his right, sliding to a halt only a few feet from Roger's car.

And the world paused.

For perhaps a full second, maybe two, the cars sat cockeyed in the road, like mirror images slashing the pavement. I was too far away to see their faces, but I could imagine the scene: one car full of stunned teenagers reeking of pot and beer, the other car with a suddenly very angry cop.

Then the driver's door on the black-and-white police cruiser clicked open. When I remember it now, I think that click unlocked the world again, set events moving, events I wish I could take back.

God, I wish I could take it all back.

He must not have seen a thing, or at least not until it was too late. I wish I could believe he didn't *feel anything*, but I have a very good imagination. I can imagine that last moment. I can imagine his gasp, his terror, his pain. He felt it. He felt what I did to him.

A silver economy sedan appeared on the right, and for a second I didn't even realize who it was. I just watched as some yahoo came over the hill at a good speed, heading toward town. Then the car began to look familiar. Very familiar. Too familiar. It was my father, driving home after work. He wasn't flooring it, but he was definitely above the speed limit. Why not? Usually the road was just about deserted, and straight as a rail in most spots.

But today, two cars blocked his path.

I heard the squeal and saw him swerve, too hard, to his right. The nose of his car ducked down, dropping into the ditch beside the road as he skidded past Roger's car. I saw the police officer — I know him by name now, Sergeant Alan Durso — as he sprang out of his cruiser, whipping off his sunglasses. Then my dad's car flew up, the rear end trying to maintain the velocity that the front end had just lost. I saw the dark underside of the car take to the air in a sudden burst of dirt and smoke. The car turned end over end, a pinwheel in a strong breeze, a toy car thrown by an angry toddler. A loud, dull pop sounded as the car landed on its roof amid the bushes of the roadside embankment. Dirt, grass, glass, and other debris rained down, and then finally the car was still.

The world paused again. Not the whole world, probably, but definitely mine.

My father was pronounced dead at the scene, from multiple traumatic injuries, at 6:27 p.m. that day.

11

The clouds spread thick, damp, and grey along the sky on the day we buried my father. Holly wore a black dress that perfectly matched her hair and offset her pale skin. But she sat in her wheelchair looking away, as if uninterested. We knew she probably didn't understand what was going on at all.

My mom wept uncontrollably. It was hard, as a kid, to figure out your parents most times. They seemed infinitely, impossibly older, adult and all-knowing. The one thing parents almost never seemed was... *young*. As I watched my mom shudder with heaving sobs, I realized how young she really was. How unexpected this was. How she had planned to spend many, many more years with my father. And how fragile she could be.

It made me hate myself for what I'd done.

Blame. People like to hand it out. But of course, no one knew I was to blame. How could they? I wasn't in any of the cars, wasn't even there at scene until the crash was over and done. A lot of people actually pitied me. I'd witnessed my own father's death. That no one knew I caused it made their pity even worse. I was angry at the people who pitied me. But the friends and neighbors and teachers and counselors considered my anger a *coping mechanism*. The spiral of my guilt and anger, combined with other people's compassion and sympathy for me, seemed to have no end. The more they *cared,* the more I *raged.*

The three high school kids, Roger, Lawrence, and Zach, were never charged with any wrongdoing. Roger claimed his brakes had failed momentarily, and when they inspected his car — that old green rust bucket — they found it had so many existing and potential mechanical problems that they believed his story. I suppose that was for the best. I can't imagine I'd have felt better knowing Roger had been charged in my father's death when I was really to blame.

Once the police had concluded that the accident was solely my dad's fault, they even considered slapping him with a couple of posthumous citations: speeding, reckless driving, failure to give way to an emergency vehicle. When they called with that news, my mom screamed into the phone. I think I learned more curse words from that one conversation than I had in my entire preceding 14 years. But Mom's anger was a front. As soon as she hung up, she fell to the floor of the kitchen and cried, for what seemed like hours.

I should have been just another kid unhappy about the start of the new school year. In retrospect, those days put the whole *I hate going back to school* argument in perspective. I would have been happy just to be in class. As it was, my mother kept us out the entire first week. On Wednesday, we buried my dad.

Sitting in the front row at the funeral services, I clenched my fists, open, closed, as a local pastor spoke. I guess one benefit of organized religion is that they know what to do when bad things like death happen. My family wasn't particularly religious, so it was actually one of our neighbors who called in the pastor. Otherwise, I guess we would've all sat around the coffin silently, wondering what the hell to do.

My shoulders tensed; my fists kept opening and closing. The air itself felt stifling, like it was constricting me, falling over me like a heavy blanket. It was hard to breathe.

Then a hand lightly grasped my shoulder, and a voice whispered to me. "It's gonna be okay, John." It was my Aunt Cindy, all in black except for the white hanky she used to dab at her wet eyes.

At that moment, what I wanted to do was push her away, push everyone away. But I waited until I was able to force a weak smile. She squeezed my shoulder twice, then took back her hand, turning again to face the pastor.

Looking across the top of my father's coffin, I could see Bobby and his parents. I'd sort of expected Bobby to be there, but his parents were another story. When Bobby and I hung out, we never did so anywhere near his parents. And they certainly didn't interact with my parents, ever. The fact that they wore their best Sunday outfits and came out for Dad's funeral was both nice and another contributor to my guilt.

I made eye contact with Bobby, and he looked at me, a blank expression on his face. We were just kids, after all. We might have something strange inside our bodies, but we still had no idea what to do in these sorts of social situations. The whole day was a blur, but I don't think Bobby and I ever spoke.

I was so wrapped up in myself, my anger, and the weight of my new burden, that I didn't see it right away. Neither did Mom. Aunt Cindy must have known that my sister and I would need extra attention on that terrible day. Because she saw it first.

When Aunt Cindy stepped in front of me, in front of Mom, my first reaction was *how rude!* What the hell was she doing, stepping in front of a grieving family at a funeral? I turned my head to follow her, and saw her rush to Holly's side.

Holly was convulsing. It was like a wave, from her feet, upward through her legs, her body, outward to her head and arms. A seizure. Aunt Cindy knelt beside Holly, held her arm, checked to be sure she wasn't choking on her tongue. For a full minute, Holly shook.

Then finally, Holly's head tilted forward, and her body gradually became still. Aunt Cindy stayed where she was a few moments more, then rose back to her feet, giving me and Mom a sorrowful glance.

In the heat of the moment, the heaviness of the day, I guess we had all forgotten what Holly's seizures had been foreshadowing in those days.

Like the wave that rolled up Holly's body moments before, a wave rippled under the land, from the trees in the distance, across the green hills dotted with white tombstones. The blue canopy that had been erected to shield the mourners from the strong late-summer sun shook and danced. The pastor, our friends, our family, they all bobbed and moved, staggering about, trying not to fall.

The world around us shuddered from the strong earthquake, like the ground had turned to water and we were ships bouncing madly on the high seas. Unable to do anything more than hold on, I stared straight ahead at the shiny brown coffin perched on the simple metal stand, the box that held my dad's body, thinking only one thing.

Oh my God, please don't fall over. If Dad can't keep his life, at least let him keep his dignity.

12

For days, the house was quiet. Holly watched TV sometimes. Mom made meals when she needed to, and did a lot of cleaning, but I think that was just a distraction. Still, it was obvious where her mind was. She'd move a paper on the countertop, something simple and innocuous, but it would have Dad's name on it and she'd start to cry.

I sat with Holly a lot. She didn't seem to judge me, at least nothing like how I was judging myself. I wanted to comfort Mom, but I was so... *responsible*... I just couldn't manage it. How was I supposed to say I killed him? My own dad. Her husband.

Late one morning I sat on the couch, staring at the TV, which wasn't even on, when the door bell rang, stirring my mother from the kitchen. She walked to the hallway, then paused. She was looking away, but it seemed like she was steeling herself. Trying to put on a normal appearance. She'd been doing that a lot. To all the people who came offering sympathies, some carrying a lasagna or another meal for us to reheat. Finally, with a sigh, Mom opened the door.

It was Bobby.

"Hey, Mrs. Black, I'm… well, I'm real sorry. I, uh." He paused, not sure what to say. My mom let him off the hook.

"Thank you, Bobby. Please come in. How are you?" she asked, nothing but polite, although I imagine she didn't care a bit about whatever his reply might be.

"I'm fine, thank you. Is… is Johnny available?" he asked. I leaned forward on the couch so he could see my face, and he smiled and waved, relieved to get out of the crucible of talking to a widow. "Oh, hey, Johnny!" I managed a slight wave in response. "You wanna hang out for a bit?" Even where I was, how I felt about everything that had happened, and about myself, I really appreciated Bobby at that moment. Sure, we fought, but he had become like a brother to me. I nodded, slowly.

"Sure, Bobby. Let's go to my room."

* * *

There was an awkward silence as we sat, him in the chair by my desk, me half flopped on the bed.

After several long minutes, he spoke. "So. Johnny. I, I really don't know anything smart to say, but, you know, I'm… sorry. I can't believe what happened to your dad."

I nodded as tears came to my eyes. I looked away, embarrassed.

So Bobby continued, trying to break the ice. "I mean, that accident… It's so… *random*." He tossed up his hands in a gesture. *What're you gonna do?*

It wasn't his fault. Not his fault at all.

But I got so incredibly angry.

"It isn't *random* at all," I spat.

Bobby said nothing. I didn't know if he was thinking about what I had said, or if he'd just run out of ideas. But after a couple of minutes, he came back to it. "Sure it is, Johnny. It's called an *accident* because it happened by *accident*. I know you're really upset, and you should be, but it was just an accident. Coulda been anyone. Coulda been *my* dad."

I clenched my teeth. "It *wasn't* an accident." I was full of rage. I could see Bobby pull back. Was that fear in his eyes?

"What're you talking about, John?" He spoke low, unsure, leaning away from me.

I almost told him then, but I couldn't. I shook my head, hard. "Nothing. It's nothing."

"Hey, man, I know I don't have any right to try to assume how you feel," Bobby said. "But we're friends, and so I can try to help, right? I mean, do you want to get outta here and just, you know, do something? To get your mind off it?"

Do something other than smother myself with my own guilt? At that moment, nothing sounded better. Timidly, I asked, "Like what?"

Bobby thought about it for a moment. "We could… hang out at the warehouse…?" He said it innocently enough.

But I snapped.

"The *warehouse*? You mean, the place just down the road from where my dad died? The place where you shot yourself? *That* warehouse?" I stood up, furious.

Bobby put up his hands, palms out. "Hey, sorry, it was a bad idea…"

"You're right. It was a *terrible* idea. If I hadn't gone to the warehouse the last time…" My voice broke. "I wouldn't have kil—" I stopped myself before I could say it.

Bobby didn't miss it. He frowned. "You wouldn't have… what?"

I put my fists up to my eyes, anger and pain and sorrow, all together. "Nothing!"

Bobby stood up, right in front of me. "You wouldn't have *what*, Johnny?"

I couldn't hold it back any longer. It came out in a rush, like the air from a popped balloon. "I wouldn't have *killed my father!*" It was a loud whisper. I couldn't hold in my emotion, but couldn't bear the thought of my mom overhearing.

Bobby took a step back. "What're you talking about?"

I pounded on my chest with each statement, each admission of guilt. "*I* made Roger drive into the intersection, right in front of that cop car. I did it for spite — to try to get back at him! To try to get him in trouble, after what he did to me! *I did it with my mind. I* did it! That's why my dad had to swerve! That's why he crashed! That's why he's *dead!* He died because I was mad that a couple of jerks dumped a beer on me! He died because I have these *damned things I can do!*" I thought for a moment, looking down at my hands. "Because I have these *damned things inside me.*" I went to the desk, and Bobby cringed back.

Opening the top drawer, I pulled out the scissors that were kept there. Not kid scissors with safety blades. My parents trusted me with real, sharp scissors. My parents trusted me. My *dad* had trusted me.

I clutched the scissors in my right hand and stabbed at my left arm, a harsh cut that should have opened a huge gash in my arm.

Instead, my arm sluiced away, and I was left unharmed.

Boy, that made me mad. I mean, even more mad.

I stabbed and slashed, mercilessly, at my own skin. I wanted the *thorns* out of me.

But nothing worked.

I couldn't hear him, but Bobby was talking to me. Not shouting, talking. Finally, he put his hands on me, and one or two of my slashes misfired and would have hit him, but of course, his skin moved away, too. I saw the futility of it all.

And I heard him, at last. "Johnny. Stop. Johnny. Stop. Johnny. *Stop.*"

So I stopped, the scissors thudding to the carpet.

God damn it, I thought. *This is a curse.*

I'm cursed to live.

13

Just before bed that night, I saw the scissors still on the floor and thought, *I should get a bandage*. Then I laughed. More of a scoff than a laugh, I suppose. What was there to bandage? Nothing was wrong with me.

At least on the outside.

I was a teenager, but of course my mom still tucked me in like I was five. I suppose she needed those rituals then more than ever. I did, too.

In a low, ragged whisper, head ducked down toward the floor, she spoke as she stood in the doorway. "Good night, John. I love you."

"Mom," I said, sitting up in bed, using that tone kids get when they're not sure how to start a conversation with a parent. "Are you okay?" It was the best I could do.

She shuddered a bit, still not looking at me. "Not really, John. But I'll be okay. We all will." She reached up and wiped at her eyes. "I'm not going to stop missing your dad. Or stop loving him. But we… you, me, and Holly… we need to keep going."

I sat still a moment, then nodded. I simply couldn't tell her. I fell back into my pillow and Mom closed the door, leaving me in a darkness that couldn't compare to what was inside my soul.

* * *

Lying awake for over an hour, I did nothing but think.

And I made a decision.

I would never — *never* — use my mental powers again. Clearly, I couldn't stop my body from protecting itself. I should have been in a hospital, slashed to pieces by the scissors. But I showed no injury. So my body would do what my body would do. The thorns were alive and kicking. But I was in control of my mind. I would never do it again.

Even the sad, the angry, the hateful, the scared… even they have to sleep.

So eventually, I did.

* * *

I woke up to a sunny new morning, feeling oddly good about myself. The previous night's distress, while painful and traumatic, must have done me some kind of good. Or maybe it was my decision to stop using my powers against other people's minds. Whatever it was, I felt like a page had been turned. Like I could overcome what happened.

I hadn't expected it, but I was still just a kid, and so intense pessimism could easily be replaced with something else. Not joy. Not happiness. Not quite. But at least the absence of anger and sadness. It was a start.

I got dressed, made my bed — Mom demanded this daily — and headed for breakfast. Mom and Holly were already there, Holly chowing down on some cereal.

"Morning, John. Did you sleep well?" Mom asked. I nodded. I guess I actually had. "What do you want for breakfast?"

I pressed my forehead against Holly's for a moment. Our little thing. Then I pointed. "What's she eating?" My mom nodded toward a cereal box on the counter with a colorful cartoon monkey plastered across the front. "Okay, I'll have that." I grabbed the box, found a bowl and some milk, and soon I was eating contentedly next to my sister.

For a moment, my mom looked... happy. Or at least she looked like she understood what she still had, despite her loss.

There was nothing else remarkable. It simply was a *good breakfast*. At the time, that seemed like a big deal. I headed to the bathroom feeling like a cloud had lifted.

As I brushed my teeth, I heard a commotion outside.

"What the heck...," an adult male voice said, surprised.

Normal human curiosity called me toward the window, where I brushed back the thin curtains to see what was going on.

There, out on the sidewalk, was Mr. Cooper, one of my neighbors. He was standing, body twisted, looking way off down the road. I followed his line of sight...

...and saw Bobby running down the street, headed away from my house.

14

It burned me the whole school day. *What the hell were you doing, Bobby?* We shared classes, but Bobby avoided me in between, and after school as well.

I had to follow him.

I could tell he was walking intentionally fast, well ahead of me, on his way home. I called out to him once or twice, then watched as he left the normal route, heading instead toward the shops in the center of town. Just as I realized we were right there, at the building where Bobby tried to jump his bike, he turned and ran down the alley. Startled, I raced after him.

As I rounded into the back parking lot, I realized I was alone. Bobby had vanished. *What's he hiding? Why was he at my house? Why is he running away?* It didn't make sense.

But I knew Bobby's abilities, same as mine. Invisibility wasn't one of them, at least as far as I knew. I stood still for a moment. And felt something above me and to the right.

Bobby was motionless on the fire escape.

As soon as our eyes met, he let loose a gush of air and started up the ladder, fast. Running to the dumpster, I leaped up to the lowest rung to follow suit. "What the hell are you doing, Bobby?" He didn't reply. "Why were you at my house this morning?" He continued to the roof.

He turned once, looking down at me. "Go home, Johnny." Then he disappeared from view.

Finally, I reached the roof and pulled myself up onto the flat surface. Bobby was maybe 20 feet in front of me, waiting.

"Why were you at my house this morning?" I repeated.

He said nothing.

For a moment.

Then all of his built-up frustration came out at once.

"Because," he said, mouth bursting open like flood gates letting loose a torrent of water. "Because you need to snap out of it. Because you need to stop pussyfooting around. You're *special*, Johnny. You can do things no one else can. *Make something of it*. Stop blaming yourself and bottling things up. I'm sick of it."

I was stunned, realizing what he'd done. Realizing that my newfound sense of peace that morning had been a lie. "You pushed my mind? While I was *asleep*? What the hell is wrong with you, Bobby? I thought we were *friends!*"

"We *are* friends, Johnny. And that's why I can't sit back and watch you do nothing. Watch you let your powers do nothing. I mean, I get it. Your dad is dead, and nothing's going to change that, and it's terrible. But it's *not your fault.*"

"Yes," I nodded vigorously, a manic smile on my face. "Yes, Bobby, it *is* my fault. I put the car in front of him with my power. I killed him."

We began to circle each other slowly, neither wanting to get closer.

"No, Johnny. You tried to get back at a couple of punks. You had no idea your dad was anywhere near there. You can't blame yourself." His tone was half plaintive, half angry. It was like he was coming to the end of his patience with me, like a parent tolerating a belligerent kid.

I stopped, standing still, and Bobby echoed me. From the roof, the afternoon sun stared down at us, a few clouds rolling overhead among the blue. "I won't use it again," I said. "I won't use the mind powers."

Bobby's shoulders fell, and a sort of weariness overcame him. "Ah, come on, Johnny. This is really getting old."

"What?" I asked, incredulous.

Bobby looked up. "It's really getting old, having to push and pull you to *do* anything. First the simple things, now this. I mean, I'm ready to move on. To move *up*. No one else can help me. Just you. You know, we should be a team. On the same page. Instead…" He waved a hand left and right.

"Bobby," I said, having a hard time believing I had to explain myself, "my *dad died*. Because of something I did. I can't just ignore that."

Kids aren't always rational. I wish I'd understood that, then. Bobby stepped within inches of me, looking me in the eye. I couldn't read his thoughts. I didn't see it coming.

"Ah, Johnny. Would you just *get over it*." As he spoke those last words, his hand came up, palm outward, and he struck me, like a hard push.

My body tried to sluice away, but Bobby was faster.

It felt like when I'd been hit by the car. Like metal slamming into my body. Instantly, I knew. *He's figured out how to do it. How to be a weapon.*

I flew back, slammed into the brick half wall at the rooftop's edge. Sure, I was used to being a punching bag for bullies my whole life, including Bobby. But now things were different. This was... *unexpected.*

I staggered back to my feet, shaking my head, brushing myself off. "What're you doing?" That was all I managed before he came at me again. Standing so close to the edge, I felt vulnerable, so I dodged left. Bobby's arm, still palm out, came down like a hammer.

Well that, at least, was something my body was used to. My shoulder sluiced around the blow as I dove to the side. "Bobby, cut it out!" I yelled.

He turned and struck again, this time a sideways slash into my ribs that my body managed to only partially avoid. The blow tossed me several feet. I could see Bobby was enjoying this. A real opportunity to show off his skills. He'd clearly been training, on his own, perfecting himself for a fight.

I hadn't.

The only time I'd been a weapon was when Bobby tried to hit me in my room, and that was by accident. I didn't even know if I could make it happen again. I tried to concentrate, and before I could bring my hand up, Bobby was there. Another blow, unavoidable, sent me flailing to the far side of the roof. On one knee, I tried to stand, wincing and tentative, hoping Bobby would see my distress and let up. He didn't. Another punch fell. And another. And many more. Bobby could see that the blows, while connecting firmly, weren't doing my body much harm.

Yes, each one hurt like hell, but my body twisted and sluiced and reformed.

Frustrated, Bobby increased the attack. He seemed determined to make me cry uncle.

Left, right, up, down, and again to the side, his strikes fell, and I was tossed about. But slowly, I came into my own.

I had been a weapon once. If I could only remember.

Bobby hit me twice, left then right hand smashing into me, sending me sprawling again. I found myself up against the edge of the half wall, for a moment tilting precariously over the side. The same one Bobby had jumped his bike over. Sure, he'd fallen and lived, but he'd been *flattened*. Ideas on what that felt like raced through my mind. I dodged another blow as Bobby approached. "Bobby, stop it!" I yelled, tumbling to one side. As I fell, I thrust one hand up, wishing it to become steel. Bobby fell against it, and let loose a loud *oof*.

"That's it, Johnny!" He was actually smiling. "Show me what you can *do*!" And before I even knew it he was beside me, his entire body sluiced and he was on top of me. "I can do *this*!" He thrust both hands into me. Did he know my body could take it and live? It was really hard to know for sure. His hands battered into my stomach like freight trains; my skin and bones and muscles tried to outrun him but I was sent airborne. I saw the edge of the half wall approaching, knew I had to grab it or I'd be sent off the edge and plummet to the ground far below.

With both hands, I keyed on the top layer of bricks… and barely managed to grasp the edge. My feet dangled toward the street as I hung off the top of the building.

For a moment, the only sound in my ears was my ragged breath, in out, in out. I dared a single look below, and realized it was worse than I thought. Not only was it two stories down, but the flight path was obstructed. If I fell, I'd hit several segments of the fire escape, and then the side of the dumpster. It would be far from a smooth landing.

I have to admit, I was terrified. My eyes bugged out as I looked down. Then I heard him coming. Letting loose a loud yell as he ran toward me, Bobby was silhouetted against the afternoon sun. All I saw was a shadow, beams of blinding sunlight arrayed around him like a halo. Bobby's hands were up, like a football player diving for a huge tackle. But I knew those hands weren't going to grab on and pull me to safety.

They'd be like iron.

I watched as they descended in an arc toward me, the world slowing as it happened.

"No," I said in a calm voice. To this day, I can't be sure I even said it out loud, but I think I did. It didn't matter. Bobby had made his body into a weapon. But I had my mind.

Bobby didn't stop, he *bounced* back, like he'd hit an invisible wall. There was a loud thud as he fell to the roof. His body twitched, once, twice, three times. Then he was still.

I was certain of two things.

First, I knew that by using my mental powers, I'd already violated the promise I'd made myself, although my dad was less than a week in the ground.

And second, I was certain that my friend Bobby Graden was dead.

* * *

Staggering, stumbling, I half-tumbled down the fire escape, eager to be free. I ran toward home, raising eyebrows all along the way. Finally, as the sun was setting, I pushed the door of my house open. I slammed it behind me, gasping, startling my mom. "John. Be careful," was all she said. Panting, looking through drips of sweat falling from my forehead, I nodded.

I walked into the living room and fell onto the couch, beside Holly in her chair. The TV was on, and I mirrored Holly's stare, blankly taking in the screen. The nightly news. I knew Holly hated it. But I was too exhausted to get up and change the channel. The remote was nowhere to be seen.

Slowly I caught my breath.

He wasn't dead.

I thought I'd killed Bobby with my mind, but he was still breathing. I'd knocked him out, which was just as well, because he'd been about to kill me. Or at least hurt me really bad. With him unconscious, I ran. Of course, he'd know where to find me. I wouldn't be safe here for long, if he wanted to fight again.

I was thinking about where to go, what to do, considering what I'd need to do to make a truce with him. His attack was unexpected, yet expected. Was there a way we could work it out?

On the TV, a breaking news report took over the broadcast. The governor's mansion, at the state capitol, was shown in a live shot via helicopter. I paid no attention to it. Bobby was the only thing on my mind.

He was strong. He was fast. He'd obviously been training without me. Even though he said he wanted me to help him, I had the distinct impression he might be happy with me gone. Once a bully... always a bully?

As my eyes wandered around the room, I saw something moving. Twitching.

Holly's fingers on her left hand. It could have been nothing, but I thought it was a small seizure. I looked into her eyes, but she continued to stare at the TV.

I turned to follow her gaze, and my jaw dropped. The helicopter camera showed police and security all around the governor's mansion, guns drawn, as a lone man walked from a balcony into the interior. He was only on screen for a moment, but I was sure.

It was Branco.

As I stared at the glowing screen of the television, the house rumbled slowly in an aftershock.

PART THREE

NOON

1

Two days after I saw him on the news, Branco offered a single reporter the chance to interview him, within the governor's mansion that he held hostage.

That's right. Branco had somehow walked into the governor's mansion and taken over the place. It made no sense. This person, this random stranger I'd met on the boardwalk the day I turned 14, was suddenly all over the news. I knew he was like me, and that was scary enough. But what was he doing with his powers? Certainly not keeping them secret anymore. The reports said he had killed four guards getting into the mansion, and when the police came after him… well, stories were unclear. Perhaps he dodged bullets. (On that point, the reporters were more right than they knew.) The talking heads on the news shows guessed he might be using some sort of mind-altering chemicals, because the officers killed themselves with their own guns. (Here, I knew the reports were very, very wrong.) But one thing was clear: Branco said if anyone tried to confront him again, the governor would die.

It was Branco, the charming, friendly guy who had given me an extra ticket to ride The Hurlstorm. But this person was so different. His charm and laid-back style had curdled into full-on arrogance. And apparently he was going by the name *Sol*. Sounded pretty pompous, if you asked me.

Like most of the people in the neighborhood, we were glued to the TV. When the interview with Branco aired on the third night of the siege, Mom and I watched it, transfixed.

The picture showed him calm, confident, relaxed. Below his face, next to the Action News logo, was the text *CRISIS AT THE CAPITOL*.

"What is it that you want, exactly?" the reporter asked, her tinny voice echoing from off-screen.

Branco — I had a hard time taking the name Sol seriously, but okay, *Sol* — sat across from her, the picture of confidence and serenity.

"What do I want?" he repeated, looking casually around the room, his tanned skin offset by an open-collared white shirt, sleeves crisply rolled up. The camera pulled back to include the reporter. Sol paused, then turned his head to stare directly at her, his icy blue irises constricting ink-black pupils down to a concentrated dot. He shrugged, and continued in his sonorous baritone, clearly enunciated English tinted with his Portuguese accent.

"Everything. Nothing. To be seen. Heard. Revered. Loved. Feared. To have power, to exercise that power. What do I want? It is such a strange thought for me now, as I have changed." He let that sink in. "It is not necessarily what I want, you see. It is what I shall have, what I shall do. But your question, if I may paraphrase it, is asking what my motivation is, am I correct? What leads me to do the things that I do?" The interviewer nodded. Was he using his mind to alter her thoughts? In the split-second cut to her face, I could have sworn she displayed not only professional journalistic interest, but something more. Fear? Probably. Attraction? Maybe. Was it that Sol was now so commanding, so confident, so powerful, that she found him attractive despite her situation? Or was he influencing her with his mind?

"I have attained, to put it simply, a clear level of *superiority*. I am no longer like you." He nodded toward her, then toward someone off-screen, maybe the cameraman. "Or him. I suppose you could say I have evolved, but even that is a crude way to describe it, since this is not the work of time and many generations. I was born like you. I am now no longer so limited. From what you have seen so far, you clearly understand I possess an unnatural — or shall we say, a *supernatural* — level of both physical and mental ability. My skin is not susceptible to your bullets. My thoughts amplify, project, become your thoughts, to the degree that there is no resistance. And my mind can do many other things as well." The camera shot switched to one showing both the interviewer and Sol, sitting on opposite couches in a classically-appointed office within the governor's mansion. The governor himself sat at his large wooden desk, dutifully addressing paperwork, oblivious to the pair sitting just next to him, or the cameras, or lights, or crew. Sol gestured toward him. "Your governor is perfectly happy to continue to allow both my presence and yours. In his mind, there is not even cause for alarm. He looks at me as someone he simply *expects* to see here now. With a thought, all of his fight-or-flight instincts have left him, just as it leaves all others who might come to oppose me."

The interviewer looked down at her notes, adjusted her light-blue suit jacket. She stole an uncomfortable glance toward the governor, licked her lips, nervous for her next words. "What about the National Guard, gathering outside these walls? They seem very ready to fight you."

Sol tilted his head down and gave a dismissive little chuckle. I knew that sound. That laugh. He leaned forward, uncrossed his legs, put both of his designer loafers on the rug. He steepled his fingers in front of his face and stared at the interviewer, studying. The camera caught his intense gaze, locked on the woman across from him.

"*Experience teaches us that it is much easier to prevent an enemy from posting themselves than it is to dislodge them after they have obtained possession*," Sol recited. "I believe that your General George Washington said that. Well, here I am, in possession. I will not — cannot — be *dislodged*." He said the words as if they tasted foul in his mouth, then turned to address the camera directly. "Hear me, all of you who might oppose me. I am more than you, more than all of you combined. At this very moment, your governor lives because I allow him to do so. This woman," he nodded toward the interviewer, "and her crew, live because I allow them to as well. Outside these walls, the great military of this powerful state awaits me. Hesitantly. Fearful. Knowing I have *possession*. Of this place, your leader. How can you attack me and not destroy the very thing you wish to preserve?" Even through the flat interface of the TV, Sol was intense. Sharply, scarily focused.

Then he settled back into the couch, the picture of ease. He re-crossed his legs, closed his eyes briefly. "What can you, the military, in fact the world entire, do to me? For, with a single thought, I can kill. With a gesture, I can topple buildings. I possess more power than you could possibly understand. And my powers continue to grow." He slowly raised a hand, one finger pointed up casually in a slight curve. "In fact, I could simply lift my finger and black out the sun."

From somewhere outside, a tremendous explosion rocked the building, a low solid boom followed by incoherent shouts. Car alarms blared. A crystal globe on the governor's desk toppled and cracked. Sol closed his eyes as the television program went into a frenzy, splitting the screen to juxtapose the relaxed scene inside the governor's office with the world of mayhem outside. The anchorman's voice called for a field reporter to explain what was happening. In response, a dark-haired man leaned into the camera view outside the building. Behind him, large billows of black smoke arose from the husk of a crippled tank, its long gun barrel snapped and hanging off the turret.

The reporter did his best to respond. "It appears the tank behind me, I believe one belonging to the National Guard, suddenly exploded from the inside. We don't have word on casualties at this time. We're checking —"

"They are all dead," Sol interrupted, suddenly regaining the attention of his audience, the world. "I would be happy to provide a further demonstration of my diverse capabilities, but I think we all realize it is unnecessary. May I suggest that the commanding officers outside these walls consider backing their forces up by, let us say, at least one kilometer? You have one hour to comply. Otherwise," Sol smirked into the camera, lolling back in his seat and casually gesturing into the air once more, "I may decide to wave my hand again." He chuckled briefly, then looked toward the cameraman off-screen. "I believe we are done here."

The view immediately went dark.

KEITH SOARES

2

Sol.

Branco.

Meeting him was no coincidence. He had power. Like me, Bobby, even Walter Ivory.

No, he had *more*. Way more. Sitting calmly, he made that tank explode, barely moving his hand. How the hell did he do that?

I was in my room after the news broadcast, sitting at my desk, thinking. Mom was probably still in front of the TV, or maybe distracting herself looking after Holly. I was certain my encounter with Sol at Playa Beach was no coincidence. I think he'd been looking for me. Or, perhaps more accurately, he'd been looking for people *like him*.

Which only meant…

He might do it again.

I shuddered.

I wasn't big on geography, but my class had done a report on our state a couple of years before. I still remembered some of it, at least the basic layout of the state. At the top, near the shore on the right side — sorry, *east* — was Playa Beach. Close to the bottom, on the left/west, was my hometown. The capitol sat roughly between the two.

Was Sol coming for me?

My hands shook. I mean, come on. I wasn't even 15. Fighting Bobby, my supposed *friend*, was one thing. Fighting Sol? Impossible.

I was freaking out.

My mind wandered. If we were the same, me, Sol, Bobby, Walter, then we should — with the right practice — be able to do the same things. Could I blow up a tank?

A yellow No. 2 pencil, slightly gnawed, sat on my desk.

I was all too familiar with the ability to influence someone else's mind with my mind. But blowing things up? That was a joke. I didn't think I could even move the pencil sitting right in front of me.

So I tried.

Move, I thought. I concentrated. For dramatic flair, I held out one hand, fingers splayed, toward the pencil. Why? I have no idea. It didn't improve my ability, nor did it seem particularly necessary. But that's what people did in the movies.

I lowered my hand, dejected. Nothing happened.

But I *did* have powers. Maybe using them wasn't my problem. Maybe my problem was *not understanding them*.

I thought about my dad, the day he died. I still thought I was to blame. I knew it as pure and simple as I knew my own face in the mirror. I played out the scene in my head every day, dozens of times. What could I have done differently?

If I could move objects, like Sol had, could I have stopped Dad's car, saved him from the crash? Maybe. But I couldn't even move a pencil. No, there had to be something else I could have done.

The answer was obvious.

When I walked past the bullies, what was stopping me from pushing their minds? Just making it so they didn't even see me? Easy. And I could have done it. Sure, there were three of them, that might have made it a little tricky, but I was pretty sure I could have handled it.

And Dad would be alive.

I got up, went to the bathroom, and looked at myself in the mirror. Skinny kid, small for 14 years old. Black mop of hair. Normal looking in most ways… but my eyes. My eyes told another story, one that wasn't *normal* at all. They held a story. This story.

Staring into the reflection, I made myself a promise.

I have no idea why I have these abilities, but I do. And so, I'm going to use them.

To protect my mom, my sister, my family and friends. Heck, even Bobby. Maybe I'd read too many comic books. It seemed ridiculous to consider myself a superhero, but I definitely had powers other people would call *super*.

Seeing Sol, I knew what I didn't want: to use my powers to hurt people, for my own gain, for reasons I could only call *evil*.

If I was going to use the powers I had, I was going to use them for good.

It was a noble thought, even if it failed miserably.

KEITH SOARES

3

If there was a moment during that time when you could turn on the TV and *not* find coverage of Sol at the governor's mansion, I must have missed it. Whenever I'd click on the tube to catch one of my shows, or pop on something Holly liked, I'd invariably have to switch away from the news. Mom seemed obsessed.

That freaked me out. Sol was a good-looking guy, an attractive, charismatic guy. Was my mom interested in the story because of that? Of course not. That was a ridiculous thought.

Monday morning, the first Monday back in school after my fight with Bobby, I wanted to distract myself before heading out. I decided to catch a few early cartoons. This meant watching the preschool shows that Holly tolerated. Honestly, so did I. They were far beneath my so-called intellectual level. I didn't so much laugh at the jokes as groan, but it was better than nothing. As I turned on the TV, I saw the news instead and started to change the channel.

"Hold on!" Mom said from behind me as she came into the living room, setting down a bunch of colorful flowers tied up in a red bow. I looked at her, confused, then back to the TV.

The screen showed a wall of tanks, artillery, soldiers, all surrounding the governor's mansion. But not idly. They were preparing something. The tension in the news reporter's voice made that clear. The tanks and guns were obviously some sort of absurd show of force. I mean, were they really going to blow the governor's mansion to bits to get one guy out? No way. Plus, Sol had already destroyed one of their tanks. I got the feeling they were testing him.

"Look…" Mom said, pointing at the screen. Sol walked out onto a balcony, seen from the high, shaky lens of a helicopter camera.

"We're seeing movement on the balcony. Sol has come outside. Perhaps he has something to say—" The reporter's voice cut off abruptly. *Pop! Pop! Pop!* Gunshots? They sounded much different filtered through news microphones and TV speakers. Not the deafening blast I'd heard in the warehouse bay with Bobby. More like the startling but harmless sound of balloons popping.

Then I realized: They weren't testing Sol. They were drawing him out.

It was hard to see clearly from the angle of the camera, from the distance, but it reminded me of the time I had shot Bobby in the stomach. Sol's body seemed to open around the shots, several at once. He fell. The resolution wasn't enough to say that's what had happened for sure, but I could imagine. I'd seen it before.

"He's down!" the reporter said. "It appears that military snipers have taken out the governor's captor. Several shots — it sounded like three, total — have been fired, and Sol is down. I repeat, Sol is down." Mom gasped. The view on TV showed troops rushing in from several sides.

Hold on, I thought. *That couldn't have killed him. Bobby shot himself in the head at point-blank range.* Assuming Sol was even more powerful…

The figure on the balcony began to move. Then he sat up. Mom made a small, surprised sound, barely audible.

The reporter noticed it, too. "Wait, there's movement. Yes, Sol is now sitting. From this vantage point, it appeared that all three shots were on target, yet he's sitting up. No — he's getting to his feet, and…" The camera shook as it zoomed out, showing a view that included Sol standing on the balcony and the troops massing on the lawn just outside the mansion doors.

Beside me, Mom trembled, the fingers of one hand raised and covering her mouth. "I can't believe all this is happening *so close to us*," she said.

I turned. "What?" Was she shivering?

Absently, my mom waived her hand toward one wall. "I mean, the capitol is, what? Twenty-five miles that way? This… this looks like a war zone. It's terrifying." Her eyes remained locked on the television.

That way…

I stared at the wall, the direction Mom had indicated, off toward the capitol. And felt it.

But what was I feeling? Something strange I hadn't noticed before. Some compulsion, some pull. *That way…* Did it suddenly happen, or had it been there all along, unrecognized? I didn't know, but what I did know is that it was there, like a splinter in my mind.

Sol is calling to me.

I shook my head. Despite the obvious reality of our powers, I felt like a fool. Calling to me? From so far away? Ridiculous.

I turned back to the TV. And he was staring at me.

Even through the shaky gaze of the helicopter camera, I would have sworn Sol was staring at me. Sure, he was probably just looking in the general direction of the camera. But if felt directed. At me.

Below him, the advancing troops broke ranks, Sol's sudden resurrection throwing them into disarray.

No, I thought at Sol. *Don't.*

He did.

One soldier turned, fired at the man next to him, who fell. Two more soldiers took shots. The whole scene devolved. Random directions, bullets, people falling, blood. So much blood. Sol made them pay. For what? He wasn't even hurt — I could tell that, even if the reporters and my mom were still confused. Still, Sol had his vengeance. There was blood. There was death. In the end, there was silence.

Even the reporters were quiet, which was possibly an awkward first in television history.

Mom turned off the TV without a word. Several moments passed. Then she turned to me.

"John," she said, clasping my shoulders in a serious manner. "I need you to listen to me." I nodded, and she continued. "This is *not normal*. What you see happening here is... well, it's not something that will affect you." I pulled back in a way that indicated I was scoffing at her, and Mom pushed harder. "Seriously. You go to school. You have a normal day, and forget about all of this." She kissed me on the forehead, but I think I saw a tear in her eye.

"Mom..." I pulled away slightly. "Dad's gone. Some crazy person is killing people on TV." Then there was me. Bobby. Walter. The fact that I knew this Sol, this Jose do Branco. I almost said these things. Instead, all I said was this: "Nothing's normal anymore."

Mom looked up at the ceiling, eyes closed, tears streaming, but she didn't say a word. After a long hug, she let me go and I was off to school.

Where I was still terrified Bobby would try to kill me.

* * *

Bobby.

At school, I was a mess. I tuned out all of my teachers. Every slammed-shut text book, every dropped binder was Bobby appearing behind me.

Oddly, my body seemed to ignore the perceived threat. My skin didn't turn to stone at every sound. Although I was too afraid to realize it at the time, that was an interesting turn.

I was scared, but my body seemed... ready.

Through third period, I hadn't seen Bobby anywhere, which was very strange. As the bell rang, I gathered my notebooks and backpack, heading for the hallway.

A hand slammed down on my shoulder and I nearly dropped everything. Hell, I nearly peed myself.

It was Steve. "Hey man, I kinda forgot to do the homework for Social Studies. Can you... *ya know?*" He pointed at me and winked. Yeah, sure, I *knew*, but I was busy with other issues.

"Have you seen Bobby?" I said.

Steve rolled his eyes. "No, remember? He's *your* girlfriend, not mine. I don't even have his number." He paused, waiting for a laugh that I didn't have inside me. "Besides, man. Haven't you heard? Everybody's saying he ran away from home."

My mouth opened, closed. I must have looked like a bass fresh off the line. "What?"

Steve threw up his hands. "Sorry, man. I would've thought you'd have known. That's the word. Bobby Graden is *gone.*"

KEITH SOARES

4

The roof. I had to check.

I mean, I *thought* he'd been breathing when I left, but… Anyway, I had to check. I climbed the rusty ladder, took the stairs as far as they went, then a final ladder to the roof itself.

Just shy of the top, hanging from the last rung, I waited.

Bobby was my friend, I thought. Then I shook my head. *Was?* Did I think he was already dead? I *knew* he was alive when I left. Or at least, I thought I knew it.

I peered over the edge.

The roof was empty.

I let loose a huge sigh of relief, so much that I lost my grip and nearly fell backward off the damned ladder. I shouted some curse word or other, slapping and then grabbing the rungs to regain a solid position.

So he wasn't dead. Or he wasn't dead on the roof where we'd fought, at any rate. Where else might he — ? *The warehouse bay*, of course. I rattled down the fire escape to the pavement below.

At first I ran flat-out, heading toward the rows of bays behind the lumber yard without a second thought. But as I got closer, I realized something: I hadn't been back to the place since the *accident*. Out on the road, at the end of the long straightaway, I could see the hill. The same hill my dad drove over just before he died.

Taking in the view, I imagined the moment. My dad, expecting nothing more than a few minutes' drive before seeing his family, maybe wondering what was for dinner, or thinking about something that happened at work that day. Then the hill, the realization that a car was blocking the way, the swerve. Never knowing that I was the one who'd put the car there. I jammed my eyes tight, trying to wish the tears away. I had things to *do*.

Finally, I opened my eyes. I was going to go to the warehouse and look for Bobby, and that was that. If I never set foot on this ground again, I'd have been happy, but I had something to *do*. I walked toward the intersection with the little side road, the one that led back toward the warehouses.

But to get there, I had to walk right past the place where it happened. Where Dad's car ended up. I saw a small blot of color by the side of the road, something red flapping in the light breeze. Closing my eyes again, I thought, *Damn it. I know what that is.* The red ribbon. Flowers. Meaning my mom had left them, just hours before.

That was hard. I mean, me dealing with my *own* issues was one thing. But thinking about the pain my mom held inside, the daily struggle she went through with Dad gone. That was a mind scramble.

I shook my head and moved on, taking the turn toward the row of bays, then around back to the door of Bay 6. I knew it would be unlocked, and it was. But it wasn't open.

With an echoing sound that was more moan than creak, I pushed the door out of the way and stepped into the darkness.

"Bobby? You here?" I thought either Bobby would leap out at me like the villain in a kung fu movie or I was talking to myself. I stepped forward, willing my eyes to adjust. "Bobby, if you're here, I just want to talk, okay? No fighting."

As the blackness turned to greyness, then eventually gained detail, I could see I was alone.

Except for a single sheet of paper left almost in the exact center of the floor, weighed down by Bobby's gun. Sliding the gun to one side, I picked up the note and took a couple of steps toward the door, tilting the paper to catch the outside light.

* * *

J —

Not gonna write a lot here, since I don't know who might find this, but wanted you to know I'm OK. Sorry about the fight we had. Geez, this sounds sappy. Anyway, I'm leaving. I've got a lot to learn and now I know how to start.

This thing we have makes us special. I have to use it. I know you have your reasons, but I hope you use it too.

You got skills, man. Knocked me out cold. Don't worry. I'm not mad. Prolly deserved it haha

See you soon,

B.

* * *

I tucked the note in my pocket. As for the gun, I just kicked it into one of the darker corners of the bay. I didn't figure I'd need it, since it didn't do any good against people like me anyway.

Despite the fact that Bobby was gone, I smiled. *You got skills, man.*

Yeah, I suppose that was true.

5

"Listen to me," Sol said, eyes glinting in the harsh artificial light. "The time is almost upon us. For all of you out there, busily wandering through this fool's errand that is your life, soon you will know." He looked around, and the image cut to the governor's office.

A week later, and once again Sol had been granted a live TV interview. Politicians always say, "We don't negotiate with terrorists." They've chanted the phrase so much that it's practically lost all meaning. But the media was a very different story. Sol meant ad revenue and ratings points for them. They'd preempt the Sunday church hour for him, if he asked for it. And what better time for him to be on TV, anyway? It was clear, this time, that Sol was hardly being interviewed. He was giving a sermon.

"As I have told you, I have changed. I am *more* than what I was, more than any of you. This may surprise you, insult you, perhaps frighten you. But there is something else I want you to know." For a moment, he sucked in air between his perfect white teeth. "I am not alone. There are others, and they are joining me." Even the interviewer, the same woman, wearing yet another smart, professional skirt suit, couldn't help but gasp. Sol noticed, and he smiled. "Yes. Yes, you are surprised, I understand. But it is true. And you have seen with your own eyes the things I can do. Take a glimpse at the future! It's a world where I, naturally, am in charge, where *we* are in charge. We who are strong. Though I have said before that my changes are not an evolution, these changes simply *are*. The world must evolve to accept our rule."

Mom and I gaped at the TV in the near dark, transfixed.

"The others like me. They are coming," Sol said. I saw my mom shiver.

The others like me. *Well, not all of them, Sol. I'm staying put. To hell with you.*

"I'm willing to be reasonable about this, of course," Sol said. Then he cleared his throat. "*The time is now near at hand which must probably determine whether you are to be freemen or slaves; whether you are to have any property you can call your own; whether your houses and farms are to be pillaged and destroyed, and yourselves consigned to a state of wretchedness from which no human efforts will deliver you. The fate of unborn millions will now depend, under God, on the courage and conduct of you and your army.*" Sol paused. "Once again, I borrow words from your own George Washington. But his sentiments ring true. I am willing to let men live in peace who follow me." He leaned closer, and his face filled our TV screen. "But those who oppose will find nothing but defeat and despair." Sol's eyes held the camera for a long moment.

And again, I *felt* his stare. Like he was looking at *me*. Only me.

At the end of the couch, Holly suddenly erupted. She flailed her hands and thrashed in her chair, enraged by something we didn't understand. Her plate of mac 'n' cheese flew, coating the wall with runny orange goo. The mess stunned me. I mean, yeah, sometimes Holly made messes. Hell, sometimes I made a mess, but not often. Usually she was more... I don't know... sedate. Another swing and a cup of milk went flying. White puddle spreading across the couch, plastic cup bouncing on the floor.

"Holly, honey, please!" Mom rushed to her side to try to calm her.

I didn't know what to do, but I had grown up with Holly, so I knew one thing: When you don't understand what's going on, take care of the things you do understand. I grabbed the cup and the plate, started cleaning up the mess.

This wasn't a seizure. It seemed more like… anger. As Mom tried to calm her, Holly kept going, waging some unknown war. She pushed at Mom to get her away. Behind us, the TV blared commentary about Sol's latest words, but it was all empty conjecture, just talking heads trying to keep their jobs by looking important and drumming up fear. "John, turn that thing off, please," Mom said without turning, still close to Holly, trying to soothe her.

I took the plate and cup to the sink, brought back some wet paper towels, and cleaned things up as best I could. Finally, Mom seemed to get Holly under control.

"Mom," I said.

"Yes, hon," Mom said, wiping beads of sweat from her forehead with the side of her hand.

I watched Holly as she closed her eyes, clearly worn out from her rampage. "Do you think she knows?"

"Knows what, John?"

"About… Dad?"

My mom slowly closed her eyes, a gesture I'd seen before. Resignation. Pain. Sorrow. "I think so, John."

"Really?"

"Really. Isn't it about your bedtime, by the way?"

I nodded. "Yeah," I said, standing. "But how could she know?" Mom exhaled heavily. She opened her mouth to speak, but before she said a word, her eyes slid past me, to Holly. I turned. Holly had begun to twitch.

Shaking her head, Mom went back to consoling her daughter. "No, dear, just relax. Lie still." Thankfully, the seizure was brief. When it was over, I found myself holding on involuntarily, waiting.

Nothing happened.

"Huh, that's strange," I said.

"What?" Mom asked, still holding Holly.

"Usually her seizures have come just before those earthquakes, like she can feel them before the rest of us. But this time, nothing."

Mom stood, considering but not replying. "Come on. Time for bed," she said, gesturing for a hug. I went to her, then went to Holly. To do that thing we always did — pressing our foreheads together.

As I leaned in, I whispered, "Good night, sis."

But Holly pulled away.

Interlude

The sounds are all there, all busily chattering. But there is something new. Not just a sound, but a call. Not a distant echo, but a voice floating on the wind.

It has purpose. It has direction.

The voice has words, though it is not made of words. It evokes feeling, compulsion, a need deep inside.

Though it says nothing, the voice speaks.

Come to me.

KEITH SOARES

6

"John. He's... gone," Mom said.

I rubbed my eyes with the back of my hand, rolling over to avoid the light from the hallway. "Uh-huh," I mumbled, fading back to sleep.

Mom shook me. "John. He's *gone.*"

"What? Who?" I said in a muffled voice, face still half-buried in my pillow.

"Sol."

I blinked. "You mean they... *killed* him?" I sat up quickly.

"No, no, not that," Mom said, waving her hands in frustration. "He disappeared. The news said he left the governor's mansion without a word. No one even saw him go."

"That's...," I said, trying to think of an appropriate word, "Crazy."

"Isn't it? And I can't say I feel much better. I mean, if he's just suddenly *disappeared*, where will he appear next? It doesn't make any sense. None at all."

Nope, none at all, I thought. Unless it was a fishing expedition. A marketing campaign, if you will. Get every pair of eyes on you for miles around, then say you're joining up with others like you. Even if it wasn't true, Sol had the attention of every man, woman, and child in our time zone. Including anyone who might happen to have similar powers. Or maybe he was just on an ego trip. From what I'd seen, that was entirely possible, too. More likely, it was a little of both.

I ate breakfast, a bowl of sugary, multicolored cereal, in front of the TV as the reporters chattered endlessly about Sol's disappearance. To me, the most interesting thing was happening in the background. Men with guns and tanks, appearing lost, aimless. Their adversary was suddenly gone, and they didn't look like they knew what to do next.

Where was Sol?

For that matter, where had Bobby gone?

I dropped my spoon with a clang.

"John?" Mom called. "Everything all right?"

"Um, yeah, sorry. Just dropped my spoon." I closed my eyes and realized that I felt something. It was what I'd felt before when I thought Sol was calling to me.

And I realized that *calling to me* was the wrong way to think about it. It wasn't like a ringing phone I could pick up and find Sol on the other end. Instead, it was like a beacon. The blinking red light at the top of a radio tower, a circling beam from a lighthouse, or a distant warning siren.

Only instead of trying to ward me off, it was trying to bring me in.

I opened my eyes and looked around. Slowly, my focus honed in on one corner of the room. I realized that, if I tried, I could *feel* which direction the call came from.

Although the military and the news media seemed to be at a loss to find him, I was pretty sure I could simply walk toward the beacon and locate Sol.

Which meant, if I could do it, so could Bobby. And he was.

Bobby was answering the call of a madman.

KEITH SOARES

7

For months, I went back and forth. *Find Bobby, try get him away from Sol. To hell with Bobby, he tried to kill me, and he made his own choices.*

Actually, for most of those months, I was having fun forgetting about all the drama. Bobby and Sol were usually far from my mind. Even the pain of my father's death, while with me every day, waned enough that I was able to have good times with Steve and Tom. It's probably the last period of "normal life" I ever had. Will ever have.

But there were hiccups. Random everyday stuff that had to be hidden — little accidents or altercations that never left so much as a cut or a scrape on me. Many times I'd hear Mom or Steve or someone at school say something like "Oh my gosh, are you okay?" And of course, I was. I used the excuse that I'd been lucky, over and over. The time I dropped a steak knife on my foot. The time I fell off my bike after hitting an ice patch.

Finally, I was swayed by the pact I had made with myself. To use my powers, and to use them to protect my family and friends. It was a simple thing that set me off — something I overheard my mom say on the phone.

She was talking to my Aunt Cindy, and I could only hear half the conversation, but it was enough.

"— you're right, Cindy, of course." A pause, a nod. "Uh-huh, I know. I wasn't there, and even though I know in my head there was nothing I could've done, I can't help but feel guilty, every day. I know it's irrational, but I just can't let Phil go. I didn't get to say goodbye. He was just... *gone* one day."

Hearing Mom beat herself up with sadness, claiming the guilt for Dad's death that forever rested on my shoulders, there was no way I could just let Bobby go.

As hard as it was to believe, I decided I had to go to Sol, because I knew I'd find Bobby with him. I had no illusion that I could defeat Sol. I just wanted to make sure Bobby was okay, see if I could convince him to leave.

Then I thought of the tank. How Sol just *made it explode*. With his mind.

So, on a random day in mid-May, as the school year was winding down, I sat at the desk in my room again, staring at that same pencil.

Move, dammit.

Nothing.

But this time I was more determined. That's right, folks. Rather than waste mere minutes in my futile effort to mind-move the pencil, I worked at it for more than two hours.

Without a doubt, if my mom had walked in, I would be telling my story from inside an insane asylum. Even in my single-minded pursuit, I realized I looked crazy. I tried all sorts of poses and gestures, straining my mind. I could feel the veins in my forehead bulging.

And in the end, I finally succeeded. In giving myself a headache, that is.

I went out for a walk, to get some fresh air, stop thinking about Sol and Bobby and the exploding tank and my dad and how I couldn't move a pencil, trying to ease the throbbing in my temples. The weather was hinting at the hot summer to come, with warm breezes bending the leafy trees back and forth, whispering promises of sticky, humid nights. I slipped on my sneakers and headed out, telling my mom I'd be back soon.

Walking randomly down one street after another, lost in thought, I suddenly became aware that I was heading right toward Roger Steele. He was in front of his house, leaning against the hood of that same faded green car — the one that had made my dad swerve and...

Roger had already seen me coming, and I could feel the bitterness and anger coming off him. Did I get him in trouble? No, technically not. And certainly he had no idea that I'd made him drive through that stop sign. But it was enough, when you were a kid and someone *saw you* in the most embarrassing situation of your life. That was enough to make him angry with me. Never mind that my father died that day. In front of me, Roger had lost some portion of his cool. And he couldn't forgive that.

"Sup, jerk," he said. As always, it was clear that Roger had smarts off the charts and was clever forever.

I stopped and locked eyes with him. *This time*, I thought, *I do it right.*

Roger jerked up from his slack position leaning against the car. At first he walked with a strange, marionette-like gait, but then smoothed out to normal as he went. He came right up to me.

And he bowed.

I couldn't even stifle the laugh. It worked, and to perfection. I couldn't have made Roger Steele do my bidding more completely if he had batteries and a remote control.

I pushed again, a little further this time. A little harder.

Roger's lips started to move, and his voice came out, not quite normal. It sounded forced, like the way people do when they can't hear themselves

211

speaking. Because, I suppose, Roger couldn't hear what he was saying. I simply *made* him say it. "Your majesty." He bowed again.

I was giggling uncontrollably.

"Why, Roger, thank you. But all of this is completely unnecessary. Now, why don't you just lie down here on the sidewalk, take a nap, and forget we ever had this conversation?" Without so much as a nod, Roger sprawled out on the concrete walkway and in seconds was asleep.

I did that. Me. The thought was intoxicating.

With a huge smile, I turned and walked off, rounding the corner on the next street. I was pretty damn happy with myself. No. You know what? I was pretty damn *full of myself.* And beaming like I'd just won the lottery.

Maybe eight houses down the next street, I saw Marjorie Green. Marjorie was, if not *the* most popular, most beautiful girl in school, at least was in the running.

In other words, Marjorie was someone who wouldn't talk to me if she were strapped to a nuclear bomb and I was the only person with the disarm code. If there were layers of society at our school, she was the peak of the mountain, and I was some subterranean stratum with moldy dinosaur fossils. And not even cool fossils like a T-rex. I was probably full of trilobites or something equally nerdy.

But, like I said, I was pretty damn full of myself at that moment. I reached out and pushed her mind.

Which is why, in full sight of her father who was on a ladder, cleaning the gutters on the front of their house, Marjorie Green gave me a cute little wave, then smiled and walked right up to me. Without a glance at her dear ol' dad, Marjorie gave me a kiss on the cheek.

Even I knew pushing it further would be a bad idea. So I told Marjorie's mind to turn and walk her body inside her house. And it did it. Or she did. You know what I mean.

As her dad stood high on the ladder, staring at me, I gave him a smirk and a little shrug before walking off, whistling a happy tune.

Head swelling with my own amazingness, I got back home and went to my room. I closed the door, walked over to the desk, and spun cowboy-style toward the pencil, still sitting there. I made little pistol-shooting gestures with both hands. *Pew pew.*

And the pencil moved.

Not a lot, but it did. The pencil rolled a few inches across the surface of the desk, before coming to a stop with a slight rocking motion.

And like Marjorie's dad, all I could do was stand there and stare.

KEITH SOARES

8

The phone rang.

The phone rang several times a day. It was, as you would expect, a non-event.

So of course I ran and picked it up. "Hello, Black residence," I said. Yes, I really said that. My parents taught me manners, okay?

There was a brief silence, enough so that I felt something. I can't say it was fear. Annoyance? Anticipation? My eyes wrinkled at the corners, as if squinting and listening were connected.

Finally, a voice spoke. "It is good to hear your voice again, John, my friend."

Branco.

I looked around the living room. I was along, thank God. "How do you know my phone number?" I whispered fiercely.

"Please, John. You have no doubt seen me on your television, just a few months ago. I know many things. I can *do* many things. You did see me, didn't you? John?"

I realized I wasn't breathing, and sucked in a breath. "Yeah, of course, I saw you, *Branco*. I saw what you did."

Laughter. That light, self-amused chuckle he often made. "Ah, my name. I am so pleased you remember it. Though perhaps it is appropriate for you to forget that name now. You see, Branco is no more. Now there is only Sol."

"Yeah, well, based on what I've seen, I'm not sure I like this *Sol* person too much." My grip on the phone was tight.

"I understand, John. You may not be ready. Yet. But I wanted you to know something. *I think you are important.* I know that not many people think that."

"And why would I care what *you* think about me?"

"If you do or you do not care, either way is fine with me, John. But you *are*. And so, of course, I am *paying attention* to you." Sol stopped, taking one long, easy breath. "I know where you are."

My eyes grew wide, and my heart rate kicked up several notches. If he knew where I was, he knew where my mom was. He knew where Holly was.

"What the hell do want with me? I'm just a kid!" I shouted, then remembered where I was, at home. I looked around, but still no one was there.

On a set of shelves near the phone sat some of my father's things, stuff my mom couldn't bear to move. Some knick-knacks from past travels, a carved whale, a miniature wooden sailboat. On the top sat a marble chessboard, with rows of ebony figures on one side mirrored by ivory ones on the other. Dust filled the carved crevices and left a thin coat across the surface of the board. As I spun to glance around the room, I bumped the shelf and some of the chess pieces toppled. An ebony pawn fell over and threatened to roll off the board, so I snatched it up with one hand.

"True, true, you are quite young. But then again, so is Bobby."

Bobby? Although I knew in my heart that Bobby must have been with Sol, hearing his name spoken gave it new weight. "Bobby is a friend of mine," I said. It was clear that I meant that partially as a threat.

Sol chuckled again. "So he is. So he is." Then the laughter stopped. "But John. That's what I am trying to tell you: I am your friend, too. Just come to me and see."

So there it was, out in the open. *Join me.* Not an invitation so much as an ultimatum. With the terms implied... *I know where you are.*

"What do you want with Bobby?"

"Ah, John. I think the better question might be, what does Bobby want with me?"

I tilted my head down, chin to chest. Was it already too late? I had waited so long, the guilt of my inaction suddenly heavy.

There was a rustling sound on the other end of the line as the phone changed hands. "Johnny?" It was Bobby's voice, all right.

"Bobby? Ah man, what the hell are you doing, Bobby?"

"Listen, I know you don't understand. You never really wanted to... *push it.* But I do. And Sol, well, he knows how to help." More rustling as Bobby apparently cupped his hand over the phone in an effort to be discreet. "Johnny, I know what he's done, and that's not what I'm trying to do. I'm just trying to, I don't know, get stronger. He *is* stronger. He's shown me how to do things. *Amazing* things."

"But Bobby —"

217

There was a dull thump as Sol came back on the line without a struggle. "Your friend is right, John. I am strong. You could learn a lot from me. Bobby certainly has. So I repeat: Come to me and see."

This arrogant jerk. This murderous bastard. I was angry at Sol for everything he'd done, from tricking me into a short-term friendship, to pulling Bobby away, to the killing he had done. But mostly, I was mad because here I was again, being bullied.

"I know where you are, too, you son of a bitch," I said.

On the other end of the line, there was silence. Until finally, that deep chuckle came again, barely audible. "No, John, you know *approximately* where I am. That is because I am smart enough and powerful enough to conceal myself until I deem the time right. Bobby came to me because he felt the same call that you no doubt feel right now. But it was not until I revealed myself to him that he actually found me. Of course, I would like for you to join me, so I will make it easy for you. I am still in the capital city. Not so far from the governor's mansion, in fact, although no one who sees me remembers much about that whole episode. I *encourage* them to forget. Do you know the capital, John?"

"No. I've never been there. And never will."

"We'll see about that, John. I think you will come. And when you do, find a park called General Tulloch Park in the center of town. In the middle of that park is a statue of the late General Tulloch himself, on horseback. Once you are there, I may reveal myself to you. Do you have a pen? I shall give you a phone number where we can talk once you're near." He rattled off a number, which I didn't write down. "Or…"

Sol trailed off, and I was speechless. The game we were playing was cat and mouse, and I most definitely wasn't the cat.

"Should you choose not to come, John, I could always come to you. I never did get to meet your mother and sister. Holly is your sister's name, correct?"

Cat and mouse. I looked down at my hand, realizing that I was squeezing something hard in my fist. The pawn from my dad's chess set, a set he and I had played on countless times. I realized that the game I was playing with Sol wasn't cat and mouse, it was chess. I thought about Bobby, the school bully who used to terrorize me, and yet I had knocked him out. I smiled, but my expression held no joy.

If my dad taught me one thing about chess, it was this: Even a lowly pawn can take out the king in the right circumstances.

"You should be careful what you wish for, Sol. If I come to you, I may be more than you expect." Sol was silent, so I pressed on. "And if you come for me and my family, I promise that I'll destroy you, even if it kills me." I hung up the phone without another word.

* * *

Putting down the phone was like taking the plug out of a giant balloon. I wilted and crumbled to the floor, shaking uncontrollably.

I wasn't even 15. Sol was an adult. I had beaten up a friend once, another kid. Sol had killed who knows how many police and soldiers.

He was going to kill me. I had no doubt.

What the hell was I going to do? Go to him, like he wanted? Come on, that had to be a trap, right? But if I waited for him to come to me, what would that mean? Barricading the house, living like an outlaw holed up in some old Western? Both choices completely sucked.

Since the day of the car accident, I had lived in secrecy. Not even my mom knew about what I could do. It seemed that was all about to change.

Go and die?

Stay and die?

What were my options? Tell my mom? Maybe she could help. But how? Guns and tanks couldn't hurt Sol. Mom could be a royal terror when she was mad, but she wasn't a tank.

I sank against the wall, one fist slamming the floor. I didn't ask for this. I didn't ask to be in this special club of extraordinary people whose president was apparently a psychopath.

I could run away. Go somewhere that no one else could find me. Then Holly and Mom would probably be safe. What would be the point in Sol hurting them?

But I could *feel* Sol. Somewhere in the distance. Maybe he could feel my presence, too.

Running away wouldn't work.

I either had to tell my mom, or…

Oh, God. After what I'd done, what had happened to my dad, the thought turned my stomach. But I could.

I could push my Mom's mind. I could make her drive me to Sol. Or just have her accept that there were perfectly valid reasons why I wasn't around for a little while.

Who was I kidding? If I left to confront Sol, whether I told my mom outright or tricked her mind, I wasn't coming back. Eventually she would know.

I had to tell Mom what I could do.

And what I had to do.

9

After making the momentous decision to reveal my supernatural abilities to my mother, I did what any 14-going-on-15-year-old boy would do on a school night. I ate dinner (spaghetti), watched TV (replaying shows I'd already seen), and went to bed.

When my alarm went off the next morning, I could hear there was trouble brewing already. Not life-threatening trouble, but the kind of everyday "oh crap, someone's in a foul mood" trouble that every family probably deals with.

Mom was rushing around trying to get things done, get us all ready to go for the day, and for whatever reason, it wasn't going smoothly.

By that time, Dad's life-insurance money was coming in, but it wasn't enough to make us rich. In fact, it wasn't even enough to live off, so Mom found a job as the front-desk clerk in a dentist's office downtown. From what I could tell, while the hours weren't too long, the pay was just so-so.

Without Dad around, mostly it meant that instead of just getting Holly and me ready for school, Mom had to maneuver all three of us out the door. Holly was picked up by a specially outfitted bus that took her to the elementary school each weekday. Being older and in middle school, I never saw the place, just heard about it from my parents. It didn't sound like much more than free babysitting, but Holly didn't fight going, so maybe she got something out of it. Because it was a special program, Holly got picked up first. That left Mom and me alone for a few minutes every morning.

It was time to talk, to spill the beans. "Mom, I—"

Mom, still huffing around, having a bad morning, walked toward me, past the shelves holding Dad's old knick-knacks. She must have turned quickly or bumped it or something, just like I had when I was on the phone with Sol, because for a moment the whole thing teetered. Honestly, those shelves should have been moved to some less-trafficked place in the house long before, but now it was too late. The chessboard, which jutted out because it was a bit too wide to fit neatly on the top shelf, lost all its pieces as they tumbled to the floor below in a series of thud-clacks. One or two of them might've chipped in the process, but seconds later that was immaterial. The board itself slipped, fell heavily, and cracked into three jagged pieces on the floor. Mom froze.

The board was *Dad's*. There was no way to replace it. I realized instantly from the look on Mom's face that the chessboard was more than just a thing, a tchotchke. It *was* my father. It was part of him. And suddenly, Mom had to face that it was gone. She didn't fall or even sit heavily; she drooped to the ground, hands covering her face, shoulders shaking.

I went to her and put my arms around her. "Mom, it's okay. I can clean it up."

She looked up, eyes red and wet, forcing a wry smile onto her face. "Thanks, John. It's not that. It's…"

"Because it was Dad's," I said, and she nodded. I didn't have anything else to say, so we sat that way for a while.

Finally, Mom looked at her watch. "Oh, God. I'm going to be late. I'll have to clean this up later." She sighed, wiping the last tears from her eyes. "What were you going to tell me?"

"Huh?"

"You started to say something, just before I—" She nodded toward the mess.

What was I supposed to do? Drop it on her then? *Hey, yeah, Mom. I know that Dad is dead and things are very hard on you now, but I just wanted to let you know that I have superpowers and I'm going to need to go confront the psychopath you saw on TV causing death and destruction at the governor's mansion. Cool?*

I couldn't.

But I had to help Bobby. I had to go.

So...

I *pushed* instead. Yes, I felt guilty. I still do.

Nudging her mind, I said, "Mom, I need to go to the capital. I'll take a bus or something, and I'll be back in a couple of days. This is all perfectly normal. Just tell people that I'm visiting Aunt Cindy. She's a little sick, nothing serious, and I'm just helping her out around the house. You'd have gone, but you need to stay here for Holly. That's what you'll tell people. And don't worry about me. *Okay?*"

With glassy eyes, Mom made a perfectly normal smile. "Sure, honey. Have fun. See you when you get back." Five minutes later, she was driving off to work and I was left at home, alone.

* * *

It didn't take long to see how Sol could get around the capital without being noticed. I'd ridden my bike to the small bus stop in town, not too far from our house, and locked it to a rack. The place wasn't a bus *station*, just a stop; a covered bench. There was nowhere to buy tickets or snacks or anything like that. But I needed to get to the city and, at fourteen — superpowers or

223

not — I had no idea how to drive. So I hopped on the first bus I saw idling at the stop. "Excuse me, sir, are you headed to the capital?" I asked the driver. He started to give me a strange look, like *What the hell is a kid doing trying to take a bus to the city by himself?* So I pushed his mind a little bit. While I was at it, I did the same to the other half-dozen or so people scattered throughout the bus.

"Nope. Bus for the capital is over there," he said without another concern, pointing across the small parking lot to a green and white bus emblazoned with the words "ROAD STAR." Through the large front windshield, I could see the driver, feet kicked up. Dark sunglasses covered his eyes, but I was pretty sure from his position that his eyes were closed.

"Thanks," I said, stepping back down to the street. The door of the second bus was closed, so I knocked lightly on the glass. The driver stirred, looking at me over his glasses. Then he simply pointed. On the dash, a white placard read, "CAPITAL, 11:00 a.m." I didn't have a watch, but estimated it to be no later than nine o'clock. For a moment, I considered pushing my way in, getting the bus moving. Then, considering the many challenges already awaiting me, I realized that hijacking a bus might bring me all sorts of attention I didn't want. So I gently nudged the driver's mind to forget having seen me, and I waited.

* * *

Fifteen minutes before departure time, I remained on the covered bench, watching who — and how many — passengers boarded the capital bus. Thankfully, it was light. I didn't know how hard it would be to push a busload of minds at once. Instead, I only had to deal with 11: the driver and 10 random travelers.

Pushing here and there, I made them all ignore my presence, especially the driver, who was collecting scraps of paper from each rider that I assumed were tickets. Another push and he overlooked the fact that I didn't have one. I sat near the back, against a window in an empty row.

A few rows ahead was a fashionable young woman wearing a short black jacket over a long-sleeved striped shirt. She may have dressed well, but she was loud and obnoxious, flailing her hands while talking on her cellphone in a voice that I could only describe as grating. From what I could hear, she was headed to the city to meet up with friends and have a wild weekend. I pinched two fingers over the bridge of my nose, a gesture I'd seen my father make many times, only now really understanding it as I felt the beginnings of a headache coming on. I wanted her to shut up.

So, of course, I made it happen. In fact, worse (or better, depending on your point of view), I made her stand up, walk to me, and give me her phone. I realized that I needed it.

I nodded at her and gave a friendly smile, although of course it wasn't necessary. Still, I thought it best for appearances. When she sat back down, I checked out her phone.

Not surprisingly, it was one of the latest model smartphones. I began to dial.

Somehow, from a memory I didn't think I had, I remembered the number Sol had given me. After punching in the last digit, my finger hovered over the green CALL button for just a moment.

And the bus engine rumbled to life, a deep throbbing sound, all bass. The driver closed the door, and without another thought, he dropped the bus into gear and began to drive.

I pressed the button.

Within moments, there was a click, then the strange, open sound of a connected phone call, like listening to the wind on another planet. "Hello?" Sol said.

Good, I thought. *At least he isn't so powerful that he can tell it's me.*

"Sol," I said, and nothing more.

"Ah John. So good to hear from you. To what do I owe the pleasure?" Typical smug bastard.

I steeled myself for one final moment before speaking. "You got your wish. I'm coming for you."

Sol drew in a long breath. At first I thought maybe he wouldn't say a thing, but of course he did.

"Good, John. Very, very good."

10

Now, if I lived in a movie, the bus would have zipped along the highway so that, by noon, I'd be standing in the middle of General Tulloch Park, facing off against Sol like gunslingers in an old Western.

What I didn't understand about the bus I'd chosen was that it was a "local." That meant it stopped a lot. I mean, *a lot.* I gave up counting after the twelfth time. People got off once in a while, but mostly people got on. More and more and more people, heading to the capital. I was pushing and pushing and pushing, trying to keep from being noticed. Until finally I realized something. These people simply didn't care. The life of the long-distance commuter is one of mindless process. Get from point A to point B, with as little fanfare, as few problems or interruptions as possible. They couldn't care less that a kid was sitting in the back of the bus. They didn't know me, my life, and they didn't want to know. So I relaxed.

Anyway, it took hours. A lot of people on the bus slept. They were clearly used to this routine. Others read, or talked or texted on their phones. But no one, and I mean no one, interacted with anyone else, unless they came on board together.

Adults are crazy.

But it helped me stay in my little bubble of anonymity.

I didn't know the way, and had no idea what to look for in terms of landmarks telling me when we'd arrived. But gradually the buildings started to get larger, then much larger. And finally, the riders all started to do things: wake up, sit up straighter, gather belongings. It was clear something was about to happen. When the bus came to a stop next to a wide, dingy building, the other buses around made it clear we had arrived at our final destination. I followed the rest of the passengers out, being sure to apply little pushes here and there. No need to get caught at the last minute.

The capital city. Or at least, the dingy backside of it.

I had no clue where I was or where to go. For a moment, I stood motionless on the sidewalk as people brushed past me from every direction, heading in every other direction. The city was a lot busier than I was used to, and despite my special skills, I found myself scared. Or maybe just intimidated. I didn't have enough knowledge of the world at large to even come up with a plan to figure out how where I was.

Seconds went by, maybe a minute. I had come to the city to face an enemy who likely could kill me with a single thought. And yet the bad thing happening to me at that very moment was so much simpler, so much more frustratingly basic; I was lost.

The crowd of anonymous people finally ebbed. I guess that each new arrival and departure created a small maelstrom at the bus station that abated shortly after. As the sidewalk slowly cleared, I saw something of use. A large kiosk with a map of the city. *Thank God,* I thought, letting out the breath I didn't realize I'd been holding.

YOU ARE HERE proclaimed a red dot in the center of the map. Scanning across the surface, I looked for parks, any park. Green spaces, I assumed, were usually shown in green on maps. General Tulloch should have been easy enough to find. That is, it would have been if it were a park where I came from. In my town, the parks were good-sized, with plenty of grass and trees. Apparently in the city, they called just about any square inch of land a park if it didn't have a house or office building on it. It took me 15 minutes to find the tiny rectangle of General Tulloch Park on the map. Sure, Sol had said the park was in the center of town, but the map I was using was centered on the bus stop, on the city's outskirts. General Tulloch Park was far up and way to left of the red dot where I stood.

Some friendly cartographer had placed concentric circles on the map showing distances. Quarter-mile, half-mile. Tulloch Park was much farther out than any of these helpful rings, meaning it was well over a mile away. That was fine. I could walk. I got my bearings from the map, noted some street names, and started off.

Early afternoon in the late fall, the sun was still up and the temperature was decent, so no one took too much notice of a kid wandering the city streets alone. Whenever I felt someone's eyes on me, a quick push solved the problem. Still, it didn't save me from getting turned around.

The capital was mostly north-south and east-west streets, but where it got confusing was the big traffic circles with radiating spokes that seemed to go off in any old direction. I didn't realize that until I think I'd walked two or three miles, far more than I actually needed to walk. Feeling foolish, I closed my eyes and just... *sensed*... for a moment. The beacon was still out there, but now it was behind me. Turning around, I backtracked for a while, noticing that the sun was setting over the tall buildings. That's when I realized I'd be spending the night alone in a strange city.

Or worse.

I'd be with Sol.

Engrossed in this rather terrifying thought, I came to an intersection where six streets connected to a box-like square. In the center of the square was a grassy space, not as tiny as it looked on the map. Park benches and cement walkways spread in various directions around a central hub: the large statue of a man on horseback who had to be General Tulloch. My heart first skipped a beat, then, to make up for it, decided to beat double-time. I had arrived. Sol was near. I could feel his presence, although the direction had become less clear. Like something was jamming the signal just a bit. Just enough distortion to obscure the true source.

Foolishly, I walked directly up to the statue, standing below its pedestal and staring up, oblivious to my surroundings. Letters chiseled into the base confirmed my thoughts: General Avery J. Tulloch. It noted his year of birth and death, which to me sounded like dates from another epoch. I'm pretty sure dinosaurs were a daily threat back when General Tulloch roamed the Earth. Above me, the horse reared on two legs as the general thrust out his sword, a gesture frozen in time.

Did you really fight with a sword? I asked. Looking again at the dates, I thought it was very well possible. In the shadows of the looming buildings of downtown, I imagined a man on horseback waving a sword against the combined forces of police cars and military tanks. I figured Tulloch had about as much chance against them as cars and tanks currently had against Sol.

Sol...

I whipped around, expecting an attack.

There was nothing, no one, just random pedestrians ambling through the park, following the journeys of their various unknown lives. I scanned left and right, saw nothing unusual, so I began to edge around the statue, keeping the good general to my back as I sort of crab-walked around in a large circle.

When I returned to the front, back under the raised legs of Tulloch's stone horse, I stopped. Sol wasn't there.

By then, the sun was behind the buildings to the west and streetlights were beginning to turn on automatically. I was no city slicker, but I had seen enough movies and TV shows to know that hanging out in a city park after dark was inviting trouble. But where the hell was I going to go? Not only did I have no place to go, no place to eat dinner or sleep, I didn't even know where to begin looking. Homesickness hit me hard, like an emptiness in my belly that no hot meal could fill.

And that's when I saw it.

Rustling lightly in the soft breeze, a piece of paper was perched at the top of the statue's pedestal, near one of the horse's rear hooves. I had seen plenty of litter during my walk through the city, paper scraps and bits of plastic that skittered by. But this one held firm, anchored by something I couldn't see, and so it kept my attention.

The pedestal was maybe seven feet tall, meaning the paper was well out of my reach, but I could get to it with a little climbing. I knew it was for me, and that it was from Sol. He'd left me a note. How considerate.

Conveniently, the note was directly above a small sign: NO CLIMBING OR SITTING ON STATUE. I froze, looking around, worried who might see. Always the nerd. When I realized that I could simply push the transgression from the mind of any passing police officer, I laughed at myself, then stepped onto the protruding lower section of the pedestal. With a little effort, I was high enough to put my hand on the paper. The tape that held it down came loose in my hand, and I jumped back down to the ground.

If anyone had seen or cared, I couldn't tell. I opened the folded paper and found just what I'd expected. A note from Sol.

* * *

John

Welcome to the capital city, my friend! Unfortunately, I am rather preoccupied today. Many wheels are turning. I'd greatly prefer to meet you tomorrow, here in this very spot. Shall we say noon?

Sol

* * *

So after all that, we would face off like gunslingers at high noon. Not that I had a gun. Compared to Sol, I felt like I had no weapon at all.

I stared angrily at the paper in my hand, and it crumpled into a ball. But my hand hadn't crushed it, hadn't even moved. I looked at the ball of paper through squinted eyes. *How'd I do that?* I was sure I'd used my mind, but unlike when I rolled the pencil around on my desk, this time I hadn't even been trying.

I decided to try to flatten the paper with my mind, reverse the trick. Nothing happened. I gave it another shot, staring at the paper intently.

"Son, are you okay? Are you lost or something?" a woman's voice said, just beside me. I nearly jumped out of my skin, turning to see a kind-looking elderly woman in a black coat, eyes looking at me with concern through thick glasses.

I had let down my guard so much that someone had noticed me. Maybe several someones. Quickly, I reached out to push her mind, too fast and hard at first, then controlling myself. She was just a kind old woman trying to help me.

Her expression changed from focused concern to blank indifference, and she began to walk away. Then I realized I needed something from her.

"Ma'am?" I called, and she half-turned back toward me.

"Yes, dear?" she said, slowing but not stopping as she walked away.

"Is there a hotel nearby, maybe one with a restaurant in it?"

"Oh yes, of course, there are a few."

"Could you please point me in the direction of one of them?"

The woman paused, thinking, then pointed down one of the main streets radiating from the square. "Just down there, on the left. The Lexington. Give that a try." Then she was off, moving like she had to be somewhere without actually knowing why. Apparently I was getting really good at pushing.

Minutes later, I was standing outside the front door of the Lexington Hotel, the nighttime city lit up with a thousand lights around me.

11

"Wake up, John, it's time for school," my mom said, gently nudging me.

"Just a few more minutes, Mom," I grumbled, turning over.

The phone rang, startling me fully awake. Not the digital beeping I was used to, echoing down the hall from our phone's place near the kitchen, but a blaring chime that felt like it was coming out of my own head. I rolled over, pushing white puffs of something out of the way.

Comfortable, fluffy billows of cloth. Stacks of posh pillows.

The phone rang again, jarring me to sit up.

Where the heck am I?

Then I remembered. Thanks to the benefits of mental suggestion, I had spent the night in a junior executive suite at the Lexington Hotel.

At the foot of the bed, the TV flashed, some show I didn't recognize, with kids getting ready for school as a laugh track backed up every single statement they made. Next to me, the phone rang a third time and I jumped to pick it up, if for no other reason than to stop the noise.

Holding the handset to my ear, I heard a robotic voice: "This is your. Wake-up call. The time is. Nine o'clock. A.M." There was a click and the message repeated, so I hung up the phone and took in my surroundings.

What was it, a queen-size or king-size bed? It didn't matter. Compared to what I was used to, it was an ocean of comfort. I briefly considered how many geese had to be plucked to make the mound of pillows I'd been sleeping among. Across the room a small table was flanked by two well-appointed chairs, and on the table sat the remains of the previous night's dinner, mostly just a salad that was essentially untouched. No trace of the cheeseburger and fries I had ordered remained. I remembered other things on the menu with much higher price tags, but when I saw "cheeseburger and fries," my stomach double-flopped and I knew I had to have it. The empty remains of three sodas finished the picture.

As delicious as the burger had been, my stomach growled, reminding me that breakfast would also be a really good idea. Fully adapted to the junior-executive-suite lifestyle, I picked up the phone and pressed the button marked ROOM SERVICE, waited a moment, and a man answered.

"Room service, how may I help you?"

"Do you have bacon?" I asked.

"Sir?"

"Bacon."

"Yes, sir, of course. But was there a specific dish from the menu you wished to order?"

Oh, crap. Menu. Stretching the cord, I could just reach the dinner menu still sitting on the side chair where I had dropped it the night before. I scanned the thick, expensive-feeling paper and saw no breakfast items mentioned, but flipping it over found what I was looking for. "Ah, here it is. The, uh, the omelette. It's called the Hearty American. Bacon and cheddar. Can I get that? And some orange juice?"

"Absolutely, sir." The man recited my room number and I confirmed it.

Thirty minutes later, there was a knock at the door. I didn't bother to get cleaned up, since I was already dressed. I'd only brought the clothes on my back for my little journey, so although they were rumpled from a night in bed, they'd have to do. I opened the door and a twenty-something man walked in with a covered tray smelling of delicious food. The tantalizing scent of bacon wafted through the air, and I followed like a cartoon dog, nose up, taking it in. The deliveryman looked at me sideways, but a little push fixed that. He even left thinking I'd given him a sizable tip, and took the dinner tray with him. Of course, I hadn't actually given him a tip. I didn't have any money on me at all. I guess I should have felt bad, basically stealing a hotel room and all, but honestly it didn't seem as important as what I had come to do.

I sat alone in the large suite, many times the size of my bedroom at home. Hell, it was probably as big as our entire house. The omelette was delicious, the bacon stuffed inside wonderfully crunchy, but it left me hollow.

Mom and Holly were home, and the only reason Mom didn't miss me was because I'd lied to her and bent her mind. I hadn't done any such thing to Holly. Did she know I was gone? Then of course there was my dad. He was just... *gone*. A fact that would always be my fault. No mind push was going to change that.

And by the end of the day, *I* might be gone, too. I looked at the clock. 9:58 a.m. My meeting with Sol was two hours away.

I took another bite of my breakfast, washed down by a swig of pulpy orange juice. And I broke down in tears.

"Mom," I said, sobbing. I spoke the words aloud, even though the room was empty. "Mom, I'm sorry. Holly, I'm sorry. If I don't come back, remember I love you. And Dad. I just want you to know, there's something *the same* about me, and Bobby, and Sol. So I have to do this. And I have to try to get Bobby away from him. But I don't want to die."

I sat there a long time, thinking of what to do.

12

Sol approached as I sat on the park bench, the one closest to General Tulloch and his horse, their likenesses frozen in time and stone, oblivious to the downtown park around them.

With a dark hoodie pulled up over my head, I raised one hand to Sol. *Stop.* I pulled out the cellphone I'd borrowed from the loudmouth woman on the bus and dialed Sol's number.

It rang once, then twice.

Sol, taken aback or just annoyed, paused. He may have even chuckled. But he reached into his pocket and pulled out his phone, pressing the button to accept the call.

"Yes, John?" he said, staring at me across the park as he raised the phone to one ear.

"Stop where you are," I replied.

"I understand, John," Sol said, relaxing his shoulders. "This is all very new, very strange, very hard for you. But as I have told you, I am your friend." He took a step forward.

"No," I said. "Don't get any closer."

"Come now, John, isn't this a little... silly?"

"I don't think so. You and I both know that our powers have a limit, at least in terms of distance. That's why we can only bend minds when people are nearby."

"Indeed, you are right," Sol said. "But John, you are well within my limit even now." The bastard smiled.

I didn't stand up, didn't visibly react in any way. Didn't give him the pleasure. "Yes, I know," I said. "And you're well within mine." Sol froze. Now he wasn't sure exactly what to expect from me. He stayed a good 40 feet back, fidgeting a bit, but not getting closer.

Instead, he changed the subject. "In truth, John, I need your help."

"Really? *You* need *my* help? For what?"

Somewhere in the distance a bell tower rang out its chimes as the clock struck noon. One... Two... Three... My heart pounded. Four... Five... Six... Sol began to answer, but the chimes were loud enough to interrupt him. Seven... Eight... Nine... Three people walked by, the park getting more populated at lunchtime. Sol glanced around, not concerned, but calculating. Ten... Eleven... Twelve... The last tone hung in the air, like it was unwilling to hand the day back over to silence once again.

Sol gestured toward the statue, an offhand move. He was, as always, suave and charismatic. He began to lower the phone, trying to speak to me directly. "John, let's be done with talking on the phone."

"No!" I said. "Stay on the phone, and stay away. I won't talk to you if you put down your phone or get any closer." Sol seemed legitimately surprised, holding the phone out to one side, eyebrows raised. "Do it," I said, "or I'm leaving."

Sol raised his phone again. "John, this is absurd. If I just walk forward a few feet, you could hear me without this phone. We could just talk. Are you even going to look at me?"

"I don't want to talk," I said. "And I don't want to look at you. Stay on the phone, or I leave."

Sol hesitated. Then he smiled. "What makes you think you could leave now even if you wanted to, John?" He stared at me, letting the threat linger. Then, he gave a little shrug and rolled his head around on his shoulders. He gestured toward the statue. "Do you know the story of General Avery J. Tulloch, John?" A random question, but Sol enunciated the general's name with an air of importance.

"Nope." Impertinent. I was being a jerk on purpose. To knock him off his game, maybe, but really because I was a kid and I thought he deserved it.

"Well, then, let me tell you about him. I think you'll find the story quite interesting." Sol licked his lips, as if he were preparing himself. "When he was a boy, Avery James Tulloch was one of 14 children, raised in an extraordinarily strict household. His father, also a military man, but of significantly less stature than Avery would one day achieve, ruled the home with an iron fist. They lived on a ranch, so everyone had to help out. His father's harsh approach wasn't an exercise in manners or discipline. They lived on the rugged Midwestern plains, and back then, if you didn't do your part, you or your family might die. Starvation was a very real problem. Avery and his 13 siblings each had jobs, and they were expected to do those jobs without question and without fail. But of course you suspect what happened, correct?"

Sol waited, but I didn't answer. "Yes, of course you do. One winter day when he was only seven, Avery was sent to deliver a wagon of vegetables to a market in the nearby town. He did, and he got paid. And he didn't steal the vegetables or the money, or go off and misbehave, not even a little bit, but he did do one thing wrong. Avery saw some other children playing in the street. You see, the children in town had a lot less to do than those who lived out on the ranches. Their lives were by no means what we today would consider easy, but still, they actually had time for games. Avery thought it was wonderful to play with these other children, some of them his own age. It was cold and he didn't think his father would notice that he was gone an extra hour or so. He thought it was great fun. Until, of course, a few days later, when a friend in town spoke to Avery's father and told him what had happened, not at all trying to get the boy in trouble. In fact, the friend remarked *how nice* it had been to see Avery having so much fun. Do you know what happened next, John?"

Interested despite myself, I shook my head. "He got in trouble?"

"Oh, indeed. He *did* get in trouble. Quite a lot of trouble. Avery's father decided he could no longer trust his son, and made Avery sleep outside as a punishment. This went on for *four nights*. It was January, and there was snow on the ground. Avery was allowed the clothes on his back and the blanket from his bed, which was thankfully thick wool, though full of holes. Years later, General Tulloch was quoted as saying that he thought he would die on those nights. The first evening or two, he called to his father for mercy, but after that he suffered in silence. It was probably the silence that saved him from having to sleep outside on the fifth night. His father finally let him back in, and Avery never again wavered from what he was told to do. Which, of course, made him a perfect candidate for military training. But he was also very smart, so he rose through the ranks quickly. Discipline. Intelligence. And a healthy fear of the deadly consequences of failure."

Sol paused again as a young woman walked past him in the park. She may have noticed us, but Sol's gaze fell upon her and I'm certain that her mind told her she saw nothing. Sol continued. "As a captain, Avery Tulloch led a charge against an entrenched enemy position and won the battle without a single loss of life on his side. In fact, his entire story is riddled with impressive successes like that, things the average person would find impossible to accomplish. Still, it wasn't until he became a general that he truly excelled. Have you heard of the Battle of the Empty Hand?"

Sol was as charismatic as always, I'd become enthralled by the story he was telling. When he stopped to ask this latest question, it was like a dream being interrupted. Was he slowly pushing my mind? "No. No, I don't think so."

"Pity. May I tell you about it? It's really quite remarkable."

"Sure," I said, still frozen on the park bench.

"The Battle of the Empty Hand happened in a remote place out west, called *el Desierto de las Tres Manos.*" Sol reveled in the words, emphasizing them with his deep voice and accent. "That means *the desert of the three hands.* It's a hot, barren place, just jutting rocks and fields of sand ranging out in all directions. The rocks can reach hundreds of feet tall, forming random ravines and canyons throughout the desert. The natives called it *Tres Manos* because if you climb onto any of the plateaus and look down, it looks like three giant hands pressed into the rock, flattening it all the way down to the smooth sand and leaving steep-edged canyons. Some of the canyons cut all the way through, but many did not. Many formed box canyons — that is, canyons with only one entry point. These box canyons were great for herding livestock. Once you went in, there was only one way out, so keeping track of your cattle was fairly easy. But in war, these closed-off places could mean death."

"I assume there's a point to all this," I said.

"Yes, of course. You are young, John. You prefer... what is it they call it? Ah, yes. *Instant gratification.* So I will jump ahead. General Avery James Tulloch had only been a general for about a year when he found himself commanding a force that was charged with providing security for the remote areas of the desert, protecting them from enemy patrols. The fear was that if no one kept these places safe, the enemy would be free to sneak through and attack something actually important, such as one of our more prominent southwestern cities. So while Tulloch's task might have been thankless, he was providing a tremendous benefit to his nation. One day, a routine patrol group came charging back into camp, having nearly killed their frothing horses. The soldiers reported that the enemy was not just nearby, but had almost surrounded Tulloch's camp. And, he was told, they outnumbered his men nearly five to one. The newly minted General

Tulloch had a choice to make. Do you know what that choice was, John?"

"No idea." Okay, maybe he had a point about instant gratification. I wanted to hear the good part.

"Well, of course, he could fight, but the odds looked to be very much against him. He could negotiate. There is no cowardice in that, only reality. Or he could prepare to surrender. As you might expect, General Tulloch hasn't been remembered with this fine statue for his ability to quit. Instead, he readied his forces. And he and his men rode straight into the canyons, into the heart of *el Desierto de las Tres Manos*. All of them. They went in great haste, kicking up a massive cloud of dust behind them. The enemy commanders must have laughed at the sight. And their much larger forces simply followed behind, knowing that Tulloch's army would tire. Into the deep, steep-edged canyons the soldiers went, tracking their prey. Ahead of them, Tulloch's army reached a crossroads, where one thin path broke off from the main, much wider way. Both directions led to death, for these were two box canyons branching out in front of them, as Tulloch knew well from scouting the area. There would be no escaping out the other side. But Tulloch was clever. He ordered half his mounted forces off their horses and into the thinner canyon, followed by the other half, still mounted. They proceeded slowly and deliberately, for the walls were close on either side. Down the other canyon, Tulloch sent the riderless horses at a quick trot, with a few men to keep them going. Tulloch himself then waited, in hiding near the crossroads. I do not know the man's mind, but from what I have read, I suspect he had an idea of what to do no matter how his opponent reacted. Not long after, the enemy approached in great numbers, a huge and fearful army. In their hubris, their commanders saw the lingering dust cloud of the fleeing horses and assumed what they saw to be the truth. They took the wider way. And when they reached the end of that box canyon, they found the *hand* to be *empty*. There were only riderless horses and the few men who guided them. Even as the enemy commanders realized their folly, Tulloch's forces fell upon them from behind, trapping them against the dead-end walls of the canyon, killing them *en masse*, each one of his men killing several of the enemy. When the majority of the enemy was dead, the few men remaining begged for mercy and surrendered."

Sol took a long breath, and again I felt like I was coming out of a dream I didn't realize I had fallen into. "That's a lovely story," I said. "What does it have to do with you and me?"

"Ah, good question, John." Sol took a step forward.

"Ah ah ah. No closer," I said, and he stopped with an audible sigh.

"The reason I told you this story, John, is simple. Before I began, I asked you if you knew anything about General Tulloch. You said *no*. Yet from the tale I just told and many other tales of his fine abilities as a commander, we see that Avery Tulloch was a remarkable man. By the end of his life, he was nearly a god among men. People revered him, loved him. Songs were sung in his honor. They would listen spellbound to the tales of his deeds. He was asked many times to run for president, although he never chose to do so, finding politics distasteful. Still, none of this matters now. The world has forgotten him. Do you understand now?"

"Not really."

"John, I don't wish to be someone *important*, even someone *great*, who is then forgotten as the creaking wheel of time turns around. Tulloch is no more relevant to the people who walk through this park than is the sidewalk, or that bench you sit upon. I wish for something much, much more, John."

"What, then?" I asked.

Sol smiled. "I want to be *eternal*."

13

Sol took a confident stride forward.

"Stop! Stop where you are!" I shouted.

"Enough of this triviality, John." Sol spoke with zeal now. "The question now lies before you: Do you wish to be *nothing?* Or *immortal?* Between you, and me, and Bobby, we can *change things*. We won't have to consider how we might offend those in power, we will *be* those in power." He was much closer now; maybe 20 feet separated us. Yet I sat still on the bench, cellphone still tucked into my hoodie. I was unwilling to move.

"I'm just a kid," I said into the phone. "Just a teenager. What would I do? How would I rule the world?"

"You've shown greatness already, John. You got here. Do you think any of your schoolmates could have managed that?" I'll admit, I raised one eyebrow, mentally patting myself on the back. "And Bobby told me of the fight between you two. How you beat him. That…" Sol said, "…that *really* impressed me."

Why? I thought for a moment. Sol could destroy tanks. What did it matter that I had fought with Bobby, that we had both used our supernatural skills, and that I had won? It's not like—

Hold on.

I'd fought with Bobby, and won. Bobby and I were alike, as was Sol. Hell, Walter Ivory was like us, too. That meant, technically, that I had gone up against two people with these powers, and both times I'd won.

How many others like us had Sol faced?

I truly had no idea.

But I thought the answer might be *zero*.

"Are you saying you don't *want* to be great? Don't *want* people to remember you, John?"

"No, of course not. No one *wants* to be a nobody. There are things I want…"

"You can have them," Sol said.

"But I just — I'm a kid," I said again. "I'm not really sure of what I want. Yet."

"And you shall have time to decide. With me. With Bobby. I can shelter you both. Give you the time you need to grow. And," Sol said, a tinge of hunger in his voice, "I can *teach* you, John. What is it you do not know about these powers yet? Ask me. Let me help you."

Sol reached out his free hand.

I thought of the pencil that I could barely move, the paper my mind had randomly crumpled into a ball and I couldn't willingly undo. There truly *was* a lot I could learn. Sol *could* teach me.

But…

More than anything, a single thought crept into my mind, and wouldn't leave.

If I knew more, if I was ready, I could stop living in secret. I had no idea until that moment just how powerful my desire was, to stop lying to my mom, my friends, the world.

I was different now, and like it or not, that probably wasn't going to change. I was sick and tired of concealing my powers behind a mask of normalcy.

I *wasn't* normal.

Why should I hide what I could do? Why should I hide myself?

All the things I might be, all the things I might do, bubbled up in my mind, all the injustices reversed, the life of the unpopular forever changed into the life of the unforgettable.

Sol's hand lingered, held out to me. My fingers twitched, wanting to reach out.

"Last chance, John. You know in your heart that it is right. Think of all that you can learn. More that that, John. Think of all that you can *be*."

"You'll teach me? And Bobby?"

"That is why I have called you to me, John, yes."

"But why?"

"Because of the very thing you pointed out to me when I first approached you here in the park this morning," Sol said, looking down for a moment. Whether he was pensive, contemplative, or just plain weary, I couldn't tell. "Our abilities, while tremendous, seem to have a limitation. Specifically, a limitation of *distance*. Within a certain range, I can affect people's minds, make objects do my bidding. But beyond that…" He wavered a hand, left and right.

249

"But you *called* me," I said.

"Yes! John. Yes! *That* seems to work at incredible distances. One of us calling to another. But that is because we are the same. These... *others*..." Sol gestured contemptuously at the people in the park all around us. Almost every park bench was occupied, people eating from brown bags and reading paperback novels. A few of them here and there played chess. "We can affect normal people around us, but farther away, they disappear from our influence. As do objects."

"What distance?" I asked. I was thoroughly engrossed in everything Sol had to say.

"It depends. At perhaps a few hundred feet, our direct influence seems to diminish."

"Is it something that will change in time? Like, can we grow stronger? Expand the range?"

"A wonderful question, John! Wouldn't *that* be something amazing for us to discover? *Together?*" Again, he stretched out his free hand. "Regardless, together, we could create a network of power that can overcome distance. Even if there was one of us every 100 miles, we could still rule these people. Rule the world."

My hand started to raise. I *wanted* to reach out. I *wanted* to accept the offer, to become bigger than I had ever been.

Yet my body sat motionless on the park bench, still pressing the cellphone to one ear inside the hoodie.

"And, John. When it comes to ruling the world..." He broke into a broad smile. "You can *leave that to me.*"

Something about that stopped me. The arrogance. The hint of threat in his voice. My arm lowered. "No...," I said.

Everything froze in time, even as too many things happened too quickly. Sol, furious, rushed forward, gesturing with his outstretched hand, and my body flew from the park bench and slammed into the statue's pedestal. The bench itself then flipped upward, swooping upward toward me, clamping down on either side of my body, trapping me against the base of the statue. My hand dropped the cellphone to the ground as Sol stepped forward.

"Now it is time we talked face to face, John." He nodded toward his cellphone and smiled. "And stop all this foolishness." Reaching through the iron slats of the bench that now served quite effectively as the bars of a jail, Sol pulled the hoodie down to rest on my shoulders.

And the smile on his face fell away to surprise, anger, and disappointment.

Because that's when he realized that I wasn't me.

14

"What is this treachery?" Sol hissed, stepping back. In his hand, the cellphone dangled, nearly forgotten.

Here's the thing: He never saw it coming. I was 14, and he was an adult. My mental powers could barely move a pencil, while his could blow up tanks. Sol had taken on an army, and while he didn't defeat them exactly, he didn't lose either. He had become infamous, and that rarest kind of celebrity, one who could literally go unnoticed if he wished (and rarer still, because he used his own special abilities to make that happen). Plus, being naturally good-looking and charismatic, he was used to things going his way.

All of that has to go to a person's head, right? That's what I figured.

Then, considering the almost unbearable, heart-pounding fear that I had developed for Sol, it made my answer clear: There was *no way* I was going to go sit on a park bench, waiting for him like a granny throwing breadcrumbs to the birds. Because this particular bird had razor-sharp fangs.

So I took a chance, betting on Sol's ego. And it worked.

General Tulloch Park sat near the middle of the city, which meant it was almost entirely surrounded by tall buildings. Walking around that morning, comparing options, I saw that the first level of many of the nearby buildings housed shops selling electronics, handbags, clothing, your typical tourist crap. It took three or four stops, but I was able to find a pair of binoculars. And yes, I had to push the shop owner's mind so I could take them without paying. I'm a terrible person. I know.

I'd chosen one of the shorter buildings just off the park as my target. It was six stories with a flat roof, the thinner side of the building facing the park and its wider side running down one of the streets radiating away. Making my way to the roof was no more difficult than getting a junior suite at the Lexington, thanks very much. Just had to do a little *pushing*. Once I stepped out onto the rooftop, I checked out the view. To me, it seemed pretty perfect. Near-complete sight lines on the park, plus the ability to see people coming in almost any direction.

I waited almost an hour, scouring the park with my binoculars, before I saw the kid. He was older than me by a couple years, I think, walking and talking on his cellphone, wearing a dark hoodie — was it black, dark grey, maybe a deep blue? Hard to tell from more than 150 feet away. I stopped thinking about it and decided it was black, because that would be perfect. I had a family name to represent, after all.

Reaching out with my mind, I found that it was a little tricky to cover the distance, but it worked. It just seemed *thinner*, like I was stretching against the edge of my sphere of influence. Anyway, the kid did as he was directed. He hung up the phone, walked to the park bench nearest the statue, sat down, and waited.

Not much later, I noticed Sol walking up from the left, and fear filled me. I was certain he was going to see through the trick right away, somehow catch me despite the fact that I was on a rooftop six stories up, and he was far below at street level. But he was so calm, so casual. He walked toward the statue like nothing was happening.

This was the trickiest part. I kept my binoculars focused on him until just that moment when he finally noticed "me" sitting on the bench. And I pushed his mind, just the littlest bit, terrified that he would notice even that gentle nudge. But he took the bait. "There's John," I made his mind tell him, which was really just what his mind was already telling itself. I just sort of *confirmed it.*

As Sol continued along, I made the kid in the hoodie raise his cellphone to one ear inside the hood, keeping his head down the whole time.

When I dialed his number, it was frightening and yet exhilarating. I watched Sol talk to "me" from afar, too nervous to poke much more than my eyes and the binoculars over the top of the roof's short wall.

I knew it wouldn't last forever. And it didn't. Once Sol pulled down the kid's hoodie, that was that. But I hadn't really planned my exit strategy. Chalk it up to being 14.

Once Sol realized it wasn't me, I figured it was time to get the heck out of Dodge, so I ran in a crouch across the wide, flat roof. The opposite side of the building seemed to be a safe distance, but I had no idea how long that would last.

I told myself I was a fool to do it, but I had to look. When I reached the far end of the roof, as far away from Sol as I could get, I leaned over the half wall once more and trained the binoculars toward the park. Sol was still standing there, over the dazed kid, as people around him gasped, some running for cover. He was slowly spinning, looking for me. I ducked as his eyes swept past, then came back up to watch him again.

"Let Bobby go, you bastard," I said into the phone, still connected. I saw Sol's head jerk down toward his hand. Then he raised the phone like it had suddenly become radioactive, putting it slowly to his ear.

"That was very deceptive, John," he said in an icy tone. "I'm... *quite impressed.* You're even more clever than I gave you credit for." He continued to spin, looking for me. By now, he was scanning rooftops, realizing how exposed his position was. "You *tricked me.*" He sounded shocked. I even felt ashamed for a moment, until I remembered he was a power-crazed murderer.

"I said, let Bobby go."

Sol chuckled. Damn, I hated that cocky little laugh of his. "I assure you that I am not *holding* Bobby in any way," he said. "In fact, he is not even in this city. By now, I suspect, Bobby is safely back in your own hometown."

You call yourself Sol, but maybe you're not as bright as you think, Jose do Branco. I allowed myself a smug smile. If Bobby wasn't under Sol's control, there was nothing more for me to do. I started to back away from the edge without another word, ready to find my way home again.

I was lowering the phone, about to disconnect the call, when Sol spoke again. "I presume you can see me, correct, John?"

I stayed quiet.

"I shall assume the answer is yes. Which means that you can no doubt see what I am about to do."

I crept back to the edge, finding him with the binoculars. Sol approached the kid — a kid I had randomly chosen to stand in harm's way in my stead — and my stomach twisted. With the park bench still holding him in place like Dr. Frankenstein's monster on an upraised lab table, the kid squirmed, unable to break free. Sol raised one hand and, above them, the statue of General Avery Tulloch began to shake.

"What're you doing?" I said.

Small pieces of the statue began to crack and break free, falling on the kid in the dark hoodie. "I *need* you with me, John," Sol said, his voice scarily calm. "Together, we would be a formidable team. If you won't come to me of your own choice, I may have to... provide incentive." One of the horse's front hooves snapped off, landing inches in front of the kid with a loud *clack*. It probably wasn't big enough to kill him, but would've hurt like hell if it had hit him in the head.

"Cut it out!"

"I will, John, if you do as I say."

"Why me? Why'd you let Bobby go?" I found myself slowly standing, the tension rising inside me.

"Oh, no, John, no." Again, that deep-throated laugh. "I didn't say I let him go. I just said I *wasn't holding him.*" Sol kept scanning the buildings, still trying to find me. "I know exactly where Bobby is and what he is doing."

My head was too high, maybe the binoculars glinted in the sun, I don't know.

Sol saw me. And he acted.

The park bench flew like tissue paper whipped into a hurricane. He sent it directly toward me.

Cat and mouse.

Or chess.

Either way, it was a game.

I could almost feel what his mind was thinking. *Can you stop it?*

In the heartbeat of time I had, I knew the answer was no. I could barely move a pencil. There was no way I could stop a metal park bench that was flying through the sky in an arc with me at its endpoint.

So I dove away, and the bench slammed into the bricks atop the wall, cracking several free. They fell to the street below and I heard cries and shrieks — fear and alarm. People were definitely noticing.

The binoculars skittered away as I flopped to the flat roof. But I was unharmed. Slowly, I stood. The cellphone remained tightly clutched in one hand, so I lifted it again to my ear. I took a ragged breath, and another, willing my heart to slow down.

"You missed, asshole," I said.

That damn laugh again. "John, John… there is no point in all of this."

"Yeah? Then maybe stop trying to kill me."

"I simply want you to join me, John. Me, you, Bobby. Using our powers. Connected together, almost like radio towers repeating a signal, broadcasting it farther than it might otherwise reach on its own."

"But doesn't that seem futile to you, Sol?"

"How so, John?" I could no longer see him, sprawled as I was on the rooftop. Was he getting closer, now that he knew where I was? I didn't know, but my heart said yes. And my feet leaped up in answer, heading for the door.

As I hit the first flight of stairs, I struggled to control my breath, trying to conceal that I was running. "There's just three of us. Even repeating one another, the signal won't go that far." I put one finger over the microphone as I huffed and ran down the stairs.

"Ah, but John. There aren't just three of us. There are more."

In shock, I hit the END button, disconnecting the call. Minutes later, I reached street level, stepping outside and folding into the pedestrian traffic. I figured there was a beacon in my head, one Sol could hear, just as there was one in his that I could hear. I told my mind to suppress it, and maybe it worked, because he didn't follow me, at least that I'm aware of.

Back at the bus station, I found a bus heading home and slipped aboard. It was another local. That meant another slew of hours wasted, but at least I was getting away. Getting away from Sol. Going home.

Despite — or likely because of — the tremendous tension and fear, I wasn't even aware I was falling asleep until the bus pulled up at the tiny covered bench that served as my town's depot.

It was dark when I stepped off and turned toward home. Along the way, each shadow was Sol, ready to leap out at me. Or worse, Bobby. I had visions of my former bully and current best friend, the eager student, learning at the feet of a madman.

The front door of my house was locked, of course. I didn't even have a key, so I had to knock. When Mom opened it, she started to say something, express great concern or relief. But I didn't let her. A little push reminded her of my trip to Aunt Cindy's house, made her remember that all was well. It was normal for me to show up in the dark, normal to have been gone overnight. Reaffirm the push I had given her mind before I left that everything was fine.

"Hi, honey," was all Mom said, making way for me to come in the door. Seeing the TV on in the living room, I walked over and collapsed on the couch.

Moms being moms, she assumed I was hungry. She was right. I gobbled down the grilled cheese she gave me, even doing a good number on the side of broccoli, although it was generally known that I hated the stuff. Then I asked for, and got, a second sandwich.

Holly sat beside the couch. I felt her stare. I expected it. I'd made no effort to push her mind, to excuse my long absence. She didn't speak, but I knew she knew. Was she staring in concern? In anger? I didn't know, so I didn't look at her.

I felt a deep guilt, having lied to my mother and essentially ignored my sister. I had acted the stowaway on two bus rides, stolen a cellphone, freeloaded a hotel room and food, taken binoculars. Worse than any of that, I'd put that hoodie kid in a situation in which he could've been killed.

And I felt a deep fear. In the back of my mind, the dull throbbing beacon that pointed the way to Sol still rang out. If he had the same sense, he'd be led directly to my door.

To *our* door.

Despite my cleverness at General Tulloch Park, I was far from done with Sol. Our time was coming. Our showdown.

Our high noon.

KEITH SOARES

PART FOUR

EVEN

1

I remember it clearly.

Me and Bobby. And Sol. And there were a bunch of others, too. In the dream I knew their names, because, you know, it was my dream. I got to name all the characters. There was dark-haired, dark-skinned Petrus, probably in his late twenties. He was reserved, hard to read. And tall, pale blond Margrethe, who might have been in college. She was like a Norse warrior goddess. Totally badass. I didn't want to mess with her. Plus another girl. Even the memory of her from my dream makes me want to linger, think about her a little longer. Her name was Phillipa. She was maybe three or four years older than me, with curves that girls my age mostly didn't have yet, and waves of deep-red hair. She went by Pip, a name I'd normally be inclined to mock, but not with her. She was sassy and smart. A no-nonsense girl who could roll with the punches, or throw a few of her own. It was appropriate that I made her up in my dream, because she certainly seemed to be my dream girl. There may have been others in the dream, but I couldn't see them clearly or remember any other names.

But I knew the six of us, because we all had it. We all had the power, in different variations. Petrus was good with his mind. Margrethe was a master of the physical skills — she had a karate chop that literally could cut down a full-sized tree. And Pip, she was a blend of the two. I guess sort of like me. Did I have a crush on a fictitious girl from a dream? Yes. Yes, I did. Don't judge.

The dream was long and epic, seemingly endless. At first, it was amazing. Six of us, learning from each other, growing. I mean, we were essentially the six most powerful people on Earth. That alone alleviates a lot of life's stresses. There were tons of laughs. Massive displays of ability. And of course, juvenile pranks.

One of them occurred when I was training to move objects with my mind, a skill that I apparently needed to work on even in my dreams. Sol had set up a sort of obstacle course, and my goal was to get through it unscathed. There were two ways to do that. The easy way meant using your mind to stop things from falling on you. Sol had arranged a route past stacked stones and crumbling brick walls, over a simple bridge, and even underneath a dump truck teetering on two tires. If you were good, you could gently nudge each item back into place when Sol sent it tumbling toward you. If you sucked, like I did, you had to run and duck, your body sluicing itself out of harm's way.

"John," Sol would say repeatedly, "you are more powerful than a stone, or a brick, or even that truck. If *you* have to move out of *its* way, you are not doing it correctly." At least the dream version didn't say it with that obnoxious laugh. No, Dream Sol actually seemed earnest in trying to improve my skills.

The others generally did better, so of course when it came time to pick on someone, that someone was me.

This particular prank happened while Sol was sending the things in the obstacle course flying, tumbling, or falling toward me, one by one. He seemed bored by the whole thing, like I was taking too long. I really had to concentrate, and still my ability to move something with my mind was… locked. So, like kids do in school, the others ganged up on me. Well, maybe not Bobby, and maybe not Pip. But Petrus and Margrethe did.

They pushed, here and there, from several sides. Sol must have noticed, but he either didn't care or he was curious to see what might happen. I tried. Really hard, like my mind was about to burst. But still the stones fell from one side, the walls of brick from another, and the truck threatened to crush me from above.

And I just gave up.

It was too much. I couldn't do it. The stones fell first, tumbling past me as my body rapidly sluiced in various directions to avoid them. Then, in a split second, the wall hit me, and my body again shifted, backwards this time, away from it all, to safety.

But not to safety, really. I sluiced into the path of the overturning truck. And my body was simply *stuck*. There was nothing else to do, nowhere else to go. I had succumbed to physical self-preservation, and in doing so, I wasn't prepared mentally. I didn't have time or a plan. I was going to be crushed.

Like Walter Ivory.

I started to panic.

But there was a sound. Not the chiming bells of angels, not the booming drums of doom. This was more like a *click*.

The truck flipped backward, landing on all four tires. The brick walls pushed back to their normal standing position. Even the stones flew away in radial lines, like I'd become the focal point of a silent bomb.

Everything blew away from me, and I stood, unscathed.

There was a long quiet. Then a single pair of hands began clapping. Sol.

* * *

265

For a while, in my dream, things got better. Somehow, I had passed an important milestone. Yet I didn't fully comprehend what it was I'd done, or, more important, how to do it again. Still, the six of us trained, and we became close.

Sometimes in a group, two people spend enough time together that they form a bond stronger than the others. That's what happened with Pip and me. Were we a couple? Probably not. Were we on the road to that? Yeah, I think so. Until things changed. Funny how time is immaterial in dreams. Was it weeks, months, years? It wasn't clear to me.

One day, seemingly no different from any other, Sol made an announcement. "We are now done here, friends," he said. "The time has come." He met with each of us in private, doling out orders. We separated, each one to our own city. By now we had been indoctrinated to follow orders.

I could see what Sol was doing, and it was just as he'd promised back in the real world, when we'd faced off at General Tulloch Park. Even in my dream, I was enough of a nerd to see the plan in my mind, like a diagram. We six became a network.

Pip was assigned to a city many miles to my east. Yet through the network, I could feel her presence. I had to reach out willfully with my mind to find where she was, leaping through the node that was Bobby to get to her. But I always knew she was there. That reassured me, but only a bit.

Messages came through the invisible wires of our network. Messages from Sol. Only Sol. Do this, do that. Send this material to Margrethe, or something else to Petrus. Take care of this problem. That was the worst. *Take care of it* always meant *Find who did it and kill them.*

Quite a dream, huh?

A super-powered clan linked together, scheming, maneuvering, ruling, killing, doing whatever we pleased. Quite a dream.

No. It wasn't really a dream. It was a nightmare (despite the presence of the lovely Pip). This was a vision of a future world that might be. One that Sol ruled. And he was as benevolent a ruler as you might expect a murderous psychopath to be.

Yes, we were all like radio towers. But he was the deejay, playing the platters that mattered. Spinning the tunes to which we danced. And that's all the five of us did: dance to Sol's tunes.

When I finally woke up, I was relieved to find it wasn't true. I was in my bed, in my house, and while the dream had seemed to span months or maybe even years, in actuality it was the morning after my return from the capital. As you might imagine, it was hard to come back to reality, like unwrapping myself from a spider's web. Still, once my eyes were open and the normalcy of life began to come back, I knew the dream was just a dream. It wasn't real.

And that's what stayed in my mind for a long time. The dream wasn't real. Until it was.

KEITH SOARES

2

I blinked awake and looked at the clock. 11:32 a.m. *Oh. My. God.* I leaped out of bed. I'd been asleep for more than 13 hours.

The capital was only 25 miles away. Hell, Sol could've leisurely *walked* to my house in the time I'd been asleep.

"Mom?" I called. No answer. "Mom!" I ran toward her room. The door was closed, so I knocked five times, hard. "Mom!"

I heard a low groan. "Yeah… yes, honey? Are you okay?"

"I'm fine," I tried to keep my voice steady. "Are *you* okay?" I stood with one cheek pressed against the door.

"Yes, why? What time is it?" A pause. "Oh shit," she said in a hush, and there was a rustling sound. After a moment, the door opened as Mom tied a light-blue bathrobe around herself. "Thanks, John. I overslept. Is Holly up?"

I shrugged. I hadn't checked.

Mom stepped past me, toward Holly's door. "Holly, honey, let's get you some breakfast." She said it in a sing-songy way, as if everything was fine and normal.

Until she opened Holly's door and the wind left her like she'd been punched in the stomach.

Holly's bed had side rails to keep her safe, keep her from falling to the floor in the middle of the night. There had been mornings before when Holly woke up early and wanted to get out of bed, but the rails worked. She would make a racket to get our attention, but she always needed help to get up.

Not this time. The rails were down.

Holly was gone.

3

Mom did exactly what you'd expect her to do with her daughter missing. She called the cops. Before they arrived, she sat on one end of the couch, on the edge, rocking back and forth.

I wasn't even surprised when Sergeant Durso, the officer who was there the day my dad died, appeared on our doorstep a short while later. There was no need for him to display a badge or introduce himself to my mother either. We both knew him on sight.

"Ma'am," he said, taking off his hat and tucking it beneath one muscled arm. With his other hand, he pulled out a little notebook and pen from the breast pocket of his blue uniform. "May I come in?" Behind him, another officer was getting out of a second patrol car, but the second officer made no effort to come to the door.

Mom turned so Sergeant Durso could pass. "Would you like a glass of water or a cup of coffee?" she asked. Even in her distress, she had manners.

271

I didn't say a word, but moments like that leave an impression. Mom was a good person, simple as that. As the sergeant entered, Mom clicked the door closed behind him.

"No, thank you, ma'am," Durso said. Following behind my mother, he sat on the couch. Mom took the side chair, again perched nervously on the front edge. By comparison, the sergeant was slouched back. I don't want to say relaxed or unconcerned, but he was there to do his job. He opened the notebook and readied his pen. "Can you tell me what happened here?"

Mom took a deep breath, and it was like a video I'd seen of a geyser pulling inward, just before the blast. "My daughter, Holly, she's disabled — she has to use a wheelchair to get around." Durso nodded. At least that much about Holly, he already knew. Mom went on to briefly describe the basis of Holly's condition and her seizures, but left out any mention of Walter Ivory. Given that he'd been found crushed to death under a large metal storage pod, I assumed this was for the best. The police might want to start connecting things that didn't connect. These two incidents were unrelated. Or at least, that's what I thought at the time. "When we woke up this morning, she wasn't in her bed," Mom said. "She wasn't in the house at all." Mom started to tear up, but shook her head. The job at hand, trying to work with the cops to get Holly back, was more important than crying.

"Was there any sign of forced entry?" Durso asked. Mom and I shook our heads; we had checked the doors and nothing seemed unusual. "Is her wheelchair still in the house?" he asked. *Good question,* I thought. We'd only been looking for Holly. I couldn't remember if we'd seen her wheelchair or not. That may sound strange, but when you live with something for so many years, it sort of blends in. Like, right now, is your end table still beside your bed? Probably. But are you totally sure? Okay, sure, it probably is. End tables don't have wheels, so that was a bad example.

Mom turned to me. "Is it?" I shrugged. "Check," she said and I jumped up, happy to have something to do, and ran around the house to look anywhere I knew the chair could fit. Nothing. I returned and shrugged again. "I guess it isn't, Sergeant." There was a pause as Mom looked down at her hands wringing in her lap. Then, finally, she burst. "You have to find her!" she pleaded. "She's just a little girl and she needs me. And — " Mom dropped her head into her hands, sobbing. "And I need her."

After losing my dad, Mom wasn't ready for another loss. Holly and her chair were gone, like she'd just taken a key, rolled out the front door, and locked up after herself on the way out. It didn't make sense.

I hugged Mom the best I could, and even the sergeant leaned forward and put a hand on her shoulder to console her. "Ma'am, I can personally promise you that I will do everything I possibly can to locate and return your daughter safely. I have two girls of my own." He let that rest a moment. "But I'm going to need to ask more questions. Will you be able to help by answering?"

Mom dragged her head up, strands of hair falling across her face, her cheeks streaked. With the backs of both hands, she wiped at her face, and I could see her do what so many adults have to do, whether they feel like it or not. She tried really hard to *come back to normal.* I can tell you, that's not something many kids think about, even ones who are older than me. Fewer still can accomplish the task. Most of us are in the yelling, kicking, hitting, shouting, screaming, biting stage of development until we're 10 years out of college. "Ask me anything," Mom said. "I will do *anything* to get my Holly back." Her face, though still drawn and frowning, had become firm.

Durso lifted his pen and cleared his throat.

* * *

The questions lasted maybe an hour. The sergeant took diligent notes, occasionally interrupted by a burst of noise and chatter from his radio, strapped to one side of his belt, with the talkback part clipped on his shoulder.

Finally, he was silent, flipping his pages back and forth for a moment or two. "Well, I think I have everything I need for now." He replaced the pen and notebook in one breast pocket, and produced a business card from the other. "If anything else comes to mind that you think will help, anything at all, don't hesitate —"

With a crackle, the sergeant's radio burst to life. "Durso, copy?"

The sergeant tilted his head toward his shoulder and thumbed the button. "Yup, go ahead."

Another crackle. "Need to speak with you for a moment," came the voice again. "Outside." It was the second officer, I assumed. The one who hadn't come in.

Need to speak to you... Outside. Well, if that didn't sound ominous. Sergeant Durso made some apology for the interruption, then stood and went to the door. Mom and I stayed in the living room, waiting. A few minutes passed, and there was a knock on the door. So much adult courtesy. The sergeant came back and pulled out his notebook once more, but this time he didn't sit.

I suddenly realized his eyes were firmly focused on me.

"John. I understand you've been on a little trip." *Oh shit.* I gulped, unable to overcome the guilt on my face. "Tell me about that."

How the hell does he know? I thought. Then I guessed it. *Oh man, the neighbors. Probably Mr. Cooper.* Why do neighbors have to stare out their windows and keep track of everything going on? Don't adults have anything better to do?

I had been to the capital, staying away overnight. Someone had noticed. Someone who I hadn't noticed, whose mind I never *pushed* to dismiss the notion that anything was out of place. Maybe *lots* of someones.

So of course my first inclination was to push this officer's mind, make him forget. I started to do it... then stopped cold. *It won't work. He knows, the other officer knows, probably a neighbor knows, maybe a handful or a hundred others.* Too many people, a connected chain. If I made one of them forget, that would be even more strange in the eyes of the next person in the chain.

My mouth opened as I started to formulate an answer on the fly. What was commonly referred to as a "lie." But Mom spoke first. "John was visiting my sister, Cindy. She was a little sick and needed some help around the house. I would've gone, but Holly needs me here." I just nodded, like a bad sidekick. *Yeah, damn right. What she said.*

Sergeant Durso looked skeptical. He stood unmoving for a moment, then made a slight tilt of his head, a gesture of acceptance. "All right. Can I get your sister's contact information to corroborate the story?"

"Of course, Sergeant," Mom said. "Though when you call it a *story*, it makes it sound like we're lying."

"No, ma'am, I'm not saying that at all. My job is to track down every lead until it dries up or pans out. That's all." He turned back to me. "How'd you get to your aunt's house, John?"

Out of the corner of my eye, I noticed my mom blink rapidly. This part of the story wasn't programmed into her memory. "Bus, there and back," I blurted out. I gave Mom's mind a little push so she wouldn't argue the point.

"Do you have the ticket stub or any kind of record?" the sergeant asked, scribbling notes.

"Um," I began. Of course I didn't. I'd used mind-powers to act as a sort of stowaway. Or perhaps *guest of honor* was a better way to describe it. "No, sir, sorry. I threw those out once I got back, at the bus stop." I can't say for certain, but I was pretty sure a bead of sweat was forming on my upper lip.

Durso cleared his throat and tucked away the notepad for the last time, turning back to my mom. "All right. You have my card. Call me if you think of anything. Unless it's an emergency, like if you hear from Holly, or from anyone with information about her. Call 911 first, in that case. Call me second." He looked us both in the eye, like we were making a silent promise, then he turned for the door.

Mom walked Sergeant Durso out as I followed. "But what do I *do*?" she asked him. "Just sit here, doing nothing? Waiting?"

"We're actively investigating this case now, Ms. Black.," the sergeant said, stepping outside. "So, yes. We'd prefer you just wait. Let us do our job."

He may have said something else, too. Hell, he may have broken into a song-and-dance number from a Broadway musical. I was no longer paying any attention whatsoever to Sergeant Alan Durso.

Because Bobby Graden was standing on the sidewalk across the street, one hand raised in greeting.

4

Police cars, particularly more than one of them, draw a lot of attention. It seemed that half the neighborhood was in the street, looking our way, when Sergeant Durso left the house and finally drove off. Bobby was just one of many interested faces, raising no one's suspicions except my own.

As the second squad car pulled away, the neighbors started to dissipate, head back to their homes. Miss Janice — that's what she told us kids to call her — walked over, asking my mom if she was okay, if she needed help. The Morrisons did the same. Mr. Morrison was one of the two general practitioners in town, so technically he was Dr. Samuel N. Morrison, MD, but he told everyone to call him Sam. He was always trying to help, living life like it was perpetually 82 and sunny, doing his best to radiate good cheer to everyone around him. I appreciated his bedside manner, especially that day.

As Miss Janice and the Morrisons gathered in front of our house, I noticed

Bobby turn to walk off. Was he going home? That seemed doubtful, given how long he'd been away. I had to catch up with him. I had to find out what had been going on with Sol and what Bobby was doing back in town.

"Mom, I'll be right back," I said, pushing through the crowd. She started to ask why, but didn't want to ignore our concerned neighbors. I left without turning back.

"Hey, man, hold up," I shouted, running across the street, almost unwilling to say Bobby's name in public. He didn't even look back. Instead, he reached the corner and turned, disappearing for a moment behind a fence. I was terrified he'd be gone, a mirage, never really there in the first place. But rounding the corner a moment after him, I saw Bobby walking fast, maybe a hundred feet ahead of me. When he got to the next corner, he quickly turned again and I had to hurry to catch up once more.

Taking that second turn, I saw Bobby in the middle of the street. Facing me. *Oh crap. Another fight*, was all I could think.

As he stood right in front of me, I realized I could sense Bobby's beacon, like Sol's but much smaller. But there was something odd about it. It was weirdly... resonant, like I was hearing a chord rather than a single note.

"Johnny, it's good to see you," Bobby said. "Glad I got your attention, but stop where you are."

I pulled up. "What are you doing here?" I was actually a little out of breath.

Bobby just tilted his head and looked at me. If he had been a schoolteacher wearing reading glasses, he'd have been looking over them, down his nose.

I took a step forward. That's when I realized something was familiar. "Bobby, listen. Stay away from Sol. You don't need that guy. He's crazy." Another step.

"Johnny..." Bobby calmly raised one hand, gesturing for me to stop.

I took another step. "Did Sol tell you I came to see him in the capital?" Another step.

Bobby's hand went higher. "John. Stop. Really."

"I'm not afraid, Bobby. I'll fight you if you want, but I'm not starting it."

Bobby's eyes looked left and right. "Yes. You are. Stop."

I paused. I don't know why I was trying to get closer anyway, other than maybe to just talk like old times, try to get some sense into him. But for a moment I stood frozen.

Frozen. Ice. *Snow*. We were standing on the spot where everything began. Where I ran into Bobby, just before we were hit by the little red car. "Bobby, you know where we are, right? Remember that day in the snow?"

He gazed around, indifferent and unfocused, more toward a fence on his left and a row of shrubs on his right than at the street and houses. "Huh? Oh. Oh yeah. The scene of the crime, so to speak," he said with a little laugh.

"Yeah. I think it is." Another step forward. "You were going to beat me up here, but then we became friends. Remember that part? Friends?" One more step, hands out, hoping Bobby would relax. We were still kids, after all.

"We're friends, Johnny. We are friends," Bobby said, eyes down. "But some things change. Some things aren't in my control."

"What does that mean?" I asked, taking another step.

"Stay back, John. I mean it. Listen. You've gotta come to Sol and really talk. None of that nonsense you pulled back in the city. When I heard you tricked him, well, I thought he was going to be furious. But... he was almost... I don't know. Proud? Yeah, he seemed proud of you. He really just wants to talk to you." Bobby finally looked up, into my eyes. "We all do."

I took another step, but felt like I was moving through a deep fog. "What, Bobby? Who's *we*?" One more step.

As it turns out, *that* was the step too far.

There were two blurs, one left, one right. In the blink of an eye, I felt like I was being crushed between a couple of freight trains, stuck in the middle where I couldn't move. No, not freight trains, but instead something amorphous, something that pressed on every surface equally. My body, usually so familiar with fluid escapes, was frozen in shock for a moment.

Bobby seemed upset. "Stop it, you guys!" he said. "Let me handle this!"

The my power kicked in, and my body started to sluice out of the grip. For a moment, it was working. I tried to maneuver, to turn and find an opponent to focus on, but something hit my head, hard. My body couldn't get out of the way of the blow quickly enough. I was stunned, seeing little flecks of light before my eyes. "Wha—?" I managed.

I had just enough time to ponder one thought. *I wonder what someone in one of these houses is seeing, if they happen to be watching?* Not much, I'd bet. Two boys in the street. One acting in a strange, unexplained way. From an adult point of view, this would no doubt be characterized as "boys being boys."

Bobby was upset, but not fearful. His expression seemed more petulant. Like whatever was happened was an insult to *him*. He kept looking to either side, and I felt a presence. Maybe more than one. "You guys..." he repeated.

The chord in my head grew stronger, enough that I could recognize three distinct notes. Three *beacons*. Bobby... and who else?

For a split second, I thought I saw a flash of blond hair above me, followed by another strong thump on my head.

Then nothing but black.

5

"I got it. I got it." A voice. It sounded like Bobby.

"Look, we should just take him back with us." A young woman. No one I recognized.

"That's not what he told us to do!" Bobby again, shouting the way kids do when they're being overruled by an adult.

A pause. I tried to open my eyes, but they refused to obey. I may have slept again.

"Look, I agree with Bobby," a man was saying. "Let us just go." He had an accent I didn't recognize. Actually, who am I kidding? I grew up in small-town America. I didn't recognize *any* accents. Except maybe British, and even then I was sure I couldn't tell English from Scottish from Irish from probably Australian. But his voice wasn't like any of those anyway. And it wasn't Sol's Portuguese baritone. That would have had me jumping out of my skin to wake up. This voice was something different, like he was enunciating each syllable a little more than necessary, the words "let" and "us" coming out completely separately, instead of the blurred together *let's* people normally said.

A frustrated grunt. It was the woman again. "Fine."

Footsteps. I may have slept a little more.

* * *

"Oh my God, it's about time, your majesty," Bobby said as I blinked and tried to look around. The room was bathed in shadow, but still far too bright for me. I squinted toward the sounds of shuffling footsteps on dry concrete, coming near.

"Where am I? What'd you do...?" My mind creaked forward a notch, and I realized there was a more important question. "Who were you *talking* to?"

Standing over me, still blurry in my vision, Bobby made an impatient gesture with one hand. "Friends," he said.

I rubbed at my head and tried to sit up. "Friends? What kind of *friends* are they?" I pressed my palm against my head to make my point.

Bobby sat down on the floor in front of me. "You're very funny, and one to talk. Are *we* friends?" He didn't wait for an answer. "Yes, we are. But didn't you knock me silly? And shoot me in the stomach?" He paused, lips pursed and eyebrows raised. "So you see my point. Look, friends don't always do what's *friendliest* for each other. But they try to do what's *right* for each other. That's what I'm trying to do for you. Now."

I kept rubbing my head where it ached. "Really? How so?"

Bobby stood and paced the room. "Look, do you know where we are?"

Still squinting, I scanned the room. *Ah, yes. Well, at least that was no surprise.* "Warehouse bay. *Our* old warehouse bay, number 6, I assume."

"Thank you. So you got dinged a bit, but it sounds like your brain's still working. Possibly." Glancing my way, Bobby actually cracked a smile.

I ignored it. "Was that supposed to be funny?"

"Come on, Johnny. Can't you just *listen* to me? Consider what I have to say?"

I looked around the room, the dark remote warehouse bay where I had been abducted and stashed. "Do I have a choice?"

"We *all* have choices. But the right choice is to stick together. Look at yourself. You're not tied up. You can leave if you want. I just want to explain a few things to you first."

I finally sat up straight, then felt the throbbing in my head and slid back down to one elbow. Tied up or not, I wasn't ready to leap into action just yet. "Fine. I'm listening. But this better be one damn compelling story. Like I better want to speak in tongues and say *hallelujah* when you're done. Because, right now, I think you're wrong. No, worse. If you're on board with Sol. I think you might be going crazy. And I think I'd be crazy to even consider joining you."

"Will ya shut up, Johnny? Geez. Always like that with you. Think think think, blah blah blah. Just gimme a second, will you?"

Rolling my eyes, I nodded. Bobby smirked. Both of us playing our roles.

"Johnny," Bobby started, coming closer. I could tell that whatever he was about to say was important to him. Immediately, he hooked me. I even checked myself for a moment, making sure he wasn't *pushing* me. But no. Seemed like just earnest conversation. And he *was* earnest. "Sol isn't what you think. He's not a bad guy." I scoffed. Bad start. But Bobby continued. "He's brought us together. We train —"

"Us? We?" I interrupted. "Who's that? You've danced around it so far. So, tell me."

"Sure. There are a few of us. Not a lot. People with powers, just like you and me. Well, sort of like you and me. Some of them are stronger one way or the other, mind or body. And, see, Johnny, that's it. That's the problem. By ourselves, we all have weaknesses. Sol says the individual is flawed but those united are true and strong. Sounds a little preachy to me, but I like it. I know I'm flawed. With the group, we can *do things*."

Just like in my dream. All that power, wielded in service to Sol. "That's just it, Bobby," I said. "Do *what?* What's the point?"

"There isn't just *one* point, John. *Everything's* the point! So much stuff is a mess these days, we need some changes. Some major changes. Not just you and me, but our town, our state, our country. Hell, the world. Things need to change because what we have now is a mess of injustice, poverty, hunger, war, you name it." Bobby was on a roll now, hardly looking at me. I got the distinct feeling he was repeating a sermon he'd heard, and I had a very strong suspicion about who'd given it originally. "But we. *We* can change things. We've been given a gift. A gift to finally break the world out of the trance it's been in. Are you starting to understand?"

I nodded slightly. "Sol wants to rule the world, or thereabouts. He's brainwashed you and these supposed *others*, and told you he's going to make the world a better place. Sound about right?"

"Dammit, Johnny, you've always gotta do that. Just be a nerd and a downer." Bobby turned away, heading toward the door. I thought for a moment that he'd just leave me there. That I might never see him again, or at least never again on friendly terms. But then he turned. And I saw something I truly never expected.

There seemed to be a tear in Bobby's eye. "I don't agree with everything he wants to do, no," he said. "I'm *sure* you won't either. But the Big Picture..." The words sounded capitalized, the way he said them. "Johnny, he's not mad at you about your crazy stunt in the city, but he doesn't want that to happen again. He wants to meet with you, for real this time. And he just needed to get your attention to do that."

"What does that mean?" I asked, already dreading the answer.

Bobby reached into his jean pocket and pulled out something. A crappy old flip phone. He thumbed it open and pressed a button or two, then leaned down and slid it across the floor to me. With a last look, he went to the door and was gone.

Beside me, the phone made a tinny sound, a ring coming through the miniature speaker, repeating once. Then a click. And a voice.

"Hello, John," Sol said.

I drooped in a sigh, still propped on one elbow on the cold, hard cement floor.

"John? You are there, aren't you, old friend?"

I wanted to raise one heel and lower it on the phone, smashing it to pieces. But I knew one thing for sure. I *had* to know what Sol wanted to say, this time if never before. I reached for the phone and put it to my ear. "Yeah. I'm here. Say what you're gonna say."

"Ah good, John. I merely wanted to tell you two things that I think you will find important. First, Holly is with me. She is quite safe, and seems happy. She's having cereal and watching TV now. It's a cartoon and I think she's enjoying it quite a bit."

"You son of a bitch!" I shouted.

Sol *tsked* me two or three times. "John, please. There's no need to be vulgar. You and I are better than that now."

I seethed. "Give me my sister back, or I swear to God no distance will be too far. I will find you."

"John, I *want you* to find me," he said. "So do my *friends*. That is, in fact, the point in all this."

"Build an army, Sol. Go ahead. If you don't return my sister unharmed, I'll destroy your army first. Then you."

"John, please. All of this anger is unnecessary. I just want you to come to me. To talk. To hear what we are trying to do. Yes, of course, I will try to persuade you to join us. But when you hear what we are doing, I don't think I'll have to try hard." He took a breath, letting it sink in. "But you have my assurances that Holly will continue to be healthy and happy. We are taking good care of her."

"She needs to be at home! With Mom! And me!" I stood. So angry, the remaining pain in my head was forgotten. "I can't believe it. I can *not* believe Bobby helped you do this." I shook my head despite the whorls of color that stirred up.

"Helped?" Sol chuckled. Damn if I didn't want to leap through the phone and pull his throat out, for Holly and also so that I'd never have to hear that dry, self-satisfied laugh again. Pompous lunatic. "Bobby did more than *help*, John."

I inhaled, waiting for the words I suspected were coming but didn't want to hear.

"It was Bobby's *idea*."

Interlude

Rage. Fury. Anger. A tempest, bouncing in all directions. No goal, no point, just moving. Whirling, buzzing in the darkness. And the voices are still there, and they are whirling, too.

Then, like the effect of bending an ear toward a tuning fork, the sound grows, doubled by another.

Still whirling, still moving, in the black.

Like bats finding prey, without sight.

A turn, and the sound increases. Turning away, the sound fades. Turning back, and again the sound grows.

Recognition.

I'm coming to find you.

KEITH SOARES

6

The look in Mom's eyes was nearly desperate. "You *can't* just be *gone* like that, John. You *can't*," she said. "Not now. Not with—" She looked away.

Not with Holly gone, too. I'm sure that's what she meant. "Sorry, Mom."

"Where have you been all this time, John? You had me worried to death."

"I saw Bobby, Mom, and…"

"*Bobby?* My goodness. He's back? Do his parents know?"

"I don't think so."

Mom got really worked up. I should have seen that coming, what with me just disappearing all day, Dad gone, and Holly abducted. Bobby running away from home was probably what Mom considered to be a *solvable problem.* "Then we need to call them. Right now." She went to the phone.

"Mom…" She started to dial. "Mom!"

With a wrinkled brow, she turned back. "Yes, John, what?"

"Don't call Bobby's parents," I said, palms up in surrender. I thought about pushing her to hang up, to forget I'd said anything about Bobby, but the more I talked to Sol and realized what the powers were doing to him, the less stomach I had for using them, especially on the people I loved.

"What?" She lowered the phone, half-dialed. "Why?"

"Because he's not going back. Or at least, I don't think he is. He's…" How the hell was I going to put this? "He's chosen a new life. I'm not even sure where he lives, but I know he's not alone. He told me he found a group of people and he's staying with them."

Mom looked confused. "John, that's simply not acceptable. Bobby is a *14-year-old boy.*"

"I think he's 15, now," I said offhandedly. With the summer fast upon us, my own 15th birthday was only weeks away. And Bobby was a little bit older than me.

"Fifteen, whatever. He can't just live in some sort of commune with a bunch of strangers. He needs to go back home." She raised the phone and finished dialing.

While she talked, all I could think about was how I was going to get to Bobby, to Sol. To get Holly back. I was scared to use my powers sometimes, for what they might do to others. To me. And they had their limits. I'd learned that pushing a few people's minds wasn't good enough. Someone else would see me, and my plan would unravel. I had to be more careful. I knew it would tear Mom apart, especially now, but I had to do it.

I had to run away from home.

* * *

I've often thought about how it must have been for Mom. Nothing short of terrible. I can't imagine how she felt, or how she could go on, day after day. The house that used to be so full of purpose and direction — organizing the family, cooking meals, cleaning up after countless messes, the work, the play, just the cacophony of a life where four human beings lived under one roof. And then, nothing. No noise, nothing urgent to do, no one there.

If I could have told her, I would have tried to make sense of it for her. *Mom, I can't bring Dad back. But I think I can save Holly. And that's why I have to go. I'll give myself up to save her.*

Which is exactly what I was planning to do.

* * *

Not knowing how to drive was a real pain in the ass. Sure, I could sneak out in the middle of the night, avoid having anyone see me go — and even then, who knew? — but it was really hard to make progress walking. Still, it was the best option. If I rode my bike, I'd have to follow some sort of trail or road, and that meant someone most likely would see me. Walking, I stayed out of sight. I followed my intuition — the inherent sense inside my head that somehow told me which way to go, which direction to walk to get closer to Sol. But still, on foot, I had a lot of time to think.

We didn't have any camping gear to speak of, but I packed my school backpack with extra clothes and as much food as I thought I could carry. I rolled up a blanket, lashed that to the bottom of the pack, and thought I was as ready as I was going to get. Until I remembered water.

Water has got to be the single biggest hardship for life on the road. You have to have clean water or you'll die, but it's bulky and heavy to carry. In the end, I opted for a single large water bottle, which I figured I could refill by sneaking into yards at night. I wasn't too proud to drink from a garden hose. Any garden hose.

It wasn't a precise route by any stretch. The beacon in my mind would often point me directly toward a row of houses that I'd have to circle. But I made progress.

I knew as soon as I left that I couldn't let anyone see me, like I apparently had when I went off to the capital, or it would be all over. With the police already searching for Holly, I knew there was going to be some sort of statewide manhunt setup if — *when* — two of us suddenly were gone. Turns out I underestimated. It was a massive effort that brought in every police force in three states, as well as several federal law-enforcement agencies. We captured the public's attention: Two young kids from the same family, father killed in a tragic accident, one of the kids in a wheelchair, both abducted from their home, leaving their widowed mother devastated and alone. So yeah, I should have realized that story would gain traction. Many neighborhoods lived in fear, thinking it was the beginning of a spate of kidnappings, a *serial child stealer*. When all I'd actually done was walk out the front door.

Of course, all of the commotion made my progress even slower. Turns out that pretty much the first place law enforcement looks for missing kids is local wooded areas. So while those were great places to avoid being seen by the rest of the world, they were swarming with cops. I had to be much more creative. Most of all, I had to keep my ears open. Thankfully, people searching the woods for a missing kid don't try to be quiet. Still, on at least one occasion, I felt I was too close and had to give a little mental push to make a cop head off in the other direction.

Then there was the issue of sleeping. I chose backyards carefully. The ideal candidates were homes owned by a working person or couple, with a few big, leafy trees — or better yet, dense pines — and no dogs. Thankfully, summer was just about in full stride, so the weather was uniformly warm. As dawn threatened, I'd climb a tree, find a hidden spot among the highest branches I could reach, then use my blanket and the straps of my backpack to secure a place where I could sleep without falling to my death. I figured that would be one of the stupider ways to die, or at least would hurt like hell before my body fixed itself, so I was extremely detail-oriented in my setup procedure. By my fifth day on the road, I had the system down pat. It helped that my blanket was green. Though of course by that time, like everything else I carried, it was impressively dirt-stained. Which I suppose was even better. Home-made camouflage.

I could feel that I was getting closer to Sol, inch by inch. As I settled in to sleep on the eighth day, the beacon in my head, sometimes crackling like electrical impulses, sometimes buzzing like a swarm of bees, was notably louder. I finished off my umpteenth granola bar, realizing I was getting pretty sick of them. As much as I hated to admit something my parents had told me over and over, it really did suck to eat the same thing for every meal, despite my 14-year-old disposition to want pizza three times a day.

I fell asleep knowing that soon I would be facing Sol. One way or the other, this whole thing would be over. But when I woke up hours later in the gathering dark, the sound — the beacon guiding me to Sol — was gone.

Suddenly, I was a boy, dirty and alone, hiding and running away from the law, looking down from my perch in a tall oak as night came on, realizing I had no idea which way to go.

7

Desperate, I spent the next two nights walking in the same general direction I had been traveling before, hoping that, like a human bloodhound, I'd somehow reacquire the scent.

I had a thin leather belt, a cheap thing my mom made me wear to keep my pants up, even though I didn't need it. Putting it on had become habit, and I did it even as I was sneaking away from home. In the woods, in the dark, it actually came in kind of handy. But instead of wearing it, I took to swinging it forward and back as I walked, a simple effort to take out the inevitable spider webs that I'd otherwise collect on my face. It was remarkably efficient, and every so often I'd have to stop to wipe a white, cottony mass of collected spider webs off the belt.

It was on my twelfth night away from home, walking in what I had come to realize was pretty much a due-west course, still with no beacon to call me forward, that I was attacked by wild dogs.

That sounded dramatic and dangerous, didn't it?

I'll boil it down, because otherwise you'll reach the end of this part of my tale and you might want your money back.

The "wild dogs" I'm talking about *did* terrorize me and push me along through pitch black woods for hours, many hours on that night. I chucked rocks at them. I diverted across a ravine and creek, trying to throw them off my scent, much like I'd been thrown off Sol's. I thought I'd be attacked at any minute, and yeah, sure, I'd most likely live, but the idea of becoming a human chew toy was not at all appealing. I had visions of huge Rottweilers and Mastiffs and German Shepherds and Doberman Pinschers ripping me limb from limb. In the deepening woods, spurred on by my youthful exaggeration, I wondered if the dogs might be worse still, some sort of hybrid beasts of doom. Or even wolves. They might have been wolves.

But guess what? We lived in a suburban area. Most people had Dachshunds and spaniels and terriers and plain old little mutts. *That's* what was chasing me. A bunch of *little* dogs. In many cases, *tiny* dogs. Strays. The lost dogs. The ones that had gone missing, or worse, got kicked out by some cruel human owner, and somehow managed to survive. Banded together, a pathetic miniature wolf pack. Howling and padding through the pine-needle-covered pathways of the woods. Living on the fringes, probably off the largesse of the suburban neighborhoods they circled. They're there, folks. If you live in the suburbs, they're there. Spend the night in the woods behind your house or a local park. You might find them. The little yippy discards and forgotten companions of a glut of repetitive housing projects. Born to be mild.

Still, the dogs startled me when their pack suddenly appeared.

I jumped, my belt still in my hand.

I didn't think. I didn't try. I *reacted*, whipping the belt out like a weapon, toward the nearest dog.

There was a yelp. Dogs scattered. I looked down and saw the belt, straight as a line. Instead of the limp, flopping strip of cheap leather I expected, there was a solid length of... what? It was still leather, but hard as stone. As the dogs distanced themselves from me, I reached out and touched the belt; it was like a rod of metal. Milliseconds before, it had been a floppy belt, but now...

I gave a brief laugh, thinking how silly it was to be afraid of the little dogs. At the same time, it was a laugh at myself. What was this new thing I had done?

And the leather belt drooped, slowly first, then falling all at once like melting snow finally sloughing off a roof. Within a moment or two, although I hadn't moved, it was hanging down from my closed fist.

Somehow, *I* had done it. I had made the belt turn solid. Standing in the dark, dapples of moonlight around my feet, I flipped the belt up, willing it to *happen again*. Nothing.

Over and over, pointlessly, I whipped the belt through the air, straining my mind to make it solid, turn it into a weapon again.

Nothing.

The rest of that night, I walked on and on, my best guess at a westerly route, snapping the belt again and again and getting nowhere. Like pushing the pencil, whatever I had done was lost, a random doorway in my mind I couldn't find again, and even if I could, I didn't have the key. That door was hidden and locked.

* * *

In the morning, as the sun was just barely cresting the horizon, I found a row of tall pines just inside a small suburban park. Picking the one that offered the most concealment, I climbed up, nestled into a dense section of branches, and strapped myself in.

Little did I know I'd reached the end of traveling alone for a while.

8

As night fell once again, I descended the pine, repacked my gear and hiked along the strip of road that ran along the park. Making my best guess at which direction was west, I realized I had to cross the street. I thought I was lucky to find it deserted except for a few parked cars. I scanned left and right, making sure no one saw me, then walked as casually as I could across the road to head back into the woods once more.

I hadn't even reached the double-yellow line when a strong light pinned me. Turning toward the harsh white glare, I cursed myself for being so stupid. One of the parked cars was a police cruiser.

I was busted.

The cruiser was maybe 50 yards to my right, on the far side of the road. Inside, some officer sat invisible behind the bright light. An electronic click sounded, and then his voice boomed out from a hidden speaker in the car.

"Hold it there, son," the police officer said just before the driver's-side door opened and he stepped out.

Still just a silhouette in the darkness, the officer approached, staying just outside the beam of light in which I was caught, keeping himself mysteriously hidden.

I stood frozen. Should I use my powers to send him on his way? Or could there be a second officer in the car, a partner? Did cops still do that? I had no idea.

He stepped closer, then pulled up only feet from me. "Well, son of a bitch," he muttered. "You're that missing kid, aren't you? You're John Black."

* * *

He led me back toward the cruiser, the word POLICE painted on the side in some dated blocky font that made me think I had been captured by a cop out of an old movie. For a moment, I envisioned him twirling a baton rather than carrying a gun, but a quick glance proved otherwise. A black pistol was snapped into a similarly black holster at his waist.

Walking beside the officer, I felt a whirlwind of emotion. Living on the road for nearly two weeks, I had begun to feel different — tougher, more self-sufficient. It was easy to forget where I was heading, the danger that awaited me. But with the police officer at my side, probably a foot and a half taller than me, I remembered again that I was just a kid. All the fear came crushing back, amplified by a boy's normal need to be with his mother, his family. I wanted everything to go away — the powers, Sol, Holly's kidnapping — I just wanted things to be normal.

With my dirty green blanket draped over my shoulders, I even cried a bit as we reached his parked cruiser.

Suddenly it dawned on me what I had missed. A small, deserted road next to a heavily wooded park would be the perfect place for local teens to hang out at night. It must have been common for the cops to patrol along the fringes, looking for kids making out or drinking.

Hell, this officer probably wasn't even looking for me. Maybe no one was. Maybe they'd tried and given up already. After 13 nights, would they even think I was alive? Would they think Holly was still alive?

They must have all thought we were dead.

Which meant I'd been found completely by accident. Damn, that ticked me off.

Sniffling, I saw the officer — a tall, thick man with a dark beard and the name HENSON engraved on the name plate under his badge — raising his hand to one shoulder. To his radio. Like I'd seen Sergeant Durso do.

In seconds, Officer Henson would call in that he'd found me. Then the word would go out, and I'd be packed up, taken first to some police station, then driven back home. To Mom. The idea was very appealing.

But no.

I couldn't.

I knew Mom needed me, needed some kind of normal life in the house. But Holly needed me way more, especially now. Especially if the cops had given up on her.

Did Holly know where she was, what was happening? I was sure she was aware that something was wrong. She wasn't with Mom, and that alone would be enough to upset her. I hoped that was all. But in my heart, I sensed that she knew much, much more than we could tell. She must've been terrified.

Thinking of my sister, captive and afraid, I became very angry. Then I thought of what might happen if I gave up, if I let them take me home. Would Sol let Holly go? Bring her comfortably back home? That didn't seem likely. What did seem likely was that he'd try even harder to get at me.

Would Sol harm a little girl in a wheelchair? He was crazy, I was pretty sure of that. Was he *that* crazy? I mean, would he even consider *killing* her?

She was my sister. I know that in a lot of families, kids bicker. Not in mine. How could we argue when Holly never said a word? When our closest interactions were shared glances. We had our special moment, when we would touch foreheads, usually when saying good night. I realized how much I missed that. Sol had stolen it from me. So had Bobby. Sol and Bobby together had taken my sister from me, and from my mom, too.

They weren't to blame for starting the disintegration of our family — I held that honor for my primary role in the death of my father — but we still *were* a family. We were together, until Sol and Bobby pulled us apart.

I no longer wanted to give myself up and go home.

I no longer wanted Officer Henson to tell anyone else where I was.

I was angry.

I *pushed.*

Officer Henson's hand stopped, then fell to his side. His eyes glazed over for a moment, then he shook his head lightly and looked around, not sure where he was. "Uh, what did you say, son?"

"Um, I was saying thank you for helping me find my dog," I lied, pushing a little more.

Officer Henson nodded. "Yes, yes, of course. You're, uh, you're welcome." He turned and opened the driver's door of his police cruiser, started to get in.

I felt relieved, and turned to head back into the line of trees.

Suddenly everything lit up in red and blue, and I heard another car approaching, the static crunch of tires rolling across the pavement. I turned my face toward the light. *Damn.*

A second cruiser was pulling up, windows down. From inside, the sound carrying in the quiet night air, I could hear the officer behind the wheel speaking into his radio. "I've located Henson and — oh my God — it's that missing kid! Henson found that missing boy, John Black!"

9

The place was dense with *stuff*. Chairs, desks, tables covered with papers and things, bulletin boards with barely a square inch of open space. Walls that might have once been white, now in serious need of fresh paint. A faded and chipped linoleum floor, in a pattern that screamed of decades past.

The police station was crowded, with every officer on- or off-duty coming by to see what Officer Henson had found. The missing boy. Me.

Walking through the zigzag of desks, I felt like a rat in a science experiment. Finally, I was led to someone's glass-enclosed office. Henson's? Did a patrol cop have an office? I didn't think so. Maybe it belonged to the chief of police. Either way, it was just as cluttered and in need of new paint as the rest of the place. Its only saving grace was a beat-up tan leather couch along one wall, where I was able to sit. Without asking, I sprawled out on the comfortable cushions, realizing how much better it was than being strapped into a tree to sleep. If they'd left me alone for even five minutes, I think I'd have been out cold.

"John." It was a new voice. I turned and saw an older man, bald on top, wearing a tan suit. "Hi, John. I'm Police Chief Carney. We're all very, very glad that you're here. You're safe with us now. We've let everyone know you're here, even your mom. She's really looking forward to seeing you, you know?" He smiled a thin smile.

Despite the joy of a real place to lie down, I was immediately cynical. Of course this man was glad I was here. His department found the kid no one could find. He'd probably end up on the national news, might even get a raise and a promotion.

But Holly was still with Sol.

I sat up. "Listen, sir, I'm sorry if this sounds disrespectful and all, but I really should go."

He chuckled. He actually chuckled. "Son, I know you must've been through a lot, but you're gonna be okay now. We've—"

"No, listen." I was riled up. Being out on my own had gotten to me, I suppose. My manners had slipped, but I also felt more confident. "You've already told everyone about me, so there's no sense in me lying. I need to leave to help my sister."

Chief Carney pricked up his ears at the mention of Holly, who he no doubt knew was missing as well. "Do you know where she is, John?" He crouched down beside me, seemingly very concerned.

"Yes. I do." I took a deep breath, afraid of what this stranger would think, but needing to say it anyway. "She's with Sol."

Immediately, the chief backed away, wrinkling his brow. "Sol? You mean... you mean that guy who took over the governor's mansion? *That* Sol?"

I rolled my eyes even though I knew it wasn't terribly polite. How many *Sols* did Chief Carney know? "Yeah, him. He took her —"

"But no one's seen him in weeks. And why would he take your sister?" He shook his head.

"It's true, Officer — I mean, Chief Carney," I said. "He did it because he's trying to get to me."

Instantly, the chief stood. "John, listen. I think you're tired. We don't have to talk about this right now. You're safe, that's what matters." *Damn it*, I thought. *He's already decided I'm lying. Or maybe crazy.* "Look, we can give your mom a call, let you talk to her. Would that make you feel better? Forget about this whole idea of Sol for now."

Forget about Sol. I wish. Still, I *did* want to talk to Mom, very, very much. "Sure," I said, sighing. There was no use in trying to convince him — pushing him or otherwise — as far as I could tell. Too many people were already part of it.

Chief Carney went to his desk, picked up the phone, and asked someone to call my mom. He hung up, and a couple of minutes went by before the phone rang. Carney picked it up on the first ring. "Yeah? Okay, thanks… Yes, hello, Mrs. Black! Yes, oh, you're most welcome, ma'am. I'm very excited to be able to make this call. I'll put him right on." Carney stretched the long spiral cord of the phone out so I could take the handset. Then, with a nod, he left the room, pulling the door shut. Even though he didn't believe me, Chief Carney seemed like a decent man. I remember hoping he'd get that raise and promotion, but I honestly don't know if he did. I never once set eyes on him again after he closed the door.

"Mom?"

"John? Oh my God, it is you! Thank God! I thought you were gone forever!" She started to cry.

"Don't cry, Mom, I'm okay."

"How did you get so far away, John? What are you doing there? No one is telling me anything."

"Mom, I know you don't want to hear this, but I can't come home yet." I cringed, waiting for the reply.

"*What?* What are you talking about, John? You've got to come home, just as soon as they can bring you here. Wait. Is this something to do with Bobby? You said he was off living somewhere, not going home. Are you with Bobby, John? What're you two doing? You're too young for this. You've got to come home."

"Yes and no, Mom. It has to do with Bobby, but not the way you think." I closed my eyes and took a deep breath. *Here goes.* "Mom, I need to tell you something. No, I need to tell you pretty much *everything*. Things aren't what you think, Mom."

"What are you talking about, John? I —"

"Hold on, Mom. Just let me talk. I know this is all going to be really hard to believe, but you're going to have to try. Okay?" I waited. Outside the glass walls of Chief Carney's tiny office, cops came and went, the miracle rescue of the missing boy already fading into history.

"Uh. Okay, okay, John," Mom said. "You can tell me anything. I'm your mother."

Now or never. "Mom, I'm not really sure were to begin, but a while ago, I started realizing I could do things. Strange things, like avoid burns, stop punches cold, make people change their minds. I know it sounds totally crazy, but I have these… abilities now. Things other people can't do. Sort of like superpowers." Silence on the other end of the line. *Oh, crap.* I just continued. "Bobby does, too. It happened around the time we were both hit by that car, but I don't think the car is what did it. Because there are other people, too. Definitely at least one more person. Do you remember that guy named Sol who terrorized the governor?"

"Of course, but what does that —"

"He's like me. Or maybe I'm like him. Bobby, too. The reason Sol could

308

walk in and take over the governor's mansion was because he could make people's minds do what he wanted. And his body can sort of automatically dodge bullets."

"John, this… This sounds…"

"I know it does, Mom, but just wait. There's more. I met Sol before all that stuff at the governor's mansion happened. When we went to Playa Beach over the summer, when I went to the boardwalk to play games — he was there. Just some guy I ran into accidentally. At least I thought so. But I found out he had the same abilities that I did, and I sort of freaked out. Then, with what he did, killing those people in the capital, well… I didn't want to have anything to do with him again. But he found me. Called me. Asked me to come meet him in the city."

"John. This isn't making any sense. I can't —"

"Mom. I went to the capital. You know I did."

"You went to help your aunt, because she's *sick*."

"No, Mom, I didn't. Call Aunt Cindy. Ask her. I was never there." I let that sink in for a moment. "Mom, Bobby is with Sol. Sol called to him with his mind, and he came. The three of us can bend people's thoughts, and we pretty much can't be hurt. Not by bullets or fire or falling off a building. So Sol wants us to all join together. This sounds crazy, but you have to believe me that it's true. Sol called to me, too. But when I went to the city, I didn't do what he expected. I didn't just walk up and join his little party. In fact, I sort of tricked him. And to pay me back, he took Holly." I left out the part about it being Bobby's idea. Even I couldn't comprehend that yet.

On the other end of the line, I heard my mother gasp.

"Mom. Holly is missing because of me, because Sol wants me to come to him. So that's what I'm going to do. I have to. But I'm not going to join Sol like Bobby has. I'm going to get Holly back. No matter what."

There was a long silence. After a while, I wasn't even sure if she was still on the line. I shifted the phone to my other ear and opened my mouth to say something when she finally spoke.

"Is that what happened to my sewing needle?"

"Huh?" At the moment, a sewing needle might have been the furthest thing from my mind, but as soon as she said it, I knew exactly what she was talking about. Was she going to make this decision based on that mangled sewing needle?

"The time you and Bobby bent my sewing needle. It shouldn't have bent. It should've hurt you instead. But I knew something was up that day. Neither of you were hurt, were you?"

"No. Not at all."

"And the needle bent from what? From touching you?"

"That was Bobby, actually. He put his finger under it while the machine was running, and the needle bent. It couldn't go through his skin. Like I said, we can't really be hurt."

I was certain she didn't believe me. But you know how moms have an almost magical knack for detecting lies? Well, they must have the same ability to detect the truth. Or else my mom took one hell of a leap of faith.

"Okay, John. Go. Get your sister. And if there's anything, *anything at all*, that I can do to help you, you call home immediately. I mean that. Sitting around here on my hands is the worse thing I've ever done in my life."

"You... believe me?" I said. "And you're not mad about it?"

"Believe you? I want to, John. You're my son. It's all very hard to understand. In fact, it's the hardest thing to understand that I've ever heard of in my life. But I believe *in* you. And no, why would I be mad? It sounds to me like you're in something you didn't ask for, and you're trying to help Holly. It'll take me a while to come to grips with all the other things you said, and I'm scared as hell to say this to you, but go and try to help your sister. But I mean it. If I can help, you *have* to let me. Otherwise, I'll go crazy here by myself."

That was when I looked out through the glass wall again and noticed several of the officers face down on their desks. *What the hell? Did they fall asleep?* Then a shudder rolled through my body.

Or are they dead?

10

Another officer walked into view through the glass, at first studying some papers he held. Then he stopped, noticed the other officers, and stammered something. I couldn't hear him, but it looked like he was saying *What the—*

Then, like an old tree giving way and falling, the officer drooped to the ground, unconscious.

I pressed my hands against the glass wall of the chief's office. I was trapped. The only way out was through the room full of sleeping officers. *No, they're dead*, my mind insisted.

It could only mean one thing. Who could do this? Who *would* do this?

Sol was somewhere near.

I became aware that I could hear or maybe feel a sound. A beacon.

And out of the corner of my eye, on the far side of the outer office, I saw movement. A shadowy form.

I stepped back from the glass, steeling myself as best I could. I was deeply afraid of Sol, but I had chosen this path. Sure, meeting him when I was blocked from all escape wasn't in my plans. Hell, I didn't have a plan. But if I'd bothered to make one, it would have been different, for sure.

Sol wore a dark outfit with a hood, his face remaining in shadows as he approached the door. He stepped over the officer on the floor, around the desks with sprawled bodies.

I backed up, almost bumping against the rear wall, then cursing myself for looking scared. Intentionally, I took a step forward. *This is for Holly, one way or the other.* I would not meet Sol while cowering in a corner.

The door opened and he walked in, lowering his hood.

And I didn't recognize him.

Except I did. It wasn't Sol.

"You... ," I said, trying to conjure the name from my dream. "Your name is Petrus."

The dark-haired, dark-skinned man in front of me laughed once, a dry bark. "That is very good, John," he said. "Yes, you are correct. I understand Sol's interest in you a little better now. You will have to show me how you did that."

How I did what? I thought. I had a dream, he was in it. But how much of a dream was it when he turned out to be *real?*

"What are you doing here?" I asked. "What do you want?"

Petrus gave a little bow. "Consider me your escort," he said. "I am here to take you to Sol."

"How can I trust you? You killed all those men," I pointed to the officers in

314

the outer room.

Petrus laughed again. "No, I did not."

"Then who did?"

"No one, John. Please. Just because I have *power* does not make me *mad* with it. These men will wake up in a few hours." Petrus even rolled his eyes at me. I immediately didn't like him.

"Okay, fine. But why should I go with you?"

Again, a scoff. "You will do as you wish, John," he said. "But I have been waiting for you, monitoring the police bands. As you can imagine, finding you was big news. But you're trying to find *Sol.* And he has dampened his sound. You know the sound I mean?"

"His beacon?" I answered before stopping to consider that maybe I shouldn't.

Petrus wrinkled his brow, considering. "Beacon?" He gave a smirk and a little nod. "Yes, that's a decent name for it. Yet, now it is gone, correct? Or mostly so." This time I nodded. "No matter. If you come with me, I will take you to him. Then, what happens between the two of you is your business and his. Again, consider me your escort." Even trying to sound pleasant, there was a tinge of something in Petrus's voice. Anger? Bitterness?

"And if I refuse?"

Petrus shrugged. "Your sister — Holly, correct? — she is with Sol now. If you refuse, then I suppose you may never see her again." He didn't sound terribly concerned, either way.

Involuntarily, my fists clenched. I was damned, no matter what I chose. Somehow I'd hoped my time on the road not only would lead me to Sol but also would help me come up with some sort of plan. Then, finding him on my own, I could assess the situation before making a move.

315

But without the beacon, I'd been flying blind, unsure of where to go. I either rejected Petrus's offer and kept flailing, probably never getting anywhere, or I accepted and let him deliver me to Sol like a package in the mail, practically gift-wrapped.

I couldn't let Holly down.

"Let's go," I said, picking up my backpack and walking past Petrus through the outer room, not even looking back to see if he was following.

11

A nondescript four-door sedan was waiting for us in the parking lot. Petrus slid behind the wheel and unlocked the passenger side for me.

"I think you'll find this slightly more efficient than walking," he said, giving me a sideways glance.

I tossed my pack in the back seat and got in, and within minutes we were on the main road. We drove in silence. I noticed from the road signs that we were heading north. *I was going completely the wrong way.* If nothing else, at least that made me feel vindicated for choosing to go with Petrus.

Miles flew by before he decided to try to break the ice. "Tell me about yourself, John Black," Petrus said.

"No."

"You are an angry one, it seems."

I turned to face him. "Why should I tell you anything about me?" I said. "You've been waiting for me, you're with Sol, and he knows enough about me. You probably know *a lot* about me." Petrus made a little smirk that told me I was right. "But I don't know anything about *you*."

"Not true, John. You know my name. How is that?"

I remained silent, thinking the less he knew, the better. Besides, he might laugh if I told him I'd had a dream about him.

"As you like it," Petrus said. "I will tell you something about myself, then. You've already gathered my name, somehow. Do you know where I am from, as well, John?" I shook my head. "Ah. Well, I am originally from Indonesia — do you know of Indonesia?" This time I nodded. Bunch of islands in Southeast Asia. "But as you might suspect, I have not been there for some time. I have been living in a small city to the north, just a couple of hundred miles from your own hometown, for the past, hmm, 10 years or so. I came to this country to go to college, then graduate school. I have a master's degree in mathematics, but do you want to guess what I was doing for a living before my powers came to me?"

I shrugged. "Solving math problems, I guess."

"Hardly. The most complex math problems I faced on a daily basis were what change to give my fares. I drove a taxi cab, John." Then Petrus laughed again. "I suppose I am doing so again, right now. Will you be able to pay the fare at the end of our trip together? I wonder."

In the other lane, a police car crested a hill in front of us, heading in our direction. Although I knew Petrus was my only way of getting to Sol and helping Holly, I secretly wanted him to be seen. But of course, Petrus had powers, too. I sensed him concentrating, calmly directing his mind toward the officer about to pass us.

And the patrol car sped by without so much as a second glance. Barring a miracle, there was no way anyone would spot us along our drive.

"You know how that was done, yes, John?"

"Yes. It's easy."

"Well, I am glad you think so. So your abilities lean toward the mind, is that correct?"

"Hard to say, actually. I'm pretty good in a fight, too." I was being a jerk. I don't think there were any ground rules saying I had to be nice.

"You see, John? I get to learn more about you all the time." Okay, Petrus was being a jerk, too. "Where was I? Ah, yes, I drove a taxi. It was not something I desired to do, I can assure you. With no offense to some of the very nice drivers I met and became friends with, I wanted to be a professor of mathematics. I applied to every university and college I could, but there was nothing available. Or, when a decent job was open, someone else got it. I was feeling quite disheartened by the whole 'American Dream,' you see. I spent a lot of time by myself, stewing over these disappointments, wondering if the future held any brightness at all. And one day, a bitter cold winter's day, I remember returning to my apartment and wishing all of my bad fortunes would just go away. Do you know what happened then, John?"

"You won the lottery?" Staring out the window at the passing miles, I listened to Petrus's story only because there was nothing else to do. Though I have to admit there was a part of me that was curious how *others* came to be the way that I was. Not everyone got hit by a car.

"Ha. No, not in the way you mean, but in another, more profound way, yes. Yes, I really did win the lottery. As did you, it would seem. I was sitting in front of a small table, and as I made my wish, the table was pushed away from me, by my mind. It moved several feet, so it was not simply my imagination at play. I am no *dukun*, though I have known a few during my life — a dukun is like a shaman, a sort of healer or even sorcerer, where I come from. In any event, the idea of mystical powers is not so foreign for my people. I didn't know what I had done to awaken the powers within me, but I quickly accepted it as real and something I could control. With practice, I realized I could move objects, control minds. It was really quite an amazing time. I am sure you must have gone through something similar."

319

"Yup," I said, feigning that I was ignoring him, when truly I was fascinated. His powers had just come to him. Maybe his disappointment with life was the catalyst he needed. My car accident, it seemed, was a significantly more dramatic jump-start. Somehow I knew that if I looked at Petrus's cells under a microscope, I'd find those little thorns. And I had my theory about where the thorns came from, and how we had all become hosts for some alien parasite. I considered saying all this to Petrus, but again opted for silence. I wasn't ready to play any of my cards just yet. After a long pause, though, I did realize I had one question. "But how did you end up with Sol?"

"Well, I think everyone saw him on television, probably worldwide. As soon as I did, I knew he was like me, had powers. In fact, he seemed *more* powerful. Then I felt the… *beacon*, as you call it, and I knew I wanted to follow it. No question. If he could help me tap more of my inner strength, I could become, well, really, whatever I wanted. No more sitting at home angry over no future. I had an opportunity to become the future, and I took it. I followed his beacon and found him in the capital. It was like fate." Petrus then gave me a long, slow look. At the time, I had no idea what it meant. But I found out soon after. Very, very soon after. "I was the first, John. The first to join Sol. You could say I am sort of his right hand-man. Or his top lieutenant. Which is of course why he chose me for the very important job of bringing you to him."

It was a total lie.

12

Rolling along highways I'd never seen before, we kept going, generally north.

After a while, I grew bored — even more bored than when I first started looking out the window, trying to tune Petrus out — and did what kids generally do on long car rides. I began to fade off to sleep. Several times I jerked my head up, willing myself to stay awake, not trusting Petrus one bit. But I had been sleeping in a makeshift hammock in trees. In comparison, the soft fabric of the car seat was too much. In time, I was out.

I fell into another dream. Not as clear or lifelike as before, but it felt real nonetheless. I was in a desert, vast and empty. No, not quite empty.

Petrus appeared before me. "This way," he said.

There was a dark form on the horizon, and we began to walk toward it. It may have been a mirage, because we never seemed to get closer. The shape was always just a black dot on the edge of our vision. Still, we kept walking.

Petrus didn't say another word, didn't even turn around. He just walked. I followed.

Above us, the hot sun sat locked in perpetual noon, scorching the land. Although it was a dream, I swear I could feel myself wilting under the harsh glare, wishing for two things over and over: to reach the dark object on the horizon, and to block out the sun.

Forever later, a voice called from behind me. I turned.

Sol was there, far in the distance. "Where are you going, John?" he said.

Confused, I stood motionless, the heat shimmering in waves off every surface. The image of Sol wavered, then disappeared.

Too close, Petrus's voice shattered the silence. "What makes *you* so special?" Turning back, I found him standing right next to me. Slowly he raised one open hand toward me.

I wanted to run, but I couldn't. I wanted to keep his hand away from me.

I felt an itch. Something inside me. Something that I didn't want there. But still, I felt I could do nothing.

I pulled inward, wishing for it to stop, to simply go away. Outwardly, I huddled down on the sand of the desert, hands coming over my head to protect me from... what?

Just as I retreated into myself, an object caught my eye. Somehow I knew immediately that it was the object that had forever been on the horizon, and it was suddenly quite near, quite clear.

A wheelchair.

An empty wheelchair.

The itch continued inside my mind, but it was inconsequential compared to what I saw. The wheelchair was empty. My sister was gone.

"No!" I shouted in my dream. The Petrus in front of me flinched, his hand no longer pointing to me, instead holding one side of his head. I screamed: "Get out!"

I woke up just as the car swerved violently, across the double-yellow line, just missing a passing car, into the wrong lane, then past that, to the far shoulder. Soon we would careen into the line of trees that flanked the road. We were moving fast, so I knew the impact would be bad. I braced myself.

Beside me, Petrus's head lolled toward the steering wheel, then suddenly jerked up. He slammed the wheel right and regained the road. As luck would have it, traffic was sparse and Petrus got us back in the northbound lane without further incident.

What was that? I thought. But I knew what I had felt. That itch. Petrus had been in my mind while I was sleeping. Had he pushed some idea there? Would I even know if he did? What if I'd just become his puppet?

No, I didn't think I'd have those sorts of thoughts if he'd gained control. After all, I assumed the first thing he'd do would be to push my mind to trust him, and I still didn't.

Trying to act like nothing happened, Petrus looked over and gave a weak smile. "Everything all right, John?"

Oh sure, everything's fine. You just tried to take control of my mind. But it didn't work, you bastard. "Stay out of my head," I told him.

His eyes remained on the road ahead.

13

Petrus drove through the night, only stopping once for gas and a quick visit for both of us to the restroom. Yes, even people with superpowers have to pee. Still being a complete juvenile, I had a vision of facing off with Sol only to have to ask for a potty break, which made me crack a little smile that unfortunately Petrus noticed.

"Is something funny?" he asked. I just shook my head. "You know, John, there are a lot of things we could teach you. That *I* could teach you. You'll see."

"So I've heard, but since I got in this car, the only thing you tried to do is push my mind while I was asleep."

Petrus shrugged. "It's true. And I suppose I owe you an apology for that." That was the last he had to say on the subject, which I don't think counts as actually making the apology. "You have said you can make people do as you wish with your mind."

"Yes," I said.

"And can you move objects?"

"Yes, of course," I lied.

He gave me a quick look, which made me think he saw right through my lie. *Well, I can. Sometimes. By accident.*

"Tell me how you knew my name. Who told you? Was it Bobby? Did he speak to you about me, or about any of us?"

"Not by name, no."

"Hmm. Then Sol mentioned me?" Petrus sounded a little too eager, like a puppy seeking its master's attention.

So, of course, I toyed with him. "Oh, definitely not."

He hid it well, but I think he was a little crestfallen by my response. *Take that*, I thought.

"Then how?"

"You really need to know so bad?" I asked.

"John, I think very soon you and I will come to an agreement, a resolution of our viewpoints, so to speak. My question is merely curiosity. If you join the fold, we all work together, learn from each other. If you do not..." He turned up one empty palm.

"You told me," I said.

"*I* told you?" Petrus asked. "How so?"

I admit I completely and utterly lied, trying to upset him. He'd tried to push my mind, and I wasn't about to forget it. Despite his talk of my 'joining the fold,' we weren't on the same team, and nothing would change that. So, I lied.

"When you walked up, your mind revealed your name to me." It sounded like a lie coming out, mostly because I knew it wasn't true. Of course, the truth — that it came to me in a dream — didn't sound terribly plausible either.

Petrus considered what I said, trying to make sense of it. Which was probably hard to do since it wasn't a sensible statement in the first place. "Like, what?" he finally said. "Like picking up a radio broadcast? Or like I was speaking only to you?" I didn't answer, but he seemed to ponder my silence, like he was working out a complex math problem. "Interesting. Perhaps it is a bit like the sound you call the beacon?" As he drove on, his brow was furrowed and the fingers of his right hand twitched on the steering wheel. This went on for some time until at last he stopped with a little *huh*, like he had come to a conclusion that satisfied his curiosity. The rising sun was just beginning to color the sky pink and orange to my right, between the passing trees.

Petrus's foot eased off the accelerator as we approached an intersection. "Well, I think we are finally here," he said, a broad smile breaking across his face. As he slowed to pull onto a small side road, I sat upright, tension stiffening me into rigid iron when only moments before I'd been slouched and lazy.

"He's here? Sol?" I asked, sounding more scared than I had hoped.

"Oh, yes. Very close now." Petrus kept smiling. He was enjoying it all, my nervousness, my fear.

Another turn had us on a one-lane road, dense trees lining both sides. I sat quietly, straining my vision forward, hoping to see *him* before he saw *me*. As if that would help at all. No doubt Petrus had already alerted Sol to our arrival.

Still, the beacon was absent. I didn't sense him in any direction, and certainly couldn't tell that we were any closer than before. I could still feel Petrus's odd beacon, like a low musical note, if I tuned myself to listen. But the strong beacon I had followed, Sol's beacon, was nowhere to be found.

Petrus pulled the car to a stop in a small parking lot with a wooden sign at the far end, so I grabbed my backpack and got out. Without ceremony, Petrus headed toward the sign. As we approached, I read the words carved into it: WIDOW FALLS TRAIL.

"What's this?" I asked.

"This," Petrus said, "is where we need to go." He proceeded to the trail, which led down into the woods. The sun had yet to reach us on its slow rise, so Petrus was quickly engulfed in the gloom beneath the trees. I followed with haste, so I wouldn't lose sight of him. I was in foreign waters, and even Petrus's back was an oddly familiar, comforting sight.

We walked down the twisting path, Petrus seeming to know the way by heart while I had to keep a sharp eye out for rocks and roots. Here and there I slid on some unseen bit of gravel or a patch of wet leaves as we descended.

Through switchback after switchback, we went deeper. I could hear the distant hiss and bubble of a river, the even more distant low bass rumble of a waterfall.

I reached out with all of my senses, trying to figure out where Sol was, willing myself to see or hear or even smell something to help me. There was Petrus's beacon, and it was slowly blending, changing into a musical chord that seemed familiar, but Sol's clear, strong beacon remained silent.

Something came to me. An agitation. *Holly's here? Down here?* I tried to imagine her wheelchair on the treacherous path, but couldn't. The distinct sense that something was wrong grew inside me. *I've got to be very careful. And ready for anything.* This thought, rooted in my concentration on Holly, may be what saved my life.

Finally, we reached the bottom. The deep sound of water thundering down was near. Another short loop around a large fall of rocks and we came to the end: the waterfall itself.

Widow Falls was bigger than any falls I'd ever seen, maybe over 100 feet tall. It was an amazing sight, and given that we had climbed down in virtual darkness, not another soul was visible. We were alone.

Alone.

"So, where are they?" I asked, panting from the hike.

Petrus turned back to me. "It would be unwise of us to reveal everything all at once, would you not agree, John? Especially after the *incident* back at the capital, your little trickery?"

I shrugged, supposing he had a point. "Then, what? Where's Sol? What now?"

"In time, John," Petrus said. "For now, tell me what you know of Sol and the rest of us."

"Why should I do that?"

"Only because we have time to pass, and this knowledge interests me."

I still felt that keeping my cards close was the best plan, but mostly due to nerves, I spoke. "You've told me more about yourself than I ever knew before. But I know there are others. Bobby, of course. I know him very well. Or at least, I thought I did." A grimace of anger overcame my face, but I paused to regain some degree of composure. "There's a blond woman, too. And a redhead."

Petrus's eyes widened just the slightest amount, but I could tell that he was surprised. Maybe stunned. "Interesting. Go on."

"I know you all train together, trying to get better at using your powers. I know that you're... *connected*... now, almost like a network. And that Sol's the leader."

"Tell me what you know of *power*."

"You all have it. Some of you are better with physical powers, some with mental—"

"No, not that power, John. *Power*. Authority. Hierarchy. Mankind's ultimate process of deciding the survival of the fittest. Tell me what you know of that."

I stood confused for a moment. "I don't know what you mean."

"Exactly, John. You have *no idea* what I mean." Petrus turned away, taking in a long breath, then spun back to begin his sermon. "Power is *all there is*, John. Every single human on Earth has some amount. The lowliest, the ones with the least power, are the newborn infants. What can they do? On their own, they would starve and die. They are completely dependent on the goodwill of other humans. And at the very, very top, there is a human who needs no one else, who can bend any person to his will, have anything, do anything, be anything. Do you know who that person is, John?"

"I can only assume you mean Sol."

Petrus smirked. Not a smile, not a grimace. A smirk. "Perhaps. Sol is very, very powerful indeed. You, too, have great powers, as does Bobby, as do the others, and, humbly, even I." He made a disingenuous little bow. "Sol tells us that we each have weaknesses, flaws. He tells us that *together* we can rule the world, a sort of *network*, as you say." With one hand, Petrus made a series of little gestures, like putting pins on a map. His whole performance reminded me of Sol talking his head off back at General Tulloch Park. Clearly, Petrus had been taking notes. "As I told you, I once sought to be a professor of mathematics, so it should come as no surprise that I prefer to do my own analysis of situations. Solve my own problems. If for no other reason than to 'check the math,' as they say."

"And what does your math tell you?"

"A wonderful question, John, and actually one that even Sol has never asked me. *My math* tells me that, although there *is* strength in numbers, a network is only as strong as its weakest link. Infiltrate the network at the weakest link, and it is *possible* that the network will fail."

"Like a virus," I said, mostly to myself.

"Correct, John. *That* is what's wrong with Sol's idea."

"So what's the solution?"

"Well," Petrus said, clearly enjoying the attention to his ideas. "I myself prefer a *closed system.*"

"What, you mean a single person with all the power?"

Petrus shook off the question, changing the subject. "Not quite. Do you know how Sol's network works, John?"

"Like a radio, sort of. Or at least that's how I think of it. But, hold on, when you say a *closed* system, what happens to the rest of us?"

He ignored my question. "Radio, yes. That's a good analogy. Can you try to reach out for that signal, John? You know, like tuning in a radio station?"

"I haven't felt Sol's beacon for a while now."

"No, not Sol's. Mine. Just try."

"But you didn't answer my question. What about the rest of us?"

Petrus waved a hand. "Just try to find the radio station, the one that is me. In your head, John."

I sighed, but decided to try. I didn't trust Petrus enough to close my eyes around him again, although I was still tired from the long, mostly sleepless drive the night before. The sun was just beginning to dapple down through the leaves, and I tried.

I tried to tune the radio in my head.

By opening my mind to what was out there. Like opening all the windows and doors in a house, trying to catch a breeze on a hot day.

For a moment, just the tiniest moment, I felt something. Not the blaring beacon I'd felt before, but something like little lights in my mind. Some were very far away. One was right in front of me. I understood in some way that these were the radio towers — the people with power. The one in front of me, of course, was Petrus. I honed in on him, his radiating beacon.

And that's when I fell to my knees, a pain like hot metal stabbing into my brain.

Taking the wide-open opportunity I'd given him, Petrus was trying to kill me.

14

I kept falling. Not just to my knees, but all the way down to the ground, sprawled flat on my back.

Near the base of Widow Falls, with the beauty of the morning sun glinting off a hundred thousand water droplets spraying through the air, I writhed in pain. Everything faded to white. Nothing but blinding white. The bone-shivering bass sound of the crashing waterfall disappeared into nothing but a single high-pitched note, a whine like ears ringing.

I was dying.

The white light, the white noise. The searing pain that felt like it would cut my mind in two.

I never even made it to Sol. I'm sorry, Mom. I'm sorry, Holly. My last conscious thoughts.

I gulped at the air, a fish on dry land. Twisting into a ball on the ground, I made myself as small as I could.

Involuntarily, I did the same in my mind, curling my thoughts, my awareness into a ball. Tighter, ever tighter. A solid ball. Tension was the only thing there was, other than pain. The twisting tension of the ball getting smaller, smaller.

Still the white light, the white noise, the searing pain continued. In moments, I would break and everything would be still. The thought of the coming release eased the tension somewhat. I was letting go. I think I was letting go of life.

Then, the tension inside me resumed, and amplified, like it wouldn't permit the release. Like it would transform me into a ball of iron despite my desire to give up. It was my power, and its bone-deep instinct for self-preservation. I curled, inside and out, more and more.

Finally, the ball was solid. I was iron, of body and mind.

An iron ball with a blade of sheer fire piercing the center, the source of all pain.

Then the blade pushed deeper.

And the iron refused.

The blade pushed deeper still.

And the iron refused.

The blade burned stronger, hotter, a fire like the sun burrowing inside the ball of iron, pushing beyond all resistance.

And the iron refused.

The blade's fire dimmed, unable to maintain its fury. Unsure, the blade pulled back.

And the iron refused.

The blade became frantic. Now it was trapped, unable to pull away. It thrashed left and right, pushing in again, pulling back again.

And, against all attempts, the iron refused.

The iron tensed once more, and twisted inward one final time. And, as the iron wound into the tightest, most impossibly compressed ball, the blade inside it snapped.

Seething and boiling in the remains of the blade's fire, the iron turned to liquid metal and raged upward along the length of the broken weapon, following its path back. Unraveling and untwisting, the tension released into a molten bolt.

I uncurled on the ground and slowly stood. I was the liquid metal. Petrus, the broken blade. My anger, my heat, my *power*, followed the line of his blade to the very core of his mind.

"Oh my" was the last thing Petrus ever said.

We faced each other, and the deadly thrust of my attack exploded within him, not just breaking his mind but cauterizing it, leaving it a burned, useless husk.

The man, the being, the body named Petrus lived on, still standing right in front of me. But the mind, the mathematician, the object of power died in that instant, burned away for all eternity. The body took a step forward, stumbled, and fell onto its face, a drooling shell.

"No!" came a woman's shriek from somewhere behind me. A form rushed past as I teetered on my wobbly legs, exhausted from the burning power.

I was no longer iron, no longer liquid metal.

I was John Black. Still a 14-year-old boy. And I was tired. So tired.

Like peering through a distant lens, I saw the tall blond woman rush to Petrus, reaching for him, wailing, cradling him with her arms, lifting his limp body. "No!" she cried again.

I know this woman, I thought. *Margrethe.* It came as no surprise that she was real, the woman I had seen in my dream. After all, Petrus was real.

The flash of her golden hair reminded me of my last meeting with Bobby. Being trapped, being knocked out. Overhearing the conversation in the dark between Bobby and two other people. A man and woman. Petrus and Margrethe. I was sure of it. Sol's army had come to life. But there must be some conflict among them, some descent into factions.

Why did Petrus try to kill me? I thought, in the milliseconds that passed as I watched Margrethe rock his mindless body. *Was he just doing what Sol told him to?* That didn't seem right. I thought of Petrus talking about power just before he attacked me. And it hit me. *This is his closed system. Just him and Margrethe.* Seeing how she cradled him, I realized. *They... they were partners.* I imagined they had become close, become a couple, during their days training with Sol.

And if Petrus and Margrethe were a closed system, that meant...

That meant they wanted to get rid of any competition. Including Sol. And Bobby.

And me.

I had allowed myself to be led to the slaughter.

And, although I had defeated one enemy, another one sat right before me. I thought about my dream, what I knew about Margrethe. *She was amazing with physical skills. A karate chop that could cut down a tree.*

I was tired. No, exhausted. If she attacked, I wouldn't even be able to defend myself, not after what I'd done to Petrus.

Adjusting my backpack, I stumbled headlong into the woods. Anywhere to get away from her.

Behind me, there was a horrible scream of anger, despair, and vengeance. I expected to be struck down at any moment, so I dodged left and right as I ran, ducking behind trees, making my way on an irregular path.

I thought of the network, the way our minds might find each other, and I thought of the iron ball I'd just become. Not the liquid metal of attack, but the iron of defense. I imagined thick metal forming a wall to block the signal, to block those little lights I'd seen in my mind — or, an even worse possibility, my own beacon. The idea that I had a beacon now terrified me. I needed radio silence.

My body buckled countless times as I ran, and I nearly fell. I dropped to a knee once, but fought to regain my feet. Slowly I rounded a large outcropping of rock and began to make my way up, up, away from the waterfall's basin.

Somewhere behind me, I heard a voice. A male voice. "He's gone this way!" the voice shouted. "Come on!" *That sounds like Bobby. Son of a bitch, he's helping her, too!*

Another voice, female. Margrethe. Some kind of argument. I couldn't make it out. Thankfully, it sounded distant.

I ran harder, with all my remaining energy, still following a zigzag path, trying to give no sense of a pattern, no indication of where I was going as long as I got farther away.

But I was so tired. Each step was agony, and my mind was spent trying to keep up the wall of silence. I pushed myself to the absolute brink, getting as far away as I could.

Finally, I spied a large tree that had fallen, pulling up a huge circle of roots. Where the tree once stood, a deep and dark opening now beckoned. I tumbled in with my last bit of strength, putting my back against the upturned roots and dirt. At least I'd be facing them when they found me. I was covered in sweat and mud, embedded in the wet clay of the hole in the ground. I sat tensed, waiting to be discovered, knowing I couldn't do anything when it happened.

Almost instantly, I fell asleep.

* * *

When I awoke, the sunlight still dappled the branches. Had no time passed? No, that wasn't right. Hours had gone by. It must have been near sunset.

Blinking, I looked around. A small red fox stood just a few yards away, staring at me like I was an alien dropped from space. I looked back into its eyes, unsure what to do. Was it a threat? Despite all that had happened, I laughed out loud. "Shoo," I said, waving a hand, and the fox bounded off into the underbrush. *A threat? Hardly.*

I thought about Petrus with a mix of difficult emotions. I had no love for him, that was sure, and I knew he had brought everything on himself. But I had emptied him. Destroyed the life of another human being. And now I had to live with that. I was still just a boy, in so many ways. I sat with tears stinging in my eyes for a while.

Finally, the tears were spent. I'd done what I had to do. And there was more to do. Sol was still out there, somewhere, with Holly.

I leaned forward and pulled off my backpack, then fumbled through it, pulling something from the bottom.

The flip phone Bobby had left me.

Sitting on the damp ground, I dialed the number Sol had used to contact me before.

He answered on the first ring. "John, is it you?"

"Yeah, it's me."

"To what do I owe this pleasure, John? I had begun to think you weren't coming, after all."

"Where's Holly?" I asked.

"She is still here with me, still quite safe, I assure you."

"She better be," I said. "And where are you?"

"Oh, I think you know, John. You and I have always been going in the

338

same general direction. Think about it."

I grimaced, having no idea what he meant. "Fine. But listen. I don't think it's all peace and happiness with your little army."

"Oh? And what do you mean by that, John?"

"Petrus. And Margrethe. They tried to kill me."

Sol chuckled. That damned chuckle. "Ah, so you all have met. That's wonderful. And you are still alive, so despite their disregard for my orders, all is well, it seems. I can deal with Petrus and Margrethe in time. We'll all come together. You'll see."

"Well, maybe not all of us, Sol."

"You're still holding out. I know, John."

"Yes, but not just that. Petrus."

"What of Petrus?"

"He's done."

"What does that mean, John?"

"It means that he tried to kill me, but instead, he got what he deserved. He isn't dead, but he isn't going to be any use to you anymore. His mind is gone." I felt both elation and deep sorrow describing what I'd done.

There was a long pause on the other end of the line.

"Good, John," Sol finally said. "Very, very good."

PART FIVE

DUSK

KEITH SOARES

1

I stole again, something I hadn't done since my trip to the capital. I'm not proud of it. But I had to. I was darn near starving.

I walked into a roadside convenience store, gathered a basket full of the most nutritious food I could find, avoiding too much salty-snack crap and opting for things with at least a smidgeon of protein. And three bags of chips. Hey, I'm not perfect.

The place was deserted except for the cashier, so I just walked out without a word, stuffing everything into my backpack as I left. Of course, I had to do a little mind push. That was the stealing part.

I was alone in whatever strange place Petrus had driven me, and there was no beacon to follow. The only thing I had to go on was Sol's insistence that I should know where to go. Only... I didn't.

Now that Petrus's northbound train had derailed, I was back to traveling west. Wandering down a two-lane street for a while, I wasn't even terribly concerned that I might get picked up by the police. I was sure the manhunt continued, but Petrus had driven me many, many hours north. I'd have to stay cautious, but I suspected the majority of those looking for me would be centered around the police station where I'd last been seen — the one where a bunch of cops had been left unconscious on the floor, possibly dead — and then spreading in an ever-growing circle from there. And I was still exhausted, and scared that Margrethe would appear at any moment. By this time, she was cemented in my mind as a Norse god of vengeance come to life.

I devoured a bag of chips, then tore into a granola bar, washing them down with a bottle of blissfully non-garden-hose water. The bottle said it was pure spring water from France. Hell, maybe that was the sign I was looking for. Maybe Sol was in France. I laughed bitterly to myself as a car drove by, the driver ignoring me. I was just some kid walking home, a little dirtier than most, but so what?

The pack was heavy on my back, but despite how it weighed me down, that felt good. It meant I wouldn't starve, at least. I might have superhuman abilities, but starving was starving.

Cresting a hill, I looked down the nearly straight line of the road, seeing it enter a small town. *I'll have to go around*, I thought. Staying just inside the tree line that surrounded the town's outlying buildings, I skirted the congested areas until I came to something that stopped me cold.

A self-storage building.

Pods, for heaven's sake. Wow. It wasn't eight stories high, like the one Bobby and I used to call Mount Trashmore, but still. The memories flooded back.

More than anything, I thought it might be a safe place to hide and get some rest. Wondering if this place had the same level of lax security I'd come to know from Mr. Gerald, I tried a side entrance. It didn't pop right open, but it didn't take all that long for me to power through it, either. I was inside.

The building was only one story. In a corner there was a ladder next to a sign reading ROOF ACCESS. I didn't see an elevator. Without one, I suspected the roof had few visitors, since it would be near impossible to get pods up there. The occasional maintenance man was likely to be the only person to ever use the ladder, which meant a pretty high percentage chance I'd have the place to myself. So I climbed up, popped open a little hatch, and crawled out onto the roof.

It was late afternoon, the sun drawing long shadows on the flat roof. I made sure to close the hatch, so I wasn't advertising my presence. Then I sat on the rough tar surface, still warm from the day, and had a little picnic of pre-packaged food, just a bit more, rationing. Afterward, I propped my back against a short wall and watched the sun go down. I was asleep before the light was gone.

* * *

"You're predictable," came the voice that woke me.

Bobby?

I opened my eyes. It was him. I tensed, rolling back against the wall, raising my hands in front of me defensively. "Stay back!" I said, too strong, sounding too afraid. I felt defenseless, caught in yet another trap.

Bobby raised his own hands, and I braced for an attack. But he held his open palms out toward me, a gesture of peace. "Hold on, hold on," he said. "I'm not here to do anything except say what I've gotta say."

I sat up and pushed into the wall, levering my body into a standing position. "And what the hell exactly is that?" I said. "Sol told me all about your *ideas*, Bobby. That you were the one to suggest kidnapping my sister."

At the sound of my words, Bobby sagged and fell, like his bones had turned to soup. He dropped onto the roof with a thud, crossing his legs and sitting in one fluid motion. His hands came up to his head and his body shook.

For a long moment, I stood tensed, waiting for... something other than what I was seeing. I didn't know what sort of ploy or tactic Bobby was trying, but I was ready.

Then, finally, I realized: He was crying.

All of a sudden, I felt like a regular 14-year-old kid. I had no idea what to do. The weight of everything, the conflict, the power, the confrontation awaiting me, disappeared for a moment, and I went to my friend. My best friend.

"Bobby?" It was all I could think to say.

He looked up with wet eyes. "I'm *sorry*, Johnny. *Really, really* sorry. It *was* my idea, and I hate myself for thinking of it. I'll hate myself forever about it. Sol is just so…" Trying to think of his next word, Bobby gave up, throwing his hands in the air, exasperated.

"Did he force you?"

"No. And that's the thing. He *didn't* force me. It's all my fault. I… I just fell under his spell, sort of, you know? He's, I don't know, so…"

"Charismatic," I said.

"Huh, what's that?" Bobby wasn't the best student, if you recall.

"It means he's extremely charming, makes you feel good being around him. You want to do things for him, and you want to do what he says."

Slowly, Bobby nodded. "Yeah, all that, for sure. And maybe he has a way to push our minds a little, too. But it's my fault. The idea came to me and I just said it. I never thought through how *real* it would be. Especially for Holly."

At that, I lunged forward, grabbing Bobby by the collar. "Is she okay? She'd better be okay. Is she scared? Hurt?"

"Yeah, yeah, I mean, no. Both. Yes, she's okay. I don't know if she's scared or not, but she isn't hurt. Most of the time, Sol keeps her calm with TV, makes sure she has whatever she likes to eat. She likes cereal a lot. And sometimes mac 'n' cheese. She definitely doesn't like orange juice, though. Sol gave that to her one time and she spit it all over him."

I stepped back, looking Bobby in the eye. And, despite the tears, he cracked a smile. I couldn't help it, so did I. "She spit OJ in Sol's face?"

"Like a freakin' citrus fountain," Bobby said.

I fell onto my butt, suddenly cackling. Bobby's smile erupted into full-on laughter, too, and then we couldn't stop. Two kids, laughing our asses off, crying from laughing so hard. When it started to die down, a single chuckle would escape from one of us and we'd be back at it.

Of course, the joke wasn't all that funny. It was what it *meant*. Even in the middle, when I could barely breathe, I knew one thing.

I was glad to have my friend back.

KEITH SOARES

2

We walked side by side down mostly empty back roads. Both of us knew people might be looking for me, but the landscape we wandered through seemed deserted so it wasn't hard to duck behind a tree when the odd car went past.

Bobby was quiet, we both were. Could I really trust him? Or was Bobby leading me into a trap? Like Petrus, in a way. No, I could feel Bobby's relief. He was glad to be free of Sol. And I could feel his genuine guilt over what he'd done to my family, to Holly. But there was something else.

Underneath, Bobby seemed angry. At himself. At Sol. Below the surface, I felt a quiet resolve. Bobby wanted to finish this, too. To make things right.

After miles of walking, I realized that I actually felt bad for Bobby. Yes, the same Bobby who'd given Sol the idea to kidnap my sister. But really, here I was, on the lam, police everywhere looking for me. Same with Holly. All-points bulletins and such.

What about Bobby? Was anyone looking for him? Hell, were his own *parents* looking for him? Knowing what I knew of them, my guess was no. They were probably sitting back, letting inertia have its way with them. Or worse, actively arguing with each other that *you* should call the cops, no, *you* should. Then sitting and watching their nightly mind-numbing game shows and crappy sitcoms all the same. I mean, how many kids are there just like Bobby every day? They disappear and no one cares. People just let them go. Let them disappear forever.

I realized *I* was the anomaly. Me and Holly. Someone actually gave a crap about finding us. We were lucky. Really, really lucky.

Even though I really didn't want to be found again. Not yet, at least. Maybe not ever, for me. Holly was the important one. I had to get her back to my mom, no matter what it meant for me.

But who knew what that might be? Walking beside Bobby, I started to have a different attitude about myself and my chances against Sol. All along, I'd assumed that I'd be the sacrificial lamb, and give up myself to save Holly. But with Bobby on my side... was something more possible? I began to hang all hope on the two of us, working together, riding in to save the day. Maybe I believed Bobby partly because I felt I need him. Two against one.

Assuming that no one was with Sol anymore. Which was a really big and highly unlikely assumption.

Still we walked. For a long while, we just followed the road, no idea where it was taking us.

"Are we going the right way?" I finally asked.

"To get to Sol? As far as I know, yes," Bobby said. "I know he's headed west. You were at least right about that part. But that's all I know. I have no idea when he'll stop, or if he'll stop, or where." We trudged on. "Sol said you'd know where to find him?" Bobby asked. I nodded. "How?"

I just shrugged. "He didn't tell you? Weren't you, like, part of the gang?"

"Yeah, but Sol's not like that. He doesn't say much about his intentions.

Likes the mystery or something."

"But west is definitely the way?" I asked.

"Yes. I mean, would I keep walking this way with you if it was completely pointless?" Bobby looked at me a moment before continuing. "Don't answer that."

The sun was rising behind us, so we were doing the best we could in terms of direction. "Okay, then," I said. "We keep going." I pointed a finger toward the horizon, hoping we were actually getting closer.

I had no idea how long Holly would last. Or how long Sol would wait for me.

* * *

"So he never told you anything?" I asked Bobby after a long, quiet stretch of walking.

"Huh?" Bobby tossed a stone into the low brush on the side of the road. "No, that's not it. He would tell us stuff, sure, just not his *plans*."

"Then what did he tell you?"

"Well, we were training. That was the whole idea. He would try to guide us, make us better."

I frowned. "That's one thing I don't understand." I kept my comet theory to myself, knowing Bobby wouldn't like talking about it. But I was still curious about how our powers developed. "How come Sol's so much better than the rest of us?"

Bobby shrugged. "Don't know. How come I'm good at taking a beating, but you can snap minds?" He looked sideways at me. "I saw what you did to Petrus."

My head hung. I would never be proud of what I'd done. "You knew him?"

"Yeah."

351

"I'm sorry for what I did."

Bobby patted me on the shoulder. "Nah, don't be. He was a dick."

We both laughed, but I couldn't sustain it, knowing that Petrus was still alive but essentially dead, because of me.

"But Sol did teach you things?" I asked, not sure what I expected him to say.

"Oh, yeah. He tried. I mean, most everything comes from inside you. You have to *get it*, you have to do it yourself. But it helps an awful lot to see what someone else has done, to emulate it, to hear *how* they do it."

The sound of a distant engine from behind sent us scurrying into a depression on the far side of the road. We waited as the car drove slowly past, just someone out for a leisurely drive through the country, it seemed. We started walking again when the road was clear.

"Have you learned how to move things with your mind?" Bobby asked.

I didn't answer at first, then turned the question around instead. "Have you?"

"Yeah. It was hard, though. Pretty much the opposite of what you'd expect to do."

"How so?" Remembering my lame attempts to move a pencil, I was curious.

"Well, you'd think you have to *force* your will onto whatever you want to move, command it to move. But it's... different."

"Go on." Did I seem too eager to hear this? I bet I did.

Bobby stopped walking, so I did, too. "Let's see." He looked around. "Okay, there. You see that large branch, the dry brown one by the pine on the right?" I nodded. And then Bobby made a simple sweeping gesture, and the branch flew across the road and into the woods on the other side.

"Whoa." That's all I could think to say.

Bobby grinned. He always did like to hit the next level, achieve the next goal, show off. Compared to my skills, Bobby might as well have been an illusionist making the Great Pyramid disappear. What he had just done was so advanced, it was like magic.

He made me wait a really long time. But finally he said, "I've gotta assume by your reaction that you don't know how to do that. Wanna learn?"

"You're damn right I do!"

* * *

An hour later, still walking west, I stopped again. "That's it?"

"Yeah," Bobby said, the proud smile on his face suddenly falling when he realized my mood. "What?"

"You're telling me that your big advice — after the amazing training you supposedly got from Sol and the others — was just one word? *Relax*. Are you kidding me?"

"No, Johnny, seriously." I started walking again and Bobby rushed to catch up. "Johnny?" I wouldn't stop, or even look at him, until finally he grabbed my arm and turned me around. "Johnny. *John*. What's the problem?"

"Don't you think I've tried that? Don't you think I've tried relaxing and clearing my mind and *everything*?"

"Actually, no. I don't."

"What's that supposed to mean?"

"Are you trying to move something now?" Bobby asked.

I stormed off again. "I should try to drop a rock on your head."

"Sure. It won't work."

"No shit it won't work, Bobby. That's what I'm trying to tell you!"

"Not because it's never worked before. Because you most certainly are *not* relaxed."

"Piss off," I said. It wasn't my most eloquent comeback.

"Seriously, Johnny. Calm down. Then try again."

So I stopped. Took a breath. Hell, I took 10 breaths. Closed my eyes. Imagined puppies. Thought about baseball. And then I opened my eyes again, spied a piece of paper — a scrap of discarded paper on the side of the road — and willed it to move.

Nothing.

"Piss off," I repeated, and walked off in a huff.

3

The next morning, I stretched, trying to work the kink out of my back put there by a walnut-sized stone I hadn't noticed when I went to sleep the night before. Despite the soreness, I was glad of two things: sleeping at night rather than during the day, and having someone with me.

I looked over at Bobby, who was still out cold, and couldn't help but smile. My friend, willing to come with me on a probable suicide mission.

I thought about my failure the day before. My inability to glean anything from the advice Bobby had given me. *Relax*. So much easier said than done, especially when you're a hormonal, super-powered kid heading toward your own certain doom.

But on this particular morning, fresh from sleep, I felt better. Calm, even. The woods were thick, so we'd been able to camp not far off the road. I looked up into the canopy of trees, the early light peeking through in bright dots. I heaved a sigh, not of frustration, but... was it contentment? I don't think so, but I was at peace, at least for the moment.

I stood up and turned around, then looked down at my filthy clothes, jeans torn, shoes clogged with dirt. Just beyond the toe of my right sneaker was the rock, the little one I must have slept on. My back called out in pain again, and I reached one hand back to massage the spot.

"Stinkin' rock. Go away," I said offhandedly, making a flicking gesture with my fingers.

And the rock flew off into the woods, cracking into the trunk of some tree.

The sound was enough to wake Bobby. "What was that?" he asked.

I didn't answer him. "Well, son of a bitch," I muttered to myself.

* * *

Walking all that day, I was practically in a Zen state. Utterly calm, in fact, nearly rapturous in my glee. I had a new skill! I felt like a videogame character who had just gained a power-up.

I flung rocks, tossed branches, flicked acorns, scattered pebbles. Over and over and over, a big smile on my face, as we walked on.

When we finally took a break, a few yards into the woods in case a car happened by, Bobby broke my joyful silence.

"Ready for the next step?" he asked.

"I actually think so, yes." It was a confidence in my powers that I hadn't felt before. I had *learned* something. That meant I might learn other things, too. "What?"

"Okay, so now you can move stuff, and that's great. But what about the opposite?"

"Huh?"

"I mean, can you make something *not* move?"

I thought about it. "I don't know," I said. "Do you do it the same way?" I asked.

Bobby made a wavy gesture with one hand. "Sort of. But there's more to it. When you push something away, you just push and that's it. It flies off, wherever you sent it. But when you want to *stop* something from moving, you have to pay more attention. Just because you stop something once doesn't mean it's gonna *stay* stopped."

"Makes sense," I said. "Let me try." I looked around, trying to find something that was moving. Other than branches slightly swaying in the light breeze, there was nothing. "Hmm."

"You need a target," Bobby said. "A person."

"The only person here is you."

"Exactly. Stop me." And he took off down the street, running away from me.

I was surprised, to say the least. But I thought I knew what do to. I took a long, calm breath, Bobby getting farther away with each moment. Then I reached out, willing him to *freeze*. For a split second Bobby hesitated. It looked almost like he had bumped into something. But he bounced off it, still running.

"You're going to have to hold me in place," he said over his shoulder. By this time he was a good distance away.

"Hold on!" I shouted at his back.

"No!" he said, sounding quite pleased. "You gotta make me stop." Still he ran. I think he may have been laughing.

I tried again, willing myself to hold on to the calm that had worked before, at least when it came to pushing objects around. I raised a hand toward him, closing a fist, visualizing him locked in place as if my fingers had grabbed him. And Bobby stopped. Mostly. I let out a short, triumphant laugh.

And he broke free and ran again.

"Not enough. You have to hold on!" His voice sounded awfully far away.

"Wait!" I ran toward him, feeling like I should close the distance. "Wait!" I was getting upset. I don't think that helped.

Bobby kept running. "Come on, Johnny. Keep trying!"

I came to a stop, panting. Once more I reached out my hand, virtually closing my fingers around him, willing him to *stop*, straining to hold on. But I was flustered, and my mind wasn't focusing. Bobby didn't so much as slow down. I dropped my hand to my side, my head tilting up to the sky in frustration.

After a moment, I looked back toward Bobby, who was still running. "Stop it already," I said, with a dismissive flick of my wrist.

And Bobby went sailing into the bushes on the side of the road.

I had tossed him aside, as if he were a rock or branch. "Oh crap," I said, running toward him, hoping I hadn't hurt him.

The bushes shook and Bobby stood up, laughing. "What the hell was that?" he asked.

"Sorry, Bobby. I —" I didn't know what to say.

"You couldn't stop me, so instead you threw me in the bushes?" He raised an eyebrow at me as he dusted himself off, and I looked down in embarrassment. Bobby walked over and clapped a hand on my shoulder. "Hey man, it's okay. I never taught anyone anything before. Maybe I'm just a crappy teacher." He laughed, bits of leaves and dirt still clinging to his cheeks, his hair, his clothes.

Soon I was laughing, too.

4

After promising Bobby I wouldn't throw him in front of a moving car or anything, we practiced the *stop* trick a few more times. The best I could do was slow him down. I could make it seem like he was running through deep mud for a little while. But I never got him to stop. Always the underachiever in these little competitions with Bobby, it seemed.

The next day, we awoke and set out west. But after a paltry breakfast — the stolen snacks in my backpack were going fast — I was in a foul mood. A half-hour later, I was standing motionless in the middle of the road.

"What's the matter with you today?" Bobby asked.

I was silent.

"Look, Johnny, you'll get it. The stop trick is just harder, that's all."

"It's not that," I said.

"Then what?"

I turned to Bobby, not angry with him, but still... *angry*. "Where are we going? West, every day, forever? How far west is he? Will we ever get there? Or did we already pass him?"

Bobby let me rant for a moment. Neither of us knew the answers, so there was no point saying anything that would just start an argument. The moment lingered, until Bobby finally spoke. "What exactly did he say to you? Can you remember?"

I rolled my head around in a circle, nothing if not overly dramatic. "I wasn't trying to memorize it, but I told you — he said I'd know where to go."

"Anything else? Anything at all?"

I thought about it, hard. "He said we were both *going in the same general direction*. But I don't know what that means, either, since he came from Playa Beach, south to the capital, and now somewhere west. I never planned to go west before all this."

"Keep thinking about it," Bobby said. I nodded. Figuring out Sol's location was about the only thing I thought of all day long already.

We plodded on, but our spirits dropped. The high of being back together waned after repetitive days in the hot summer sun. Even my joy at learning new skills was severely tempered by my failure to master the stop trick. We didn't talk much. We were nearly out of food. And we had no idea where Sol was. Hell, we didn't even know if we'd be able to find a convenience store to rob before we starved to death.

The following night, as we prepared to sleep, Bobby asked me what had happened between me and Petrus, and without thinking about it too much, I told him the whole story. How I'd first encountered Petrus at the police station, how he had taken me on that long drive, and finally how he'd attacked me.

"But, I knew Petrus," Bobby said. "He was pretty strong with his mind. How'd you do it?"

"I don't know. I was just trying to pull back into my own head, make myself small, and something happened."

"Could you do it again?"

"I don't know," I said. But I think even then I knew it was a lie. I had a terrible power inside. It scared me. Could I do it again? *Yeah, I think I could.*

One part of my story stuck with Bobby: the whole thing about me knowing Petrus's name before I'd actually met him, and knowing about Margrethe, too. "How did you know that stuff?" Bobby asked, both of us staring up at the stars.

I shrugged, about to hide in another lie before I figured there was no point. "Do you want to know the real truth?" Bobby nodded. "I had a dream. It was the night Holly disappeared." I could feel Bobby shift uncomfortably next to me at the mention of it. "I dreamed about you with Sol, and these others, and even me. All of us were training with Sol, doing little tests and stuff. Petrus was in the dream. So was Margrethe."

Bobby seemed confused. "But, how? I mean, other than you being with us, that's what we were *really doing.* How'd you just suddenly get that in your head? It doesn't makes sense."

"I don't know, really. But you wanna know what I think? At least, it's my theory."

"More theories, Johnny?"

"Well, it's not like there's a user manual for what we've got, is there?"

"Guess not. What do you think happened?"

"You took Holly from my house, didn't you? I mean, you personally. Not Sol."

"Yeah. At least she knew me. Look, I'm really sor—"

"Stop. That's not what I'm getting at. I think that when you took Holly,

361

somehow I read your mind."

Bobby was quiet, frowning. "Well, isn't that new and different?" he finally said.

"I take it that's not a skill from Sol's school for wayward super beings?"

"Definitely not," Bobby said. He turned toward me. "Can you do it again? Can you tell me what I'm thinking now?"

I concentrated, my eyes boring holes into Bobby's skull. "You're thinking… you're thinking… about a nice pastrami sandwich."

Bobby rolled his eyes. "Nope. I'm thinking I'm going to bed."

5

I was asleep. I knew I was, but still things seemed real. Was I reading Bobby's mind again?

I saw Sol, with Holly — God, it made my heart ache to see her that way — and he was preparing to go somewhere. Somewhere far. He had a maroon minivan, wheelchair accessible, packed with supplies. Sol pushed Holly in and secured her chair.

"Where are you going?" a voice asked. A female voice. I couldn't see her, but knew who it was. Not the warrior Margrethe, but the dream girl Pip, once again in my dreams. In my mind's eye, I turned to find her, but she wasn't there.

"Where I go is my own business for now," Sol said, climbing into the driver's seat. "I will send for you when the time comes. For all of you. All you need know for now is that I go west." He started the engine.

As he began to drive away, I saw my sister looking out the window, directly at me.

I assumed she must have been looking at Bobby, that this was a memory I was somehow stealing from his mind. But her eyes penetrated into me.

It was like that day in the hospital, after the car accident, a day that seemed like a thousand lifetimes ago. She saw through what I was doing.

Somehow Holly could see me.

Still, the van drove off.

Then the dream changed and I was back in the capital, tricking Sol into believing it was me sitting in the park, below that statue. I peered over the edge of the tall building, looking at Sol down below. He approached the hooded figure he thought was me, a step at a time.

Only things were different. Sol reached out, sweeping the hood down to reveal a face: Holly.

Again, she looked directly at me. Not speaking, but seeming to know everything.

Still in the dream, I fell back onto the roof of the building, unable to keep watching.

Finally, I gathered my courage and slowly looked over the edge again.

They were both staring up at me, Sol and Holly, under the statue of General Avery Tulloch on his horse. Only this time, they weren't in the park. Or they were, but the park wasn't in the city. It was like I was looking into a life-sized diorama. Sol and Holly were inside the largest box I'd ever seen, three sides of cardboard, with the front open to face me. Their eyes never left me.

I felt the earth begin to shake, and I woke up in a cold sweat.

It was the middle of the night, with a nearly full moon beaming down through the leaves of the trees. Just a couple dozen yards away, the road was empty. The air had cooled down, and moisture was clinging to me, to the rocks, the trees, the grass around me.

I tried to go back to sleep, but for a long time I couldn't.

Each time I closed my eyes, I saw Holly staring back at me.

Awakening

Disjointed pieces, a puzzle of endless dimension. Yet a boundless knowledge. Slowly pieces click, one after the other.

The answer is there. I can feel it, itching inside my mind.

Tiny whirls and whining sounds, like an orchestra tuning, each instrument seeking the same note until they are all as one. The sound increases, becomes deafening. It proceeds from deepest bass to highest treble, resolving into a sound beyond hearing.

A sound of understanding.

I know.

I know.

6

"I think I know the answer, Bobby." He was just starting to stir but I'd been awake for more than an hour.

Standing and stretching, Bobby stifled a yawn. "If the question is, *do you have to pee, Bobby?*, then I know the answer, too," he said, turning to head off into the woods.

"The answer to where we're going."

Bobby froze, turning back to me. "Yeah? Where?"

"The desert."

"Anything more specific? There's gotta be, like, what, a million deserts?"

"A specific desert. The one where General Avery Tulloch fought." I rubbed my hands together to warm against the cool morning.

"Who's *General Avery Tulloch?*" Bobby spoke the name with a sort of puffed-up mockery.

"Let me ask you something different. Were you there when Sol drove off to the west?" Bobby nodded with an almost inaudible *uh huh.* "Was he in a maroon minivan?"

Bobby didn't answer, instead squinting his eyes at me. "You in my head again, Johnny?"

I shrugged. "Not on purpose. I had a dream last night. Well, more than one. In the first one, I saw Sol and Holly in the van. Then later, I saw them in the capital."

"But that's way behind us, back east!" Bobby's hands flew up.

"The city itself isn't important. It's the statue. The one of General Tulloch, where I met Sol — or *sort of met* him —that last time. He told me a story about this general fighting an impossible battle in the desert. In a box canyon. And in my dream, I saw Sol and Holly in a box."

"Are you psychic now, Johnny?"

I shrugged again. "How the hell should I know? Do you really understand *your* powers?" Bobby didn't have an answer. "But it makes sense. Sol said I would know, he said we were heading in the same *general* direction. I'm sure that's where he is."

"Then what are we waiting for?" Bobby said with bristling excitement. "Let's go!"

I held up a hand. "Couple of problems. First, I don't remember the name of the desert. Second, the only deserts in this country are like a thousand miles away. It would take us forever to walk there. And third, even if we got there by some miracle, it's a *desert*. It's gotta be huge, and it's supposed to be made up of a bunch of twisted box canyons. I have no idea where they'll be."

"I don't think that last problem is really a problem," Bobby said.

"How so?"

He came over and sat down next to me, putting an arm around me. "Because Sol *wants* you to come and find him. If we get all the way to that desert, he's not going to hide. He's going to draw you right to him."

"Wow, that's reassuring," I said.

"I know, right?" Bobby was all smiles.

* * *

A few miles along, we came to a small general store on the side of the road, and once again we had to steal. Definitely not racking up karma points, but what could we do? Bobby seemed to have fewer qualms about it than I did. We took a paper map of the United States, and a free brochure titled *Granite County: Your Guide to Fun!* I hadn't heard of Granite County before, and so I was unaware we were smack in the middle of it (and all of its potential *Fun!*) until I leafed through the brochure. It included a handy map of the surrounding area, showing parks, lakes with water activities, an old mine that offered tours, and various towns and hamlets. Ahead of us on our route was a small town called Percetville.

Lucky for us, there were still public libraries, and Percetville had one. (Although in the back of my mind, I wondered why the library was listed on a brochure about *activities* in the county. How sleepy was this place?) It helped that libraries weren't hotbeds of criminal enterprise, so we hoped we wouldn't be busted the moment we walked into the place. In fact, we figured that if we cleaned up a bit, the staff might think we were there to do homework. If people were still looking for me, my hair was somewhat longer than it had been the last time anyone had taken my picture, so I was hoping I'd be hard to recognize. Skirting the town proper as much as we could, we eventually weaved our way in and found the Percetville Library.

In the back, there was a single computer. And, of course, it was occupied. A grey-haired man slowly tapped individual keys, doing some kind of search, forcing Bobby and me to look busy among the stacks for nearly an hour. I was too nervous to read anything, but when I finally noticed the old man get up and waved to Bobby to get his attention, I saw that his nose was buried in a superhero graphic novel. "What?" he said, following me to the idle terminal. "It's sort of like research."

I opened a window on the computer and started a search for General Avery Tulloch. "Of course," I said as the information appeared. Butchering the pronunciation, I read the name of the location of the general's most famous battle: *el Desierto de las Tres Manos*. The Desert of the Three Hands. "That's where we need to go."

"Can you look up how far it is?"

"Yeah, hold on." I clicked a few more options, jumping over to a map. "Crap." The results stared back at us like a curse. *2,135 miles*. "Gee, that's only twice as far away as I'd thought. No problem."

"Awesome! Look!" Bobby pointed the screen where it said *32 hours travel time*. "We can be there in a couple of days." I spun around to look at him, my expression no doubt conveying what I felt at that moment: *Bobby is as dumb as a box of rocks*. "What? What's with the look, Johnny?" he asked.

"That's *driving* time, idiot." I toggled a button. "There. *Walking* time."

Bobby looked at the screen again. "Shit." *684 hours*. "What's that in terms of days?"

"Well, how many hours do we walk a day?"

"A *lot*."

"How many?"

"I don't know, like 14?" I suspected it was actually 12 or less, but to humor him, I pulled up a calculator on the computer and divided 684 by 14. The result was staggering. "Forty-eight-*plus* more days. Of walking. Are you up for that?"

Bobby looked at his feet. Like mine, I suspected they ached. The idea of almost two more months of walking and sleeping in the woods did nothing to raise our spirits. "What the hell are we going to do?" he said. "I mean, is

Sol even going to wait that long?"

"I was just about to ask you the same thing," I said.

We looked at each other, two kids, miles from home, no ideas, no plan of action. I turned off the computer and we walked outside.

At the door, a boy and a girl about our age ran by, coming from a car at the curb. Inside the car, a woman, probably the mother of one or both kids, called out, "I'll see you in two hours!" The kids waved but didn't reply.

I felt an intense jealousy. Kids just being kids. No powers, no dangerous encounters, no hiding in the woods. No worries about a journey they had to make but had no idea how to accomplish.

All these kids had to do was get their mom to drive them somewhere they wanted to go.

I froze.

"Hold on," I told Bobby. "I've got it."

7

"You've got to be freaking kidding me," Bobby said when I told him what I wanted to do.

"And you have a better idea?" I asked, hands on my hips.

He thought. For a minute, at least. In terms of the least introspective 14-year-old on the planet, it was impressive. It meant he *really* didn't want to accept my plan. "I got nothing," Bobby finally said.

"Then we're agreed?"

"Sure, fine, whatever. Call."

I pulled out the flip phone. When it powered up, the little battery indicator was nearly invisible. I figured I'd have one shot, maybe a minute of talking. I dialed the number.

She answered on the second ring. "Hello?"

"Mom! It's me," I said with more relief than I'd felt in a long time. Shocked, she launched into a litany of questions, so I had to yell to interrupt her. "Mom!" Finally, she relented. "My phone's gonna die. Bobby and I are in —" I checked the brochure again. "— Percetville. Granite County."

"What? Really? You mean way up north?"

"Yeah, Mom, listen. We need you to come up here. If we're going to get Holly back, we need a ride." Bobby rolled his eyes.

"John, the police watch me all day long. Because you two are missing… They say it's for my own good, even though I tell them I'm fine. Maybe they think something else will happen here. I'm not sure. I don't think I could go anywhere without them knowing."

I sighed. It was the only idea I had. "Is there any way? Any way *at all?*"

Silence greeted me on the line for a moment. "Hold on, I think I know what to do. Most days around lunch, the officer on duty here asks if I want anything to eat. I say no, but tomorrow I could say yes. Ask him to go pick up something; sometimes they do that, leave me here alone for 10 or 15 minutes. There's only one officer, and I could make sure he's gone long enough for me to disappear."

"That's perfect, Mom! Just don't get caught. Back streets only. Or get another car."

"Hm. Okay, how about this? I'll drive to the capital, and hide my car in Aunt Cindy's garage. She'll let me take her car, I'm sure of it." Mom sounded positively *happy.*

"Okay, Mom. Percetville. We'll look for you by the library. Honk three times, like you're picking up kids. We'll be waiting."

"I won't get there until the day after tomorrow, if I have to switch cars and all. Will you be all right?" Worry crept back into her voice.

My phone beeped. I looked at the screen and saw the battery icon blinking red, then quickly lifted the phone back to my ear. "We'll be fine. Mom, I have to go. I love you. Thanks!"

"I love you, too, John." I reached for the END button on the phone, but she spoke again. "Oh, and John? Thanks for trusting me."

I started to reply, but the phone died.

* * *

"Seriously, Johnny?"

"What?"

"It's so… I don't know. *Embarrassing*." Bobby made an exaggerated gesture, like the worst of all possible things had come to pass.

"Do you want to *get there* or not?"

"Of course, I do. But…"

"But *what*?"

"We're, you know, like, super-powerful and stuff…"

"Uh-huh?"

"And we have to get a ride from your *mom*? Jesus. Like I said, it's so embarrassing."

"You want me to call her back? Have her bring juice boxes? Maybe PB&Js, too?"

Bobby socked me in the arm. "No. And you're not funny." He wandered off, but I knew the truth. Despite what he said, despite the embarrassment and his sudden teen angst, I knew Bobby *liked* PB&Js and juice boxes.

* * *

The next two days were simultaneously the most boring ones I'd had on the road, and the most anxious. At night we camped in the woods outside town. During the day, we tried not to draw attention to ourselves, and when it got to be around the time we thought Mom would arrive, we hung back from the library, able to see the front of the building from afar. Every time someone pulled up, we jumped in case it was her.

Bobby kept asking me if I'd recognized the car, but the truth was that I had no idea what my Aunt Cindy drove. So we jumped at every car equally.

Finally, late in the day, with the library already closed, a car that could only be described as *old school* drove up slowly and came to a stop.

"Is that her?" Bobby asked.

"I don't know." Then the horn blew, almost timidly. Once, twice, three times.

It was Mom.

We hurried across the street and over to the waiting vehicle. On the way, Bobby couldn't help but offer a critique. "A wood-paneled station wagon? Really? Your aunt still drives a wood-paneled station wagon?"

All I could do was shrug it off. "Don't people call them *woodies?*"

"That's not helping," Bobby said.

I got to the passenger window and looked inside, almost afraid of who I'd see, but sure enough, she'd come. My mom. Seeing us, she threw open the door and ran to me, giving me a long, tight hug. When she was finally done, it was Bobby's turn. "I never thought I'd see you again, Bobby." Then she stepped back, taking us both in. "Actually, I never thought I'd see *either* of you again." There were tears on her cheeks.

Okay, *now* Bobby truly was embarrassed. "Um, thanks, Mrs. B. But we really should get going. Right, Johnny?"

"Yeah."

"Hold on," my mother said, eyeing us. "There's one thing I need to know. Actually, it's something I need to *see*. So I'm sure."

Normally, I might have been offended at my mom's lack of trust, but I knew right away what she meant. I'd asked her to take a leap of faith bigger than the crossing of an ocean. She deserved to know it wasn't bullshit. I looked at Bobby, who seemed confused, and I nodded.

Twisting, I took off my backpack and placed it on the sidewalk in front of me. Then, with a quick flicking gesture, I sent it slamming into the wall of the library. Mom's eyes nearly bugged out. Still, she regained her composure and looked at Bobby. And he made his own flicking gesture, sending the pack flying back toward me. At the last second he made a clenching motion with his hand and the backpack froze in front of me, then settled into place where it had started.

Mom shook her head in disbelief, but walked to the driver's door. "Thank you, both of you. Come on. Get in." That's all she said.

We tossed what little gear we had in the cargo area of the station wagon and hopped in, me in the front passenger seat, Bobby alone in the back. Mom looked around, already used to making sure no one was watching, then slowly drove off.

Within an hour, Bobby and I were asleep. Mom drove on, hour after hour. Somehow she'd stocked up on cash, because when she did stop for gas, she never used a credit card. We were still living off convenience-store food, but at least we weren't stealing it anymore.

We did only four hours that first night, the three of us sleeping in the station wagon semi-hidden in some trees on the side of the road, but managed 15 hours the next day, getting us past the halfway point. The landscape outside grew flat, with long stretches of farmland growing wheat and other grains. On the third day, we abruptly reached foothills, which led to mountains, first small, then much, much larger. Snowcaps. We followed the highways and switchbacks threading between the high peaks.

Everyone's spirits were high — we were making great time, and we were even comfortable, for the most part. Bobby and I had cushioned seats instead of sore feet. Mom must have been miserable doing so much driving, but she never complained. And the car, despite its age and ridiculous appearance, ran well.

Right up until disaster struck in the form of a woman scorned.

8

I was nearly asleep, even though it was mid-morning, not midnight. In the back of my mind, I felt guilty, having Mom drive us the whole way while all we did was lounge around. Bobby was already snoring. He'd been awake for maybe two hours that morning.

As we came out of the mountains, the weather got warmer, the landscape more orange and brown, less green. I'd like to blame our laziness on the heat, but in truth we'd also slept while Mom drove through the cold mountains, the cool foothills, the dry plains, and the shady forests.

The trip had turned into a series of naps for Bobby and me.

"So you can move things with your mind?" Mom said, startling me back awake. She spoke in a low voice, trying not only to let Bobby sleep, but to keep the conversation between just us. "That's called *psychokinesis*, right? *PK*?"

"Is it? I've never heard that word in my life." I blinked and rubbed one eye.

Mom kept looking straight ahead. It seemed like she was trying to make casual conversation, but I could tell from her strained tone that she wasn't feeling terribly casual about the whole *superpowers* business. After all, I was her son. "I've been thinking about it, since your demonstration at the library. I've had a lot of time to think." She gave a little laugh and thumped the steering wheel with one hand, reminding me again of how long she'd been driving.

"Well, yeah, I guess we have... PK. But there's more. Our bodies are, like, impervious to injury. Well, maybe not *all* injury, but the basic kind — we can avoid it. And even when we do get injured, we heal really fast. Plus, I can harden my skin, my flesh, like stone. Become a sort of weapon. In fact —" Realizing I'd been ranting, maybe even bragging, I glanced over at my mom, and found her still staring straight ahead. It was like she was unwilling to look at me. "Mom...?"

"Yes, John. Please continue. What else can you do?" Her bottom lip quivered just a little bit, like she was trying to hold in a tide of emotion.

"Mom." I leaned over, putting my head on her shoulder. "Mom. I didn't ask for this. I didn't ask for any of this. You have no idea how many times I've wished it was all a dream. That I was just a normal kid. I don't know why this happened to me, or Bobby."

Her emotion ebbed, enough so she could control it, and she put her arm around me. "Oh, John, I'm so sorry. I wish I could do something to make it better. I'm so, so sorry." She squeezed me as tight as she could at the awkward angle.

"There's only one thing that's going to make me feel better now," I said. "Getting Holly back. Nothing else matters." I closed my eyes.

And my mom let out a horrified gasp, stomping on the breaks and bracing herself against the steering wheel. I lurched forward, opening my eyes as the car started to slide, its front end slipping to the left. Behind us, Bobby flew into the foot well with a sharp yell. There was something in the road, and we hit it, hard, with the passenger side of the car. Abruptly, we skidded to a stop.

I had half a second to wonder what happened when my door was ripped open, nearly off its hinges, and the Norse god of vengeance stood above me, hell with blond hair.

Margrethe had found us.

She reached in and grabbed me by the shirt, pulling me forward, then tossed me into the air. I slammed against a rock wall beside the road. If I were just a normal kid, I'm pretty sure I would have died on impact. But my body responded quickly, becoming solid and protecting me. I thought of hummingbirds, their wings too fast to see with the naked eye. My body reacted on hummingbird time. Shaking off dirt and bits of rock, I stood.

In front of me stood a very powerful and very angry woman, blocking my way back to the car. I could see my mom sitting in the driver's seat, still gripping the steering wheel, mouth agape, eyes bulging, probably wondering how I lived through such a collision. The rear door on the far side of the car opened quietly and Bobby slipped out.

I had to distract Margrethe. "What do you want with us?" I shouted.

"Not with anyone else." She pointed at me. "With *you*. My business is with you alone. You *killed him*. You killed Petrus!"

I raised my hands, palms up. "He *attacked me*. He tried to kill me. What was I supposed to do? Besides, I didn't kill him."

She scoffed. "No, you're right. You *didn't* kill him. You did worse. You destroyed him. You ruined his mind and left *nothing*." She let loose a pained sound, a shriek. "He couldn't speak! He was just a shadow. I had to help him eat. I had to help him do everything! With what you'd done, he wasn't *there* anymore. I gave him mercy. But his blood is on your hands."

Her words hurt me, the accusations were like daggers, but I realized that they were also making me mad. Bobby had crept around the car and was positioning himself behind Margrethe. I had to keep my cool, and maybe throw her off-balance. "No, you didn't give him *mercy*," I said. "If Petrus is dead, you did it, not me. When my sister had a seizure, a long, long time ago, she was left unable to speak. We had to help her eat, we had to help her do everything. But we *did*. We didn't just give up on her. If you loved Petrus, then you've betrayed him."

"How dare you speak to me this way?" Margrethe stood in shock at my words. A mere boy had just condemned her, and she didn't know what to do. I could feel the conflict inside her, the rage boiling ever hotter. Maybe I could use that to our advantage.

"I can't predict the future, and neither can you. Petrus might've gotten better. But now you'll never know. And now, we're going to save my sister. And no heartless witch like you is going to stop us."

Moving fast, Bobby appeared, coming around the back of the car. He attacked her in her moment of confusion, using his mind to drag her violently toward him. His fist turned to steel, and he delivered a double-strength blow, both striking at her and pulling her in at the same time. As she slammed into him, Margrethe's body went rigid and I could tell she was unharmed. She bounced and staggered away, then recovered. She gave Bobby a quick look of hatred and swung hard with her own iron fist. Bobby sailed across the road, skidding to a stop a good distance away.

Figuring my only chance was when she was distracted, I jumped forward, willing Margrethe to be struck by my mind. She fell back against the car, but immediately turned. My body solidified, but I found myself once again flung wildly through the air.

It was Bobby's turn again. He leaped onto the roof of the station wagon, looking down on Margrethe. To me he yelled, "Together!" and reached out to hold Margrethe frozen in place. She struggled against it, and I thought that she'd quickly wriggle free. So I reached out with my mind.

Despite her defenses, the razor-thin blade of my attack pushed through, into the very core of her brain. Margrethe shuddered at the violation, but her spine weakened and Bobby's hold stayed true.

I paused, the hot dagger of my attack lodged a hair's breath away from killing her. "Stop! I don't want to hurt you!"

She growled. "But I *do* want to hurt *you*." Her teeth were clenched and her eyes gleamed with fury. "You're going to have to do it, or as soon as I'm free, I will kill you."

"No," I said, wavering.

A small smile crept onto her face. "Yes. Let me go. Let me kill you for what you've done." She jerked to one side and Bobby flinched, working hard to keep hold of her.

"No," I repeated. Past Margrethe, inside the car, my mother still watched, terrified. I realized that if I acted, my mother would see me kill another person. I couldn't do it. The molten blade I had used to cut through her mental defenses started to cool. Then I had an idea. "No. You're wrong. I don't have to kill you."

I reached forward, redoubling my efforts to get into her mind.

Bobby yelled, a combination of fear and exhaustion. Holding her for so long, as she fought hard against it, was wearing him out. "What're you doing?"

"I'm trying something!" I replied, closing my eyes. Seeing Margrethe only with my mind. There, inside her, I saw flashes of her life... Looking up at a woman much taller — was that her mother? Then a boy, maybe a brother. Many things flashing by, people, places, even a dog. Then a moment... An important moment came into my view — confusion, joy. It was the moment she realized she had power. I mentally waved at the scene and it faded. Then another. Meeting Sol. Again, I waved it away.

Following so many pathways, flicking so many invisible switches.

Margrethe's body stopped fighting. Then she went limp.

"I think you can let her go," I said to Bobby. He just shook his head, terrified she'd turn around and try to crush him. "Really, I mean it."

Slowly, Bobby released the hold, then fell back, expecting her to rage.

Margrethe just stood, looking around, like she'd never seen us before.

"Are you okay?" I asked her.

"Ye — yeah, I think," her voice said. A different voice. Not angry, not hateful. Confused, afraid, maybe shy. "Where am I?"

Bobby and Mom continued staring, no idea what had suddenly changed. "Where are you from?" I asked, trying to sound reassuring.

"Uh, Pine Vale. Why?"

"I think you're a long way from Pine Vale." I smiled. I couldn't believe it, but it seemed to have worked. "Do you want to go back?"

"Yes. Yes, I really do. I don't know how I got here, but if you all could help me get back to Pine Vale, I'd be so grateful. But wait — I don't even know your name." With the anger removed, I could see Margrethe more like she must have been before all this happened to her. Tall, athletic, muscular, pretty. And very polite.

"My name's John. That's Bobby," I said, pointing. "And that's my mom. And sure. We'll help you." Behind Margrethe, Bobby gasped. I turned to my mother. "Right, Mom? Can we give her a ride to a bus station or something?"

"Uh. Okay. I guess," she said, finally remembering to breathe. She gave me a look, a look that every kid knows well: Mom was going to want a pretty serious explanation.

* * *

"I made her forget," I said as we watched Margrethe wave and turn back toward the bus station. Mom had helped her get a ticket, even paid for it with nearly the last of her cash. The station wagon had a huge dent on the side and the front passenger door seemed to be hanging on by a thread, but looking around the bus-station parking lot, I saw many other cars in various states of disrepair. We hardly stood out.

"What do you mean, John?" Mom asked.

"Yeah, Johnny, I mean, I know all about pushing minds, but that was *serious.*" Bobby still couldn't believe what had happened.

"That's all. At the moment, Margrethe has no idea she has powers at all. She's forgotten the entire thing. Me, you, Sol, even Petrus." I felt guilty about the last part, if they truly had been in love. Somehow it seemed worse than taking him from her the first time. "But honestly, I'm surprised it worked so well, for this long. As far as I know, she might sit down on the bus and remember everything. So we'd better get out of here." I turned back to look at them so they'd know I wasn't kidding.

Mom started the engine.

9

We drove on in the damaged car, putting as many miles between us and the bus station as we could. With Margrethe on a bus heading east, each mile we traveled doubled the distance. I could only hope the many adjustments I'd made to her mind were enough to keep her away. At any rate, if she wanted her vengeance on me, it would have to wait. Sol and my sister were my only concern.

Gauging the miles, Mom said the words I had longed for and yet dreaded. "We should be there tomorrow, you guys."

Bobby didn't say anything, instead slumping back into his seat, looking out the window at the passing landscape. Rugged hills, the color of rust, sped past. The endless repetition of phone and power lines, pole, slow curve of wires, pole, over and over and over, enough to mesmerize you. Soon, Bobby closed his eyes.

The sun was setting in front of us. It was a beautiful sight, orange and pink and purple sky coloring the land, rocky hills and outcroppings silhouetted in black and tinged with light. I stared at it all, transfixed, though even the fading brilliance of the sun was enough to burn temporary blind spots in my eyes. With every blink, I saw the landscape in negative.

I figured this would be my last night alive, so I might as well watch the sunset one final time. I'd never been big on admiring nature, but it's funny how impending mortality changes your opinion of such things. I mean, I wasn't trying to be pessimistic or anything, but seriously. Two kids going up against an adult whose previous experience included keeping the entire power of the police and military at bay?

What could be easier?

I was scared. Bobby was snoring. And Mom was clearly worried.

"Mom?"

"Yes, honey?" The last rays of the sun cast an eerie array of pink and purple on her face, like I was looking at an angel.

"I just want you to know I'm going to do everything I can to get Holly back."

She turned to me with a smile, but her eyes quickly grew wet. "I know, John. In just a couple of days, the things I've seen you do... Well, they're just *incredible*. I have faith in you. And thank you. From Holly, too."

"You don't have to thank me, Mom. If it weren't for me, Holly would be home. She'd be fine. Sol took her because of me."

"That's not your fault, John. This... *Sol* person is a monster. Stealing helpless children. I hope they lock him up and throw away the key."

I sighed. "I don't think that's going to happen. Remember how easily he got away, back when he held the governor hostage? They won't be able to arrest him. I've got to deal with him." She didn't say a word, but I could tell she was holding herself in, trying to be strong, knowing her son and daughter were both at great risk. "But Mom..."

"Yes, John, is there something else you need to tell me?"

"Yeah. But I don't know how."

She looked at me sideways, still watching the road as the dark came on. "You can tell me anything, honey. Anything at all. Okay?"

"I know, Mom. It's just that it's not easy to say it." I swallowed hard before continuing. "I don't think I'll be coming back after tomorrow."

I expected an argument, empty reassurances, something. But Mom had just witnessed the full fury of one bad person with power, and Margrethe was only a student. Sol was the master. And I was the outsider. I'd never even studied.

Still, she was my mom. "John. I know what you're about to do is dangerous, the most dangerous thing in the world. And I know you're doing it for Holly." Through her tears, she kept driving, west into the darkening sky. "My instincts tell me to turn around, to take you away from Sol, not toward him. But he has Holly. We can't just leave your sister with him. So as much as I want to protect you, as I *need* to protect you, I believe in you. I know you're strong."

"Okay, Mom, okay, thanks." She had me crying, too.

"But I want you to know two things."

"What's that, Mom?"

"First, I've seen you in action. What you did back there against that woman was nothing short of unbelievable. If you can do that, then I think you can do anything."

I blushed. "Thanks, Mom, but really —"

"But nothing. It was incredible. You don't just have power and skill, you have compassion. I'm sure you could've done much worse by her, maybe even killed her, right?" I nodded. "But you did the right thing. And that means you're a good person."

There was a long silence. The only sounds were the low hum of the engine, the tires on the road, the wind outside. "What's the second thing?"

"Just this," she said. Her tone had changed, become hard. I never heard my mother speak so forcefully in my life. "Sol is an evil son of a bitch, and if I have to pull him limb from limb myself to get *both* of my children back, I will."

I couldn't help but crack a grin as we rolled along. Somewhere ahead, Sol was waiting for us, maybe laying a trap. But we were three determined people, each powerful in our own way, and at that moment I thought Sol was in for a load of trouble.

A rustling sound from behind got our attention. Bobby was waking up. Drawing a hand through his mop of hair, he yawned, one cheek red from pressing against the seat.

"What'd I miss?" he said with a dopey grin.

10

We arrived late morning the next day, after a long stop overnight for Mom to get some much-needed sleep. Amid the dull, sand-scrubbed monotony of the desert, something finally popped out: a wooden sign, painted a deep, even brown, with simple capital letters carved into the wood and painted white. They read:

EL DESIERTO DE LAS TRES MANOS

DESERT OF THE THREE HANDS

NATIONAL PARK & HISTORIC SITE

Below that, a green metal sign warned PARK CLOSES AT DUSK. *Oh good, thank you. We'll be sure to wrap up by then. Wouldn't want to break any rules.*

I was so nervous, I giggled at this silly thought. Mom and Bobby each gave me a look, eyebrows raised. I waved it off with a quick apology.

There was no ranger station, no visitor's center. Just an empty two-lane road that lead to a parking lot.

The lot sat empty except for a single vehicle. An old maroon minivan.

Sol.

Mom parked and killed the engine. Bobby and I sat still. I guess he was as afraid to get out as I was. We sat in silence for a couple of minutes.

"Man, I'm really thirsty all the sudden," Bobby said. "I mean, it's a desert and all, right? I think there was a store, maybe 10 miles back. We could —" I tossed him a full water bottle from the pile of random stuff we'd accumulated on our brief stops. "Oh. Okay. Thanks."

I faced the two of them. "Bobby, it's time. I've got to do this. I'd say I wouldn't blame you if you decided not to go, but I will. You owe me, and you owe Holly." Bobby nodded, eyes to the ground. "And Mom. I can't have you follow us. It's too dangerous."

"John —" she started, but I cut her off.

"I know it's crazy. I'm 14 and you're my mom. You should be the one telling me what to do. But you saw what went down with Margrethe. It'll be that, times 10." I took a deep breath. "Maybe times a hundred. I want you to stay with the car, here."

"It's not that," she said. "And you aren't 14. Not any more."

"Huh?"

"I nearly forgot myself, with all the hiding and driving and powers and such, but it's true. I'd sound like a fool wishing you happy birthday while I'm sending you off to fight a madman, but it *is* your birthday. You're 15 now, John. And I love you. I'll stay back, but I meant what I said. I want *both* of my kids back today." Bobby cleared his throat dramatically, and Mom laughed despite the situation. "*And you*, Bobby!" She tousled his hair and he smiled.

There was nothing else to say. No way to really prepare otherwise. So I opened the door to get out. Mom gave me a short but intense hug. I didn't want it to end, but it did. I stood in the parking lot outside the car.

God, it was hot.

Late morning in the desert, it must have been in the high 90s. Any last semblance of cool from the AC in the station wagon quickly evaporated. I leaned back into the car and grabbed my backpack, filling it with four water bottles, leaving two for Mom.

As I stood and slipped the backpack onto my shoulders, the ground started to vibrate. It came on slow, but built up steadily.

An earthquake. I hadn't felt one in so long. Just thinking about it felt strange. They'd been so common at one point, even the news had stopped reporting on each one. I thought of Holly's seizures, how they could predict the earthquakes.

Sol, you're doing this. It's like your calling card. And each time you do it, you're hurting my sister, you bastard.

The fact that Sol could move the earth itself did little to bolster my confidence, but there was nothing left to do. "Come on, Bobby," I said, and we both set out.

Bobby pulled at his collar, trying to loosen it, even though he was wearing a light t-shirt. To me, he simply mouthed one word: *hot.*

I gave my mom a final wave just before we crossed over a little hill and disappeared behind a rocky outcropping, hiding her and the car from view. My heart sank, knowing it was likely the last time I'd ever see my mother.

* * *

We followed the easiest path, no doubt the one any tourist would follow after parking in the small lot. It wound between growing rock walls, a sandy flat path into the deepening canyons.

These are box canyons, I reminded myself. *We need to be careful about dead ends.*

We were tense, alert. Expecting an attack at any moment as we rounded turns left, right, right, left again. The canyons were a maze, the walls towering over us. Countless times, we'd turn blindly into a new area, expecting Sol but finding nothing. Eventually, our state of readiness diminished.

Which of course was when we turned into a wide opening. On the far side two branches of the canyon split off, one left, one right.

And in the very middle stood Sol.

"Hello, my old friends. Thank you so much for coming to visit me. I've been waiting for you." Bobby and I nearly fell over each other getting into stances like amateur karate masters preparing for hand-to-hand combat. Sol chuckled. Yes, he did. That damned chuckle. Again. "Boys, please. Lower your arms. Can we not talk? Are we not, in many ways, brothers? Even if brothers-in-arms? We should seek to resolve our differences as such. Please." He held out one hand in a gesture of peace, his charm working overtime.

I saw Bobby lower his arms, and felt myself doing the same. Bobby took a step forward.

"No," I said with as much force as I could, willing myself out of the daze Sol was putting us in. "Bobby, stop. *He's* doing this. He's trying to push your mind to give up."

Another chuckle. "Ah, John. So clever. Well, you can't blame me for trying, can you? There's really no need for a fight. I was just trying to... *alleviate some tension.*" He gave me a smile, bright white, perfect teeth gleaming.

I wiped my forehead, already beaded heavily with sweat, and noticed Sol wasn't perspiring at all.

The ground started to tremble again, and Sol looked down. It was brief and weak, soon passing.

"Cut that out," I said. "It's hurting her."

Sol raised his eyes to look at me again. "You mean Holly? The seizures? Yes, I am aware that she feels these tremors more *intensely* than others, it's true. Despite her otherwise complete detachment." He smiled again, giving a small bow. "My apologies, John. I shall try to control myself."

"Give me my sister back, and this whole thing can end!" I shouted.

Sol *tsked* me. "No, John. I am afraid that is not true. You see, if I give you your sister back, it resolves *your* problems. However, it does nothing to alleviate *mine*."

"What do you mean?"

"I think your friend Bobby knows what I mean. Right, Bobby?"

Bobby shook his head. "I don't know what you're talking about." His face was slick with sweat, and I could see damp stains growing larger under his arms. Still, Sol seemed oblivious to the heat.

"Ah, Mr. Graden, have my teachings had such little impact upon you? That's disappointing. You don't recall what I've told you — indeed, what I taught *the entire group*?" He spat the words like they tasted bad. "Don't you remember what I said about *allies*?"

Bobby wrinkled his forehead. "You said, 'Those who are not our allies are our enemies.'"

"Good," Sol said, smiling. Not only wasn't he sweating, but he was immaculately dressed, a pristine grey button-up shirt tucked into neatly pressed black pants, a sliver of gold flashing from the buckle of his thin leather belt. As usual, Sol was tanned and handsome. Even his hair was perfect. In contrast, Bobby and I were disheveled and probably smelled horribly. We'd been on the road and in the car for so long. Still, in the desert, we seemed to *fit*. Our clothes picked up many of the colors of dirt, like the rust-hued walls of the canyon around us. Unlike us, Sol wore pristine shoes — some kind of fancy type, maybe alligator? — So gleamingly perfect that I wondered how he'd come to stand in this place without scuffing or dirtying them. "So there we have it, John. If I hand over Holly to you, you go home, but we remain enemies. That does not help me to achieve my agenda."

"And what *is* your agenda, Sol?" I put my hands on my hips, defiant. Or at least trying to look like I was. Beside me, Bobby tensed.

"Well, I've already explained it once to you, John." He spoke with the perfunctory wave of a hand, like his words were so obvious he was insulted to have to say them. "I wish to be eternal."

"But what does that *mean*? And what does it have to do with *me*?"

"It's simple, John. Allies or enemies. If you join me, we can become eternal together. Change the world, bend it to suit us. And the others will return to us in time, I have no doubt. There have been so few people throughout history who were truly eternal. Think about it. Christ. Mohammed. Buddha. Mahavira. Moses. Or, in more secular circles, Aristotle, Khan, Napoleon, Einstein, Hilter. People who changed the world forever, left an indelible mark."

I scoffed. "You realize how crazy you sound, right? You want to be put on a list that includes Buddha *and* Adolf Hitler? Jesus *and* Genghis Khan? And you think that sounds appealing to me?"

Sol stepped forward, radiating an intensity that spoke of his power. "Think about it, John. Genghis Khan was brutal, it's true, but he lived in brutal times. Do you think it was *easy* to unite the nomadic tribes of Mongols, scattered as they were across a harsh landscape, unwilling for someone else to bring them to heel? But he did, and in so doing he changed their world, giving them something they'd never had before. An *empire*."

"He gave them servitude. Just like you'd like to enslave people now."

Sol nearly spat. "What use would I have for a horde of human slaves? No, Genghis Khan *enlightened* his people. Education, religious tolerance. Did you know that Khan promoted his deputies by their merit, not by who they knew or which family they came from?"

I was no history genius, but I did go to school. Genghis Khan was someone we'd spent some time learning about the semester before in Mrs. Setzer's class. "Wait. Didn't he divide his empire among his sons when he died?"

"So?" Sol clearly wasn't someone used to being questioned on matters of intellect.

"Are you telling me that, of all the people who lived in his time, his *sons* were the most worthy?"

Sol gave a smug smile. "Perhaps they were, John. They learned at the feet of the master, after all. And that is what I offer you. Join me. And Bobby, I will forgive you and allow you to rejoin me as well. Let us come together to change the world."

I took a deep breath, knowing this was the last moment, perhaps my last moment of peace in life.

"No," I said, arms falling flat against my sides.

And from my right, without warning, Bobby launched an attack.

Sol was surprised, but not nearly enough. Bobby used his mind to pull down a section of the canyon wall behind Sol, and rocks the size of watermelons came tumbling toward him. But Sol simply pivoted and swept his hand back and forth, parting the falling rocks like one might sweep away the crumbs after a meal.

I was too stunned to move. I realized Bobby and I had absolutely no plan, and wondered in that instant how we had spent so many hours on the road, in the station wagon with Mom driving, without coming up with a single idea. Suddenly I realized that Bobby was only creating a distraction. With Sol's back turned to handle the small avalanche, Bobby leaped forward. His arms and legs shot out in front of him, becoming rigid as steel as he slammed into Sol's back. It was far from elegant.

Sol lurched forward, then quickly caught himself. Turning around, he had a look of pure hatred on his face. More than any other affront, it seemed, Sol couldn't stand being embarrassed. And although he had only staggered a few feet, even that was more than he could tolerate. "It appears that I have your answers," he said with a sneer. "So be it."

With one quick gesture, he pushed Bobby away. Bobby flew like a dart into the far wall of the canyon, then crumpled to the sand below, broken.

Torn between launching my own attack or helping my friend, I hesitated.

And Sol ran away, laughing as he disappeared down the left branch of the canyon.

11

With Sol at least momentarily gone, I went to Bobby. His body was twisted in an unnatural way, legs bending where they shouldn't, even his back arched horrifically over the stones he landed on.

But he was alive.

Not for the first time, I saw the effects of the power we held and wondered if they were more curse than blessing. Still, Bobby's body moved. Seeking to put itself right, it jerked and spasmed back into more normal positions, then sluiced and rippled until everything was smooth. His face was disturbingly blank the whole time, and I wondered if he was there in body only.

At last, he took on a natural form, almost like he'd simply been sitting on the rocks, like he'd taken a short rest.

He blinked once or twice, then looked up at me with a smirk. "Thanks for the help."

I stiffened. "What? I —"

"You what? Wanted me to take care of him by myself? Listen, doofus. Next time I jump at him, next time I've got him distracted, *that's your cue, okay?*" Bobby slapped at his pants, trying to get the rusty dirt off, but it didn't help much. He stood up and cracked his neck, like a boxer getting ready for round two. Red dirt stained his clothes and was plastered to his sweaty face. He looked like some kind of ancient warrior, face paint and all, hair shaggy and splayed in all directions. And, in his own way, he was thinking more clearly about how to handle Sol than I was. I have to say, I was pretty impressed. In my mind it was easy to categorize Bobby, to still think of him as the old class bully, the guy who'd use his fists before his brain.

But, although it was a simple one, at least Bobby had finally come up with a plan: He'd attack first, then I'd follow through. If only I had a clue what my part would actually be.

"Where'd he go?" Bobby asked, looking around.

Standing on the hot, packed sand of the canyon floor, I pointed to the left branch. "That way," I said.

"Okay, then, what are we waiting for? Let's go get the bastard." Bobby launched into action, following after Sol.

But something was wrong. "No," I said.

Bobby turned around, confused. "What? We drive, like, seven million miles to get here, and now we're *not* going to go after him?"

"No. Something's wrong here. Why'd he have us come all this way to the desert, and then as soon as we meet up, he runs away down that canyon?" *That canyon?*

"How the hell should I know?" Bobby said. "But I have an idea. I hurt him. And now he's afraid, because there's two of us and only one of him."

"Wait! Is that right? Did *everyone* desert him? I wasn't there, I only had a dream about it. But in the dream, there was Sol, and you. Margrethe and Petrus. And —"

"Phillipa!" Bobby said, slapping his forehead. "I forgot about her. She was always really quiet around me."

I suspect I had a stupid-looking grin on my face just asking. Thankfully, Bobby ignored it. "She's real?" I asked.

"Of course she's real, idiot. And she's good, too. Not just a fighter. Not just a thinker. Her name is Phillipa, but she goes by —"

"Pip," I interrupted, knowing it was true.

Bobby pulled up. "Whoa, dude. You're freaking me out with the whole mind-reading-dreams business."

I shrugged. "Anyway, we don't know where she is, so we have to assume that she's still working with Sol. She could be anywhere around here," I said, gesturing to the high walls all around us. Still..." *Why did Sol confront us, then just run away down the canyon? Down this* box *canyon.* "Of course. *That's* why we're here." It was so obvious that either Sol was much less intelligent than I'd given him credit for, or there was more to his scheme than I knew.

Bobby waited for me to go on, but for a moment I was lost in thought. "Um. Hello? Not all of us read minds. Care to give your dumb old friend a clue?"

"Very funny," I said, walking over to the place where the canyon split. I raised one hand and pointed down the left branch. "Listen, Bobby. Sol *wants* us to go after him. When I saw him in the capital, the time I tricked him, he told me the story of General Avery Tulloch — you know, the whole reason we're in this desert in the first place? He was a real guy and fought a real battle, right here where we are. He used these box canyons to set up a trap, and then wiped out his enemy from behind."

Bobby's eyes grew. "So you're saying if we'd run down that way, Sol or Pip would've snuck up behind us?"

"I think so."

"What a little cheat!" Bobby said, genuinely irritated. "Geez. It's one thing if he kills me when we're face to face, sure. But if Sol kills me by sneaking up behind me, I am *not* going to be happy."

He said it with such conviction, I really didn't want to laugh. Still, my body betrayed me, first shaking, then finally bursting with giggles. "You're going to be one upset dead person." I kept giggling, couldn't stop. Finally, Bobby's mock-angry face vanished, and he laughed, too.

"So, smart aleck," he said. "What do we do now? We can't go after him because it's a trap, and we can't just sit around here giggling like babies. Should we ask your mom to drive us to the movies or something?"

"We go up," I said, pointing to the steep walls of the canyon. "The only way out of the dead-end part of the box canyon is up if you're blocked in, but those people Tulloch killed didn't have time to climb because it's almost straight up. We do. As long as we don't walk right into Sol's trap, we can take our time. Go to the top, circle around. Find him before he finds us." I put on a big grin. "In a way, it's like what I did to him back in the city. He's going to think we're down here on the ground, but really we'll be above him, looking down."

"Oh, that'll really tick him off," Bobby said.

"Good."

We started climbing.

＊ ＊ ＊

Near the top, we pulled water bottles out of my pack and drank, our bodies eager to replace the moisture that was oozing out of every pore, soaking our clothes briefly before evaporating away. We were covered in a rust-colored dirt, our clothes ripped and worn from the sharp rocks.

The ascent was difficult, especially since neither of us had much skill or experience at rock climbing. But in time, we made the top ledge.

Far in the distance was a strange darkness. A storm of some kind. I vaguely hoped to be done with Sol, one way or the other, long before that storm hit. But a new fear filled me, and somehow I knew I'd be fighting Sol and the elements all at once.

Once we'd had some time to catch our breath and drink our fill, we packed away what little water we had left and began to trace the upper edge of the box canyon, looking for a place where we could peer down on the dead end.

The top edge itself wasn't flat. Rocks more than twice our height seemed to jut up everywhere, forcing us to take a winding path toward our goal. Most of the time, our visibility was limited. The only direction in which we could easily see was outward, toward the yawning openness of the full canyon, and down, toward its sandy bottom.

Rounding another set of tall rocks, we finally saw the end of the canyon, the box.

It was empty.

"Where the hell is he?" Bobby whispered with surprise.

I just turned up my palms to say *I have no idea.* "Let's keep going around. Maybe he's tucked in a crevice or something down there."

Bobby pushed past me, making his way farther along the rocky edge. In only a moment he disappeared from my view, and I scrambled to catch up.

As I rounded the last tall monolith of orange rock, I saw them both: Bobby, standing frozen only feet from Sol. Not frozen with fear. Held still, in the invisible vice of Sol's grip. Bobby screamed in pain, but it sounded muted, like he didn't have enough air.

"I am flattered, John," Sol said.

"What? That I didn't fall into your trap down there? Yeah, I remembered your story about the General. You're not getting rid of me that easy." My words dripped with spite. Was I trying to upset Sol, throw him off his game? Maybe. But in general, I think I was just pissed.

"And what of Master Graden, here?" Sol asked, pointing one tanned, well-manicured finger toward Bobby's forehead.

"Please stop! It hurts and I can't breathe!" Bobby pleaded. I remembered our day in the hospital, Bobby pleading with his parents. He sounded like that again, but worse. Bobby was being crushed to death by the power of Sol's mind. I heard cracking sounds that I assumed were Bobby's ribs, and a *whoosh* of air blew from his mouth like dying wind.

"Let him go, Sol!" I shouted. "I'm the one you want, right?"

"In many respects, you are correct, John, yes. Ever since we met, that seemingly chance encounter at the beach, I have been most intrigued by you."

"But why? Why do you care about *me* so much?"

Sol chuckled. I could live a thousand years and never wish to hear that sound again. "You really do not know, do you?"

"No," I said, feeling the dry heat deep inside me. Like the very air I was breathing could burn my lungs. I was exhausted and outgunned. Confused and tense. Each breath, every heartbeat, even just blinking my eyes, these things seemed *forced*, like I had to work for each millisecond.

"John Black. You and I did *not* randomly meet. I was looking for you."

"What? Why?"

"Because of what is inside you, of course. I would call you a diamond in the rough, but that is inaccurate. You are more like the entirety of the Crown Jewels, but as if they were tarnished, dirty, and forgotten. You only need someone with the right eye to find you, clean you up, bring out your shine, and..." Sol made a wide sweeping gesture. *And what? I could have the world?*

The day was rapidly growing darker as he spoke. The wind was dry, but increasing.

"I don't understand what you're saying. I'm just a kid. I didn't ask for these powers, and I don't really know how to use them." I realized as soon as I said it that it was a bad thing to reveal. Ah, well.

"John, you have felt me calling out to you, yes?" Sol asked.

The beacon, once loud, now gone. Even standing feet from him. "Yes."

"Well, I cannot hear it, or feel it, coming from me. But from *you*. It is like this profound *note*. This tone, one of great clarity and strength. In fact, it is so strong that when you are near, as you are now, it feels like it is coming from everywhere at once."

I raised an eyebrow. "That's why you didn't guess my trick in the capital? You didn't know I was on the rooftop, not right in front of you?"

"Correct," he said.

"But your beacon — uh, that's what I've been calling it — it's been gone for a while now."

"Yes, it has. Once I felt yours, and those of Bobby and the others to various degrees, I knew I must have one myself and that it must be strong." Always humble, that Sol. "I learned to control it. But I can turn it back on." Suddenly a deep bass chord filled me. I knew it wasn't a *real* sound, an audible sound, but still I took a step back, almost to the ragged drop of the ledge, and the sound abruptly cut off. "Now, John, careful. As you can see, I have even learned to amplify the call."

I lowered both hands, though I hadn't even realized I was covering my ears.

"Okay, so you've been looking for me, and now I've been looking for you." In front of me, Bobby squirmed, just a little, and Sol clamped down with his invisible hold, stilling the motion. "Can't you just let Bobby go, then?"

"As you wish," Sol said. With a whipping gesture as fast as lightning, he sent Bobby flying over the edge, down into the box canyon, bouncing horribly off countless rock formations before smashing into a jagged outcropping that finally stopped him. He tumbled with a sickeningly smooth motion into a low, dark nook, falling out of sight. The last I saw of him, his body looked more like a bloodied amorphous mass than a person.

"You son of a bitch!" I shouted. My entire body tensed, and this time I could actually feel the cells rearranging themselves into stone. I swallowed. Even that was hard to do, too dry. I was so tense, the power building so strongly in me, that I felt I wouldn't have control. That I would be at the full mercy of the parasites within me.

A sharp wind snapped at my shirt, and I noticed the distant sky again. Much darker, and that darkness was much closer. And much bigger. It spread as far as I could see on the horizon behind Sol. Slowly, I spun around, taking in the sky in all directions.

The wall of darkness filled the horizon. Everywhere.

"What... is *that*?" I asked, mostly to myself, but Sol answered anyway.

"That, John, is a very large, very deadly sandstorm."

"But it's coming from every direction at once."

"Yes. It is not what you would call a *natural* weather phenomenon. It is almost exactly circular, and it is contracting. Shrinking toward this spot. Soon the circle will collapse upon us, John. Are you prepared?"

"Why?"

"Because I am, John. Because I need you to decide, a final decision, in these final moments. Join me, or the storm will tear you apart and even your formidable powers will not stop it."

My hair whipped around as the hot wind spiraled. "But you'll die, too, then. And if that's what I have to do to save Holly, I will. I'll stand here and let the storm destroy me, just like it will destroy you. Then she'll be free."

"Not exactly, John. I have no intention whatsoever of being here when that storm arrives. I have my own means of escape, I can assure you. But you do not. And Holly does not. If you will not choose to ally yourself with me, then both you and Holly will die. Here."

The sandstorm seemed visibly closer already.

"Then I'll have to give you my final answer," I said, lowering my eyes to the ground.

"And what, pray tell, is that, John?" Sol crossed his arms, waiting.

"I'll do it." I let out a huge breath, terrified at what I was saying, what I was about to do.

"Now, finally, some sense from you, John. Good. You will find that I am hardly the monster you think I am."

"I'll join you."

"Yes, good." Slowly Sol nodded, white teeth bared in a wide smile, contrasting sharply with his dark olive skin.

I looked up, holding his eyes with mine. "I will join you, and stay with you until the end." And with furious vengeance, I reached out with my mind and locked Sol in place, his arms still crossed against his chest. He was frozen, posed like a mummy in a sarcophagus. Whatever means of escape he'd planned was useless, and the sandstorm was closing fast. "I'll stay with you until the bitter end," I said, "and we'll watch each other die when this storm crashes down upon us."

Sol raged against me, trying to break free, but my grip was iron. I was determined to hold him. I knew I still wasn't any good at controlling or stopping objects, holding them, but I was going to try, with everything I had, to my last breath. Sol's face twisted into a gnarled mask, the only part of his body that could move, and he screamed in a hateful rage. "John Black!"

I nodded. "And when you're dead, *Branco*, then I'll know my sister is free from you, you bastard."

12

Honestly, I was surprised it worked at all, that I could hold him even for a moment. I believe now that my exhausted resignation to simply *do it* and to keep doing it until we both died was the secret that made it stick.

Sol struggled, veins bulging on his forehead, but the rest of his body was motionless, held firm. He uttered a low, guttural sound. He was a bear with his leg in a trap, wanting nothing but escape.

And then I could feel the push. At first it was as ineffective as holding your hands up against a rushing stream to keep the water from touching you. But his efforts grew as mine waned. I used every ounce of fury in my body to hold him, but my grip seemed to slip faster the more I tried. Soon, I was joining him in yelling through clenched teeth.

Finally, my hold broke, like a dam finally giving way to the great flood behind it. I didn't release him gradually, but all at once. Suddenly he was free, I was staggering backward, and he was attacking.

Sol leaped toward me, swinging his hand in a terrifying arc. When his flat palm struck me in the stomach, I couldn't do anything to stop myself from flying backward, like a ping-pong ball hit with a baseball bat.

I was launched out over the box canyon, and soon found myself plummeting to the sandy floor below, just like how Sol had dispatched Bobby.

But I couldn't let Sol get away like that. I wouldn't let myself be crushed on the rocks below without one more try, one more fight. As I fell, I sent a mental dart deep into Sol's mind, small but meant to cut. Whether it was the effect of my powers or simple human adrenaline, I saw it all in slow motion — me tumbling downward, Sol reeling from my attack. Then I dropped down and our line of sight was broken.

I knew that somewhere below me was a craggy wall or pile of rocks, something that I would soon be landing on spine-first. Yet I could think of nothing to stop it.

I crashed hard into several rock formations at once, too many to rationally understand. My head, back, right arm, each was smashed and cut and broken. Then I bounced and tumbled, slipping through a small gap in the rocks and flipping over, ripping up my hands, tearing my face. I vaguely noticed blood, my blood, spraying everywhere. Finally, I came to rest on the sand, crumpled like discarded paper.

I pulled in a ragged breath. Then another. Near me there was nothing but silence, but farther out, from every direction came the sound of the storm, closer still. The storm is what made me move. The storm would kill my sister. I had to move.

Forcing my will upon my body, I directed it to reassemble. Like a scene from a horror movie, my back bent over until it found its original line. My legs straightened. My skin pulled gashes back together. Slowly, slowly, minutes or days later, I stood.

"You see, John. *This* is why you are special." Sol's voice echoed from the lip of the box canyon. "Why you matter so much to me. Could Bobby do what you just did? No, he is still somewhere, either dead or healing slowly. But

412

you. I can see it. You have forced your body to heal, and to do it *now*."

My neck rotated awkwardly, like it was snapping back into position, and finally I could see him, coming down from above. Not climbing down. *Drifting* down.

How the hell is he doing that? I thought. *It almost looks like he's flying.* In the moments while he descended and the last parts of my body corrected themselves, I think I understood. I was seeing Sol's getaway car. He was using his ability to move objects with his mind, only the thing he was moving was himself. *Damn, I wish I'd thought of that.*

Sol landed gracefully only feet away. "John, I would very much like to extend my offer to you once more, one final time." He grinned, a wide and charismatic grin. Then it fell. "But you have now tricked me twice. I will be forced to move ahead on my own. And you, John Black. You will now die."

Suddenly, I couldn't breathe. An invisible fist clenched around my lungs, pushing out all air, clamping down on my heart.

I raged. I tried to fight it off, screaming my anger and desperation. I knew that if I couldn't stop Sol immediately, I would die. Powers or not, he was preventing my heart from pumping blood, my lungs from getting air. I had minutes to live, maybe seconds.

Again I screamed. I was letting everyone down. Holly, Mom, Bobby. I felt the guilt of all the people Sol would kill in the future, or enslave, or whatever he had in mind. Every cell in my body tensed, awaiting the end that I could no longer forestall.

It can't end like this. I have to fight harder!

But there was no greater rage to tap. No larger pool of energy or anger.

Sol came close, standing right in front of me, looking down into my eyes. "For what it is worth, John, I did not want it to come to this."

And he raised one hand over me, the executioner's axe.

I closed my eyes.

And accepted the reality of my death.

13

As soon as my eyes closed and the outside world disappeared, a calmness came over me, replacing all the rage.

Forgive me, Holly. Forgive me, Mom. Forgive me, Bobby. I failed. Forgive me, Dad. I couldn't protect them.

The calmness grew, expanding throughout my body, and became a peace. The peace of the dead.

Milliseconds slid past like years. I faded into nothing but that peace.

And somewhere deep, deep inside that peaceful feeling, that feeling of waiting for fate, there was something different.

A beat.

A very tiny beat.

My heart was beating.

Calmly, I mused on this, considering it to be inconsequential. The last heartbeats of a dead person.

My mind escaped my body, I suppose. I wasn't above myself looking down, I was simply more *of* myself than I'd ever been before. The peace invaded my arms, hands, fingers. My legs, feet, toes. The surface of my skin felt warm. Not hot and dry and parched, like it had been in the desert, but warm with the glow of life.

Life?

I sipped a small breath. Although only the tiniest amount, glorious air came into my lungs. I sipped again. More air.

I could feel the blood flowing through me, each drop. I could feel the air oxygenating that blood. I could feel every cell in my body being nourished and returned to life. I could feel myself becoming... *alive again.*

And I felt not just Sol's grip on my lungs and heart, but the *nature* of that grip. Like discovering the key to a locked door, I suddenly understood how it worked. How it could be dismantled.

Slowly, calmly, as if in a trance, I opened my eyes.

Again, the earth shook with a quake. The leading edges of the storm were whipping at the top of the canyon walls. In moments, the whole thing would crash down upon us.

Still, I moved in slow, calm motions, deliberate. I looked into Sol's eyes.

He was smug, happy. With the thinnest tendril of my mind, I reached into his thoughts, although he was completely unaware. I saw Holly, sitting in her chair on the sandy floor of a canyon, somewhere nearby.

And then I found something so unexpected that I nearly lost my control.

Sol was terrified.

But of what?

From his point of view, I was near death, my lungs and heart still crushed by his grip. He was only waiting for the inevitable. My calmness, to him, was merely the first stage of death.

I sent the tendril deeper.

What are you afraid of?

The storm. The sandstorm, massive and encroaching from all directions. Strong enough to rend our flesh and body, rip apart our very cells, destroy us both.

The sandstorm.

Sol didn't make it.

He was desperate to escape, terrified of what would happen if he didn't leave.

I sent the tendril deeper.

The storm wasn't the only thing he was afraid of. The earthquakes. He hadn't been making those, either.

Sol was frightened that there was something much more powerful, more powerful than himself, or me, or both of us together, and that it was on its way to us.

This was Sol's great need for me. He knew there was something very strong out there in the world, and that only with my strength, the strength of others like me, might he have a chance against it. But I had spurned him, made it clear I wouldn't join him. A world with some unknown power *and* me aligned against him was unacceptable. He needed me to die *now*. And then, he very, very much needed to escape.

The heavy blow of his fist finally came down, intended to crush me as the air and blood had already left me. With all of Sol's physical power gathered close, pulled in for one massive strike, he hit me. In my new calmness, I could discern the sheer force he put into the blow, and to me it seemed that such an attack might crack the very surface of the world.

And yet, I didn't flinch.

His hand hit its mark and fell aside. Almost bounced aside. There was a sound like a dull metal gong, but I was unharmed.

"What's this?" Sol asked, looking at me in complete confusion.

With a slight gesture, I swept aside his hold on my lungs and heart, his power falling away like droplets of water. Sol's eyes were huge, bulging. The terror that he'd kept hidden now came to the surface, multiplied by the new fear of what I'd just done. He stepped back.

Any semblance of composure was gone. Sol was raving, a lunatic consumed by fear. The dry, gritty wind whipped his hair, framing his twisted face in a mane of frenzied motion. "I am destined for greatness, John Black. You know this to be true."

"No," was all I said.

Sol screamed, a wordless sound full of hate. The charismatic, powerful being was gone, replaced by a hideous, panicked demon. "If you will not die," he spat out with all the bitterness of his twisted soul, "then *your sister* will."

"No," I said again.

Sol made it one more step.

The tendril I'd put in his mind sparked and flared like a magic wand, and every molecule of water within his body, making up most of Sol himself, came together and *froze*. I didn't simply hold him in place: that was no longer useful to me.

Calmly focused on his feet, I leeched the heat from his body. The water in his toes froze first, his skin quickly frostbitten and blackened. Then the

418

arches of his feet, his heels. Working up through his ankles, legs, into his torso. From bottom to top, Sol stiffened as my peculiar magic did its work.

It happened quickly, sliding relentlessly upward, but still deliberately enough to be agony for him. In my peaceful trance, I saw the pain, but it seemed more curiosity than concern. The wave of ice continued, reaching his core, freezing his lungs.

And with his last breath of air, he rasped at me. "You have beaten me, John. But you have also beaten yourself. And Bobby, and your sister. Look!" His eyes flicked upward, toward the top of the canyon walls. "The storm is upon us! And so we will die together. The new powers of this world shall be extinguished in this very moment because of you, and the human race will continue its pathetic and futile march into the bleak winter of its nothingness."

I slowly tilted my head up, thoughtfully pondering the raging storm, nonplussed by Sol's ranting.

"Even now, Holly is dying!" he shouted.

Then I raised a single digit, the index finger of my right hand, and placed it to my lips. *Shhhhh.* And the ice froze Sol's neck, his chin, his entire face. Only his wild hair remained free, shooting in every direction above his head.

Even in my detached state, I thought Sol looked like a mad version of the man who once had his greatest victory on this spot, General Avery Tulloch. There would be no victory for Sol here, nor anywhere else. The process was complete.

Sol was frozen solid, wretched in his anguished appearance. A devil who had threatened not only my family but the world, now caged forever.

I let my finger fall from my lips, and reached out toward him. Extending my arm, I tapped the center of Sol's chest with a resonant *thud* that seemed to echo off the canyon walls.

And Sol exploded into a million pieces, perhaps a thousand million. Ice and whatever else he'd been made of, in so many tiny, glinting fragments. Puzzle pieces that could never be made whole again, scattering in the whirling wind, gone.

14

My senses began to come back. My peaceful state began to dissipate. I began to step back into the normal world.

My ears began to hear. The throaty yell of wind howling through the canyon. The endless peppering of rocks and sand thrown together, blasting each other to nothingness.

My eyes began to see. The world was almost completely dark. The storm had come, and it had blacked out the sun.

My skin began to feel. The wind scraped at me. In my head, I heard the screeching sound I associated with the thorns in my cells. They were screaming, dying as each layer was peeled away.

I stood amid the howling hell of the sandstorm as it tore apart the world around me, and tore me apart with it. I blinked once, twice.

"Holly! Where are you?" I shouted. Sol had said she would die in the storm; she must be near.

I turned and tried to run, away from the dead end of the box canyon, back to the spot where the two branches split. I had to fight against the wind, coming from all directions at once, pushing me forward and pulling me back, making any progress nearly impossible. Still, I pressed on.

In a narrow crevice, something bright stood out against the grey and black and orange and brown of the world around me. Bobby.

His body was pulling itself back together, healing after his fall, but slowly, as he'd been pummeled nearly into pulp by Sol's blow and the hard fall into the canyon. I made my way to him and hefted his irregular form up and onto me as best I could, and we staggered together, leaving the left branch of the canyon and entering the right.

It twisted through ever-narrowing passageways, partially blocking the storm's harsh winds and providing us with a little relief. Making it a little easier to move. Then finally, the passage opened onto a clearing, the dead end of the box canyon.

Through the deafening roar of the storm, I could sense a single note, a beacon. Nothing like Sol's, more like Bobby's, which I had mostly come to ignore. But a new note, one I'd never heard before.

The canyon walls were hard to make out in front of us, just patches of orange in the darkness. High on the far wall, I thought I saw a human form, climbing up and away from us. I squinted my eyes to block out the flying sand, but it was impossible. The figure, if had even been there to begin with, disappeared into the distance and darkness of the sandstorm. The new beacon in my mind diminished.

"Look," Bobby said through a still-mangled mouth. He couldn't point with his hand, but his eyes were focused. I turned to follow his gaze, lower, closer.

And I saw my sister, sitting alone in her wheelchair near the middle of the box canyon, the wind spiraling around her, building little dunes against her tires, in her lap. Her head was down, hair raised up and whipping like black fire above her, and I couldn't tell if she was alive or dead. Lowering Bobby to the sand, I ran for Holly.

But my feet were swept out from under me almost instantly. The sandstorm was a fury, circling through the canyon, picking me up and spiraling me around. I was only a few feet from Holly, but I couldn't reach her, instead spinning around and around her, out of control.

Then the storm's winds changed and I was flung directly toward my sister. I grabbed hold of her wheelchair on one side, still thinking I would save her, when I couldn't even save myself. I pulled myself toward her, into a huge hug, tapping my forehead against hers, hoping she was still alive.

As the skin of our foreheads touched, Holly looked up at me.

She was alive.

And yet...

Her eyes were different than I'd ever seen before.

Holly wasn't just alive, she was ablaze, seething with rage. Tears streamed down both cheeks, only to be instantly caked with orange sand. She looked like she'd been painted with a warrior's mask, pagan and mysterious.

"Holly, it's me, John!" I shouted above the din of the storm.

The chair came loose in the sand. The winds converged on us, and we were lifted off the ground, only inches at first. Me, Holly, and the wheelchair. We spun upward like a balloon accidentally let go from a child's hand.

"Holly! I'm trying to save you!" But even as I said it, I knew it was foolish. I was a fool. I had come so far, across the country, face to face with a madman, and for what? What was I doing beyond simply hanging on? "I'm trying to save you. But I don't know how. I'm sorry, Holly. I love you, but I don't know how to save you."

Our foreheads were still pressed together, that old ritual that used to give me… what? Peace? Reassurance? A sense of connection to my sister? Yes, but more. It meant we were there for each other. In these last moments, did Holly feel the same? Her eyes continued to sparkle with rage, the tears still falling, tracing through the grime on her face.

"Holly, can you hear me?" I'd always thought she could, on faith. But…

I realized that I had another way.

I reached out with my mind and gently touched hers. *Holly, can you hear me?* Of all the times I had pushed minds with my powers, I had never before tried simply to speak to someone else. It felt like I was a ship, floundering on rocky seas, a lighthouse in the distance. And when I called out to Holly, the light turned toward me, quickly, like an accusation. A beam so bright it obliterated all darkness.

First, there was only a sound. A tone, like a single, clear note played so loud I thought I would never hear again. Then a word came through, erupting out of the intense sound.

WALTER!

I fell back in shock, nearly losing my grip on her and the chair. "What?"

Holly's mouth quivered, so tense, so full of hatred.

The storm spun us around and around, higher and higher, straight up above the canyon floor, so that I could only barely see it anymore in the darkness and spiraling winds. I was dimly aware that skin and cells were continuing to be flayed from my body.

Holding tightly to Holly, I reached out again with my mind, bracing myself. But now, instead of that feeling of floating in darkness, everything was white. The tone filled my senses. The complete focus of her attention was waiting for me.

WALTER!

I shied back, but wouldn't let myself fall away again. *What, Holly? Walter*

Ivory?

Louder than before, near deafening in my mind's ears, she screamed. A horrific banshee cry. *WALTER IVORY!*

The words blew over me, stronger than the storm around us. *Holly. What about Walter Ivory?*

HE DID THIS!

Still spinning, I could no longer see the ground. We were somewhere high in the storm, dull and formless hues all around, wind still stripping away cells, gradually pulling me apart, gradually pulling us both apart.

He did what, Holly? Made this storm? I don't understand.

The whiteness I felt inside of Holly grew hot. *HE DID THIS TO ME!*

I exhaled powerfully, with the sort of deep regret that only suffering can bring. Suffering for so long, so many years. Walter Ivory was the root of Holly's isolation, the catalyst that took her from us so many years ago. But he was gone. *Holly, Walter Ivory is dead. I watched him die myself. He can never hurt you again.*

The white light flickered, the tone faltered, like her concentration waned.

And we fell from the sky, plummeting down into the storm, toward an unseen end.

Just as abruptly, we stopped. The light that was Holly focused on me once more.

BUT. DADDY?

Did Holly know what had happened to our dad? I suddenly felt filled with guilt, to add to my regret. It was hard to breathe.

We were going up again. Quickly now. Far too quickly, going far too high.

It was hard to breathe.

I didn't answer her. What could I say?

WHERE IS DADDY?

Still, I didn't answer, and her rage grew twofold. We were speeding into the thinning air. Holly was doing it, I realized. Holly was the sandstorm. She was all those earthquakes. She was the unknown power Sol had feared. Living right in front of him for so long now, his ego unable to see her.

Nor could I. Holly, my sister, right under my nose this whole time, had power greater than I could comprehend.

And in her rage, she was killing us both.

He... I began, but lost my courage.

WHERE IS DADDY? she screamed again in my mind.

There was almost no air left. I was becoming lightheaded.

He's dead, Holly.

She uttered a scream so loud I thought my mind would burn away. And the physical Holly, the one clutching the chair, uttered a wailing, pitiful moan.

Our speed increased, toward the edge of the light.

I had to tell her. We were going to die together, so she deserved to know.

Dad's dead because I killed him, Holly.

This time the scream was like fire. Something inside me snapped and was burned away. But I continued.

I can never say I'm sorry enough, Holly. It was an accident. I... I didn't know my powers and I was just trying to punish some kids who had hurt me. I didn't even know Dad was there, but then, there he was. It was a car accident. He died in a car accident that I'm responsible for, even though I never, ever meant for it to happen.

We flew higher and I was fading from life. There was no air, no atmosphere at all. I saw nothing but darkness above us. And dots of light. Stars.

Holly, I didn't know how to control my powers, and that's what killed Dad. I'm sorry. I'm so sorry. For however long I live, I will be filled with guilt and regret. But I came here to try to do something right. To try to save you. But your powers are about to kill us both. Please, Holly.

I may have just been losing consciousness, imagining the worst things I could, but it seemed her rage began to tear apart everything, even time and space. Flashes of light appeared and died out. Bolts like lightning crackled past us.

To my left, the darkness appeared to rip, and three giant shapes fell out from the gap, plummeting to Earth below like huge fireballs.

Still we climbed, and despite my powers, I was at the end. I was going to die.

I'm sorry, Holly. I am so sorry. I loved Dad so much and never meant to hurt him. Or you.

And in that moment, something dawned on Holly. Something changed. The whiteness of her rage became brighter than a thousand suns, and then… diminished.

We stopped climbing and then gravity reversed our direction in a slow arc. We picked up speed, falling back through the atmosphere, air gradually returning.

My consciousness came back slowly, and along with it came the very real fear that we were falling, perhaps farther than any living soul had ever done before, with no idea how to stop. But something held the friction of the air at bay, keeping us from burning to ash in the atmosphere. Holly's power.

All I could do was hold on.

I wouldn't plead with her again. She was my sister. It was hers to decide. I had killed our father in a terrible accident. If Holly chose to do the same to me, I couldn't do anything to stop her. I didn't want to.

We fell, faster and faster.

The landscape became familiar. The box canyons were below us, now free from the dissipating storm. Their orange and brown walls were brightly lit by the afternoon sun, and we fell to meet them and our doom.

Without warning, our speed waned, like we were suddenly falling through water, not air. We slowed, being guided by an invisible hand toward the ground.

And at last, the wheels of the chair settled into the sand, on the same spot we'd left an infinite time before. We touched down so gently, I barely felt it, didn't even hear a sound.

Exhausted, I collapsed on the sand at Holly's feet, then looked up to see if she was still alive.

Holly was staring back at me. Her mouth quivered again, and for a moment I thought she would trigger another earthquake.

Then I heard the sound.

Holly was trying to speak.

It was low and muffled, from a tongue and lips years out of practice.

Eyes locked on mine, she said only a single word.

"Johnny."

THE END OF

FOR I COULD LIFT MY FINGER AND BLACK OUT THE SUN

but

JOHN BLACK WILL RETURN

in

AND IT AROSE FROM THE DEEPEST BLACK

Keith Soares

By day, Keith Soares runs an interactive game, web, and app development agency. But by night, his imagination runs wild. A fan of classic authors such as Stephen King, Robert Heinlein, Arthur C. Clarke, and newer writers like Justin Cronin, Hugh Howey, and Andy Weir, Keith writes stories of science fiction, the apocalypse, fantasy, revenge, and horror. He lives in Alexandria, Virginia, with his wife and two daughters, who are all avid readers.

Sign up for the Keith Soares new releases newsletter:
KeithSoares.com
Get release news and free books,
including private giveaways and preview chapters.

Like Facebook.com/KeithSoaresAuthor
Follow Twitter.com/ksoares